"POOR JENNY...
THINGS WOULD HAVE BEEN SO MUCH EASIER
IF YOU'D ACCEPTED MY OFFER."

He approached her slowly. The trapped look in her eyes seemed to delight him as much as her previous willingness.

He took her face in his hands. "I really don't need your cooperation..." Leaning forward, he brushed her unmoving lips with his own. "...but I do need *you*."

His lips moved on hers, lightly at first, and then again with deepening intimacy. As if she were a department store mannequin, he began undressing her...

Shapes

A Romance of Horror

RICHARD DELAP AND WALT LEE

C
CHARTER BOOKS, NEW YORK

SHAPES

A Charter Book/published by arrangement with
the authors

PRINTING HISTORY
Charter edition/February 1987

All rights reserved.
Copyright © 1987 by Richard Delap
and Walter Lee.
This book may not be reproduced in whole
or in part, by mimeograph or any other means,
without permission. For information address:
The Berkley Publishing Group, 200 Madison Avenue,
New York, New York 10016.

ISBN: 0-441-76103-8

Charter Books are published by The Berkley Publishing Group,
200 Madison Avenue, New York, New York 10016.
PRINTED IN THE UNITED STATES OF AMERICA

For Cindy Lee Kimmick, whose valuable assistance helped shape this book.

—*Walt Lee*

This book is dedicated in loving memory to
Decco
a soul-mate who was more than a cat, a true extension of my spirit, with me from the first word of the book to the last, until he died on September 10, 1986.

You are with me always, my little friend.

And this one is also for those people who helped: Leona Delap and Carolyn Delap, Mr. and Mrs. B. Lerke, John Wells, Joe Sanchez, Carol Canode, Michael de Gaetano, Harlan Ellison, Shigeo Morioka, and Mildrid Jansen.

And most particularly, Barbara Delhotal, who knows what it takes.

—*Richard Delap*

*What might this be? A thousand fantasies
Begin to throng into my memory,
Of calling shapes, and beck'ning shadows dire,
And aery tongues that syllable men's names
On sands and shores and desert wildernesses.*

—John Milton, *Comus*

prologue

THE *THING* LISTENED.

Even through the shield of the forcecage cylinder that imprisoned it, the monster could hear the telepathic screams of the Cepheans. They were going to die, and in their final moments they could do nothing but cry out in despair.

The cityship contained hundreds of them—crew, scientists, technicians—all dedicated to the peaceful exploration of myriad worlds of the vast and daunting universe. But they had made a fatal mistake. The thing the Cepheans had taken on board to study, a creature both primitive and voracious, had not been content to lie dormant. The cylinder imprisoned it, but it had watched . . . and waited . . . and listened.

One of the Cepheans had been careless, and it had been ready. Then, when it had finally found a way to tap into the vast biocomputer of the great ship, it had done so with nothing on its mind but destruction—and murder.

As the cityship emerged from hyperspace, its magnificent globes and spires were reduced to debris and dust. The thing had done its work well.

There was only one survivor.

The cylinder had been built to withstand the most tremendous forces imaginable, and it slipped through the transfer point into normal space, as slickly as if it had been greased with cosmic oil. Falling through space, it was captured by the nearest gravitational field. The energy walls protected the monster within them—first from the vacuum of space, then from the heat produced by friction with the atmosphere of the world below.

A great ocean waited to cushion the impact of the fall.

A planet waited to be plundered.

A planet called Earth.

Part I

Convergence

one

HER APARTMENT HAD a comfortable, bemused look about it. The colors, rich earth tones with black and white accents, soothed Jenny the moment she looked at them. It had that effect on her after a hard day in the tense and professional atmosphere of the lab, and it had that effect on her now, very early in the morning.

Over the tawny linen couch, two art posters smartly framed in brass proclaimed the Paris exhibition of Piet Mondrian and the Metropolitan's lavish opening of last year's Impressionist Collection.

In the corner, perfectly at home and in daily use, stood Jenny's pride and joy, her grandmother's antique oak writing desk with its twenty-four beautifully crafted little drawers. The drawers still smelled of old forgotten lavender. There was a tiny spring at the base of the bottom drawer on the left that opened up a hidden compartment. As a child she had kept her paper dolls in there.

She'd always wanted to tell Brad about that little compartment, and her dolls, but she had never done so. It remained a trivial but intimate secret, close to her core. To share it with Brad—well, her little treasure had become a symbolic barrier to ultimate sharing. The barrier had trembled at Brad's masculine touch, but somehow it had never fallen. Now, it looked as if it never would.

"Keep watch for the van," Brad called from the kitchen. "It's early, so they probably won't honk."

Just like Brad to explain even his simplest command, Jenny thought as she turned to survey the living room for any forgotten items. Brad wouldn't think twice about blasting a horn at five in the morning, but he was right about Duane and Maria. Rather than jar the neighbors out of their sleep, either one would be more likely to write a note and, with a quiet tapping, slip it under the door. They were polite people.

Jenny moved nearer the front window of her second-floor apartment, close enough to see that the space Brad had vacated to make room for Duane's van was still there. Jenny tried to keep watch on the street, but found that she couldn't stop her gaze from drifting to a closer range. Another step forward and she would be able to see the tiny patch of ground that passed for a front yard. She wanted to take that step, to look at the cramped lawn below with no fear of what she might see—or of what she might imagine.

Step/eye contact/*trigger*. She knew well that her mind might be taken over in an instant. Was it merely a few weeks that the inexplicable visions had been troubling her?

The visions crossed over from fantasy to reality with great suddenness, and she'd told herself repeatedly that they were only a release created by her subconscious. It made her feel safer to channel her logic toward self-analysis, to regard her odd dreams and strange visions as a self-created distraction from her real problems with Brad.

But perhaps it wasn't so simple. During the two years of their relationship—their meaningful relationship, as the mass-market magazines called it—Jenny had sensed a change in herself.

She felt a growing estrangement between herself and Brad. Somehow the fun and the freshness were gone and there was little left to sustain the relationship. Maybe it happened to everyone.

Was something really missing or was she expecting too much? He was pressing her to marry him, but she found herself backing away from it, or at least from giving him an answer.

What else could she want in a husband? He was a professional with a secure future. He was tender, protective, affectionate, and sentimental. He was a "catch."

Brad couldn't do enough for her. Sometimes Jenny felt as though she were his pampered pet. He enjoyed zipping her around in his Jaguar-XL, and everything about him was first-class all the way. He earned a lot, spent a lot, and lived the good life now that all those horrendous years in medical school were over. He took her to all the "in" places, as well as those intimate restaurants where the nouvelle cuisine was inventive as well as expensive. Brad knew the places that would delight her. He had a knack for such things.

She sighed. She was probably just picking on him because she was tense and depressed. Brad had a heart of gold. An insufferable ego, but a heart of gold.

And besides, he was good-looking. That was what had attracted her to him in the first place. Six feet hit him at eye level, and his head drifted in a tight mass of soft brown curls, dramatizing the handsomeness of his angular jaw and pale, liquid-blue eyes. He smiled easily, a dazzling display he called his "two grand" smile, referring to the amount of money his parents had paid out in braces and other orthodontic atrocities when he was a kid.

He was also an athlete, with powerful shoulders and legs that he kept in shape with daily karate workouts, and with three sets of tennis a week. Which he always won . . . except for the time he was about to serve for break point and Jenny had—in an unsporting action—unzipped the bodice of her tennis dress. He had protested heatedly and shouted foul, but she had claimed *that* game.

It was impossible for her to picture Brad as his patients undoubtedly did: methodical, efficient, confident. If they could only see him at home, scruffy and unshaved, his hair tousled, crouched behind the sports page as he ate his oatmeal with wheat germ. That was the real Brad.

And yet for all the time they spent together, they almost never sat down these days for heart-to-heart talks about their lives, where they were heading, their innermost feelings. It was as if they were frightened of what they might find out about each other.

But her logic had little influence on these confused emotions. And none at all on her effusive hallucinatory visions.

If you can't keep your finger off the trigger, you shouldn't play with the gun.

Jenny could almost hear her grandfather's voice reciting his favorite homily, like a warning thrown out from the flotsam of her memory. As a little girl, clutching the old man's corduroy pants where they hung loosely over his bony knees, she had accepted such statements without question. But when they floated to the surface of her adult mind, they were encrusted with symbols and double meanings, the polysemous junk of hard-sell advertising in a world gone mad.

So, now, were her fantasies, dreams, and recurring visions a result of the world's insanity or a cry of simple truth? Jenny felt alone with the question. And Brad wasn't proving to be much help.

Half an hour earlier Brad had asked her to move his car to the garage while he finished packing, and they had a mild tiff when she said no. He hadn't given her a chance to explain why she refused, why she feared walking alone, in the dark, past the scrubby front lawn, past the curb of the sidewalk. Buttoning his chinos and throwing her a look of annoyance, he'd hurried out the door and down the stairs to do the task himself.

Just another indication of the growing emotional distance. The responses she could eke out of him were getting to be weak tea: annoyance instead of anger, smiles instead of laughter, affection instead of passion.

She had no business berating him, though. While she kicked Brad for his failings, she knew she should take a few kicks in return.

Why didn't she push harder to explain to him the fearful response she'd been having to her recent visions, or hallucinations, or whatever one called them? She had tried, she told herself, but each time she mentioned her bewildered state of mind and odd dreams, Brad's face automatically assumed the patronizing smile he used with people who presented minor difficulties to him at the hospital. It was a smile he slipped into as easily as he donned a surgical gown and gloves, and he wore it too often these days.

Jenny had come to hate that look. It not only disregarded her professional standing as research technologist, it also dismissed her as woman, lover, even as a friend. In his eyes she became a defective creature known in the profession as a *patient*—something to be patched up, watched briefly, then dismissed from the active file. His smile explicitly told her: I am the doctor; you are the patient. I will take care of your body, but keep your mind submissive. It gets in my way.

For a woman whose work daily kept her in search of answers, the lack of answers in her personal life had become intolerable. She no longer mentioned her emotional problems, fears, or fantasies, and the chasm between them continued to widen.

Worrying about it simply made her angry and she prowled nervously around the room. Snatching up an extra scarf, she stuffed it into the top corner of a bloated overnight bag. She spotted two tiny chess pieces that had somehow worked their way out of the rug's deep pile, and mindlessly grabbed them up and dropped them into the checkbook pocket of her shoulder bag. It gulped the pieces greedily before she slapped its lips shut with a resounding smack.

A metallic clatter drew her to the kitchen doorway. Brad had all the lights on, even the bright spot over the sink, which flooded the room with a disagreeable intensity. Beside a carton in the middle of the floor lay a colander.

"You missed."

Brad climbed down from the counter top, waving a paperback book he held in one hand. "Look at this!"

She glanced up. "Why do we need a colander?"

"I've been looking for this for weeks," he said, brandishing *Rules for Card Games*.

Jenny remembered hiding the book after Brad and his hospital cronies had spent one long and loud evening hunched over a card table in the living room, draining endless cans of beer and cackling maniacally over winning hands they called "gynecological flush" and similar medical crudities.

"Surely, Miss McGregor, it wasn't thee hid our rule book with the canned beets?" Brad clutched her hand and kissed her fingers in mock knightly servitude.

"The only thing I hate more than beets is poker." She jerked her hand away and tucked it under her other arm. "You should have heard yourselves that night, until three in the morning. Every time I woke up I thought the three witches from Macbeth were partying in here."

"Why didn't you kick our asses out, then?" He sounded truly puzzled. "Why hide the rule book with the beets, for Christ's sake?"

"I don't know, really." Why did she, she wondered. Hiding the rule book wouldn't keep the guys from playing cards there. She was too tired and slow to dredge up an answer. It was just too early in the morning. "Somehow it seemed the right thing to do."

Brad studied her momentarily, and Jenny felt that he wasn't going to respond with his usual wisecrack, the kind he spouted when he wanted to avoid a question or a confrontation. Was he really trying to see into her, comprehend her emotions? Although it might be only a reflection from the overhead light, she thought she detected a questing warmth in his eyes and had an urge to smile, to reach out and touch his face.

He turned and moved away, and the moment was lost.

"Oh well, nevermind." His voice was distant as he nudged the box across the floor with his foot. He began rummaging once again, this time in the floor cabinet, his rear end hovering just above the heels of his Nikes.

With nothing to do, Jenny began to pace once again. Her bags stood packed and ready at the door, filled with light summer clothing and one formal dress for Maria's wedding.

It was going to be a fine vacation. They would travel up the California coast to Point Locke, staying with Maria's mother until Duane and Maria's wedding in a small town, woodsy setting, far away from the Los Angeles summer smog. Jenny could already smell fresh air wafting a clean scent of green, growing things into her lungs.

Small sounds continued to echo from the kitchen and she glanced across the room. Brad was determined to play out his fantasy of combining some camping out with the trip for the wedding celebration, packing junk that would never get unpacked, much less used. There wasn't that much time, and of course they would be involved with the wedding festivities the whole week. Perhaps the fact that Maria and Duane were putting a clear sign of permanence on their relationship was giving Brad his silly nervous energy.

Maybe he thought the sentiment of seeing her best friend's marriage would induce Jenny to try it for herself. Brad Knowlton's first marriage had ended in divorce shortly after he'd finished his internship, and he liked to make Jenny feel it was her duty—"as a woman"—to marry him. "Make me legit," he would plead with a crazy chuckle, bulging his eyes as if he were playing a scene for Mel Brooks. "A famous surgeon can't shack up all his life with a pretty technologist. You know how a hospital gossips."

Jenny had thought about marriage—thought about it quite seriously. But she didn't feel she had achieved the inner contentment or warm stability that could sustain a permanent relationship with Brad.

Brad's mock-serious macho-stud image, which had become his stock running gag, had secured an existence beyond joke-filled chatter with residents and scrub nurses. He carried it like a suit of armor protecting his ego, and Jenny was no longer sure that the exterior disguise was separate from the man at all. The gentle, but willful man who had swept her off her feet two years ago, the man she had invited into her bed with a fevered passion she was sure was love—perhaps that man no longer existed inside the protective shell.

To her, marriage was more than a contract. It meant making a commitment to one another that would be strong enough to stand up to times of serious adversity. She was, quite honestly, no longer sure of her true feelings for Brad. How deep did they really go? And the answer kept coming back with a hollowness that saddened her: not deep enough.

What had created the widening chasm between them? Did the growing distance create her fears and her fantasies, or was it the other way around?

Brad's exterior might look tough, but she thought she could see the day when he would have to face, as all must, his own special demon of fear. Would he crumple in its clutches? Would there be something left for her then?

Jenny gave a deep sigh. She knew she would have to find answers soon, and this short vacation was surely the perfect opportunity to search for them in peace. She would have to be firm, look at herself and Brad clearly to decide if they could ever regain the emotional bond that forgave evenings of habit and turned sex into something more than mere physical release. She would also have to determine if she had encouraged Brad's present attitude by trivializing herself inadvertently, by standing back when she should have stood up.

Perhaps they *could* find a common ground once more, one of respect rather than of convenience. They should try, Jenny thought. They really should try.

"Hey-hey-hey, there's a kerosene lantern here. You think we should take it? We could use it if we go camping."

Jenny groaned. The pounding and clattering told her that

Brad was already dragging the damned thing out from the deepest corner of the cabinet.

"I used to have a grill for cookouts, Brad. It might be in there too." She wanted the line to sound funny—silly—but it came out in an icy voice.

"No kidding? That's great. Maybe . . ." His voice, muffled, rumbled between the low kitchen shelves.

Don't try to explain, just keep him happy and occupied for the time being. "Keep looking, Brad. I'm sure it's in there somewhere."

She'd thrown the grill out months ago, but it was better to have him rummaging in the kitchen than waiting with her in here. He could be restless and impatient, and she wasn't in any shape to calm him down.

While pacing aimlessly in the living room, Jenny caught sight of herself in the mirror. She stopped and looked at her reflection critically. Tilting her head to the side, Jenny smoothed her hair down. Ash blond hair framed her face carelessly, and beneath her long lashes her bright green eyes were alert. Too alert. They betrayed the inner torment she had felt of late.

A few new lines were now etched around her eyes, but all in all she was pleased with her appearance. Her body looked slender and lithe in the skinny-knit sweater and blue jeans.

Jenny peered at herself closely and smiled. She licked two fingers and leaned forward to pat down an errant wisp of hair along her forehead. In the mirror, the front window of the apartment loomed into view behind her head.

It wasn't the cool morning air coming in from the open window that breathed a shudder down her spine. She detected an eerie glow outside, neither the soft illumination of the street lamp nor the icy sharpness of moonlight. The glow hovered with a sickly gray-blue color that seemed to press against the window like heavy fog.

But it wasn't a fog. The street lamp offered a clean silhouette, and beyond it the stucco exterior of the condo across the street was clearly visible.

Jenny clenched her fists and turned away from the mirror slowly, unwillingly. She inhaled deeply, her nostrils flaring, and looked at the window. The glow was gone. Only a trick of the light, she thought. Unconvinced, she stared wide-eyed until her eyes glazed over. She finally blinked. When the glow did not return, she moved toward the window to reassure herself that all was indeed normal. Her hands remained clenched.

Something was happening in her head. There was a sound in her ears that seemed to reach her through a million tons of water, as if she were riding a heavy current near the ocean floor. Moving toward . . . what?

There's nothing out there, you fool, nothing but your crazy imagination. It's not real, not true, only a fantasy. Jenny repeated the words over and over, but her body continued moving forward.

She reached the window. She could see that there was nothing outside, and yet she could hear her grandfather's voice, muffled by the layers of years, as if it were warning her from a great distance.

You shouldn't play with the gun . . .

The familiar scenery outside was abruptly replaced by chaos. Bits and pieces of memory—hallucinations?—crowded their way into her jumbled consciousness. Images of darkness and flashes of glowing red pervaded her mind.

Think of something else, Jenny, something . . . anything. She grimaced, even though she knew, deep in her mind, that this was all in her imagination. I'm not fighting hard enough!

. . . if you can't keep your finger off the trigger.

With an effort, she resisted, but she could feel the blood in her heart responding, a pounding tide. Around her she could sense the unseen ocean, deep and wild, succumbing to the force of a ruling moon.

Keep your finger off the trigger.

All her emotions were now sublimated to the invisible touch, the aroused panic. Something was trying to engulf her. And the very thought of what it wanted to do to her sapped her will to resist.

The trigger

The visions and nightmares that had haunted her for weeks at last rose up and fused hideous shadows into a reptilian image she feared more than death itself.
Trigger
The lizard coalesced and advanced toward her.

two

JENNY'S SCREAM REVERBERATED in her mind as her lips pressed together in agony over clenched teeth. She knew that no scream had left her throat. It was all in her mind.

There was nothing outside. She stared through the window, down at the patch of lawn. Everything was normal.

The early morning was calm, incredibly peaceful. Laurel Canyon slumbered undisturbed between the restlessness of West Hollywood and the coma of the San Fernando Valley.

She could tell there was nothing on the lawn, knew it as surely as she knew she was heading for a mental crack-up if she didn't get control of herself. Nothing on the lawn, nothing on the street. Nothing waiting or beckoning. Nothing but the nightmares in her mind.

Only the fear was real—something to be conquered, a troublesome psychosis to be beaten and whipped back into the dark with decision and logic.

The strange gray-blue color must have been a trick of reflection as heavy dark clouds tumbled across the bloated moon. Duane's bright orange van was not yet in sight. She tried to imagine it coming up the street, its brilliant color dispelling her gloom, but the street remained as empty as the shadowy windows in the building across the way. Jenny gripped the window sill with her aching hands and shook her head in anger.

Shit, I can scare myself with all sorts of visions, but to soothe my nerves I can't even conjure up a familiar van.

Her eyes returned to the lawn below. It sprouted a stunted palm and attendant hardy shoots of ivy that apparently never grew or died. Nothing waited in the shadows here. Nothing living, nothing dead.

The small lizard corpse was gone, probably picked up and flung unceremoniously into the furnace by Mr. Domenico, the ever-watchful landlord. All that remained were her memories of it, memories that were being transformed into bizarre nightmares by her troubled mind.

I'm not seriously searching for the dead lizard.

The thought drifted across her mind like an offhand remark, and she recognized the dishonesty of it immediately. The thing had appeared at dusk, then reappeared in broad daylight, and the mystery of it was not in its appearance, but in its effect. Her fantasies were never bound by temperance, but this was something new. Something she didn't understand, something dark and terrible.

It had begun several weeks earlier when she had arrived home, tired after a long day at the Institute. She had expected to see Mr. Domenico pop up from his bench near the garage entrance, where he often worked in the early evening and would remind her to lock her car door. "You know, Miss McGregor," he would say, "if we don't mind our *P*s and *Q*s, our *A-B-C*s will be stolen right out from under us."

Frank Domenico was a kindly and neat but sometimes nosy landlord. With his gentle Spanish accent and fumbling grasp of English metaphor, Jenny was never quite sure if his monotonous smile indicated mild concern or just mild incomprehension. She knew he didn't approve of Brad sleeping over so often. He was never directly critical, but there was something about the way he said "*Miss* McGregor" and "*Doctor* Knowlton" whenever he saw them together that made her squirm.

Jenny had hurried up the sidewalk, glad that Mr. Domenico was not at his bench. She came to a halt as her shoe met a small resistance. She saw the lizard and wondered if she had stepped on the creature, perhaps even killed it. Guiltily she bent forward and with the pointed toe of her shoe she cautiously nudged it. There was no movement.

The dusky evening light helped it blend into the shadowy concrete with the efficiency of a chameleon hiding from predators. It lay along the narrow crevice between the curbing and the plane of the walk. Even its tail lay straight along that concrete cleft, as if the creature had rolled there to die and rigor mortis held it in place.

As she leaned closer Jenny realized that the death image that had sprung to mind was appropriate. The lizard was undoubtedly dead, but she watched, as if to make certain she didn't miss even the feeblest twitch of life.

It had become so very dim that she thought she could detect the light washing out to nothing as she waited.

As the street lamp switched on automatically, the pavement began to glow with a soft haze. Yet it wasn't the faint crackle of the bulb coming to life above her that made her heart leap. It was what the light revealed that jolted her so severely.

Even when alive, reptiles often look dead when seen lying motionless in the shade of a leaf, or baking on a tree limb or rock in the afternoon sun. But this lizard had been dead for some time. The body was slick with corruption, and the head was crawling with tiny ants.

Even as she pulled back in disgust, Jenny's perceptions fooled her for a moment. The lizard looked not *quite* dead, as if only a brush with living flesh would revive it from timeless slumber, destroy its plunderers, strip away its rot. And she felt strangely drawn to it.

Could her nearness discharge a spark of life? Was this something the lizard craved and compelled?

Perhaps its dead eye would open. The ants would flee like routed soldiers as moisture returned and the iris caught a glint of light. As the mouth gaped, the tongue darted out and back. As the reptile curved its flexible body and rolled over, stretching its deep jaws, drawing in a sucking breath, moving toward her . . .

Jenny blinked. She emerged as if from a cloud, momentarily dizzy and disoriented. She looked down at the lizard. It lay along the curb. Unmoving. Dead.

Jenny had never had a hallucination in her life, but she felt she'd just had her first and it frightened her more than she dared acknowledge.

A minute later she was in her apartment. She quickly fell into her normal routine, dismissing the lizard from her mind entirely.

Or so she thought.

The following days found the lizard crawling out of the dark places of her memory. Unbidden and unwanted, its image would surge up before her. The suddenness of these hallucinations was startling, since they were obviously no more than mental projections, fantasy images flicked on and off her retinas like fast-changing slides.

Her co-workers noticed Jenny's uncharacteristic actions—blank stares, odd hesitations, and once a dead stop in the middle of a stride across the room—but none of them would have considered confronting her with a direct question. Staff asked questions about patients, not about staff. There was *gossip* about staff, which was something else entirely, and these days Jenny was getting her share of that, especially among those who believed that marriage was the answer to her problem.

Jenny was as puzzled over her actions as everyone else.

In the lab she would hesitate before opening a refrigerator door, although she knew exactly what she would find: shelves of culture dishes and specimens, each labelled with a name, room number and date, some to be checked and discarded, others to be left for twenty-four or forty-eight more hours. Overflow work from the hospital lab kept the shelves crowded these days, but there was nothing out of the ordinary about that.

Knowing what she would find inside apparently did not prevent her mind, now so willful and inexplicable that she almost thought of it as a separate entity, from playing its new little tricks.

One time she opened the door and saw the lizard, alive and agile, uncorrupted, doubled in size. It weaved over the slender metal shelf rods, gulping the plates of agar, drinking the stored chemicals. It spun and hissed at her, its eyes shining, then lunged forward, its cold skin snaking back from the teeth and jaws as if it were smiling. Hideously.

This happened in a second or two, a dream superimposing itself seamlessly over reality. As she stood with the open door in her hand and an astonished expression on her face, the pressure of a hand on her upper arm made her gasp and jump. She smiled nervously at Joan Kranz and explained that, no, she wasn't ill, perhaps a little tired. The date for Maria's marriage was still firm and, yes, the vacation would probably do her a world of good. She just needed a little rest. Yes, she had, yes, she could, yes, she would. . . .

The conversation with Joan, as no-nonsense a woman as Jenny had ever met, pushed her fantasies back into the darkness. She returned to the reality of fluorescent lamps, to counters loaded with diseased cultures and slices of flesh, to rubbery tubings of congealed blood, to dyes washing away the look of health and coloring the appearance of death.

Ah, yes, reality.

Jenny reached the dubious conclusion that the dead lizard had triggered some obscure obsession pulled from a cobwebbed corner of her memory.

Since the lizard's body had disappeared from the sidewalk by the next morning, it had been easily forgotten. She knew her fantasy images did not reflect an obsession with the actual reptile, and she tried to dismiss the whole matter as some weird psychological fluke that would resolve itself when she decided how to confront the other tensions in her life—namely, her escalating dissatisfaction with Brad and their relationship.

The following Saturday morning, Jenny had hurried out the front door of her apartment building, slowing to fish sunglasses out of her purse. As her hand crept through the bag's jumble, groping for the familiar feel of the worn leather glasses case, she caught her foot in a tangled shoot of ivy lying across the sidewalk, and stumbled. As she nudged the plant off the walk, the leaves trailed after her shoe and the remains of the lizard were uncovered. It rested on its back, near the palm tree, its body badly decomposed. Her lungs froze. The dead creature made a disgusting smell and sight, but it didn't have the impact of the first encounter. It was merely unpleasant.

Or so she thought.

If her repeated hallucinations had become an annoyance, Jenny's second actual view of the dead lizard triggered the opening of a new mental corridor for the visions to haunt.

The daytime episodes ended and the night siege began.

Brad was attending to an emergency at the hospital, which had cancelled their plans for dinner with Duane and Maria. Jenny reveled in her unexpected evening of solitude. She carefully opened her writing desk and cleared the work area of the clutter that always seemed to accumulate there. She admired the clean surface briefly, then she placed on it a plate of Graham crackers, a glass of milk, and a stack of unpaid bills. She turned on the bright desk lamp and settled down to pay her debts.

This was the sort of tedious log work that drove her crazy at the Institute, where it seemed triplicate forms outnumbered the atmosphere's oxygen molecules about ten thousand to one. But at home, with the radio tuned to a station playing music from the 40s, 50s, and 60s, Jenny felt like she was in a time machine. She found the work as calming as a sedative.

By the time she'd pressed stamps on all the envelopes, it was ten o'clock. Television news wouldn't start for another hour, and she didn't want to watch some tired situation comedy or figure out the plot of a half-finished movie.

Leaving her desk in a mess, Jenny closed the cover over it. She switched off the lights and peeled off her clothes as she ambled toward the bedroom. There she fell across the bed with a sigh, luxuriating in the cool clinging texture of the sheets. She was asleep almost instantly, easily and without fear.

When the dream began, Jenny sleepily groped for the cover she had kicked aside in the night. The bedroom was so chilled that she thought she'd left the windows open. Hazed with drowsiness, her eyes seemed touched as well with the damp night mist that sometimes crept through the city's hills and smothered the darkness.

Jenny rose to shut the louvered window but saw that the windows were already closed. Not a breath of breeze slipped between the glass slats to ruffle the lightweight curtains. Her gaze skated across the window to the ivory walls of the bedroom, walls that glistened like wet porcelain.

She touched a wall. It even felt like porcelain, cold and slick. What had happened to the walls, to the room? Everything was lit by a blue-gray glow.

Jenny was shivering uncontrollably now and snatched a cream-colored blanket off the bed. She wrapped it tightly around her shoulders and her fingers left dark wet stains on the soft material. She glanced down at the stains and gasped. The floor was gone, replaced by metal crosshatching pressing painfully into the soles of her feet.

She regarded herself as an animal caught in a trap, but the concept didn't really frighten her. Everything was suffused with a sense of the familiar. There was the reassuring acidic odor of the lab to the room, an odor of chemicals reacting with human flesh and waste.

Even in her sleep Jenny had always been able to tell the difference between realistic and fantastic dreams, and she was never captured by them in the way a child can be swept up in their fury and immediacy. To most people dreams vary in their intensity and sharpness, but Jenny, as an adult, couldn't remember having a dream that she did not know at the time *was* a dream. Even her infrequent sex dreams, emotionally cloudy but accompanied by quite convincing physical sensations, never seemed "real."

But her present dream confused her.

She realized it was a dream, but this did not reduce the dread that was beginning to press against her, imprisoning her in an unreal temporary world. She could accept the combination of her home and work environments, for the substitutes and symbols almost explained themselves. But there was no basis, no "why" to this dream. The images were devoid of meaning. The growing unease had no cause.

Her distress intensified when the room's blue-gray light, coming from nowhere and everywhere, began to creep around her like shadows on a pool at twilight. She knew that its source was now behind her, yet all the will power in her mind couldn't convince her that the bedside lamp and its funny bubble shade could produce this eerie effect.

The light began to pulse, slow and steady. Rhythmically. Enticingly.

There were too many oddities now and Jenny could no longer deal with them directly. In a nervous habit that lingered from childhood she pulled her hair over her shoulder and began to twist little strands of it with her fingers, concentrating on those strands to the exclusion of all else. But she couldn't blot out the light.

It was such a silly way for an old table lamp to behave, she sighed, and thought, I can probably fix it myself. She flicked her hair back over her shoulder with a sweaty hand and, sighing once again, turned.

Instantly the blood drained from her face. The bed, nightstand, and lamp were gone.

In their place was the lizard.

It lay on its back across the wire crosshatching. It had grown much larger, almost as large as a human child of five or six years. And it was still growing—rapidly.

She watched the body elongate, taking weight. The tail twitched briefly but the eyes remained closed; the legs gained muscle yet remained limp. The light came from the thing itself and intensified as it grew larger. The dream image incorporated the putridity of its small sidewalk counterpart, but the light seemed to be healing the lizard's corruption.

It became difficult to see what was happening, for the light turned dazzling.

There comes a point in dreams and nightmares where the bizarre is so predominant that the dreamer's logic screams with sensible questions. As the dream proceeds the dreamer begins to reject it, even while still moving through it. The dream becomes a play that must reach a conclusion, no matter how unconvincing. So the child in Jenny retreated as her adult sensibilities once again took hold.

Questions were raging, but by then it was too late. As if sensing that she was fighting its illogic, the lizard rose to its hind feet. It was now the size of an adult human.

Using the tail for balance, it took a step forward and hissed in her face. Turning its head to the side so that she could see the scales glisten along the damp line of its mouth, it hissed again. The sound was deep, rhythmic, enticing. The eyes, closed till now, sprang open, bright yellow and filled with . . . hatred? desire? It was impossible to tell.

The lizard stepped closer, snaking out a long tongue that licked softly at Jenny's neck as the creature pressed on its own chest with lank front feet.

It was then that Jenny looked down and saw she was garbed in a surgical gown. Her right hand held a nine-inch scalpel.

There was a throbbing sensation in her head, a sense of unbalance, almost sensual, irresistible. There was also an overpowering sense of danger which drove Jenny to grasp the handle of the blade in both hands and lift it above her head.

There was no time for consideration or question, no time to wonder.

With a wail she plunged the scalpel into the lizard's chest, pulling the blade down through the middle of the abdomen, feeling it tear soundlessly through gristle and meat.

Her gloveless hands and the sleeves of her surgical gown were instantly drenched in a colorless ichor that ran slow and sticky from the creature. Blood leaked from its body in widening rivulets, turning the slow-running ichor red.

Jenny began to sob with unbearable shame. She'd been degraded, violated, used. What she had done was murderous, not sexual, yet she felt like a whore, opening to a stranger whose face she couldn't see. Didn't *want* to see. Tears flooded her eyes and spilled hotly down her cheeks.

And through it all her mind desperately grasped again for logic. This makes no sense; it isn't real. Her brain stabbed messages at her: *Don't look! Don't listen!* She tried to concentrate, and as she listened the warnings seemed to strengthen. The room and the horrible creature before her grew dim.

She was almost free of the dream when, with incredible suddenness, it surged back and gripped her with a strangling power.

From inside the lizard's incision, a man's hands appeared. The reptilian body began to fold and crumple as the strong hands tore the creature's flesh away. Jenny thought she could hear the bones snapping. There was a popping, bubbling sound, as if internal organs were being pushed aside, rearranged.

Within moments a tall, swarthy, naked male stood before her. He looked familiar, but for some reason she couldn't tell who he was. Someone she knew at the Institute? The hospital? The man was not embarrassed, perhaps not even conscious of his nudity, but he looked at Jenny and desired her. His arousal was evident.

Jenny herself was once again naked. Experiencing pleasure from her own surging desire and shame at its lustful aspect, she trembled and crossed her arms over her chest, her limbs cold against the heat of her breasts. But neither the shame nor the lust survived the onslaught of the new emotion that crushed her when the man came a step nearer.

For the first time in her life she felt the iron grip of unrelenting terror.

She couldn't run, couldn't move her body except to tremble, but her thoughts bolted into the wild, writhing with revulsion and horror.

The man reached and held her shoulders. He smiled, and as he smiled Jenny began to shudder and cry because he kept smiling. His lips pulled back, the face disappeared behind a row of shiny objects that had to be teeth—but looked like steel blades. The jaws opened with a hiss and she could see—blood, everywhere, *blood*!

Jenny threw her hands to her mouth but could not scream. Gagging, choking, she thought she would die of suffocation.

He—It—was on her over her with her *in* her. It was beyond what she could endure. Beyond anything, beyond everything, beyond life itself. She could not, *would not* admit it was something that seemed like pleasure. It mingled sensuously with her terror and disgust. The union was obscene. She would rather die. Die . . .

And then she was awake, eyes stinging with the sweat that poured into them, her body aching with the tension that had twisted every muscle into agony.

It was several minutes before she began to breathe normally, several more before her body began to relax from its adrenaline high. She rubbed her hands over her cold face and pushed the damp hair off her cheeks where it clung like a fungal growth. The window curtain puffed inward on a cool breeze; the bedsheets were wringing wet.

The dream's images lingered abnormally, drinking up the last drop of fear.

She didn't sleep for a long time. The terror refused to fade. For a moment she hoped that Brad would come by, but the thought of a man's hands on her made her cringe. She could still feel the lizard-man's hands on her body, feel them gripping, holding, pulling her into—

"Hon. Hey, wake up. Duane and Maria just pulled up." Brad waved a hand in front of her eyes.

Jenny blinked, her memories scuttling back into dark

storage. She placed a hand over Brad's, which rested on her shoulder with a warm secure pressure. "I wasn't asleep. Just daydreaming."

"Can't daydream until the sun comes up." He kissed her briefly on the neck, then whispered, "If you'll carry the heavy stuff out to the van, tonight I'll let you play with my—"

Jenny jabbed her elbow into his ribs. "*You* carry the heavy stuff and I'll buy you a deck of cards. Then you can play with yourself."

Brad lifted two suitcases and started toward the door. "You know, you've got a very sexist attitude." He winked as he walked out.

You fight back with humor, Jenny mused, but it really isn't very funny at all.

"Self-defense, Brad," she murmured.

three

EVEN THOUGH DUANE and Maria had packed for a week at Point Locke, the wedding, and a week-long honeymoon trip to Hawaii, they were not taking as much as Brad.

Jenny's suitcase and overnight bag were small, but Brad had carefully taped shut a half-dozen boxes of food, camping utensils, and God knew what other "essentials," all in addition to his black medical bag and two hulking Naugahyde suitcases.

Duane lifted a suitcase and groaned. "Jesus, you afraid someone's gonna break a leg? Feels like you've got all the hospital's X-ray equipment packed in here."

Brad snorted, juggling the cumbersome but lightweight boxes in his arms as he shouldered open the apartment door. "That's the light one. The other has twenty-seven bowling balls."

"I think you've got enough balls already, Brad."

The men stumbled their way down the stairwell.

"Hey, that reminds me, Duane. There's this nurse who works in a prep room, see, and one day this post-op football star wakes up, takes one look at her..."

Brad's voice was cut off by the slam of the outside door. Jenny was grateful. She watched as Maria scurried across the living room to switch off Jenny's kitchen light. Was it only her imagination or did Maria seem to float across the room? Did marriage and happiness actually lift one off the floor?

Maria was small and very feminine. Her dark brown hair erupted around her tiny face in a joyful explosion of curls. She was beautiful. Everyone thought so, especially Jenny, with a slight touch of jealousy. Maria's brown eyes—the color of root beer—were expressive and lit up her face. Her lips always seemed to be suppressing a giggle... especially these days. She and Duane had been inseparable for months. Since they had announced their engagement, Maria's smile was so indelible that Brad liked to joke about her suffering from a severe muscular disorder.

Duane's looks were a perfect complement to Maria's— they made a handsome couple. He was a little taller than average, lean and trim, without having to work at it as Brad did. His eyes were a bright blue. As the summer progressed, the California sun tanned his skin bronze, while streaking his light brown hair with touches of gold.

His healthy good looks and polite, pleasant manner— plus his shy smile—were irresistible. He was just the sort of fellow you'd be proud to take home to Mother.

Maria turned in the doorway, her hand on the switch. "Did you water these plants, Jenny? You know you're always forgetting." There was no criticism in her voice. She simply knew Jenny very well.

Jenny had to think a moment. "Yes, I did," she replied. She'd watered the three plants and placed them in the kitchen window where they would have plenty of light in her absence. Not that it would do the poor things much good. They alternated between yellowing collapse when she forgot to water them, and attacks of root rot when she overcompensated for her neglect.

"Okay." Maria hit the switch and joined Jenny at the front door. "Living with you has put those poor things through plant-world equivalents of the Chicago fire and the Johnstown flood. They'll probably be grateful for a few days of relief."

"Oh, you." Jenny fumbled through a heavy ring of keys as they stood outside the door.

When the two women hurried toward the van, Duane was gallantly holding the door open for them. Jenny whispered to Maria. "There's your future husband, to have and to hold, etc. etc. Are you sure you know what you're doing?"

"Yes," Maria answered, rolling her eyes with all the subtlety of a silent movie queen.

Jenny groaned, reaching for Maria's neck with fingers arched into a threatening position. Maria giggled again and ran to the van, jumping inside and trying to pull the door closed before Jenny could catch her. The door had large block letters reading "Eastman Hardware" over a black silhouette of a claw hammer.

"All right, I give up," Jenny called. "Anyone who runs and hides doesn't *deserve* a distinguished death by strangulation."

The night was dying over the city as Jenny climbed into the van. Duane switched on the ignition. The vehicle moved up Laurel Canyon and dropped gently out of the hills down to Studio City, then turned west onto Ventura Boulevard.

How nice to get away from that environment of poison, thought Jenny, watching yet another chain restaurant—*6-10 A.M.! Breakfast Special!*—wave its garish banners and disappear behind them. In the front seat Duane, cautious and responsible, concentrated fully on the road. Maria's fingers toyed idly with the back of his shirt collar, but she too was quiet and watched the way ahead passively. As a doctor, Brad had learned to grab sleep any time or place.

He was asleep before the second Breakfast Special had been swallowed up by the dawn.

Jenny glanced at Brad with irritation. So much for a sparkling four-way conversation to get the day off to an energetic start. She leaned her head against the window glass and watched the early morning people bring the West Valley suburbs to life. An early riser herself, she identified with them as they wended their way to work. The sun would rise, the earth would spin, and these were the people who made the world move, who diligently turned the great engine over every morning.

Morning spilled deliriously over the horizon behind them as the van, now on the Ventura freeway, breezed through Tarzana, Woodland Hills, and Calabasas. The traffic moving in the other direction, into Los Angeles, was beginning to pick up. In another thirty minutes the inbound lanes would hold long, segmented snakes of metal, each segment switching from one serpent to another, slithering toward another day of viperous business.

The pace of the day, both inside and outside the van, began to pick up. It was as if everything had to absorb a certain amount of morning warmth to become animated with life.

Maria warmed quickest, as always. As she talked she turned in the front seat to watch Jenny's reactions, moving her hands with precise little gestures to emphasize her words. It was one of the things that Jenny had always admired about Maria, this clarity in everything she said and did. Maria was a woman who made decisions rapidly, who knew exactly what she was doing at all times. Such precision made her an excellent medical chemist, just as it made her a dependable friend. There was never any question of where you stood with Maria.

Jenny listened attentively, watching with an analytical eye. For a woman on her way to get married, Maria didn't look the least concerned about the coming changes in her life. But when you knew Maria as well as Jenny knew her, had seen her self-control in the laboratory with demanding supervisors and impatient doctors, then her untypical remarks to Duane—"Look out for that truck . . . Watch that entryway. . . . You're over the speed limit, slow down!" —were dead giveaways of her pent-up nervous energy.

Maria just couldn't be quiet. She chattered away, giving Duane unneeded warnings that he tolerated with amazing patience, interspersed with her little squeals of pleasure as she responded to picture-postcard roadside views.

Jenny would nod, stare fascinatedly at the scenery as it rolled past, and murmur appreciatively. Suburban sprawl was eating away the lovely landscape, burying the rolling hills in concrete. Condo villages and shopping malls clung to the earth with the heavy weight of convenience. Contractors and engineers obviously thought esthetics was something to do with arranging potted palms in parking lots. Nonetheless there were stretches along the way where the hills strained to become mountains, where nature had its way and retained a hold on the golden land. Especially after they had passed through Ventura, when the highway ribboned its way alongside the ocean, nature still ruled a majestic realm.

A refreshing breeze swept in from the water and the land responded with a bloom of color. It was going to be a glorious trip, a glorious wedding, a glorious summer. Maria insisted it would be, over and over.

As Jenny watched her friend chatter on, she let her mind drift. She could not help thinking about the Regard Cancer Research Institute. It was her career, her life, in many ways her most consuming love. Had she really been there only three years?

She thought of all the tissue samples she had examined in that time, the elevated enzymes that Maria and the other techs reported when carcinomas had metastasized. They all studied as people died, experimented as people died, repeatedly failed as people died. Would there ever be an end to these needless deaths? Doctors struggled to keep them alive for a few more days, a few more hours, as thousands of research teams around the world hunted for answers.

If we're lucky, Jenny told herself, we'll stumble over a cure just the way Duane accidentally stumbled over Maria.

It had been tragic, that day in the hospital parking lot when Duane Eastman had blundered into the car door Maria held open for Jenny. There was a glassy look in his eyes, and Maria, so sensitive to human pain and suffering, saw immediately that he was in shock. Grief and rage hung from him like ragged clothing, but by good fortune he had fallen into the arms of Maria Salina, who held him as he cried.

Dazed and broken, Duane at last had brought his emotions under control as he and Maria sat on the rough pavement. She grasped his hand tightly as he leaned his back against the car fender, closed his eyes, and began to talk. Duane's older brother, Howard, had just died, victim of a freak auto accident that had also claimed their parents.

Duane had listened to the voices of solicitous hospital personnel and the crowding horde of leeches who began to converge at the smell of blood and money. As the only surviving family member, Duane would inherit a considerable fortune, generated from his father's expansive chain of hardware stores. The leeches, all "close" friends of his parents, many of whom had tried at one time or another to buy into the business and been rebuffed, had closed in on the survivor before Howard and the parents were even cold. Duane had managed to escape them by slipping into a service elevator, then had simply wandered out a corridor exit and into the parking lot.

Jenny knelt beside them and listened for a time, finally hustling them into a coffee shop across the street. She left them in a dim corner, where they talked over steaming cups of oily coffee and bowls of lukewarm soup, and called the hospital to explain that Mr. Eastman would contact them soon with arrangements for the bodies and to sign the necessary legal papers.

The next day at the Institute Maria had been tired, but her face was radiant. She had taken Duane home to her tiny apartment and propped him up on the couch with pillows and blankets, feeding him hot tea laced with honey. They had continued to talk for hours.

Jenny knew Duane was a quiet sort, pleasant and agreeable, but a long way from talkative. It was hard for her to imagine what that night must have been like. The glow in Maria's tired eyes the following morning, however, told her that it had somehow gone deeper than veiled autobiographies and the superficial easing of tragedy. And Maria had never since lost that glow.

Over the first few days after the accident, Maria took some of her vacation and spent as much time with Duane as she could. She had helped him start his life over again. One of his wisest early decisions was to hire some competent management personnel for the Eastman Hardware chain. Without his brother and father there, Duane didn't want to spend much time at the headquarters, and that thriving concern didn't really need his attention at all. Duane was fond of saying that all he had to do was look at the books now and then to keep them honest.

If Jenny's own romantic life was troubled, it didn't dampen her enthusiasm for Maria's delighted discovery of love. Just like in the movies, Jenny chuckled to herself.

"What are you laughing at, Jenny?"

"I was just watching you. You've been talking nonstop for I don't know how long. Brad's sound asleep, I lost track twenty minutes ago, and Duane—"

Duane reached across and tousled Maria's hair lightly. "She was describing all the special preparations for our wedding night." He winked.

"Gee, Jenny. Something's missing from my trousseau. I should have picked up some of those sexy clothes we saw at Frederick's of Hollywood."

"Don't worry, Maria—just wait till you open your wedding presents!" Jenny said with a smug smile.

"You two wouldn't be caught dead in a place like that!" Duane stated with total conviction. Frederick's was known for its sexy ads in men's magazines—it specialized in scanty, erotic clothing.

Jenny and Maria exploded in laughter. Maria caught her breath first and raised her right hand as if swearing an oath. "I cannot tell a lie, Duane. I have been in Frederick's!"

"Okay, that does it!" Duane said, trying to keep a

straight face. "I'm not marrying anyone who shops in that flesh empire!" He threw his head back and laughed heartily. "Tell me more!"

"I've been there *twice*. Does that mean I have to get out of your van and walk the rest of the way?" Jenny asked, her eyes wide and innocent.

"That depends," Duane answered. "Did you buy anything?"

"*I* did, but Maria was chicken. I guess I better confess, too. I dragged Maria along for moral support; I wanted to get a new outfit for Brad's birthday."

"Tell him about the panties!" Maria urged.

"Oh yes, the panties. Well, they were skimpy to the point of being nonexistent." Jenny looked around conspiratorily, then checked to see if Brad was still asleep. Her voice dropped, as if to let Duane in on an important secret. "Some were even no-crotch models!"

"No!" Duane exclaimed, pretending to be scandalized.

"It gets better," Maria said. "Some were *edible*. They even came in assorted flavors!"

Duane licked his lips lustfully, and Maria and Jenny howled.

The women's shrill laughter woke Brad from his slumber. He rubbed his eyes briefly. "Are we almost there?"

Even Duane joined the next explosion of guffaws. Brad's expression made it clear that he thought they'd all gone totally crackers with road fever or something. Being odd man out didn't please him at all. He settled back in the corner with a sour expression, frowning a bit harder each time one of the others would glance his way and muffle another giggle.

Things had calmed down by the time they reached Santa Barbara. They freshened up at a service station, then parked in a public lot and enjoyed a brisk walk under the fan palms that separated the beach from the city. Exploitation of the town's beauty for the benefit of goggling tourists hadn't yet attained the crassness of L.A.'s environs. The laid-back atmosphere of comfort seemed to embrace them as they wandered aimlessly under the afternoon sun.

Brad and Jenny admired the city's architecture, especially the distinctive Moorish influence, but Maria was less interested in the overview than in the small details. Boldly opening closed gates and peering over garden walls, she rediscovered a courtyard off a small alley, remembered from a previous visit. The enclosure housed a series of delicate Roman fountains.

"It reminds me of Hadrian's villa," sighed Maria, who had once been to Italy with her mother. "All it needs is a couple thousand years to acquire some real character."

"It's a date," Duane said, splashing her lightly with water from one of the small fountains. "Two thousand years from now we'll all come back to admire its character." He jumped out of the way when Maria began paddling water out of the fountain onto his pants.

"Now, now," Brad scolded Maria. "Mustn't mistreat the future hubby—*eeyow!!*" Jenny had sneaked up behind him and dumped a handful of cold water onto his neck. She hopped out of reach as he flailed around the courtyard, gasping like a beached fish.

"Surgeons are such sissies," Jenny said airily, shaking the water off her hands with a show of nonchalance.

Brad's melodramatic yells brought a fat, middle-aged lady to an upper window nearby. She shouted at them in Spanish, waving them away with a yellow dish cloth, but Jenny saw her hide a smile as they moved out into the alley. The air of romance is hard to resist, Jenny told herself with amusement.

The city was full of similar delightful discoveries, and it was after noon before they realized that they had eaten little all day. Maria said she knew just the place for lunch and led them to the El Paseo Restaurant, which reeked of Old World enchantment and the mouth-watering smells of spicy Mexican food.

As they studied the menu they all tried the hot sauce that the waiter had left at their table along with a basket of deep-fried tortilla chips.

"God!" Jenny gasped as her eyes watered and her throat tried to shrivel away. She downed half a glass of water in a gulp. "What do they *put* in that stuff?"

"Red peppers and nitric acid. Mostly the latter, I think," answered Maria as she popped a sauce-drenched chip into her mouth. She didn't even flush. "Kills cockroaches, too."

Brad looked around briefly, but couldn't spot any waitresses, only waiters. He was disappointed. He liked to joke with waitresses, and his tips went up, Jenny knew from experience, with the state of their undress. A shapely, exposed leg guaranteed a generous gratuity, and a low-cut neckline had him pulling bills out of his wallet with a generosity that equalled or exceeded the exposed cleavage. Their stiff and formal waiter, with his little black bow tie and nonexistent hips would be lucky to get a standard tip. Jenny made a mental note to slip an extra bill onto the table before they left.

They ordered salads and various Mexican dishes—except Maria, who ordered a hamburger. Soundly reprimanded by her companions, she laughingly ordered red wine to go with it.

Maria's chatterbox nervousness dissipated in the afternoon sun, or perhaps it was Duane's warm attention that evaporated her earlier mood. The two pulled their chairs together, sharing a fruit salad, passing little bites back and forth to one another with smiles and satisfied murmurs. Jenny thought they looked like an advertisement for wedding rings, and said so.

"And they lived happily ever after. . . ." Brad quipped.

". . . feasting on fruit salad, passion, and love," Duane finished. He took another mouthful of cantaloupe from Maria.

"Passion and love are very nice, but they aren't going to wash your underwear or fix dinner every evening."

The moment the words were out of her mouth, Jenny regretted them. She was allowing her own bitterness to spill out in remarks such as that, and it was a selfish thing to do. This was neither the time nor the place for such self-indulgence.

Brad tried to cover. "You know Jenny—always worried about someone's underwear. . . ."

Everyone laughed, even Jenny, but she spent the rest of the afternoon silently berating herself for that slip of the tongue. She would have to be very careful over the next few days if she were to keep from injecting a somber note into an occasion that should be nothing but joy.

The remark hadn't surprised Maria, knowing as she did Jenny's distress about her changing feeling for Brad. She and Jenny had spent repeated lunches and coffee breaks in the hospital's cafeteria, balancing the philosophical scales on the values and hazards of feminine independence.

"You and Brad live together," Maria had once commented. "Oh, Brad has his own apartment, and his neighbors may say they've even seen him there once or twice. But he's at your place nearly as much as you are. The only thing you lack is that slip of legal paper."

"A piece of paper's a piece of paper, no matter what's written on it." Jenny had waved her hand in disgust. "I'm tired of the sexist jokes, the poker games, the macho image that Brad thinks is so damned important. I'd hoped he'd outgrow it, but now . . . I just don't know. It seems to be so ingrained that I can't rub it out."

"Have you told him how much it disturbs you? How seriously it affects your relationship?"

"It always becomes a joke. He thinks I'm making a stand, and nothing convinces him we're doing anything more than taking sides in a debating exercise. For him it's a game. For me it used to be a challenge, but now it's become a bore."

Maria was not so easily misled. "Are you sure that's not what Brad has always been?"

"What do you mean?"

"Maybe that's why you liked him in the first place. He was a challenge, something new and exciting. Maybe it was the challenge rather than the man you loved."

"Don't be ridiculous." Jenny had answered testily, but

the idea had startled her and she'd given considerable thought to it over the past weeks. If plans had not already been made for all of them to coordinate vacation time for the wedding, Jenny might have already been mapping a new future with plans that would not include Brad. Perhaps she only needed a sudden change in perspective to see her way clear of her present indecision.

Would a separation bring a change in Brad's viewpoint as well as her own? God knew they couldn't go on this way any longer. *She* couldn't go on this way any longer.

Jenny felt a hand on her shoulder and turned to look into Brad's blue eyes. He pointed to his watch and smiled.

"If we don't move out, we'll be trailing into Point Locke like zombies in the dead of night."

"We must get there soon," Maria added mischievously. "Mother will have the highway patrol, the FBI, and half of Mexico's illegals out searching for us. So let us please get our pretty asses in gear."

She wasn't kidding about the illegals. Maxine Salina had some of the largest privately owned vineyards in California's Central Coast region, which had originally belonged to a group of Franciscans who had moved farther south and sold the lands to Mr. Salina's great-grandparents. Scrupulously maintained by the family, the vineyards had proved successful many times over when Juan Salina met and married Maxine Hammond. Maria had been born a few years later.

When Mr. Salina died of a stroke while Maria was still in high school, Maxine buckled down and trained herself to manage the business, having had no more than peripheral interest in it in the preceding years. Juan's relatives presided over the actual maintenance of the winery and the harvesting—including hiring the illegal immigrants who flooded California with cheap labor. Maxine was concerned about this practice, yet assumed that Juan's family knew more about it than she did. As the yearly profits went up, however, political and business pressures were being applied, and these pressures were always directed at Maxine.

Jenny had not yet met Maxine, but from Maria's descriptions she pictured her as a strong-willed, determined woman whose vineyards never failed because she told the grapes to "grow, or else. . . ."

The sun slowly settled into the Pacific Ocean as they followed Highway 1 at a lazy pace, past San Luis Obispo, sidling nearer to the coast.

The moon was shining silver when they passed over a ridge and saw Point Locke spread out below. From the forest crowding right up to the edge of town in the east, to the white sand of the shoreline sparkling distantly in the other direction, Point Locke glowed with a bleary softness that was like a delicate watercolor painting in a picture book.

Duane gently pressed the brake and parked for a few moments.

The ridge beneath them sloped away gradually, as if giant hands had scooped out a gentle basin for the town. Jenny thought the trees looked like an EKG pattern etched against the blue-black sky, a tracing of nature itself, calm and regular and reassuring. The four of them were silent as they pressed to the window, drinking in the sight below.

"Heaven, that's what it is," said Duane, leaning over to kiss Maria delicately on the neck. "Heaven."

four

FROM THE RIDGE by which they approached Point Locke, the forest looked as if it had mysteriously coughed out the town intact from somewhere in New England. In spite of contemporary encroachments, the community reeked of quiet old wealth and tradition, a place where decorum had not been allowed to degenerate into mockery. The highway itself did not slice through the town. It left the shoreline instead and fled inland, plunging through the forested hillsides that crowded into the northeast edge of town.

The van glided over the silent streets as if it were a lazy pinball. Avoiding the main thoroughfares, it ricocheted along tiny side streets, corner to corner, until it reached a place where the campus joined wooded hillsides sown with scattered homes.

Maria indicated a long sloping driveway and Duane entered cautiously. The headlights swept over a row of carefully trimmed hedges bordering the drive for several hundred feet, then abruptly flooded the edge of a jungle.

At least it looks like a jungle, thought Jenny, when the brightness splattered over the wall of green leaves. As the driveway curved to run parallel with the wall, the visitors could see it was the wall of a gigantic sprawling house covered with vines. Ahead waited a great porch that gave off a gentle light, a warm oasis in the cool evening.

Maria honked the horn. It startled Jenny out of her open-mouthed awe and she glanced at Brad. He couldn't have been any more flabbergasted if he had opened up an appendectomy patient and found four-and-twenty blackbirds. It really was quite a place.

Jenny peered out the van's side window. The light from the porch was too wan to penetrate the darkness more than a few dozen feet, where the ivy crawled back into the wild shadows. She couldn't shake the feeling that the vines were growing down over the house rather than up, clawing *into* the earth as the house slowly crumbled under the pressure of green leafy fingers.

"Looks ominous at night, doesn't it?" Maria whispered in her ear, and Jenny turned to see that her friend was also staring at the vine-encrusted wall.

Jenny tried to be matter-of-fact. "What you need is some flood lamps along the drive, something to chase away the gloom."

"My room is up there." Maria pointed up into the shadows. Jenny thought she could see a window ledge, but it was so dark that she couldn't be sure.

"When I was a little girl," Maria continued, "I would sit at that window in the evening, on top of my toy box, staring at the moon. Every time I made a wish I'd pick a leaf off the ivy and drop it to the ground. I'd wish and wish and wish, but I wasn't able to make much of a dent in that ivy, it just grows so fast."

"What did you wish for?"

"After I saw *Snow White*, I guess I was waiting for my Prince Charming to just sort of mosey up the driveway and find me. But he never did find me. I had to go find him."

Duane grinned sheepishly, as if he had forgotten to rescue the girl from her ivy-covered room and was embarrassed by his oversight.

"If the place is this dark and gloomy all the time, I don't blame him for not showing up," said Jenny.

Brad patted Maria on the head. "No prince in his right mind would climb that wall in the dark, not unless you promised him a lot more than one of those chaste Disney kisses."

"Oh, I don't know," Duane commented. "Feeling around in the dark can be kinda fun sometimes, even if it is dangerous." He hugged Maria and yelped when she bit his ear.

The foursome clambered out of the van. Their happy expressions were a pleasure to the middle-aged woman who stepped through the massive front door and onto the porch. Jenny noted that the woman's face was as warm and welcoming as she thought a human face could ever be, and it made her smile just to look at it.

With a delighted cry of "Mama," Maria jumped up the steps and threw herself into the woman's arms, spinning her around as she hugged her tightly and kissed her.

It was a charming surprise to Jenny to find Maxine was *not* a slightly older edition of Maria and her vaguely rumpled, casual style. Having heard Maria talk so often about her mother and their shared confidences, Jenny saw them in her mind more as sisters than as mother and daughter. She didn't expect the patrician woman immaculately clad in a high-necked silk blouse and tweed skirt, her short silvery hair as sensibly coiffed as her feet were sensibly clad in sturdy but not unstylish black pumps.

"I'm sorry we're so late, Mama. It was such a nice day, we spent more time in Santa Barbara than we should have."

"I was concerned." Maxine Salina tried to look stern but couldn't pull down the corners of her mouth because a grin was fighting to get out. She grinned at Duane as he moved to give her a shy and gentlemanly peck on the cheek. "I thought Duane might have decided he didn't want to come visit our little backwoods after all."

The scene was mannerly and relaxed, yet Jenny was sure she detected a trace of resentment in Maxine's voice. Whether imagined or real, wouldn't a bit of motherly jealousy be normal?

After college, Maria had left Point Locke to work in L.A. During the first year Maxine had found excuses to travel down the coast and visit her daughter. She also telephoned, often. As much as she wanted Maria to become an independent woman, the mother in her could never quite let go of her only child.

Maria's psychological healthiness and new-found maturity had provided her with the outlook she needed to find a new life with Duane. The familial distancing was not severe or unpleasant, following as it did a perfectly normal human pattern, but Maria had once mentioned to Jenny that she thought her mother was finding it more difficult to be alone these days. It was the primary reason Maria had insisted on having the wedding in Point Locke, and her mother's radiant expression proved that her decision had been wise.

If Maxine's voice betrayed even the smallest trace of reserve about Duane, it was surely because she didn't know him well enough yet, Jenny thought. With her husband dead and her daughter ready to begin her own family far away from her, Maxine was entitled to some fear and resentment. It would pass.

Jenny felt her heart go out to Mrs. Salina. Brad followed her as she moved up the steps toward the older woman.

"Maxine, I'm Jenny McGregor."

"Jenny. I'm so happy to meet you at last." Maxine grasped Jenny's hand in both of hers.

They had spoken on the phone a number of times, but had somehow always just missed meeting whenever Maxine was visiting in L.A. Jenny had been sure she would like Maxine, and she did.

Jenny tugged at Brad by his shirt sleeve. "And this is Brad Knowlton."

Maxine shook his hand and studied him a moment. "Is this the one Maria calls the Ripper?" she asked with amusement.

"*Oh, Mama!*" Maria blushed.

"That's me, all right," Brad sang out. "But I'm the one surgeon who's more dangerous when he *hasn't* got a knife in his hand."

Brad had that look on his face. Jenny suspected he was prepping for a suggestive joke. Knowing that Maxine could hardly be ready for one of Brad's vulgar hospital jokes at this point, Jenny let out a low moan and shuddered theatrically before Brad had a chance to continue.

"Oh, brrr, I'm freezing. just freezing to death." The light breeze was hardly enough to ruffle the feathers of a bird, much less cause Jenny to clutch her arms and shiver.

Maxine put an arm protectively around Jenny's shoulders. "We'll go right in, Jenny. The night air does get chilly up here."

As Maxine and Jenny moved through the front door, Maria caught Jenny's eye and gave her a quick "okay" signal with thumb and forefinger, breathing a short sigh of relief. She knew Brad's little routines almost as well as Jenny did. The men gathered the luggage from the van and looked like a slow-motion Keystone Cops as they grappled and tried to carry it all inside in one trip.

The hacienda was constructed traditionally, with two floors of rooms surrounding a central open courtyard decorated with a profusion of trees and plants. A blue-tiled artesian well invited visitors to the courtyard's center, and tiny gardens dotted the expanse in low-walled, slightly raised plots. Barksea white rose vines that must have been as old as the house itself weaved along the iron grillwork of the balconies. The air was filled with the heavy sweet aroma of jasmine.

The courtyard was well lighted with strategic spots and hidden banks of bulbs. It was an area meant to be shown and appreciated. Jenny gaped with delight at the sight of the well and the flowers she glimpsed through a hall window.

Maria pointed to some small pink blossoms near the base of the well. "Aren't those the kind you kept losing, Jenny, because you left them in the sun too much?"

Jenny squinted. "I think so. I'm not sure. Brad, are those flowers the kind I had in the kitchen window a couple of months ago?"

Brad's arms were full of suitcases. An unwieldy bag of something tucked under his chin made it impossible for him to look anywhere but directly before him. He grunted noncommittally.

"That's what I thought," Jenny took one last peek then hurried to catch up with Maxine, who had begun telling them about the house.

". . . owned and lived in by my late husband's family since it was built in 1846. The house is one of the historical haciendas of the area. The old part of the house was built by Don Francisco Garcia Marquez y Salina for his bride, Maria, newly arrived from Spain. It was a land grant from the Spanish Governor and there were a thousand acres surrounding it at the time. Most of the land was eventually sold to buy vineyards from the Franciscans.

"The hills here are red clay, from which the bricks were made for the original part of the house." She pointed to the rough clay blocks that poked out from behind colorful tapestries hanging on either side of a large doorway. "As you can see, the walls are two to four feet thick, so the house air conditions itself."

In the two-story living room, massive beams supported a redwood plank ceiling. Heavy grillwork on the windows and the graceful arched doorways bespoke eloquently the Spanish heritage of the house, as did the polished quarry tiles of the floors. Their footsteps clattered on the tiles, then were muffled when the group herded across one of the deep-pile throw rugs scattered generously around the room.

Later, when they had been shown their rooms on the second floor—Maria and Duane had adjoining rooms,

Duane's having been converted from what was long ago Maria's playroom—the group adjourned to the kitchen for hot tea before retiring.

Betty, the maid, served them unobtrusively.

If she hadn't been such a pretty young woman, one would hardly have noticed her efficiency, so expertly did she appear at the table just as a cup needed to be refilled or the sweet little wheat cakes replenished. She spoke only twice throughout the hour, once to protest Maxine's gratitude at her willingness to work so late, the second time to answer affirmatively to Mrs. Salina's inquiry about whether the housekeeper, Mrs. Gordon, would be able to make it in early the next morning.

Despite its large size, the kitchen was quite cozy. Natural pine gave a soft amber color to the whole room, and the glass-topped table and chrome chairs, polished twice weekly, gleamed with reflected warmth. A fat, tortoiseshell cat was sleeping in front of the refrigerator, curled up where the warm air came out.

Maxine and Maria did most of the talking. Maria would ask after mutual acquaintances in Point Locke, and Maxine would try to speak to all her guests when answering. But eventually mother and daughter gave up trying to keep the conversation general enough for the others to follow. The guests yielded and contented themselves with listening in polite silence.

Jenny found her eye wandering over the room as the conversation receded to a gentle buzz across the table. She watched Betty clear items from the counter top, her hands moving effortlessly in familiar motions. Jenny smiled and shook her head when Betty caught her gaze and automatically reached for the teapot.

A row of small windows along the outside wall was covered by tastefully subdued curtains of pale yellow cotton. Above the sink a small vase of varicolored, slightly wilted wildflowers were a bit of color to mellow the icy stainless steel of the sink. Jenny suspected they were Betty's touch, for the maid patted them carefully whenever she passed, perhaps slightly distressed that they hadn't survived for the late arrivals.

Jenny had known that Maria's family was affluent, but this enormous house made her realize for the first time that Maria had drastically downplayed her wealthy background. There was money here, lots of it, going back for years. And with Duane having inherited his father's successful business—well, Jenny suddenly felt privileged, not at all uncomfortable but definitely out of her financial league.

Growing up in the Valley, Jenny had spent most of her adult life trying to banish middle-class attitudes infiltrating her thoughts as effortlessly as the poison-laden smog had infiltrated her lungs. It was one of the reasons why she had made the medical profession her life's work. It was a duty that allowed no moral but one—to preserve and protect life. In tissue studies, the causes of tissue degeneration and damage were analyzed and understood, never condemned. Regeneration was what mattered, bringing things back to health, to normality.

Just as she was going to have to bring her relationship with Brad back into healthy balance with a sense of equality. . . .

Jenny's silent reverie ended with a snore—not her own, but Brad's. His chin rested on his chest, head lolling slightly to one side. The rude noise again charged out between parted lips that quivered with ironic daintiness. His hands, even in sleep, held his cup and saucer steady in front of his stomach. The snoring didn't even rattle the spoon.

Such is the control of a great surgeon, sighed Jenny as she gently removed the tea things from his lap.

Maria leaned over and whispered to her mother, loud enough for all to hear, "You'll have to excuse him, Mama. He's had a hard day, riding here all the way in the back seat. We're so embarrassed. He usually does this only in surgery. . . ."

The response to Maria's deadpan line brought Brad halfway back to life. "What's that? I didn't quite . . . catch . . ."

Maxine gestured at the wall clock. "Maybe Dr. Knowlton's got the right idea. It *is* almost midnight."

"That's *it*. Everybody to bed," said Maria. "I want to hit the beach tomorrow for at least a couple of hours before we get tied up with strategies and rehearsals." She looked at Duane and snorted. "C'mon, Romeo. I want to lock you up before some local mankiller steals you away."

"Wait a minute, you mean there's more here like you?" Duane ducked but Maria caught him by the ear.

"Breakfast at nine," said Maxine.

The group assented and began to pick up their dishes.

Betty rushed forward and for the first time spoke authoritatively. "No, no, no, let me do that." She grabbed a cup right out of Jenny's grasp. "You all get to bed, right now."

Her hands suddenly empty, Jenny felt flustered. She'd seen devoted house servants in the movies, but she didn't know how to deal with one who grabbed a dish right out of one's grasp. Must take some getting used to, she thought with amusement.

As they moved into the hall and up the stairs, Mrs. Salina added, "We'll have breakfast out back, on the patio. Just go down the hall and through the kitchen."

"We'll be there, Mama," Maria answered. "Nine o'clock."

By the time she'd bathed, brushed her hair, and dressed for bed, Jenny was moving at zombie speed, but more tired than sleepy. Her eagerness to get away from the job, the excitement of the day, and the anticipation of the coming ceremony all combined to key her up to a state where she felt exhausted, but not ready for sleep.

One of the windows in her room looked out over the central courtyard, the other over the curving drive and outer yard. It was a small room with an adjoining bath, and its bed was a large, old-fashioned four-poster with a matching flouncy pink canopy and quilted bedcover.

She felt like a child in a fairy world on the edge of a dark and scary forest, in a mansion fighting for survival against an evil overgrowth of suffocating ivy, cursed by some hideous demon who lived at the bottom of the nearby ocean. It was real and fantastic at the same time, a storybook drama illustrated in deep moody colors by Arthur Rackham.

She opened the window and peered out across the dark driveway to the yard. The moon was diminishing but bright, and there was really nothing to see. The flat lawn was broken only by a single flowerbed directly across from the porch below, that split the yard down the middle like a long open grave.

Jenny cringed at the unexpected image.

Why had she seen the flowerbed as a grave? Was it the hedges bordering the drive? She vaguely remembered once seeing a cemetery with hedges like that. The lawn was neat and trim, as far as she could see in the night, much like a well-tended cemetery would look. How strange, she thought.

Resting her chin on her cupped palms and leaning on the window ledge, Jenny stared off to the west.

She couldn't see the ocean from here, but she remembered how it had looked from the bluff overlooking Point Locke. Mysterious, smoky, glittering in small odd places, it had been a gigantic speculum reflecting the lights of the universe. She had never in her life seen the ocean look that way at night, and the sight stayed in her mind, nudging inward to settle quietly alongside her visions.

Movement in the sky caught her eye. A scattering of dim lights streaked, glittered, and died—a meteor shower. It didn't last long, but Jenny felt a great sadness sweep over her. So overpowering was the feeling, that she couldn't bear to watch the night sky any longer and retreated.

She turned down the covers on the bed. The sadness became an inexplicable sense of melancholy. Jenny felt as if a cloak of iron had been draped over her small shoulders. She switched off the lamp and fell across the sheets with a groan.

The melancholy grew more intense, the iron cloak heavier. Jenny felt as if she were being shoved down into deep water.

When sleep at last possessed her, her dream/vision stirred restlessly and moved in her head like an evil creature of villainy, gnawing at her memory, scraping at her soul. Then melancholy fled into the darkness, and deep in her dream, deep in the dark water of sleep, fear lunged at her like a ravenous sharp-fanged lizard.

She woke several times during the night, stuperous and perplexed. Despite her unrest, she somehow felt as if her nightmare demon was nearly finished with her, making one desperate grab before it crept away to die.

Jenny was right. The nightmare creature *was* leaving her.

The visions were dying, and Jenny couldn't know her psychically sensitive mind had created the demon as a warning. Her subconscious had responded to a call that transcended the warped barriers of time and space. She'd been a psychic receiver who didn't comprehend the messages.

Jenny was positive that it all had something to do with her tension over Brad, with dominance and submission, with male stubbornness and female insubordination. In her troubled mind, the final resolution regarding Brad had taken form. It was a decision she should have made long ago.

A couple of hours later Jenny slumbered peacefully, her mind at rest. Blond hair swept picture-perfect over the pillow, no longer plastered to her cheeks with the sweat of fear. Her breasts rose and fell with an enticing rhythm, no longer jarred by the pounding of a frantic heart and the strain of gasping lungs. She had become the faultless embodiment of her peaceful imaginings, a little girl tucked away in the corner of a sweet fairy tale.

At last the nightmare creature had shriveled away to nothing. It was dead.

And the living nightmare was approaching as fast as it could come.

five

FIFTY MILES DUE west of Point Locke's shoreline, and about a hundred meters below the surface, the alien cylinder lay in a crevasse.

The silty muck stirred up by the cylinder's impact initially added to the surrounding murkiness, but now the ocean bottom had settled back into its forever slumber.

Millions of tiny ruptures radiated through the capsule's glasslike exterior, but the cylinder itself didn't crumble despite the pressure. The salt water abraded the invader, eating away at its intricate net of biocircuits with an alien mix of chemicals. The process began slowly, then accelerated as the circuits failed to rebind their new edges. The capsule lay like a broken galleon in a liquid world that indiscriminately accepted all tokens from above. No questions asked.

The container's generator, weakened by the forces it had been subjected to, continued to maintain the energy wall, but the exterior circuitry was already dying.

It was only a matter of time.

Something inside the cylinder employed additional pressures, finding the microfractures and insinuating thin but strong cilia. Each minute point of stress inflamed the cancerous breakdown. Alien gases began to bubble out, creating a deadly exterior brew in which a number of sea creatures died agonizingly before the mix was diluted by sea water.

As a chick breaks out of its fragile prison, the creature emerged from the capsule at last, born of blood and pressure, pushing its way into a new world. Fighting for survival.

In its escape form, with much of its mass converted to filaments and small extrusions, the pressure of the water made movement difficult. It experimented and discovered that a spherical shape withstood the pressure best. Survival instinct, rather than intelligence, guided it. But it knew that to live in this new world, it must have the proper shape.

And so began the search.

Rising through the watery environment, it sensed the living creatures around it. All were too small, too primitive. It snatched a couple of them with tentacles grown for that one purpose. Drawing the fish in and crushing them with spiny new teeth, it sucked up the cells it needed, cells that carried the body patterns. The patterns were absorbed immediately.

The alien was equipped to ingest and store all DNA structures easily. It was the memory transfer from the brain that took some time, if the victim had any sort of mental complexity at all.

It quickly discovered that fish had no useful intelligence. While essentially useless to it, the patterns, once assimilated, could not be discarded. They were merely stored, bits of information in a storage bank of almost limitless capacity. The thing's abilities had been fed by the brain of a weak-minded Cephean, and by a brief touch with the living cityship. Its hunger had been whetted with intelligence, and now it was ravenous. It could learn, and it could grow. Endlessly.

The tentacles were flattened into fleshy paddles that helped it move closer to the surface of the ocean. Its languorous movement attracted the attention of another kind of fish. A much larger, primitive fish, one without an air bladder and without scales.

The alien became aware of the shark's approach. Earth's most efficient death machine circled in for the kill, unable to realize that its massive and efficient body was of great interest to the intended prey.

Primitive and deadly, an essentially unchanged survivor for uncounted millions of years, the shark moved with unerring skill, its great jaws poised to clamp down and mangle whatever came between them. The enormous mouth closed on empty water, however, and the shark had only a split second to assess its failure before something gripped its head and extruded hundreds of spiny teeth into it. The teeth elongated into probing, sharp filaments.

The filaments plunged through the shark's eyes, reaching for the brain as the thing flattened out and wrapped itself around the dying predator. Pushing more needlelike filaments down through the surface denticles and into the shark's abdomen and cartilaginous skeleton, the thing sliced mechanically until the water turned dark with blood. It gobbled cells from the muscles, blood, and bones, but concentrated on the brain, and when it had all it needed, the awful wreckage was discarded.

What had been an accomplished biological death trap was now fit only to nourish the lowest scavengers of the deep. The water was stained with blood, clouded with ripped flesh, and in the midst of the scum came a transformation at once wondrous and hideous.

With a darting movement a Great White swam away into clearer water. It looked exactly like the shark that had just perished so violently. The parts of its body that had not been consumed to make added mass drifted in pieces toward the ocean floor.

The new shark moved through the water with incredible

grace, heading for the shoreline where its stolen memory indicated that shallower waters sometimes offered a more interesting supply of food. It swam no more than three meters below the surface of the water. The early morning sunlight filtered through rippling waves and spilled over the great body. The dorsal fin occasionally sliced through the ocean's surface as the giant rose in the water, foraging for food.

The pirated memory told the alien Doppelgänger many things—how to move through the water, how to find food, how to kill. Instinctual things.

The authentic creature had been stupid, and its mental power was limited to its instincts: hunt, kill, eat. But if its knowledge was generally useless, its body pattern was nonetheless excellent, perfectly suited to the watery world.

The monster concentrated on maintaining this efficient new shape, but there had to be something better. Something strong, yet with a useful brain. Something with intelligence it could use.

It swam toward the shore.

Hungry.

Greedy.

Searching.

Part II

Point Locke

six

THE DAY WAS already warm by the time Jenny came downstairs the next morning. Things looked different bathed in sunlight and she did not remember which of two doors led to the kitchen. Fortunately, a clue—in the ample form of the family cat—presented itself. The dark, tortoise-shell cat sat patiently by one of the doors, meowing softly but persistently. Judging by its plumpness, Jenny was sure its favorite place was the kitchen. She pushed open the door and they both stepped into the large, inviting room.

The window over the sink admitted plenty of natural morning sunlight. Here again, the appearance of the room was entirely different from that of the previous night, when her pall of exhaustion had noticeably affected her perception.

This morning, the change in mood was bolstered by a large woman who listened to a radio plugged in next to the toaster. She swayed her hips to the beat of the popular song while buttering muffins and stacking them neatly on a large silver tray.

Jenny stood just inside the doorway, enjoying the lady's exuberance. She wasn't sure her entrance had even been noticed until the woman turned and smiled, waving the butter-smeared knife in a tight little circle. She carried the song to its conclusion and swiveled with an elaborate motion that wouldn't have been entirely out of place on a burlesque stage.

It looked odd only because the woman was unredeemably into late middle-age and weighed in somewhere over two hundred pounds.

"Morning, honey, I'm Mrs. Gordon. You must be Jenny." She hummed a last few bars of music.

"Mrs. Gordon" was a ridiculously formal way to address this woman, who looked as if she would be comfortable with something as common as Rosie or as exotic as Zenobia. Maria had given the warning, however. It was always "Mrs. Gordon," even to Maxine, who was the only person in the house who knew the lady's Christian name. Any attempted transgressions would be met with hard silence and burned toast.

Before Jenny could reply, Betty slammed breathlessly through the back door with a pitcher of milk and a pot of coffee in her hands. She nodded at Jenny as she placed her burdens on the table.

"The doctor wants grape juice, Mrs. Gordon. He doesn't like orange juice." Her tone indicated that anyone who didn't drink o.j. in the morning might very well ask for gooseberry jam or something equally peculiar.

Unperturbed, Mrs. Gordon continued the task of buttering. "No grape juice. Closest thing we got to grape juice is wine or vinegar if he'd like that," she chuckled and waved a muffin at a scratch pad affixed to one of the cabinets. "Write it down on our marketing list, Betty."

"Brad—uh, Dr. Knowlton will drink tomato juice, if you have any." Jenny offered. As she spoke she knelt to pet the cat that was rubbing against her legs in a shameless bid for attention . . . and food.

Mrs. Gordon did not raise an eyebrow or give any indication that she was curious about Jenny's knowledge of the doctor's breakfast preferences. But Jenny could almost hear a mental file card with pertinent information drop into place:

Dr. Knowlton. Breakfast: grape or tomato juice. Information source: Jenny McGregor, doctor's probable lover.

Mrs. Gordon reached into one of the upper cabinets and pulled down a two-liter can with a green label. She shook it vigorously for a second or two, then placed it under the electric opener.

"It's okay, tomato juice he can have." *Shake, shake.* "Tomato juice we got." *Bzzzz, whirrr, click.* "Better'n orange juice anyway—less calories."

"Uh . . ." Jenny ventured, "I think the cat is ready for breakfast too."

"Rebecca? Oh, she's had breakfast *twice* this morning already. She's trying to con you for a third." Mrs. Gordon chuckled as she poured an oversized glass of tomato juice. She was about to hand it to Betty when Jenny stepped forward and intercepted it.

"I'll give it to him," she said as she took the glass and headed for the door to the patio. "I can't wait to get out and breathe that fresh air."

"Poached, boiled, or scrambled?"

Jenny paused, one hand on the doorknob. "Huh?"

Another song with a good beat began to play on the radio. Mrs. Gordon's hips started to sway. "Your eggs. How do you want them?"

"Oh . . ." Jenny turned the knob and took a sip of Brad's juice as she moved through the doorway. "No eggs. Muffin and orange juice are fine, thanks." The cat followed Jenny out the door, hoping, perhaps, to find better pickings outside.

Mrs. Gordon waited until Jenny had closed the door, then shook her head in motherly judgment.

"See how these big city folks are, Betty? They just don't eat right. That woman is so pale you'd think she'd been living in a cave. Needs to stay out in the sun and drink up that vitamin D."

Betty, whose complexion was almost as pale as Jenny's, knew Jenny would have to be cautious in the sun because of her scant pigmentation. She thought about explaining this to Mrs. Gordon, but they'd been through these debates before. Betty's knowledge, gleaned from health articles in *Redbook* and *Ms.*, was no match for the lurid warnings and frights the older woman extracted from the *National Enquirer*.

"I take my vitamins in capsules." Betty couldn't help her mild belligerence. "My doctor said—"

Mrs. Gordon thrust the tray of freshly buttered muffins into the girl's hands. "Oh, shee-it, honey. What has that doctor done for you except take your hard-earned money." She pointed a finger accusingly at Betty's knees. "All those vitamins and, look, your legs are *still* too skinny!"

If she hadn't had her hands filled with the tray of toast, Betty would have self-consciously tugged her skirt down, but the best she could do was to press her knees together. There was simply no answer to that sort of accusation.

Balancing the tray on one hand, Betty tugged at the back door. She held it open with her hip as she repositioned the tray on both hands, but paused before slipping outside to call back defiantly over her shoulder. "I just decided what I'm going to get you for your birthday—a book on good manners! You can keep it with the diet book I gave you for Christmas."

Jenny had already crossed the stone patio and joined the others at a long glass-topped table, when Mrs. Gordon's raucous laughter barreled through the back door as Betty scurried outside with a mischievous grin on her face.

"Must have been better than my operating-room jokes," declared Brad, eyeing Betty appreciatively, skinny legs and all.

"Anything's better than your operating-room jokes," said Maria, lighting a cigarette.

The cat had been circling the table, and suddenly jumped up into Duane's lap and began preening. Duane smiled, pleased at having been chosen for the cat's cushion. "What's the cat's name?"

"Rebecca," Jenny replied, "and don't you believe her if she tells you she hasn't had her breakfast!"

"Hello, pretty Rebecca," he said as he scratched her under the chin. "Can you say 'photosynthesis'?"

The cat haughtily ignored his silliness and settled in for a nap.

Maxine watched disapprovingly as her daughter continued to smoke. Finally, she could keep herself from commenting no longer. "Maria, you really should give those up. You see people at the hospital all the time, dying of cancer, and still you smoke."

"Brides-to-be get nervous." Maria couldn't keep the tone of amused tolerance out of her voice. "Anyway, Mama, you should talk. You smoked for years and didn't give them up until after Daddy died."

"A good reason, don't you think?" The flatness of her voice revealed a lingering pain.

Maxine explained to the others, "Juan was a heavy smoker, too. We'd fill every ashtray in the house. When he died . . . well, I doubt it was the smoking alone that caused his heart to give out, but who knows? It seemed a wise move to quit."

My God, thought Jenny, the morning's only begun and already the conversation is getting morose.

Maxine and Maria's faces became set with dour expressions. Duane would smile if Maria looked directly at him, but otherwise he remained silent, picking at his breakfast with only mild interest. Brad had become oblivious of the conversation entirely, his point of visual focus being at that moment somewhere among the trees and hedges bordering the expansive lawn beyond the patio.

Jenny couldn't stand it another second. She said the first thing that popped into her head. "Maxine, the next time you're in L.A., you must give me a call. Brad and I would love to take you out to dinner. Brad knows a million unusual places. You ever try macrobiotic pizza?"

"Ravioli, not pizza," Brad grunted absently.

"Yes, Mama." Maria reached across the corner of the table and grasped her mother's hand. "After the wedding why don't you come back to L.A. with us? Stay for a month, or longer. Enjoy yourself."

Maxine tried to sound insulted. "You make it sound as if I were a senile old woman. I've better things to do than meddle in my daughter's life." She smiled at Jenny. "But I would like to try that pizza sometime."

"Ravioli," muttered Brad.

"Mama, we *want* you to come stay with us for a few weeks." Maria nudged Duane. "Don't we?"

"And I'll make you a pizza, too. A *good* one." Duane's words were light but didn't hide the sincerity in his voice. He liked Maxine a lot. "But I have to warn you that your daughter has an ulterior motive."

"Oh, I know that. Maria always has an ulterior motive." She took a sip of coffee, yet her smile slipped onto her face too quickly to be concealed by the upraised cup. "What is she up to this time?"

"I listen to him and learn all about myself." Maria waved her hands in the air with mock exasperation. "He knows my motives better than I know them."

Unexpectedly serious, Duane leaned forward with his elbows on the table. He massaged his knuckles, a nervous habit that manifested itself whenever he spoke about things that truly mattered to him. He shifted his position, careful not to disturb the cat, now sound asleep on his lap. "I have a house up in the hills near Griffith Park. After my family died, I thought about selling it and getting an apartment, but I really love the place, and so does Maria. It needs to be redecorated, but with Maria's job at the Institute, she won't have much extra time. And she mentioned that perhaps you'd—"

Maria couldn't control her excitement any longer. "Oh, Mama, wait'll you *see* it! Right on the side of a mountain, with the city going out for miles and miles below. It's beautiful, and I want the house to look just right.

"Come down for a few days after our honeymoon,

please? Help me get the place in order. I need you, Mama, I really do."

"Of course I'll help you." Maxine would have trampled down a forest of sequoias to respond to her daughter's plea. But she was a woman as much as a mother, one who knew that a mother's love could create tensions if she didn't proceed with caution. "But I can't come down right away."

Maria's face fell like a soft scoop of ice cream collapsing down the side of its cone. "Oh, Mama . . . why not?"

"I wasn't going to mention this until after the wedding . . ." Mrs. Salina hesitated, as if searching for that final spark of courage within her before she leaped off a diving board. "I'm going to sell the house."

"What—?" Maria was stunned. "But *why*?"

"Look around you, baby. The damned thing has eighteen rooms and every one of them collects sixteen pounds of dust each day. Betty and Mrs. Gordon work like chain-gang laborers just to keep up with themselves, not to mention the grounds and the garden and all the upkeep.

"It's too much work. And there's no reason to keep the house. It's only memories that keep me here now." She glanced at the hacienda and sighed. "Sentiment gets in the way of living, you know."

"But what do you plan to do?"

"June's been showing me some houses around town." Maxine's voice picked up some enthusiasm. "I even looked at a couple near the vineyards. I thought I might find something small, maybe a little stucco with one bedroom and a cactus garden on the porch."

"Have you already picked something out?" Maria was suspicious. She knew her mother was an efficient woman. It wouldn't surprise her to learn that her mother had not only found a new house, but had purchased, furnished, and been living in it for months.

"No, not yet." She saw Maria scrutinize her shamelessly. "Really, darling, I haven't. I've just been considering . . . and looking."

Maria felt a sudden pang, realizing what her mother was facing.

Here was a middle-aged woman, still attractive but remaining married to a man who'd died a decade ago. She had tried to bury herself in work, but found less and less to actually do as the years rolled by. She would remain loyal to her daughter, to her late husband's family, and to the workers who depended on her for their wages, but all the time she would grow older, withering a little more each day. The creases in her face would deepen into wrinkles of age and loneliness. Her beautiful dark eyes would dim as images lost their sharp edges and slipped into a dusky twilight. As the world crept out of sight and out of mind, the woman would rely on shadow memories, ghosts of a time that was no more.

The series of images flashed across Maria's mind in a second, and their impact tore into her deeply. She sprang out of her chair and clutched her mother desperately.

"Oh, Mama! *Please* come to Los Angeles with us. We'll see each other every day. You'll find lots to do, new people to meet. I don't want you to be alone."

Maxine kissed her daughter gently on the cheek.

"We'll talk about it later, dear, after you get back from Hawaii." She stood, perhaps to hide the misting of her eyes. "First we have a very important wedding to take care of."

"A wedding, a wedding, there's going to be a *wedding*."

Everyone turned at the shrill singsong voice bawling from the vicinity of the kitchen door.

"Here comes you-know-who," whispered Maxine.

The door burst open to a tornado of pink chiffon that whirled across the patio with crazy grace. The yards of frilly material were gathered over the chunky body of a woman in her mid-fifties. She carried a buttered muffin in one hand and a magnum of champagne in the other. This was June Framington's trademark—inseparable conventionality and indulgence.

"Maria! My little sardine!" June's voice could be described as a barely repressed shriek. "I could just eat you up!"

June clattered across the patio stones in ridiculously dressy high heels, her arms outstretched.

"Stop!" Maria shouted as she jumped to her feet, warding off the attacking pink chiffon with outthrust palms.

The frilly lady halted dead in her tracks, flabbergasted. "Honey . . . it's your Aunt Junie. . . ."

"Don't you 'honey' me. The last time you hugged me, I got chocolate stains on the back of my dress that I never could get out. Before you take another step, put those things down."

June looked at the items in her hand with a baffled expression, then with a hearty laugh slammed the bottle down on the table and nonchalantly threw the muffin back over her shoulder. "Is your Aunt Junie acceptable now?"

"She's beautiful," giggled Maria, running around the table to give the fat woman a bear hug.

June squeezed back with enthusiasm. Snatching a napkin from the table to dab the smudged mascara from her face, she then blew her nose with the same napkin and left a black smudge decorating the space between the nose's bulbuous tip and the carefully applied moue of pink lipstick. Maria laughed and used a clean napkin to wipe the smear away.

Jenny was fascinated. Here was a woman who took stately complacency and turned it on its ear in a second. She wouldn't draw much attention in most parts of L.A., but Point Locke hardly seemed a proper place for June. She was too vibrant for a small town.

"I just can't believe my lit-tul girl is going to be a married woman." June lifted the bottle of champagne again. "It's time to celebrate! What we need is a little drinkie!"

When June Framington was in a "good mood," as she was today, it was a signal to Maxine to watch her closely. June was a woman of harmless but aggravating extremes. She'd clearly been nipping at the wine even before she arrived, and the champagne *might* last for thirty minutes.

Before the clock struck noon she would be slugging down the gin, straight, unless Maxine could slow her down.

Supervising and controlling June's excesses was an assignment Maxine had accepted for years. When Juan died, June had been at Maxine's side every moment. While her friend was speechless from shock, June had spoken up and handled the morbid details, instructing the servants on how to manage inquiries and messages, keeping an eye on the funeral arrangements, driving off the wheeler-dealers who detected easy pickings from a wealthy widow with no idea of how to maintain successful vineyards. For weeks the lawyers snuffled around like lusting bloodhounds, but June sent them scurrying with shrill, flamboyant dismissals. She was silly and impractical in her personal tastes, but one of the shrewdest business persons in town.

If Maxine had appeared resilient throughout the months of adjustment, it was June who'd been the force behind Maxine's control. She'd endured a similar ordeal and knew exactly what to do. After her own husband's death earlier, June had bought a mildly successful real estate firm with part of her insurance money and had jacked up profits considerably within a couple of years. She taught Maxine how to simplify business records and control expenses, and most importantly, how to run a business without being driven to suicide in a week.

"June, please don't break open that champagne." Maxine kept her manner light. "The youngsters are going to the beach. If you tempt them, I'll never get them into their bathing suits and out of the house."

It worked like a charm. June clutched the bottle to her protectively—with a sense of purpose. She was no longer an aging woman fogging her enviousness of youth's charm with a haze of alcohol. She and Maxine were mature conspirators allied against the newcomers; the polish and experience of age versus the impulsive carelessness of youth.

"No, of course not." June scrutinized the visitors, watching for the slightest sign of rebelliousness. "Never, *never* swim after you've been drinking." She glared at Brad as he slipped a last bit of toast into his mouth. "And you have to wait at least two hours after you eat before going into the water."

"Sure," mumbled Brad.

"At least two hours," added Maria, hugging June again to show her obeisance. The rest echoed assurance when Maria peered at them over June's ample shoulder and rolled her eyes heavenward, as if to explain that someone can be a little crazy yet lovable.

Betty appeared like the phantom from the kitchen. Catching a signal from Maxine, she snatched the bottle of champagne with the finesse of an experienced thief and carried it away.

Maria was having trouble controlling her chuckling as June tiptoed over and stood between the seated men, eyeing them appreciatively.

"I know you're only marrying one of them, Maria, so can I have the other one?" She tapped her long pink nails on their shoulders. "They're both so cute!"

Maria's frantic hand motions brought Jenny to her side. "The other one belongs to Jenny."

Duane and Brad were enjoying the silliness. Rather than spoil the game, Jenny smiled and did her best to look knowledgeably mysterious.

"Oh . . . this is fun. Like a contest!" June gushed, enjoying the moment very much. She finally pointed a lacquered nail at Brad. "You . . . must be Duane?"

"If *I* marry Maria," Brad laughed, "Duane will cut off my head and Jenny will cut off my—"

"Brad!" screamed Jenny, then clamped her hand over her mouth. Sometimes that man was absolutely shameless!

"—ears," Brad finished with a smug grin.

June reached over and patted Jenny on the head. "I know exactly what he was going to say. And if he gives you too much trouble, darling, you might take it into consideration."

Her expression was equally smug, but if there was any feminist rancor in June's remark, it was no more than a feeble attempt to be contemporary.

Duane assured her that Brad was not exaggerating about Duane's cutting off his head. "One time he gave Maria a box of chocolates for her birthday, and I got so mad I bit his toe off. Ask him to show it to you sometime."

Maria was astounded at Duane's off-the-wall sense of humor, and delighted by his impulsiveness. He'd always been so quiet in a group, and she felt she was discovering new aspects of him every moment in Point Locke.

Duane was pulling June's leg, of course, high heel and all. Brad confessed he'd never given Maria a box of chocolates, and he'd lost the end of the small toe on his left foot in a boating accident when he was six years old. He said it was the incident that inspired him to become a surgeon. Brad told the story as if it were a joke, but Maria suspected there was more than a grain of truth in it.

Away from the hospital Brad sometimes couldn't resist blurting out the truth with boyish enthusiasm, but he'd learned that if you hid everything behind a sneer or a leer, people found it humorous and didn't pry too deeply into your private life. If anything, they did just the opposite, dragging out their own deep secrets for display. The technique worked wonders with patients.

But it could create tensions among the hospital and Institute employees. Brad had let a lot of ugly cats out of bags that were probably better left tied. Like the time with Sally Newcomb, a scrub nurse who spoke with a slight lisp. She'd let it slip that she was interested in a nineteen-year-old guy named Max, who worked at a McDonald's in Hollywood. A day later the hospital's number one gossip item was about how Sally had ordered "two big Maxth" but had settled for one when she saw the size of it.

Sally had filed a formal complaint with hospital administration, and the next day she was looking for a job. Scrub nurses were expendable; skilled surgeons were not. Administration never even bothered to tell Brad about the incident.

Duane would never be a match for Brad when it came to jokes and off-the-cuff humor, but they'd been around each other long enough for the abilities of one to rub off on the other. While Duane was picking up a bit of humor, Brad was realizing that Duane's sensitivity was not necessarily a weakness. One lesson was as simple as watching for signals of unhappiness from your lover and trying to ferret out their causes. For a long time Brad wasn't even aware of these signals, but as the closeness he and Jenny had shared began to dissipate, he'd become concerned.

Awareness was only a first step, however, and a first step can be wasted if the second isn't taken. Brad's sexist jokes—he had a special fondness for stories about breasts and their various uses—had diminished at home but persisted in the hospital. The stories travelled from the operating rooms to the floor nurses and ward clerks, who carried them across the small greensward to the neighboring Institute. And Jenny seemed to get even more annoyed hearing the jokes from others rather than from Brad. She was quite aware of their source.

During their courtship, Maria had occasional spats with Duane, and talking her problems over with Brad and Jenny—especially Jenny—had helped resolve them. Now that Jenny seemed to be groping for answers, Maria wanted to help. Perhaps she could get Jenny alone later tonight and they could have a heart to heart talk about the situation.

"There's only one rose looks better when it's not in the garden."

Maria was startled out of her reverie by the ghostly voice. She stood up and fell into the arms of a grizzled man clutching a pair of sharp gardening shears in one hand.

"I ought to cut off your ears with these for staying away so long," he said, waving the shears in her face.

June, whose attention was apparently not fully concentrated on coquettish flirting, spoke up quickly. "Sorry, Happy, that joke's already made the rounds this morning."

The man towered over her and Maria clutched the straps of his overalls excitedly. "Oh my god, you look younger than the last time I was here. How do you do it?"

Happy Miles, whose real name was Hoppenstead, for reasons that were unfathomable even to the mother who bore him, *did* have an ageless appearance. His features, up close, were networked with fine lines too shallow to be true wrinkles. The flesh appeared glued to the bones beneath, giving his face the creased and crumpled look of a flattened, well-worn road map.

Jenny had watched him approach across the enormous grounds that stretched to the edge of the woods crowding the back of the Salina property. She had liked his looks then, his lanky stride, his passive face below thinning salt-and-pepper hair, and she liked him even better at close range. His coveralls and plaid shirt were soft and shiny with wear, perfectly suited to the man. He reminded her a little of her grandfather.

Maria explained to the others the private joke about Happy's age. When she was a child Happy had told her he was two hundred years old, but getting younger. When they reached the same age, he'd said, they would run away together to live in a rose garden forever more. As Maria told her story, Happy stood close at her side, one hand draped casually over her near shoulder, a guardian angel in hayseed drag. He'd been the family gardener for thirty years, living with the Salinas, suffering and prospering with them, watching them grow up and grow older, as much a member of the family as anyone with Salina blood in their veins.

Jenny smiled politely when introduced, wondering if she were passing before the unerring eye of a single-headed Cerberus. I'll need more than a drugged cake to slip by this judgmental gaze, she decided, then felt a flush of security course through her when he rewarded her with a brief smile.

Happy grunted when introduced to the two men. "Don't get up," he said to Duane, "you'll disturb Rebecca." He shook hands politely, coolly. A small frown creased Maria's forehead. She had expected a bit more enthusiasm from Happy over her choice of a husband; after all, Happy was family . . . almost. Maria's concern was vague and unfocused and her frown vanished in a moment, realizing that Happy was just being paternal. In his eyes, Maria suspected, no one would *ever* be good enough for her.

"C'mon, kids. Up and at 'em. Off to the beach." June made it a point to grasp both men's shoulders and give them an admiring squeeze before nudging them toward the house. "Happy has to work on the garden for the reception, and Maxine's got a zillion telephone calls to make. In this town, a big wedding is a B-I-G wedding!"

"Have they replaced those paving stones around the fountain yet?" Maxine asked Happy. "They were supposed to finish the job today."

The gardener pulled a mahogany-stained pipe from his shirt pocket, clamping it in his teeth and lighting it with an expensive pocket lighter.

"They're here." He sucked carefully on the pipestem and blew out a cloud of smoke. "Three kids who might be able to lay a stone if they had a picture book to show them how."

Maxine sighed. "Didn't Mr. Snow come with them?"

"Oh, sure. He even gets out of the truck once in a while, I guess just to make sure the kids haven't run away."

"Well, you know what to do, Happy. I want that fountain completed today."

Happy lifted the opened shears and closed them with a vicious snap. "I know what to do, Miz Salina." He made his way across the closely trimmed lawn, disappearing behind a maze of hedges that shrouded the fate of Mr. Snow's work crew from the patio breakfasters.

Duane watched Happy stalk off determinedly and said, "Ouch. I don't think I'd want to be out by the fountain right now."

"That's just because you don't know him," Maria laughed. "He'll just tell Mr. Snow that if the work isn't done on time, there will be a slight delay in writing a check for payment. Somehow the work always gets done. On time."

Half an hour later the four young people had gathered up their beach gear and were carrying it out to the van.

Rebecca was determined to climb into the wicker basket that held the picnic lunch Mrs. Gordon had packed for them. Jenny shooed the cat away and peeked inside to find a steaming peach pie, fresh from the oven. Its aroma made her mouth water.

Maxine waved from the porch as the van pulled away, until a sweaty palm on her bare arm sent a small shiver through her. She turned to see June's face set in a frightening grimace. She grabbed the woman's shoulders and forced her to sit down on the steps.

It was several moments before June lost her glazed look and could respond to Maxine's questions. "It was another one," she answered, gasping. "Just like the one I had when Terence died. It hurt."

June's psychic abilities were well known in Point Locke. She'd helped old ladies remember where they'd put their keys and young children find lost pets. June considered the "talent" a gift from God, not something to be used for profit.

The result of June's abilities could be pleasant or not, occasionally a combination of both. The most harrowing of her psychic episodes had happened years before when she was alone at home. She'd called Maxine the moment the episode ended, telling her in a dead voice that her husband Terence, an airline pilot, had just been killed. In her mind's eye a bluebird had fallen from a slate sky, plunging quickly and soundlessly into a tunnel that receded until its mere speck of existence winked from sight. Within three hours she'd been told that Terence's plane had gone down in North Carolina, with no survivors.

June's graying curls hung limply over her forehead now. Her hands dug into the pink folds of her dress like scurrying mice seeking a hole, an escape.

Maxine was inexplicably afraid, but she had to ask. "June . . . what did you see?"

The fat woman passed a hand over her damp face. Her voice was tiny and distant. "It was just the driveway and the lawn, there, as it always looks. The van was driving away, and then the orange color fell off, like icing melting off a cake. The color ran like water over the ground, and the ground became an ocean. An ocean that . . . that turned into blood."

Maxine's hands gripped June's arms like talons.

"The van floated and then slipped beneath the surface. one of the women made it out through the window at the last moment. She started swimming back, but she was screaming and covered in blood. I wasn't sure she could make it."

June's hands were totally hidden away in the folds of her dress, but their shivering was evident beneath the light material.

"I couldn't tell who it was."

seven

THE VAN TURNED onto St. Andrew's Place, a boulevard that looped the campus before it cut back across the north end of town on its way to the beach.

Point Locke University was stately and breathtaking. It was here that the town's New England look found its imitative pinnacle. The four-story Administration Building was especially impressive, fronted with gray stone columns starkly contrasting with the red brick walls. The remainder of the campus buildings were only slightly less honorable copies of Americana-cum-laude, loosely scattered over the gentle slopes. Alfresco walkways and gardens of California blossoms were all that belied the architecture.

Jenny couldn't resist leaning out the window to sniff at the air.

She had been East only once—Vermont in late October, in fact—and she couldn't forget the crisp and slightly damp smell of the air there. It's early summer now, but if I close my eyes and use a brush of imagination, she told herself, I'll recapture that brisk East Coast touch against my face. The cool touch of . . . of . . .

Duane turned a corner sharply, swinging the van close to the curb. One of the campus's revolving sprinklers hurled a jet of water in an arc that intersected with Jenny's hapless smile. With a yelp she pulled her head back and cracked her skull against a metal divider separating the back seat from the van's rear storage area.

Maria gasped almost as loudly as Jenny. "Hey, are you all right?"

With no chance to analyze the event, Jenny simply put her hand down to the seat to steady herself. It took a moment for the pain to subside, but she quickly realized that the warm gummy feeling around her hand wasn't a normal side effect of a bump on the head.

While Jenny's imagination had been conjuring up olfactory sensations, Brad had flipped open the top of the wicker picnic hamper to admire the real aroma of Mrs. Gordon's peach pie. As Duane turned the corner, the basket had coasted to Jenny's side and was now pinned neatly in place with her hand squarely in the middle of it.

"I hope you slice your tissue samples with more precision." Brad's face and voice were a perfect match of innocence and monotone.

Maria looked over her shoulder just in time to see a handful of Mrs. Gordon's creation deposited in Brad's mouth without benefit of fork.

Brad grabbed Jenny's hand and tried to gobble the remainder of the syrupy mess off her fingers. Despite the recent knock on the head, she laughed as she rummaged with her free hand for a napkin.

Duane glanced in the rear-view mirror and nudged his wife-to-be. "There's a maniac in the back seat—he's eating that lady's fingers off!"

"Don't be silly, Duane. Things like that only happen in the movies."

Maria had seldom seen Duane so happy. He smiled

easily, laughed at jokes and joined their games, enjoying himself every minute. His personal tragedies didn't pervade his life so completely anymore, and his private ease with her was expanding to include others as well. Duane's words were more casual, his manner less guarded. The eyes showed the change; they sparkled with pleasure instead of guilty tears. It delighted Maria so much that she could hardly stand it.

"I think you're right." Duane again glanced in the mirror. "And this one is X-rated."

Jenny wiped the last of the pie off her fingers and went after a syrupy smudge on her notably décolleté front. Brad watched, fascinated.

"The only thing X-rated back here is Brad's imagination," she quipped.

They arrived at the beach area a few minutes later. It was already crowded with summer students whose energetic running and splashing provided entertainment for the town's older residents, who lolled under beach umbrellas and simply enjoyed the show.

The closest parking lot was full, but a block farther on a Datsun pickup packed with noisy Boy Scouts pulled away from the curb. Duane scooted into the empty space quickly but imperfectly, at which the departing scouts jeered and hooted like miniature banshees. One of them managed to stuff his finger up his nose while trying to blow out a raspberry. Another turned and crouched, ready to moon, but he apparently had some trouble with his belt and was still fumbling as the pickup turned the corner.

"America's future," snapped Brad. "Fifteen years from now those little buggers will be ripping us open for hysterectomies, laparotomies, and bypasses. You ready for that?"

"Come on, Brad. What were you doing when you were that age, performing brain surgery?" Jenny said as she climbed into the back of the van. Maria joined her to gather up the blankets, towels, lotions, sunglasses, and assorted oceanside paraphernalia.

"I could at least get my belt unbuckled in time to moon someone."

"Ah hah! Now we know who started that dumb craze." Jenny slipped out of her skirt and draped a short red terrycloth robe over her shoulders.

"All kids go through that stage," said Brad. "We remember our mothers, cooing and smiling at us as they wiped our asses. We're imprinted with the idea that people like to look at us from that angle." He and Duane gathered up the picnic basket and umbrellas, while Maria struggled to fold a large blanket.

Jenny humphed. "Speak for yourself. The only thing I heard about asses was that some of them become surgeons."

"Right on, Mother McGregor," said Maria, her voice muffled, perhaps deliberately, by the blanket. Duane grunted noncommittally.

They lugged their burdens the hundred yards to the beach from where they'd parked. Jenny didn't want to sit too near a group of kids who were slinging sand, and Brad insisted on a spot where he would have an unobstructed view of some attractive college girls playing volleyball with a team of ogling jocks.

The group finally ended up downslope of an enormously fat woman who rested on a pathetically frail beach chair. They couldn't tell if she was watching as they set up their beach equipment and laid out the blankets, for no one could see her eyes behind the reflector aviator glasses. She never turned a page of the Sidney Sheldon novel she'd propped up on her bloated thighs.

Jenny suspected she was fast asleep, but a moment later the woman reached into her beach bag for a cigarette. Her ritual was fumbling and elaborate, bending back the matchbook cover and holding it in place as she removed a match, all the time pressing her novel flat to her knees and manipulating her cigarette with whatever fingertips were available. Jenny thought the lady was drunk, but a quick glance revealed no more than pop-top cans of Dr. Pepper. Jenny concluded that her judgment of human character was really off the mark today, so she shrugged and turned to watch the beach.

The town's East Coast appearance was not lost even at

the beach. A couple of chain-anchored rafts drifted fifty yards from the shore, floating on the easy waves like crispy brown waffles. They would have been more at home on the Atlantic seaboard than the California coastline, but the irregular curve of the land created a rocky cove that made surfing impractical, so the rafts merely added to the New England illusion.

If the town and its beach were anachronistic and "East Coast," the people who scurried across the sand were all contemporary and Californian. Youngsters screamed their conversation over the blare of rock music pounding out from large, battery-powered radios. College students soaked up the sun, oiled one another's backs, and played ball, managing to be only slightly less quiet. Some would scamper into the water for a few moments and then return. It was a fine excuse to sensuously rub each other's backs with lotion once again. Senior citizens complained to their middle-aged offspring about the heat, the kids, and social security, until one or the other, or both, fell asleep from sheer boredom.

When their own conversation began to break down into isolated comments about whether the baby over there was crying because he'd been abandoned or just wanted attention (the latter proved to be the case), or whether the honey-blonde's breasts were going to leap out of her bathing suit whenever the girl hit the volleyball (they didn't, but Brad was watching closely), Duane began to rummage in the picnic basket.

"Uh-uh," Maria plucked his hand out of the container. "Can't have any lunch until you do your exercise."

"If I'm going to work out, you should make it worth my while." Duane glanced toward the water. "I'll race you to the raft. If I win, I get to kiss you, and if you win you get to kiss me."

"Sounds perfectly fair." She stretched a moment as she stood and brushed the sand from her legs. Duane started to rise but Maria quickly put her foot on his chest. "I'm shorter than you, so I get a five-second head start."

Duane lunged for her legs but she sprang away with a

shout and raced down the slope. Jenny slammed down the lid of the wicker basket when Duane struggled to his feet, scattering sand in all directions as he sprinted after Maria. The couple reached the shore at the same moment and fell into the water with all the convulsive grace of mad cats dropped into a jacuzzi.

Maria was not the least bit athletic, so there was little doubt about who would reach the raft first. Jenny turned her attention back to the food, most of which had been protected from the flying sand by plastic dishes and aluminum foil. Except for the demolished pie, she noted, everything was in order.

Everything is in order but my life, Jenny thought, turning on her side and propping herself on her elbow. Brad's gaze was still eagerly directed toward the volleyball game, ostensibly watching its progress, but in reality watching with growing disappointment as the blonde's breasts managed to stay securely inside her suit, despite the laws of thrust, stress and gravity, or whatever it was that governed such matters. Brad's interest waned and he was silent for a long while. Jenny cast a sidelong look at him. His eyes were half-closed against the glare of the sun, and she suspected he was drifting off into one of his doctor's naps.

She was wrong. He suddenly shifted his weight and turned to her. His sober words were as unanticipated as a voice from an empty closet. "Jenny . . . what are you thinking? About us? You've been so distant . . . even before we left L.A."

Jenny was struck dumb. This wasn't the way she'd envisioned it. She had imagined them lying beside each other in the dark, comfortable in each other's arms, satiated with love—no, with sex, the time when Brad was most receptive and would listen to whatever she had to say. But on a public beach in Point Locke under a blazing afternoon sun, surrounded by strangers, deserted by two friends who were swimming away to be alone and dream of happy years of future togetherness? This was not the way Jenny had planned her serious confrontation with Brad.

She sat up. Too much had been left unsaid for too long, and the fact that he was willing to listen to her *now* was an opportunity she couldn't pass up. Unable to wrest his eyes away from her pale, anguished face, Brad stared unblinkingly as Jenny spoke honestly of things he had already sensed intuitively. He had been afraid to cope with them, and had banished them to the recesses of his mind, but now they were laid out in the open. And it was worse than he had imagined. Their love affair, which meant more to him than he dared to admit even to himself, was dying. In fact, it might already be in its death throes. His mind rebelled against the seeming finality. To an overachiever like Brad, failure at anything was unpardonable.

Oh, Jesus, maybe it's all in my mind, just like my dreams, Jenny moaned inwardly. I'm being too harsh, I'm being a bitch. Am I so insecure that I feel threatened if he looks at a pretty girl? Do I have to take his crude, petty jokes and his chauvinism seriously even when I know damn well that they're just a release in his high-pressure job? Am I cutting off my own nose to spite *his* face?

The question boiled in her mind like a slightly rank stew. But she kept talking, her words pouring out in a torrent. Not abusive, just steady and detailed. And Brad kept listening.

Maria lay on her stomach on the raft, propping her chin on the backs of her hands. Her dark and watchful eyes were directed toward the beach, squinting to observe Jenny's unrestrained gestures and Brad's rapt attention.

"Oh my," she murmured, "I think Jenny is finally letting the steam out of the kettle."

The raft was roomy enough for five or six sunbathers, but Duane scooted closer and put his arm over her shoulders. Both of them were still damp from the swim but warming quickly in the sun. He gave a little tug on the dark ringlets that curled behind her ears.

"You mean she's flipping her lid?"

"Jenny's not that sort." Maria cuddled her cheek into the palm of her hand. "I think she's reached the end of her rope. It's been a long time coming, but I think she's going to call it quits with Brad. She's had enough of his macho bullshit."

Duane rolled over on his back and shielded his eyes from the sun's glare with his hand. He dangled one foot off the side of the raft. "I think Brad's afraid of getting old."

Maria pushed up on her elbows. "Old? What is he, thirty-two? That's hardly an age to begin worrying about the onset of senility."

"That isn't exactly what I meant." Duane turned his head slightly and looked at her from under the brim of fingers. "He's a doctor. He knows how to take care of his body. What I'm talking about is attitude.

"Ever watch how he teases the young people, follows the fashion fads? He detests the Valley and generally ignores Hollywood. Always goes to the movies in Westwood to be among those bright, young UCLA students. It makes him feel young."

"Jenny likes to go there too. Remember, she's a UCLA graduate. It's like her home turf."

"What I mean is, Brad feels hemmed in by his profession." Duane took her hand and held it in his. "He's scared to death of complacency, but he knows it's inevitable. Each year he's more and more respected professionally, and he sees the day when he won't be able to have fun anymore.

"The nurses laugh at his jokes because they're crude and nasty, and they enjoy hearing them from a handsome young doctor. Ten years from now they'll laugh because they'll be afraid to offend him if they don't. Brad knows it. He hates it and he fights it, but he isn't ready to admit that he was never really much of an iconoclast."

"I don't think Jenny looks at it quite that way." Maria looked shoreward again. Jenny was still talking. "I think she still loves Brad, but his attitude has turned her off. She feels they've drifted too far away from each other. But it isn't just him. I know she's doing a lot of self-examination as well."

"That might be part of the problem."

Maria looked at him blankly.

"Jenny's so damned analytical," he continued. "Maybe it's her job, but life isn't a job and it isn't so clear-cut. You know what I mean? Sometimes it's just better to shrug off the bad things and enjoy the rest."

"But Jenny's so hung up on *his* hang-ups—"

"Sshhh!" Duane tapped his fingers on her mouth. "I've got my hang-ups. You're learning to deal with them, right? And unless you back out, you're gonna be dealing with them for a long time."

Maria knew how serious Duane's recurring depression about his family's death had been. Years of father-son rivalry and hidden fantasies of patricide were brought screaming to the surface after the accident. The inherited wealth only added more chains to his heavy burden of guilt.

Duane was a sensitive man, but not a weak one, and Maria had reacted to his pain with compassion and hope, not pity and despair. As their relationship grew, his resolve to be healthy and strong grew as well. Now they saw the future reflected in one another's eyes, and they could revel in the intimacy of security and love, the joy of sharing.

"If I deal with your hang-ups the rest of my life, will you be able to deal with mine?" Maria shyly glanced away as she spoke, across the water toward the open sea.

Duane cocked an eyebrow. "What hang-ups? You don't have any!"

"I can't stand being made love to more than once an hour, twenty-four times a day," she whispered. "That's my limit."

Duane pushed her away and let his mouth drop open in feigned dismay. "Why didn't you tell me we were going to have this serious, *serious* problem when I proposed?"

Maria's ever-ready laugh exploded like a bomb of joy. She grabbed his ears, shook his head, then kissed him all over the face. He slid out from under her and plunged over the side of the raft.

Pouting, she watched his head bob to the surface. "What's the matter, don't you like Maria's kisses?"

"They're great," he sputtered "Too great. For what I was thinking, I could be arrested if I tried to do it in public."

Brushing her hair back from her face, Maria tilted her nose up in the air. "Oh, Jenny, you were right," she sighed. "These men are all just alike."

Duane held the side of the raft and tried to tug his fiancée into the water, but she slid out of his grasp. "If you don't come for a swim with me, I'll have to find a little mermaid who will."

Maria waved him away. "You can get arrested for doing it in public with a mermaid, too."

"Who's gonna tell? The only things out here are clams and starfish, and they don't talk."

"If you do anything indecent out here with anybody but me, I'll never speak to you again . . . *after* we're married."

"Most men would call that a dream come true," Duane laughed as he swam to the west, thrusting himself energetically into the gently rolling waves.

Maria wrapped her arms around her upthrust knees and watched her lover. If for the rest of her life she could be even a fraction as happy as she was at this moment, she could greet every day with the delight that surely was the natural wonder and right of the human race. She breathed deeply, contented, and stole a glance at the beach, just in time to see Brad rise from the sand and hold out a volleyball to a scantily clad young woman who ran up to retrieve it.

"Thanks."

The woman was young, probably a college sophomore or junior, Brad guessed. She had a sweet, sincere expression that advertisers paid a fortune to capture in photographs. Brad still bore a stunned, drained expression from his session with Jenny.

"You're welcome to join us, if you'd like," the coed continued. "It's the women against the men—and the women are winning!" She spoke as if she were delivering a sexy challenge.

Brad responded to the challenge but not to the bait. He

turned to Jenny and held out his hand. "Want to try a game? The exercise will do us good."

Jenny took his hand and stood. She couldn't believe it. No reference to her lengthy venting of spleen, no snappy response to the pretty girl. It seemed somehow unnatural and she was unaccountably embarrassed by it, turning away to hide the flush as she slipped out of her thongs.

Yes, the exercise will do us good. How does one tell a man, kindly, that his juvenile enthusiasms are no longer honest? Can he be made to believe that his attitudes are outdated, his humor insulting?

They approached the volleyball net, which hung limp and near the ground between wobbly green plastic poles. About as steady as my own legs, Jenny thought, hoping the players would ascribe her faltering steps to the sliding sand. She studied Brad from the corner of her eye. She'd been honest with him, honest and harsh, and it was hard to tell how much of his cautious silence was bluff. Were they both evading emotional responsibility—she with words, he with calm? Guilt took many shapes, and some of them weren't easy to recognize.

"Women are not rewards," she'd told Brad. "I'm not waiting for you each night because you've been a good boy all day long. If I make you happy, I want to know it; if I make you depressed, I want to know that, too. What I want us to do is *share* our lives. Telling me jokes and finding new amusements is not my idea of sharing. Sometimes I feel like I'm living with a talking monkey, and I don't want a chattering pet who loves me no matter what I do. I want a man who respects me, who wants to give himself to me because I might enjoy him as much as he enjoys me."

She hadn't expected him to leap up and shout denials, but she'd hoped he would make some sort of stand. Enumerate her own errors and shortcomings—God knew, she had enough of them! Would he open up now for negotiations, after he'd had a chance to think it over?

The students welcomed them into the game. The men were especially pleased to welcome someone who could show these females that the world of sports was the natural domain of men. As the game progressed, Jenny wondered if the guys were disappointed when Brad didn't join their choruses of catcalls, although he was playing a reasonably good game that made the women sweat to keep up their score. He was alert and friendly, but she could almost sense his brain seething with the words she'd battered into it, examining them with surgical precision. What was he dissecting, her or himself? Both? Jenny wished she knew.

She saw Brad hit the ball over the net, but she didn't really comprehend that it was coming straight toward her until it bounded off her shoulder and rolled over the sand toward the shore. It came to a halt at the water line where Jenny retrieved it.

Maria waved at her from the raft and blew a kiss. Jenny waved back, wondering where Duane had disappeared to.

The waves caught the sunlight and, like a floating, tilting mirror, reflected it. Between the flashes Jenny caught sight of Duane. He had swum about a hundred feet or so away from the raft, where he paused and turned to wave—whether at her or Maria, Jenny couldn't tell.

The water swelled up behind Duane in a wave that buoyed an almost hidden burden. Jenny dropped the ball and threw her hands over her mouth to stifle the scream that choked in her throat. Frozen with fear, she felt strong hands grip her shoulders and knew Brad was holding her.

"Oh God, Brad . . . *look!*"

"I see it." Brad held onto her, and she could feel his weight as he lifted himself on his toes and shouted. "Get back to the raft, Duane! *Hurry!*"

They watched in horror as the sleek dorsal fin cut through the water like a scalpel.

A mouthful of scalpels.

Headed directly for Duane.

eight

MARIA HAD NEVER seen anything as terrifying as the hysteria of the people on the beach.

The panic spread through the crowd like a visible electric current. Individuals twisted and turned, jumped up from the sand, huddled in close groups—watching, watching, watching. What was so frightening was how they did it all at once. The friendly, nondescript crowd instantly became a hydra-headed multitude that made Maria's blood run cold.

Brad was gesturing and shouting frantically, but the splash of waves and the brisk salty wind held back his words. At first she thought he wanted her to dive off the raft and swim to shore. There were similar gestures from the others. Why did it frighten her so and freeze her to the spot? The sea was calm, nothing in the sky, no threat from—

She twisted to look behind her. Duane was swimming

relentlessly toward the raft. Then the wind shifted and allowed the shouts and screams of the crowd to reach her ears. Her eyes fastened on the steely glint moving through the waves as her heart battered against her rib cage like a desperate bird. One voice somehow rose above the others, shrill with terror and warning:

"*Shark!*"

The whole world shifted into a different time frame.

Maria's eyes became cameras snapping flash pictures, holding them only an instant before whisking them away. One picture did not blur into another; each was separate and alone, caught forever in her mind, a frozen nightmare of scenes that would sear her life as surely and irrevocably as scarring acid hurled into her face.

Click.

Duane's arm strained out of the heavy drag of the water, struggling to thrust him toward the raft. His hair was plastered to his scalp like a dark brown cap, only a small pink corner of his forehead showing.

Click.

Behind him, the gleaming bulge of predator flesh dropped below the surface. It might have been a gray shimmer of fog dissolving into the water, so insignificant was the tremor it caused. The calm ocean transformed into a caldron of horror.

Click.

Duane's face lifted out of the water—locating the raft, getting his bearings, filling his lungs for the last fifteen meters he needed to swim.

Click.

His eyes locked with Maria's; a tight grim smile flickered on his mouth.

Click.

Duane's fingers clawed at the air, his eyes already glazed with shock. Salt water poured into his open mouth as his head jerked down into the watery darkness.

In the last split second *Click.* the agony of dying in an unspeakable fashion *Click.* had drained Duane's face of all *Click.* humanity. Whatever emotion *Click.* it contained was put there only by *Click*. Maria's mind and soul. There was *Click*. nothing truly human *Click*. left in his *Click*. ghastly *Click*. expression *Click*. *Click*. *Click*. *Click*. *Click*.

Duane was dead.

He was dead even before his body had disappeared completely below the waves. When he had raised his head to glance at Maria, the shark had circled and closed in beneath him, its exterior sheath and underlying musculature melting and melding, convulsing in a manner that was a marvel of the unnatural. The writhing shape dirtied the surrounding water with blood lost in the transformation process, but the obscurity did not deter it from its plan.

Jagged terrible teeth divided into deadly fine tentacles and shot out like living wires. They moved as if of their own volition, marauders with a resolute mission. And the mission was invasion.

With the acuteness of thousands of elongated, squiggling hypodermics, they twisted into human flesh, mindlessly following programmed instructions to uncover the pattern of life during the delivery of death. They searched through the body for the stored information, absorbed every detail, then discarded the wreckage. The twisting filaments were thorough. The body was raped and ravaged. Devastation was total.

Bones twisted until they broke and gouged through the body's exterior, then were ruthlessly pulverized and ejected. Interior organs and muscles were shredded, the cartilage stripped. The muscles and nerves leading to the eyes were rapidly examined and all information about them was assimilated in a twinkling. The eyes were then sliced and dumped.

As the body was being disassembled, the brain was examined with utmost care and exactitude. Its storage units were picked clean, one by one. The data they contained was quickly scavenged, strained out of the jellied meat, their complexities carefully retained and reinjected into harsh new flesh. Alien flesh.

Because of the complex interrelationships between the brain's cells, their delicacy and constant need of oxygen, the storage of this information took a great deal of time. Almost two minutes.

In her stricken condition, Jenny was vaguely aware of the panic, the growing number of people behind her as they drew together on the sand. The frightened crowd was jumpy, a parade of short fuses, the buzz of human voices the sound of their burning. People sought out one another to cling to, to protect; to comfort, to seek comfort.

No one on the beach doubted that something dreadful was taking place. Maria's sudden scream became the focus of their nervousness. Their voices died as eyes were tugged to the raft-bound, dark-haired woman. She fell to her knees, her grief crushing a name out between sobs: "Duane . . . Duane . . ."

Brad's hands left Jenny's shoulders. She saw him help a young man drag a red-and-white striped canoe toward the water.

Maria had risen to her feet again and tottered on the edge of the raft. Jenny's own panic leaped as her mind's eye saw an image of Maria jumping into the water in her hysteria. Her voice was caught in her constricted throat, but her eyes and clenched fists screamed aloud—*Hurry, Brad, Hurry!*

Stretching her arms toward the deep, Maria called Duane's name over and over. The waves were mild and the raft bobbed gently until a sudden surge lifted and tipped it briefly. Maria almost fell into the water. The crowd drew a collective breath and held it fearfully.

Brad and the sandy-haired man clambered into the canoe and began to row desperately toward the lonely raft. The muscles in their heavy shoulders bunched and relaxed in rapid, regular rhythm. They moved as one, thought as one, synchronized by their determination to protect a human life.

The boat's progress was rapid, but to Jenny the distance between it and the raft shrank with excruciating apathy. A hundred thoughts rushed unbidden through her mind. If *I* were on that raft, would Brad struggle so valiantly? Would he speed ahead with such assurance and skill? Such private inquiry was too nebulous to penetrate her agony of suspense and worry. Later, however, it would whisper to her and worry her. She would be more stunned by the rude incongruity of the thought than by any speculated answers.

When Brad finally clambered out of the canoe, Maria swayed for a moment, her toes slipping on the damp edge of their perch. He lunged forward, caught her by the waist, and pulled her back into his arms. The other man remained in the canoe. As he gripped the raft with his left hand, he pulled the paddle out of the water with a sudden motion of his other hand, as if something might swim by and take a bite out of it.

Jenny glanced at the sky. The heat of the day was now heavy and stifling, as if the sun had surreptitiously sidled closer to the Earth while her attention was riveted on the ocean drama. She looked down again to see Brad edging Maria toward the little canoe. He was talking quietly, undoubtedly using his practiced and professional tone of voice, breathing all the necessary lies to calm her, to get her into the boat and back on shore. She could see his lips moving close to Maria's ear, his arms holding the small woman protectively, and Jenny felt queerly strange when her mind interpreted the image only for its sensual element.

The journey back was swift. They'd reached the beach even before the crowd could cluster around them on the wet sand. Were the spectators lingering on purpose, afraid to interfere, or just afraid to get near the water? Maria, dazed and unobservant, showed no will of her own until Brad stepped over the side of the boat and she saw his foot enter the water. Something seemed to snap. She crumpled then, her chest heaving with ragged breaths as her body trembled uncontrollably and collapsed. Brad scooped her into his arms and carried her onto the shore.

Jenny caught up a large plaid blanket as she pushed her way through the milling crowd. The red-and-black pattern screamed as she shook the blanket out and wrapped it around Maria, who had stopped trembling but would not look at her, keeping her eyes to the ocean. Tiny and frail,

Maria looked like a damp doll snatched from a forgotten corner. Her beautiful dark hair, drying in the salty breeze, stuck out in odd tufts. Jenny reached up unconsciously to smooth it as the crowd at last closed in around them.

Brad couldn't force Maria down on the sand. Her body was rigid, resisting the pressure of his strong arms, resisting the force of reality. She scanned the placid waters, her gaze returning again and again to the raft. It wasn't until Jenny gently pried Brad's hands away, adjusting the blanket more tightly around her friend's body, that Maria noticed the foreign pressures on her body. Her eyes sought Jenny's with painful lethargy, then her quivering hands clutched the towel.

"Gone . . . everything, Jenny . . . everything that mattered. . . ."

Maria's face was blank with confusion, as though she'd only just discovered a butcher knife buried in her heart and couldn't understand how she had time to comprehend it. Jenny, on the other hand, felt her chest heave as if she had felt the gash of the metaphorical blade herself. Her tears washed away that mad staring face and she groped blindly to pull Maria close, to hold that still-living corpse and transfer her own energy into it.

Brad burst through the silence of the crowd, pushing away onlookers who were drawn like silent maggots to the remains of the tragedy. He demanded to know if anyone had summoned a rescue unit, but his question was interrupted by a woman's shrill voice. She plunged across the sand, screaming *"There! There!,"* fluttering an arm heavy with jangling bracelets.

Ragged cries rose from the crowd. Incredulous eyes followed Duane's erratic, halting steps as he gaspingly emerged from the ocean. The salt water dropped away from his thighs, lapped at his knees, then the short hairs on his calves glistened with remaining droplets. He was naked.

Duane was already nearly out of the water before Maria responded to the pain of Jenny's fingers tightening on her upper arms. She looked up.

People were moving past her, toward the beach, and

Jenny's hands gripped her with the force of an Inquisition torture rack.

Maria's attention was caught by a three-year-old girl who waved her sand bucket over her head and went shuffling after the moving crowd. The child had pulled her jumper down around her ankles and stepped out of it, laughing merrily. She was just like the funny man who came out of the water.

It was enough. Maria knew, somehow, and her body was flying over the sand before her eyes had actually given her their message. Her arms were around Duane's neck and her lips crowded his face with a delirium of kisses.

Someone in the crowd wolf-whistled. It broke the ice. People whooped and yelled and danced over the sand, their reticence erased by Maria's joy.

Relief mixed with concern on Brad's face as he wrapped a towel around Duane and sent Maria to the van for his black bag so he could conduct an examination.

A quick scan revealed that there wasn't a mark on Duane's body. By the time Maria had returned, Brad had Duane lying down with his legs slightly raised. Aside from his slow movements and the slightly dazed expression of mild shock, he seemed by some phenomenal miracle to have escaped unscathed from the attack. His pupils dilated normally, and though his pulse was initially rapid, it quickly slowed to an unhurried, healthy rhythm. He might have done no more than go wading along the shore, if his present physical state were any indication.

Brad was quite thoroughly astonished, and said so.

"I'm a little short-winded," Duane replied, a trifle distantly. He breathed deeply, flexing his chest and shoulders. His lungs worked splendidly. "Underwater, it felt like my ribs were crushing me."

"Well, there doesn't seem to be any water on the lungs or any internal injuries," Brad said as he began repacking his bag. "Your blood pressure's a little low. . . ."

"It always is. I feel all right—I just have to get used to being alive. I was sure I was going to die. Was I under long?"

"Long?" Brad was incredulous. "You must have been down for over ten minutes. Jesus Christ, Duane, by all rights you should be stone-cold dead!"

"But I'm not, am I." A statement, cool as an iceberg.

"No, no, you're not!" Maria hugged him tightly. Now that the exam was finished, she couldn't bear to leave him untouched for a second, as though the slightest break in physical contact might cancel the magic that had returned him to her arms.

The persistent blare of a horn signaled the arrival of a lifeguard's orange jeep. Two muscular, bronzed young men alighted and took charge. One of them ran over to Brad while the other grabbed a megaphone and ordered everyone away from the water's edge. The crowd complied slowly, folding up their chairs and gathering their belongings. After what had just happened, they did not need to be told that it was unsafe to go into the water. The lifeguard that had been talking to Brad jumped onto the hood of the jeep and began scanning the water. Brad pushed through the people milling around Duane and took his blood pressure again.

Jenny stood, frozen in place. She kept telling her body to move, to join the crowd's elation, but it was no use.

The sun burned down on her. Although she could feel its warming rays, she shivered uncontrollably. At last, her feet began responding to her mind's commands and she began an unsteady shuffle toward her friends.

"Jenny? Are you all right?" Brad asked. "Maybe you should sit down."

"No, I'm fine. Is Duane okay?"

"He seems to be. Look, can you keep an eye on him for a minute? I won't be gone long."

Jenny nodded, not trusting herself to speak. Brad joined the lifeguard on the jeep and together they searched the dark water for a telltale fin.

The woman who had detected Duane emerging from the water, the one with the bracelets, crowded past Jenny. She spoke animatedly to a tall skinny man who nodded and paid no attention, either to the woman or to the toy poodle straining at the other end of the red plastic leash he held in his hand.

The dog acted as if its nerves were strung out to the limit. It would jump back, then circle and crouch, giving short high-pitched growls as it stared toward the group around Duane.

Jenny observed the dog's behavior for a moment, then looked up to note that Duane was also watching it. His face was impassive. He didn't seem annoyed or jumpy about the animal; rather, he watched it with the concentration Jenny might give to a slide of suspicious tissue.

She surprised herself with the aptness of the analogy that had popped into her mind. As if he could read her thoughts, Duane's eyes moved. He stared directly at her face. A deep and searching look, as if he had never seen her before.

Maria turned to follow his gaze. Seeing Jenny, she reached out for her. "Jenny! Isn't it a miracle? Stay here with Duane, will you? I want to run to the van to get him some clothes." Leaving Duane in the safest hands she could imagine, she dashed off.

Duane's gaze had not faltered. Jenny thought the whole universe had wrapped itself around her line of sight. His face seemed to lunge forward and hover within inches of her own. All she could see were dark tunnels behind the irises, and billions of miles of emptiness beyond. She was but a solitary cell of life, sucked down an artery to infinity.

With her body frozen into immobility, the moment was just long enough for a psychic dagger to split the incorporeal flesh of her quaking soul. An instant of undiluted evil, ultimate perversity. And then it was gone.

Jenny cowered under the overpowering mental assault and tried to fight back for her self-control, for her sanity. It *was* Duane. Of course it was. Who else but Duane? And yet . . . the eyes were wrong. They were too alert, too rapacious. Feral—that was the word she was groping for. Wild and bestial, hungry.

And the smile. He was smiling down at her in a way

that was completely foreign to Duane. An obscene smile that terrified her and sent an icy shudder through her.

It was a dream. Her mind was playing tricks on her again. This was very much aligned to the emotions that haunted her in her alarming dreams. It was all a dream. She would wake soon and be safe.

But she did not awaken. The nightmare intensified.

Without a word he drew her against him and his hands slid under the course blanket to caress her flesh. He desired her, that was evident. She could not move her body except to shiver, but her thoughts screamed and writhed in the agony of revulsion. His hands were all over her body, touching her, exploring her body with almost a clinical precision. It was degrading. It was indecent, shameful.

She could scarcely breathe. She was suffocating in her own guilt. This was more than she could endure. A merciful blackness closed over her and she slumped to the warmness of the sand.

It was Brad's voice that came through the darkness. She opened her eyes to find herself in the van heading back home. There was a throbbing sensation in her head, and she had not lost the sense of overpowering confusion, danger and guilt.

Maria was behind the wheel with Duane beside her.

Jenny's eyes bored into the back of Duane's skull, wondering, dreading. When he looked back at her, he smiled wearily. He looked exhausted, but his face was as right as a face could be.

It *had* been a dream . . . a delusion.

nine

As THE LATE afternoon sun slanted its light through the far windows, buoying a delicate array of dust motes in a thoughtless pavane, the foursome settled in to tell their remarkable story to Maxine.

Settle was hardly the right word, however. Everyone but Duane still seemed on an adrenaline high. Only Duane sat calmly, contributing nothing to the conversation except an occasional affirmative nod or grunt when pushed for a response. If anything, he appeared to be as much a willing and fascinated audience as Maxine.

Brad hovered near Duane as he had done all the way back to the house, convinced that delayed shock symptoms might soon manifest themselves. Jenny had overheard fragments of a long distance phone call he'd placed to a colleague in Los Angeles. The hushed conversation about oxygen deprivation and possible brain damage increased her inner tension. Brad's watchfulness pressed Maria's anxiety hysteria to the limits, prompting her to snap an uncharacteristic remark about his idiot behavior. Chagrined, Brad retreated to the rust-colored wingback, hunkering behind a newspaper and a Scotch and water.

The fading daylight couldn't disguise Maria's lingering paleness. She paced the room as she talked, and the more she tried to spare her mother the details of the afternoon trauma, the more agitated and directionless were her steps. She circled Brad at least a dozen times, traversing an invisible circumference, glaring as if she would strap him to the chair should he ask to take Duane's pulse even one more time. Brad, for all his feigned nonchalance, was sipping at a third drink by the time Maria finished her turns around his bivouac.

Maxine collected the details of the beach incident entirely out of sequence and from shifting viewpoints. She listened with astonishment, waiting for bad news and not quite believing that the story had a happy ending. Once she ascertained that everyone was safe and uninjured, she actually appeared not so much upset as she was curious and, finally, dumbfounded.

Jenny was annoyed with the entire silly charade, for the others acted as if Maxine could not stand the slightest upset or shock. Jenny shifted nervously around in her chair, trying to hide the disquietude she felt. Her eyes seldom strayed from Duane. They scrutinized him continually, waiting for him to eventually react to the afternoon's crisis. Her dove-white hands began to drift back and forth across her legs, until she noticed their movement and stilled them over her knees once again. But she could tell that they were poised, as if for sudden flight.

She could have contributed more of her own observations but remained silent. What Jenny might have told could not be said aloud. The thoughts in her head *would* shock Maxine, and everyone else. They shocked Jenny herself. They were unfocused fantasies, senseless musings that were all emotion and no logic. Yet she couldn't get them out of her mind, and her gaze returned to Duane again and again. Unfocused fantasies. Sick fantasies.

Jenny's attention was easily distracted from the meandering conversation as Rebecca the cat casually entered the room and headed for Duane. The cat was preparing to jump on his lap when she halted abruptly. Unnoticed by everyone but Jenny, the cat peered at him closely, then began backing cautiously away and finally slunk out of the room.

As Maria voluminously and once more explained Duane's astounding emergence from the ocean, Maxine could not help but blurt out: "What happened in the water? What were you doing all that time?"

Duane had stuffed a good part of a sandwich into his mouth and was caught off guard by the question. He sat on the edge of the sofa, chewing laboriously on bread and cheese. Everyone's attention was on him and he nervously choked on the last swallow.

"It's hard to remember—" He spoke haltingly, as if organizing his thoughts, almost as if trying to decide what it was that they wanted to hear. He leaned to the side, relaxing at last with an elbow on a cushioned armrest.

"Jesus, what can I say? I was lookin' across the water at Maria. It was funny because I was thinking about diving under the raft to the other side. I wanted to pop up and scare her, then pull her into the water. Next thing I knew I was at the bottom of a whirlpool with the whole ocean falling in on top of me. I couldn't feel much of anything, just a suction that swallowed me down."

His eyes were sincere, but not as sincere as his voice, the sweet low sound his friends knew so well. Jenny felt he was striving too hard for their acceptance.

"The worst part was fighting for air," Duane continued. "When I thought I couldn't stand it a second longer, I was up through the surface and almost at the shoreline."

"I still don't know how he stayed conscious," Brad grumbled, belting back a gulp of Scotch and snatching up another section of the newspaper from the floor.

"I don't care if he made a pact with the Devil," Maria blurted, eyeing Mrs. Gordon's iced honey cakes pyramided on a filigreed silver tray on the coffee table. She sat on the rug with an arm draped over Duane's knees as she reached toward the tray, then resisted and glanced at Duane. "You didn't, did you?"

Duane winked. "The Devil is a woman."

"If the Devil was a woman, she'd slap you for being so frivolous about it," Maria sputtered.

"If the Devil doesn't strike him, maybe meteors will fall on his head," Brad said to no one in particular.

"Oh, yes," said Maxine. "I saw that."

"What are you talking about?" Jenny reached across and snatched the paper from Brad's hand. Scurrying around to stand beside Jenny, Maria also scanned the page. Duane stretched briefly, then wandered across to a small bookcase, where he bent his head sideways and examined Maxine's small collection of books on business management and California history, plus a few assorted popular novels.

"I saw that last night, looking out the window before I went to sleep." Jenny continued to read for a moment. "But if wasn't nearly as spectacular as this story makes it sound. Just a few lights, that's all there was."

"Maybe whoever wrote this was watching through a telescope," Maria said. "There was no warning, it says here. Just *blooey!*—out of nowhere."

"Just think, Jenny, you and one reporter sat up last night and watched lights in the sky." Brad took another swallow of his drink. His voice had acquired a noticeable burr. "You forgot about it and went to sleep, like a good girl. But this asshole . . . well, he sits up half the night to write a *major* article about something you already knew and had dismissed as unimportant."

He finished off his drink and set the glass down carefully. "There's a major philosophical point somewhere in that."

Maxine, perhaps from embarrassment, began to gather up dishes from the coffee table. Jenny caught the hint and rose to help her, but couldn't suppress a final snap.

"More booze than philosophy, dear."

Stepping between Brad and Jenny, ostensibly to help

Jenny pick up the dishes, Maria spoke lightly. "Why don't you men go take a walk while we straighten up in here."

Jenny could see the pleading in Maria's eyes, yet the remark was so domestic and sexist that Jenny almost had to bite her tongue to keep from replying with something obscene. Her mood was getting foul.

The suggestion nonetheless had the desired effect. Brad cuffed Duane playfully on the shoulder saying, "It sounds to me as though they want us out of their hair for a while," and led him into the hallway, presumably for a walk out back.

Jenny watched them go. Her anger was inexplicably replaced by a sudden sense of dread.

Maria slipped up and snatched another honey cake off the tray in Jenny's hand, then quickly put it back. "I always eat too much when I get tense."

Jenny wondered if Maria's nervousness was only the psychological detritus of the day's harrowing event, or was she picking up the vibrations of Jenny's odd mood of despair and fear? Jenny again promised herself she wouldn't put a pall on the coming festivities.

"Hey, why are *we* doing all this?" Maria turned to her mother. "Where's Betty tonight, and Mrs. Gordon?"

"I let them go home. I thought it would be nice if we had the evening to ourselves, to enjoy each other's company." Maxine plucked the tray from Jenny's hands just as Maria gave in and reached for another cake. "But if I'd known everyone was going to be so ravenous—"

"Just one more, Mama . . ."

The older woman held the tray up high as she glided out of the room. "That's quite enough. I don't want to spend tomorrow letting out all the seams in your wedding dress."

"Duane said he wants me to gain weight, so he can have something to pinch when he grabs." Maria balanced some dishes in one hand and picked up the coffeepot, trailing close behind her mother toward the kitchen as Jenny absently brought up the rear.

"He didn't say any such thing." Maxine twisted her shoulder forward to push open the kitchen door.

"He did so. Tell her, Jenny, you were there." She held the door for Jenny, then followed and set her dishes and coffeepot on the counter. "God, I don't want to be too skinny again."

"Again?" Jenny placed her own load next to the sink and looked out the window. The back patio was empty. Duane and Brad were nowhere in sight.

"When I was in school I was so skinny that the other kids thought I was an alcoholic."

"What?" Maxine laughed. "Who thought you were an alcoholic?"

"It was just one of those gossips the girls passed around." Maria noted Jenny's puzzled look. "I was so thin that someone started the rumor that Mama was a fanatic and fed me only wine from the vineyards. Dorothy and I thought it was so funny.

"We started dressing in purple all the time. Remember that, Mama?" Maria sat, placing her elbows on the table and cradling her chin in her palms. "I even went to Mr. Stone's import store to buy those violet scarves from France, to stuff into my bra. We looked like the daughters of Dracula, with all that purple lipstick and everything."

"If my memory serves me well, that was about midway through a thoroughly exasperating series of obsessions." Maxine couldn't help but laugh again. "Come to think of it, alcoholism might have been easier to cope with than some of the things you girls did."

"C'mon, Mama, you did crazy things when you were a girl, didn't you?"

"Mostly wishful thinking on my part." Maxine moved away from the counter and put her hands on Maria's shoulders, leaning forward to kiss her daughter's forehead lightly. "But I got my wish. A beautiful girl who's found her Prince Charming and will live happily ever after."

"Yeah, that Prince Charming image has been going through my mind, too. I just wish Dorothy had found someone. We used to invent our own fairy tales, and they always ended in a double wedding." She clutched her mother's hands, then leaned back in her chair and sighed.

"What if this turns out to be some other fairy tale? What if I kiss him in church and he changes into a toad?"

"And spoil my celebration plans? He wouldn't dare!"

Jenny continued to stare out the window. She wanted to be touched by the rosy banality of the scene, but her emotions had slunk away to hide somewhere dark and isolated.

Outside the light was fading. The shadow of the house fell across the patio and onto the lawn spread out in the twilight. Neatly trimmed borders of shrubbery created a fascinating but, in the dimming evening, somehow disturbing maze of hidden pathways and cul-de-sacs. Yet it was a lovely setting for the coming reception. The yard was luxurious, spacious, attached to a warm and friendly house.

Why, then, thought Jenny, was there a feeling of *wrongness* about it all? The hysteria from the beach incident should have faded by now, but everyone seemed twisted by it, unstrung. Duane had become distant and inattentive, which she supposed was understandable but somehow struck her as aberrant.

If Duane had fallen to the floor in shock and frothed at the mouth, she would at least know what to do and would feel more at ease. But this sense of *distance*, of being removed from everything that was happening around her, made her feel helpless.

Worse than helpless. She felt frightened.

She squinted through the window, looking for any sign of the men. What was she afraid of—*really* afraid of?

Jenny determined then and there that she'd revise her nonsensical attitude immediately. She only made herself unhappy, made others nervous and apprehensive. And all of it, surely, because she simply couldn't make up her mind about taking control of her own life. It was like those bad dreams that haunted her, interrupting even the most mundane moments, reaching for her, grasping and clutching. . . .

Jenny clenched her teeth to keep from screaming when she felt something grab her shoulder.

"Jenny? Jenny, are you okay?"

"Yes, I'm fine." Jenny hadn't heard the men enter the kitchen and stepped sideways, patting Brad's hand on her arm and reaching up to cover the evasiveness of her move. "Falling asleep on my feet. I guess I'm more tired than I thought."

The room clouded before her eyes and she barely heard Maxine's recitation of the following day's schedule. The wedding rehearsal would be held in the morning, and in the evening, there would be a small dinner party for a few close friends.

By the time she was back in her room—lying on the bed, staring at the ceiling, fully clothed—she could remember nothing but Duane's eyes. He had stood at the table, the burnished coffeepot gleaming on the counter behind him, the tray of honey cakes on the table before him. He'd reached for a cake, lifting it to his mouth and taking a slow bite. "Very sweet." He was staring directly at her when he'd said it, then he'd looked away and hadn't noticed her again.

But she couldn't forget his eyes. They aroused feelings in her that she thought were confined to her nightmares and visions.

Primal feelings. Hot and musky.

ten

ALL THROUGH THE next day Jenny watched Duane. Overnight, everything he said and did had taken on great importance to her.

She watched him surreptitiously during the wedding rehearsal as he followed instructions precisely. Later, she studied his every move at lunch.

He sat impassively, his face devoid of all expression, and listened as preparations for the wedding were discussed. Guest lists, flower arrangements, and receiving lines did not interest him . . . or anyone else at the table except Maria and Maxine.

Jenny had to restrain herself from grabbing Duane and shaking him until his brain rattled. It wasn't that she or Brad were terribly fascinated by wedding etiquette, it was simply that Duane did not seem to be present mentally. Gone was the tender, loving Duane who had bantered with Maria and Jenny on their way up the coast. In his place was a blank-faced stranger.

Duane did not take an interest in anything until the conversation shifted to a discussion of the guest list for the dinner party that evening. He paid rapt attention to Maxine's and Maria's description of the three old friends of the family that had been invited.

His interest was focused initially on Boris and Carolyn Page, or the "Professors Page" as they were most commonly referred to at Point Locke University, where they taught Archeology and Anthropology. Jenny had no idea what fascination a couple of elderly professors could hold for Duane. From Maria's chatter about their accomplishments, it was clear that the Pages were not only good friends but brilliant people. Duane was no mental lightweight, but he was certainly no intellectual. When Duane's questioning became too inquisitive, Maxine cleverly steered the talk in new directions. She intervened again when Brad's joviality became too dominant and when Maria wandered too far into personal nostalgia.

No one seemed to notice Jenny fussing endlessly over her tea, adding a bit of sugar, a touch more cream, then a twist of lemon, none of which she really desired. It kept her eyes busy, however, distracting her from peering at Duane like a voyeur, waiting for . . . what? She did know that the beach incident had changed him somehow, but she couldn't for the life of her figure out what the change was.

Duane might smile or frown, but Jenny felt that whatever expression he wore was only a mask, a shroud that covered him whenever he was not responding to direct stimulation. It was as if all human thought and character disappeared whenever he was not directly interacting with someone. It was an odd thought and the more she worried about it, the more she wondered if the oddness was with Duane or with herself. The thought sent a shudder through her and an involuntary jerk of her hand caused her to spill her tea onto the white tablecloth. There was a mild buzz of words as Betty rushed in to clean up the mess and Maxine assured her that no real harm had been done. Brad made some joke that Jenny, in her embarrassment, didn't even catch.

The questions were still reverberating in her mind, but her accident seemed to have broken the spell. Lunch was over. Everyone was pushing back their chairs to get up.

In the Spanish tradition, the house quieted for a rest period after lunch. Jenny was deep in troubled thought as she trudged up the stairs with Brad trailing hopefully behind her. She felt the pressure of his arm around her waist and found herself leaning into his shoulder willingly.

His face lit up when she looked up and down the hall, determined that no one was around, and pulled him into her room.

Brad's hopes for an amorous encounter were immediately dashed. She sat on the edge of her bed and directed him to a straight-backed chair. His first thought was that she wanted to resume their talk of yesterday regarding their relationship, and he was sure he was not up to having his heart lacerated again.

He was relieved, then annoyed, and finally mystified that the subject on her mind was Duane. He studied her closely. Her face was pale and taut. He could see she needed to talk, needed comforting, but he did not know what to communicate to her beyond the tired consuetudinary phrases that were his stock in trade. Before yesterday, his way of dispelling her anxieties would have been to get off a good joke. Now, however, with his armor pierced, he felt exposed and helpless.

He had been wrong. It wasn't comforting she was after. It was cold hard facts. Medical facts. And those he could provide.

Yesterday after the beach incident, he'd been concerned enough despite Duane's apparent well-being, to place a call to a colleague at Regard Memorial Hospital. Jenny had overheard some of that conversation and was now demanding a blow-by-blow report.

It had not been a long conversation with the other doctor, and it did not take long to tell Jenny. He could not help concluding on an optimistic note. "It's been over twenty-four hours now, Jenny. He hasn't manifested any of the danger signs. He hasn't gone into shock or had a seizure. His blood pressure was a little low, but not enough to be of concern. No sign of water in the lungs. No headaches, dizziness, fainting, or signs of impaired memory. Everything seems fine. You're not the only one that's been keeping an eye on him."

Jenny felt unaccountably ashamed. Was I *that* obvious, she wondered?

"Everyone is just edgy after what happened," Brad continued. "That's understandable. Duane beat the odds, that's all."

"Yes, but he was under so long!"

"Just last year, there as a case where a little boy who'd been ice fishing with his dad fell in when the ice broke. He was under for about thirty minutes and he recovered."

"I thought brain cells started dying four to six minutes after being deprived of oxygen."

"They do. But there's an effect called the 'mammalian diving reflex' that reserves all the available oxygen for the brain and heart. It's why seals and whales can survive for up to an hour without air. In humans, it's normally better developed in kids under four, but there are precedents for it in adults. And Duane may not have even been under for the whole time."

"But Brad, haven't you noticed anything different about Duane? He seems . . . well, distant, as though he were somewhere else. . . ."

"He *is* somewhere else. He's in a little town full of strangers and he has to be gracious and polite to everyone, after a traumatic thing has happened to him. Then, as if that weren't enough, there's the fact that in a few days he's getting married. Give the guy a break, Jenny. He's got a lot on his mind."

Brad was proud of himself. He had presented the case well, he thought. Jenny had listened, considering his words, looking at him with an amazed expression, as if she had just remembered that he was a physician whose opinions might be of value.

She looked beseechingly at him and asked, "Do you really think so, Brad?"

"Yes," he answered assuredly, gaining confidence with every passing minute. Seizing the advantage, he rose and sat on the bed beside her and took her in his arms. "You worry too much. Let Maria worry about him. Why don't you worry about me? I could use some tender loving care, too."

The sincerity of his appeal undid Jenny, and she was caught up in a rush of tenderness that astounded her. His strength and sureness had given her a sense of security. At that moment it was the most wonderful and comforting sensation she had had in days. She wanted to luxuriate in it as long as possible, as long as she could make it last. She wanted him to stay and make love to her.

He kissed her, a tentative, hesitant sort of kiss, after which he drew back as if to gauge its impact. Emboldened by the invitation in her eyes, his restraint snapped.

With practiced skill he quickly removed her clothing and his hands and lips began an eager, maddeningly sensual exploration of her body.

For the shining minutes their bodies were joined in love, the world was only that small room filled with their deep, gasping breaths.

Later, as they lay side by side, Jenny felt pangs of guilt. There had been a quality of desperation about her lovemaking. She had needed the closeness of another person, wanted the refuge of his arms and body. She had felt cold and empty, in need of someone to fill her with warmth and love. She had wanted to forget her fears.

But as she had returned Brad's kisses and as her body arched against his, pressing into his strong, hard, familiar body, she had found a rekindled desire. It was a feeling for Brad that she had thought was gone forever. This did not feel like the last flush of a dying romance, the last flutter of a dying pulse.

Jenny glanced at Brad, lying naked like a *Playgirl* centerfold among the crushed pillows and sheets. His eyes were closed, a spent, but satisfied look on his face. His breathing was growing deep and regular. She played with his hair, running her fingers through it, hoping he would wake up and talk to her.

Aside from an occasional slip, Brad was becoming more aware and considerate of her feelings. He was taking their relationship seriously now, and she could see that he was trying to grow out beyond the playboy image. She smiled down at him, and decided Brad deserved an "E" for effort.

When it was clear that he had drifted irretrievably into sleep, Jenny sighed and tried not to think of the great, pressing anxieties that lurked in the perimeters of her mind, ready to spring out like a nest of evil hornets. She stared up at the flouncy, lacy canopy gracefully held up by the four slender, tapering posts of her bed. She noted the intricacies of the lace design for the first time. Her eyes followed the pattern, how it crossed over and under, over and under, in an endlessly complex, endlessly repeating intertwinement.

She was tired. She had not realized just how tired she was.

She awoke with a start. Brad was already up. She could hear him showering in the bathroom. Voices were coming from the central courtyard below, and she disentangled herself from the sheets and made her way to the window.

The shadows had grown long. She could see the gardener, Happy, standing by a wheelbarrow full of plants. He was deep in conversation with Maxine, Maria, and an elderly couple. The man was tall and thin, and the old woman's wispy white hair barely cleared the height of his collarbone. The woman clutched the old man's hand as she chattered with Maria, then placed her other arm around Happy.

They must be Boris and Carolyn Page, Jenny thought. Maria had mentioned something about the Pages being the only people outside of the Salina family that Happy considered friends.

eleven

BY THE TIME Jenny and Brad joined the group in the courtyard Carolyn was on her knees beside Happy, helping him pull dying plants out of the rectangular patch of soil. After introductions were made, Brad offered his hand to Carolyn and she accepted gratefully, wincing a bit when her knees sent small spasms of pain skittering along her spine.

"Oh my," Carolyn huffed, "when you get to be as old as I am you really have to start considering alternatives to the active sports." She brushed her hands together, dislodging damp mulch from her fingers.

"You don't look like the sort who would be completely satisfied to sit in the den and read the Bible," Brad told her with a conspiratorial wink.

Carolyn winked back, shamelessly. "Absolutely right, doctor. Those genealogical lists bore the crap out of me, and Nabokov far surpasses the Song of Solomon in the sensuality of language, don't you think?"

Brad had the good sense to know he was out of his league. He realized the professor had measured his lack of interest in the literary and was tap dancing all over his head. Brad remembered an aphorism his mother was fond of quoting: "It is better to remain silent and be thought a fool than to open your mouth and remove all doubt." Brad nodded his head and flashed Carolyn a big grin, but kept his mouth shut.

As they walked from the courtyard into the large living room, Maria, embarrassed, apologized to everyone. "I'm sorry that Duane isn't here. He took off after lunch to do some errands and isn't back yet. . . ."

"Oh well," Carolyn said, "I'm sure he'll be joining us soon."

Jenny had noticed his absence immediately. She would have thought after all the interest in the Pages he had displayed at lunch, he would have been on hand for their arrival.

As the group went by, Betty leaned out of the kitchen and started to call out. Then, apparently deciding it wouldn't gain her any Brownie points with her employer, she put on a prim expression, which was her concept of professionalism, and walked toward the group as she arranged the words of her announcement in her head. She arrived and stood for a moment, waiting for the missus to take notice and give her the floor.

"Hiya, Bets. What's in the old Mixmaster tonight?" Maria asked.

Betty giggled and forgot her speech entirely. "It's the biggest ham I ever saw! It's got all this pineapple and sticky sauce and walnuts. You're gonna freak out when you see it!"

"No, Betty," Maxine interrupted good-naturedly. "We are *not* going to freak out. But we would like to know if it will be ready by seven-thirty."

"Oh, yeah, gosh." Betty clamped her hand to her cheek, struggling to remember her lines. She re-established her prim expression. "Mrs. Gordon . . . begs me to inform the gracious guests that dinner will be slightly delayed. Until eight o'clock. Wine and *or-derves*"—she didn't quite have a grasp of that word yet—"are available in the living room."

Betty sighed and clasped her hands together, smug in her accomplishment, then added casually: "But don't get soused."

Maxine managed to gasp out *"Betty!"* before she joined the others in laughter.

"Well—that's what Mrs. Gordon *said*," Betty piped up sheepishly.

The two professors sat next to each other on the overstuffed sofa. The cushion flared under Carolyn Page's ample weight, but bone-thin Boris seemed buoyed by the soft padding, floating like a stick of balsa. Each of them held one of Maxine's crystal goblets filled with red wine. Carolyn puffed contentedly on a cigarette stuck into the end of an efficient but ugly holder. Boris did most of the talking.

Brad was again sitting contentedly in the wingback, which he apparently had adopted as *his* chair for the duration. Jenny perched herself on its arm, her hand resting lightly on Brad's shoulder as they listened to Boris speak.

Boris Page appeared so frail that Jenny felt sure that his wife, who was also elderly but quite robust, accompanied him more as guardian than companion. But his conversation revealed quite the reverse. He still taught special classes at the university except during the summers, and held a position on the board of directors. He repeatedly mentioned tinkering with the Model T he kept in the garage for what he called personal therapy.

"One day I'll take that damned thing out of the garage. Raspy will sit beside me, his big ears flapping in the wind, and we'll show these kids in their plastic buggies what a real car drives like." Boris cranked his eyeballs to the side, waiting for Carolyn's smart-ass retort. He wasn't disappointed.

"Raspy may be a dumb mongrel, but he's not that

dumb." Carolyn tapped her cigarette on the ashtray in front of her.

Jenny giggled as Boris snorted and tried to look offended by his wife's lack of sympathy.

"First you'll have to get that hunk of metal trash moving, which I think an unlikely proposition. Then you'll have to get Raspy to sit quietly while it's moving, which is even more unlikely. Next you'll have to run me down to get it out on the road." Her eyes were merry as she glanced at Jenny and Brad. "I don't want to admit to the world that I allowed my husband to commit suicide by driving that antiquated deathtrap."

"It's not a deathtrap, as you so quaintly call it. It's a good car, a real car, built the way cars are supposed to be built. To last forever." Boris carefully placed his goblet down next to the ashtray. "And if you give me a hard time I just might run right over you."

"You and what army?" Carolyn asked as she lit another cigarette. "And speaking of things lasting forever, how about getting together at the carnival tomorrow night?"

"Carnival?" Maria was delighted. "Does the old carnival still come through here?"

"It's here now! In fact, Thursday's the last night. It's probably playing somewhere more profitable over the weekend."

Boris explained that the university's annual summer celebration had been postponed from the previous month when the traveling carnival had altered its seasonal bookings. Each year the show was a bit more worn and tattered than the year before, but the family who owned it refused to acknowledge that such attractions were thirty years or more out of date. Schools and charity benefits in small California towns booked the show for a flat rental fee and hoped to pick up some profit. Each year the carnival's own profit margin was smaller, and the show's owners managed to survive only by retaining concession sales.

Maria groaned and plopped herself down on the floor. "Duane will love it! I can't believe that show is still dragging through here every year. Can they still make money with that old thing?"

"The kids love it, but I think it's probably on its last legs," answered Boris.

"Sort of like us," Carolyn piped in as she took Boris's hand in both of hers. "All worn out and broken down. But not dead yet."

Maxine sighed. "I wish you'd tell me how, if you're so worn out and broken down, you still do twice as much as anyone else in this room."

" 'Because my heart is pure,' " Carolyn replied.

Boris lifted an eyebrow. "Keats?"

"Later, later, you ignoramus." Carolyn sniffed. "Tennyson."

"Damn clone."

Throughout the exchange the Pages never once let go of one another's hand. They looked like two slightly battered toys, Carolyn a panda bear, her gray hair sticking up like stuffing working its way through split seams, and Boris an ancient tin soldier, the paint buffed away with age and the metal battered in a thousand little places.

They may be old, thought Jenny, but I'm closer to senility than they are.

As the hour grew later, the room grew quiet by inches rather than minutes. The flames sank into the gray dust of the fireplace, and as if by magic, the soft glow of lamps rescued the room from darkness.

When Duane came bustling in, his arms full of packages, the Pages had ceased their verbal sparring and sat smiling, their hands still linked.

Maria crossed the room to gather up the purchases from Duane, but Betty was there before her, snatching up the packages and piling them on a serving cart and wheeling them away.

After the quick introductions, Duane apologized profusely about being late, and went into lengthy explanations about long lines in the stores and an endless succession of "folks" who delayed him at every turn with conversation about Maria's childhood.

He then excused himself to shower and change, and Maria took his arm and left the room with him. In the corridor, they almost ran into a woman.

The plain-faced lady stood there with her chin quivering, then burst into spasmodic sobs. She pulled out a handkerchief with which she tried to soak up the flow of tears.

Duane looked alarmed. He put his hand on the woman's elbow. "Are you all right, miss?"

The woman lowered her hands. Her eyes continued to stream tears, but a tentative smile appeared beneath the torrent.

"She's all right," laughed Maria. "She always does this when she's really happy."

Now Duane seemed thoroughly confused.

"Duane, meet Dorothy, my old comrade-in-arms. And Dorothy . . . this is my soon-to-be husband, Prince Charming."

"Is he really *the* Prince Charming?" Dorothy's eyes weren't yet dry, but her voice was more in tune with the smile.

"The one and only."

"Maria always said you'd come someday. I think you were supposed to arrive when we were sixteen." Dorothy held out her hand. "But better late than never, as they say."

"I came as quickly as I could." Duane smiled cordially as he shook her hand, and then excused himself.

Dorothy watched him disappear up the stairs, and then turned to Maria. "Oooh! He's cute!" Dorothy giggled as the two women sat down on the tiled stairs for a private chat before joining the others.

Dorothy wasn't actually homely, but she was so unmemorable that people, as a way of remembering her, tended to see her that way. Her face was just too plain to easily recall, and her thick and bushy brown hair refused to be combed into the right place on her head. A spindly frame accented her breasts, making them look mismatched as they poked out pathetically under the pink dress she wore with little style. From head to foot, she was an odd duckling, and Maria loved her unremittingly.

They'd grown up together, sharing one another's heartaches and traumas, confessing fears of men and sex one day and sharing their eagerness to nonetheless experiment with them on the next. When Maria left Point Locke, it was as difficult to leave Dorothy as it was to leave her own mother. Maria would always have her friendship with her mother, but her friendship with Dorothy had thrived on their physical proximity.

Time, distance, and emotion force change, however, and the women could feel the alteration as they studied each other. Each held a brief private war with acceptance and denial of the facts. Their affection had not truly diminished, yet their reactions were transformed and muted. Different.

Maria remembered many afternoons when she and Dorothy had sneaked away from the rest of the world to a sunny corner of the garden or a secluded room in the rambling Salina hacienda.

"You're radiant. You have that glow of Oz," said Dorothy. Her voice was very soft, with a trace of huskiness. "But I always thought I was supposed to get to Oz first. After all, I'm the one with the right name."

Oz was the nickname they had given as teenagers to the state of marriage.

"Let me tell you," Maria confided, "I haven't even gotten to Oz yet and the road's already getting rocky. I think the Wizard's out of commission with a headache. What's a girl to do?"

"Kick up her heels together and *go home!*" They spoke in unison, sharing a memory that could hold them only briefly before its feathery wings were mutilated in the reality of the present.

"I was just talking to the Professors. Carolyn told me you still go to the house to help out with errands." Maria hesitated, still wondering if she could bridge the gap of years. "She and Boris really appreciate it, you know."

Dorothy blushed, acutely embarrassed as well as slightly

annoyed. Maria had echoed the words she heard too often—words that made a point of emphasizing her good deeds, as if that would disguise the fact that she was unlovely, awkward, and already as faded as old wallpaper.

"They keep telling me they're going to retire one of these days, but I think they relish teaching too much. Boris says that arguing with his grad students keeps him young, and Carolyn loves teaching too, even though she bitches constantly during the school year about grading papers. I'm just grateful she'll let me help."

"She's always been a tough cookie."

"Not as tough as you might think. Boris had a birthday a couple of months ago and I found her in the kitchen, trying to bake a cake from scratch. Her fingers were gnarled up and she was crying because she couldn't open the sack of flour."

"They're a lovely old couple."

"Yeah, and if you're still willing to bake a cake for your husband when you're nearly seventy years old, I'll come and rub your arthritic knuckles, too."

"That's a deal I can't refuse," said Maria. "And how about our dear Dr. Weitzman? Mrs. Gordon said he's as irritable as ever."

Dorothy was a receptionist for Daniel Weitzman, a short, high-strung general practitioner in his late fifties. He went through at least three blond and busty office workers every year, since a staff position with Weitzman was only temporary for any pretty woman who valued her reputation—or so the rumor went. Dorothy had worked for him, unmolested, for five miserable years.

"I'll be working for that old bastard until the day he dies, or I do. I guess it depends on which one of us gets sick to death of the other one first."

Maria continued to search for a way across the gap. She reached out and grasped her friend's hands. "Why don't you quit and go away somewhere, Dorothy, someplace new and different. A yellow brick road can lead anywhere, if you know what I mean. Make things happen, Dorothy."

"Me? Where would *I* go?"

"Anywhere, just away for a while. Carolyn Page, Dr. Weitzman, a lot of people depend on you too much. Maybe you need to shuck those responsibilities and do something for yourself for a change."

"For myself . . ." Dorothy sighed wearily. She could almost feel the hand of reality folding little bags under her eyes and tucking creases into her face. "If I went to a big city I'd end up working in another boring office, drifting from day to day. I'm not cut out for a glamorous career and romantic adventures. Not like you."

"Me?" Maria wanted to scream, but she laughed instead. "The most romantic thing in a lab is a goddam sperm count. Romance doesn't come with a job. It's the way you grab at life. So grab it and hold on."

"I'm not even interested in Oz these days, or the yellow brick road, or romance."

Dorothy hardly realized she'd been speaking aloud. She'd said these very words so many times to herself that they were an automatic and usually unvoiced litany. Maria's flinch forced Dorothy to scramble for words that would obliterate her *faux pas*.

"Ever try to walk on a brick road in heels? Makes your feet hurt like a sonofabitch."

Same old Dorothy, Maria thought. She's determined to stick it out and take no chances. She'd stay in Point Locke until the day some sympathetic youngster would notice her tired old shuffle and offer her a helping hand. Was that all Dorothy's life was worth—a helping hand to the grave?

"No!" Maria jumped up and pulled Dorothy to her feet. "Dorothy, I want you to promise me something. Sometime, while I'm still here, I want you to really do something for yourself. Anything, but it has to be wild and impulsive and selfish. Strip yourself naked before the university football team, eat a hundred chocolate eclairs in one sitting, I don't care what, just anything! Be creative!"

Dorothy's face took on the partners-in-crime look that had made her ordinary features radiate with life when they were kids. "You really mean that, don't you?"

"Damn right I mean it. Something really crazy, like the

days in purple, remember? And if you do it, then I'll find a way to equal it."

"You've got to top it, Maria. That's the way we did it before. You've got to find a way to top it."

"Bet you think I've lost the knack, don't you?" Maria wasn't sure she hadn't lost it, but the nostalgic taste of conspiracy stimulated the memories on her palate. "Have we got a deal?"

"We got a deal."

The women barely had a chance to seal their agreement with a hug when Duane came down the stairs again. Together they joined the rest of the party for dinner.

As her mother led the way into the dining room, Maria gave her a smile. "Oh Mama, we're eating in the dining room? How wonderful. It's been so long."

The formal dining room, which lay opposite the living room, across the courtyard, had been used daily by Maria's family when she was growing up; but since her husband's death and Maria's departure, Maxine served all guests on the back patio or buffet style in the kitchen and living room.

Jenny looked a shade distressed. "I should have brought more formal clothes."

"No need to dress up, Jenny," Maxine assured her. "The setting may be formal, but the occasion is strictly casual. Just family and friends."

twelve

THE DINING ROOM was long and wide, as was the ornate handcarved table that was its centerpiece, but the room was without windows and retained an edge of mustiness that revealed its several years of isolation. An empty sideboard stood at the far end of the room, near the door through which Mrs. Gordon and Betty made their bustling entrances and exits. The kitchen, oddly enough, was on the opposite side of the house, but the women didn't seem to object to the long trip through the back hallways and served everything with side dishes of prideful good cheer.

Echoes of elegance reverberated in the stones of the house, even though Maxine kept several of the upstairs rooms closed off and unused. The walls of the dining room spoke unmistakably of the changes that time had made. Outlines on the sand-colored walls revealed where furniture had once stood, and now the candlelight only emphasized the forlorn mood, flickering faint shadows over dusty stucco, settling a gold patina on the diners huddled at one end of the lengthy table.

Maxine sat at the head of the table, Duane on her right and Maria on her left. Jenny sat next to Duane, and soon resigned herself to the fact that she couldn't watch him as carefully as she would like at such close range without drawing attention to herself. She could only listen.

Duane did, in fact, become more talkative and lively than he had been since their arrival. Even Betty and Mrs. Gordon seemed to lose the reserve they generally displayed in his presence when he complimented them repeatedly on the meal. Brad did not seem to notice Duane's unusual talkativeness.

Though Duane was participating in the conversation more than usual, he deferred to the professors, especially when they were relating anecdotes about their anthropological field trips. Maxine was quite pleased the dinner was going so well. Dorothy only listened politely. Duane did not even give her a second glance.

After a period of rapt attention, Duane directed a question to Boris. "You're an anthropologist, Professor Page. Perhaps you can help me with a question that's been bothering me. What do you think really distinguishes humans from beasts?"

The question was in such contrast to the light dinner conversation that everything came to a noticeable halt. Maria paused with a wine glass halfway to her mouth. Jenny could only turn and stare. This was yet another twist in Duane's character—one for which she was completely unprepared. Apparently Maxine couldn't decide how to react either.

"That's no lightweight question, Duane," Boris said after pausing as though to make sure he had heard correctly. "It's a topic for at least a four-unit course. But my own opinion is that what really sets us apart is our ability to store knowledge beyond what one individual can remember and pass directly on to another."

"You think, then," Duane asked, "that the ability to

read and write is what sets humans apart as an intelligent species?"

"Reading and writing allow individuals to make permanent contributions to our culture so that generations can add to our knowledge. It is critical to progress."

Duane spoke slowly with dawning comprehension. "You're saying that writing was *the* critical achievement for humans, that it sets them apart from beasts because it's essential for the evolution of culture and technology."

Jenny thought what Duane was saying sounded odd. The way it was worded sounded strange to her. She didn't understand why, but everything about Duane seemed odd to her now.

Boris, in contrast, was intrigued. He nodded in agreement with Duane's statement. "Yes. And once cultural evolution starts, it far exceeds biological evolution in importance for the survival of the species."

"I can see that," Duane said. "It's like a species waking up and taking evolution into its own hands, developing telescopic eyes, radio hearing, microscopic vision, underwater lungs . . . maybe even computer-augmented brains."

Boris was impressed with Duane's quick absorption of concepts.

"But what about values?" Duane asked out of the blue. "Good and evil? Is there any moral distinction between intelligent species and beasts?"

Boris looked at Duane carefully. Here was someone he had just met, someone from God knows where, asking the very questions he had spent much of his life pondering. His natural response, conditioned by years of academic life, was to answer them as best he could.

Carolyn, too, was fascinated by the conversation, but she was content to listen. Everyone else at the table was listening too, fidgeting uncomfortably as they did so.

"Now," Boris was saying, "you're getting more into philosophy than anthropology, and I don't think I have a simple answer to the problem of values. I think we have to find what's best for us. That is, we're in an amoral universe and we have to establish our own values."

"By 'us,' " Duane asked, "do you mean as individuals or as a species?"

"Very perceptive question!" Boris exclaimed as though congratulating a favorite student. "The ultimate good, Kant's *summum bonum*, must be the survival of the species . . . because individuals just don't survive very long."

"But what about other species?" Duane asked.

The conversation was getting into unfamiliar territory now and the professor spoke carefully. "Our experience has been that we can live with some species to our benefit. Sometimes the benefits are mutual . . . sometimes they're not."

"I meant other *intelligent* species."

"There could be conflict I suppose," Boris grinned, "but we haven't encountered a rival intelligent species yet."

The professor looked around the table, realizing that he and Duane had been selfishly monopolizing the conversation. Brad was feigning polite interest and concentrating on enjoying the food. Jenny was trying to make sense of this new permutation in Duane. Maria was eating sparingly but draining glasses of wine in rapid succession as she watched Duane with a look of confusion on her face.

"I think we're boring everyone else, Duane. Come over to our place some time and I'd be glad to continue this conversation."

Carolyn sincerely echoed her husband's invitation, and Duane smiled as though he were grinning at some private joke. "In that case, maybe I will come over and pick your brain in more detail."

Now that Boris had indicated that the conversation should take a more general turn, Duane himself realized what was happening. He then overcompensated, being charming, attentive, polite—beyond what was needed, beyond what was reasonable.

To Jenny, his conduct bordered on the mind-boggling. Was this the sweet, sincere, thoughtful Duane she'd known and respected? If she had not seen or heard him, she would not have believed him capable of such a strange performance.

The meal seemed interminable. By the time they pushed their chairs back from the table, Jenny could not avoid the feeling that what they had been through was an ordeal of tension rather than an evening of relaxation. No one had really enjoyed the gathering, with the possible exception of Duane, who seemed to be trying too hard to fit in.

It would be easy to attribute it to the fact that the room itself exuded an aura of Salina family history and faded memories of happier days. Too easy, Jenny told herself as she folded her napkin and placed it on the table.

There is a strangeness here, she thought, and it has nothing to do with the house. Her eyes met Duane's as she turned toward the door, and she looked away quickly, as if she didn't notice his ready smile.

It's *him*, she realized, confronting the idea directly. Duane is not the man we knew before. He's become someone else—someone distant, unpredictable, untouched by the world of the past, unmoved by the world of the present.

And what of the future?

The possible explanations were many. His close call with death in the ocean. The curious and judgmental attention of strangers in Point Locke. His approaching marriage. The small-town milieu so unlike his lifetime in a sprawling metropolis. But none of the excuses were equal to the oddness of his manner, his shifting moods and impenetrable withdrawls. And tonight, the strange questions he had posed. He was . . . a *stranger*. No longer one of their group.

The more Jenny thought about it, the more certain she became that her conclusion was correct. Even as she searched her own mind, sifted her own emotions for motives to misinterpret Duane's actions, her resolve strengthened.

Maxine, who had been silent most of the evening, suggested they watch a movie, but the Pages quickly begged off, saying they were exhausted. Jenny had seen the look on Maria's face that told her that she needed some private family time, and she and Brad also filed out quietly.

As Jenny mounted the stairway, she turned back to see Maria, Duane and Maxine at the door waving to the departing guests. She heard Maria call out laughingly: "And listen, Dorothy, if I need medical attention while I'm in Point Locke, I'll come to your office."

By the time Jenny had reached the landing, she heard the massive door close and saw the trio heading silently back to the living room. What will they talk about—mother, daughter, son-in-law/husband-to-be? How will they break down the strange barrier that has grown so quickly, so unreasonably?

It was a question that would return to her later. But the answer, when it came, would be couched in a moment that would bring her previous nightmares screaming together. She would at last face something that would eat into her psyche with the appetite of eternal greed and the terrible promise of the ultimate perversion.

thirteen

IT WAS A slow day in Daniel Weitzman's office.

Dorothy glanced up once again at the clock over the entrance and couldn't repress a disgruntled yawn. Of course Dr. Weitzman stepped through the doorway at the moment Dorothy's mouth was stretched to its limit, her face molded like rubber in an expression of utter boredom.

The doctor was leaving the examination room with Mrs. Fields, whose scarecrow face bobbed and smiled as he propelled the tall skinny woman toward Dorothy's desk. Babbling on about her insomnia, migraines and her other assorted aches and pains, Mrs. Fields pulled a checkbook from her oversized and notably expensive purse. Dorothy handed her a ballpoint and a bill. The charge was exorbitant but, as usual, the lady didn't bat an eye. She filled out the check and signed it with a swirling flourish exactly timed to a heavily orchestrated version of "The Sound of Music" piped in over hidden radio speakers.

After Mrs. Fields had exited, blowing meaningless kisses behind her, Dr. Weitzman turned to Dorothy and scowled, jabbing his folded hands into his hips and thrusting his rounded belly forward with exasperation.

"Miss Roosevelt," he grumbled, "I'm sure my patients would appreciate it if you confined your clock-watching and yawning to a more appropriate place."

Dorothy didn't even bother to glance around the office. She already knew that all the chairs were empty. To be honest, she couldn't think of a more appropriate place for being bored to death. She wanted to roll her eyes and yawn again but didn't dare.

"When Miss Greenwood arrives, then you may note the time . . . as you leave for lunch." He folded his arms and tried to temper his severity, speaking as if to a child who deserved punishment for a mild misbehavior. "I don't know what I'm going to do with you, Dorothy. I never have this sort of problem with Irene."

Speak of the devil, thought Dorothy, as Irene Greenwood hurried in through the front door. Dorothy glanced quickly at the clock when Dr. Weitzman turned away. It was twelve-fifteen. Irene was fifteen minutes late.

If Dolly Parton were two inches taller and two inches bustier, she would look like Irene, who poked at her platinum blond wig with long red fingernails and took a deep breath.

"Oh my goodness, Doctor. I'm sure I'm a couple minutes late and I'm just so sorry. I had to help Billy catch his poodle. Little Curly jumped out of the Mercedes and ran away down the street. It took forever to find her. The little booger ran into the bank and piddled on the floor." Dorothy could almost feel the breeze as Irene batted her lamp-black eyelashes. "Poor little thing was just shakin' like a leaf."

Weitzman put his hands on Irene's shoulders and squeezed, pulling her a little closer. His eyes careened down the slope of her low-necked coral blouse as if watching tiny skiers drop into a bottomless crevasse.

"Don't worry your head about it. We've been managing just fine." He slid his arm around Irene's shoulders and gave her a firm hug. "Why don't you go to lunch now, Dorothy. I'm sure Irene will have plenty to keep her busy while you're gone."

Sure she will, thought Dorothy, as she pulled open the lower desk drawer and retrieved her purse. She'll answer the phone for an hour, mess up the files, and scatter enough face powder over the desk top to write code messages in. Although there was no need for code around this place. Dorothy knew exactly what was going on.

"Don't be late, hon," Irene called after her. "I got an appointment for a manicure."

Dorothy shut the door with a bang.

Standing on the stoop a moment later, she took a deep breath then moved down the steps, wondering if the sandwich shop on the corner would have even a counter seat left. Her hand suddenly tightened on the iron railing, as if it had a life of its own, and she paused on the last step. Same old anger, same old frustration, same old sandwich. She thought about what Maria had said to her. Self-gratifying, that's what she had told her, do something self-gratifying.

Without another thought she took the last step and turned to her left. The new Garden Building, with its expensive rooftop restaurant, was only three blocks away. It was frequented by successful businessmen who felt comfortable with the extravagance. Dorothy wasn't sure if the women who accompanied the men were executives, secretaries, or mistresses—she had heard stories each way—and she knew she would get embarrassed the moment someone stared at her as if she didn't belong there.

It didn't matter. She'd made up her mind and her steps were strong and sure. She didn't even see the orange van parked across the street or the driver who sat behind the wheel and watched her as she walked away.

Duane tapped his finger lightly on the steering wheel as he watched Dorothy's determined gait. He glanced across the street at the building she had just left. Painted on the window in severe gold letters, he read: *Dr. D. Weitzman, M.D.*

Dorothy was winding her way through a crowd of boisterous young pedestrians as Duane reached forward and twisted the van's ignition key. Dorothy turned to cross the streeet at the light. She was imagining all the things that might happen once she reached the Garden Building restaurant. Her fantasies ran riot. None of the people in the crosswalk seemed to notice her preoccupied expression. None of the drivers passing through the intersection even saw the plain woman in the loose shirtwaist and colorless sweater fastened in place with a brass clip.

Only the driver of an orange van noticed as she passed in front of him, her purse brushing the headlight as she marched determinedly forward.

fourteen

THE MAKESHIFT MIDWAY cut across the campus between Royce Hall and Sherman Auditorium. It was a tacky affair, lined with game booths, refreshment stands, and mildly vulgar sideshows under sagging strings of colored lights. The vendors looked tired but no less rapacious for that. The amusement park rides were fewer than Maria remembered from years past. Perhaps they broke down year by year and simply were not replaced.

The professors chattered endlessly but charmingly, their conversation sprinkled with an endless array of esoterics and solid knowledge of their respective specialties. Maria listened politely, but with no more than half an ear, and Brad's main attention was on Jenny. He was only briefly distracted by the flattering smiles of college girls and the mechanical gyrations of the midway dancers. Jenny kept an eye on Duane. As at dinner the night before, he seemed captivated by every word the Pages uttered. Had it not been for the noise and the crush of the crowd, Jenny was convinced, Duane would have badgered the Pages with his strange questions.

Everyone laughed when Boris suggested they take a ride on the Whip-Bang, and none of them quite realized what was happening as he pulled a handful of passes from his tweed jacket and herded them past the ticket-taker. Only Duane managed to pull back at the last second, pleading motion sickness and promising to wait for them on the midway.

Maria looked disappointed and a bit confused. She and Duane had been to almost every amusement park in Southern California, gone on every ride in sight, and Duane had always bragged about his "cast iron stomach."

"What's wrong, are you chicken?" Brad threw the taunt over his shoulder as the Pages prodded the group up the ramp.

"No, it's the hot dogs. I want to keep them in my stomach for a while."

Jenny strained to watch Duane as the attendant snicked the bar into place over her lap. He strode resolutely away as if he were on an important errand and disappeared into the crowd milling around the entrance, waiting their turn. Jenny clutched the bar as the ride began and wondered if it was only the sudden motion that made her stomach lurch.

Happy felt uneasy, too. But he wasn't on the Whip-Bang and his eyes had no trouble following Duane, who had come across the midway and begun speaking to a plain woman who munched distractedly on a cotton candy. Dorothy Roosevelt.

Moving beside a booth where the attendant duped the public into throwing quarters in an effort to win dishes that were worth only pennies, Happy leaned against the narrow counter next to a motionless mechanical doll. He watched Duane and Dorothy carefully, only vaguely aware of the attendant and a teenage girl who leaned on the counter next to him.

The attendant absently flipped a switch and the mechanical doll began to sway from side to side, the cellophane grass skirt swishing quietly across Happy's hand. The skirt tickled his fingers and he snatched his hand away with a start.

It was the dilapidated condition of the doll that held his attention. The face, stylish during the Forties, was now a hopeless ruin and it seemed as if it wanted to remind him of his own mortality. The most recent facial renovation could have been house paint slapped on with a single crude stroke from a gigantic brush. A large area on the left cheek was split and peeling, and the grim disaster of the doll's face held his eye a moment too long.

When Happy looked back across the midway, Duane and Dorothy had vanished.

The attendant and the girl turned when the man in coveralls standing next to them muttered "Oh, shit!" and hurled himself into the crowd, bobbing up and down as if searching for someone. The girl then glanced at the doll before her eyes locked with the attendant's once again. She rolled her hips imitatively, holding her scarf in front of her where it waved like the doll's cheap skirt, and the jumpy stranger was immediately forgotten.

The doll danced, oblivious to the ravages of time, caught in the grip of an automatic motor that ground on and on and would continue to do so until the hidden mechanism could no longer stand the strain. The cogs would slip, the gears would grind, and finally the spring would break with a spasmodic fury. It could happen at any moment.

And the doll would stop. Permanently.

At the tap on her shoulder, Dorothy had turned and smiled. A smear of cotton candy at the corner of her mouth caused her skin, under the garish midway lights, to appear cracked and peeling away.

"Well, hi and how are you and all that sort of thing." Dorothy brushed the smudge of feathery candy from her face, searching briefly for Maria's distinguishing dark brown curls. "Now don't tell me . . . you've already misplaced your fiancée. How very careless of you."

Duane responded to Dorothy's cheeriness with a forced little grin. "She's riding the Whip-Bang with the professors."

"Oh." He seemed edgy and Dorothy didn't know quite how to respond.

Pushing forward into the crowd, he tugged at her elbow. "I need a little exercise. Will you walk with me?"

She dropped her candy into a trash container and followed him, loosening the clasp on her sweater which she draped over her arm. Fanning her face with her free hand, she saw that Duane's face was also damp with perspiration. "It's all the people and the lights, and no breeze from the ocean tonight. That's what makes it so hot."

They sidestepped a group of noisy children who wailed inconsolably as they shuffled in a ragged circle around a spilled box of popcorn. Dorothy patted one little boy on the head as she passed, causing him to cry harder in his bid for sympathy.

Duane shaded his face from the low-wattage bulbs that blinked a maddening rhythm over a stage where women, most well past their prime, danced heedless of the crowd of onlookers. The dancers appeared to be following the clock of a mental metronome that had no rhythmic relation to the scratchy music blaring over the loudspeakers. Duane stopped and actually covered his eyes with his hand.

Dorothy looked at the women on the stage—gyrating, mindless puppets—and wondered if Duane were really so prudish as to be offended by the display. Perhaps he had strong religious leanings. Actually, she knew almost nothing about this man her friend would be marrying.

"Did Maria make you promise not to look at the girls?" She tried to make light of it, but when she placed her hand on his arm, she found it was damp and warm, but shivering. "Are you all right?"

"It's the lights," he said, turning his back on the stage. "The lights, they make me dizzy."

Placing her hand on his back, she propelled him forward until they were near the end of the midway, near the west wall of Sherman Auditorium. They stopped by the corner of a large gray tent, where Dorothy turned to face him, placing the back of her hand across his forehead.

"You *do* seem too warm." She felt awkward, her concern transformed in a moment into an emotion she was afraid to identify. His blue eyes, deep-set and intense, bored into her own with an unwavering gaze. She looked down, fumbling with the clasp on her purse. "I can give you an aspirin. . . ."

Suddenly he smiled a dazzling smile. "You medical people are all alike, always pushing drugs."

The tenseness of the moment dissipated in the glow of his amusement. "Oh, so Maria told you what I—"

"I saw you leave your office this afternoon as I drove by." He paused. "You were in such a hurry."

"I was late for lunch." There was vagueness in her answer, but she didn't want to remember the lunch she'd had, standing at a sandwich counter on the ground floor of the Garden Building, afraid to take the elevator to the upper floor, afraid to face a room full of successful men with their Irene Greenwoods.

She wondered what Duane would think of Irene, with her stiletto nails and silly wig. No, he'd like a woman who was simple and real, a woman who didn't fuss. A woman like Maria, or like herself. Not like Irene.

From the front of the tent they stood by, a barker used a megaphone to urge the crowd to come inside the Hall of Mirrors. Though it was still relatively early in the evening, his voice was ragged and hoarse.

". . . Inside, inside this tent, ladies and gentlemen, see it all. Once you're caught in the Hall of Mirrors, you're a fly in the spider's web. The mirrors see all, tell all, and there's no escape. *No escape!*

"Are you a midget, a giant? Is there really only one of you, or a hundred? It's a challenge, ladies and gentlemen, a challenge to find your real self once you enter our maze of illusion and surprise. It's all here. Inside, inside this tent, ladies and gentlemen, see it . . ."

Dorothy didn't know where to steer their perfunctory conversation, so she turned to watch the barker whose spiel, for all its extravagant promise, was enticing no customers. He used his megaphone, its red plastic split across the rim, to tip back the straw hat on his balding head, pushing his shoulders over the top of his rickety prefab booth when he thought he had Dorothy's attention.

"How about you, young lady, is one boyfriend enough?" the barker teased. "Take him into the Hall of Mirrors, turn him into a dozen. Think you can handle that?"

The barker's leering wink left her speechless and embarrassed, and her silence gave the man encouragement. He motioned the couple forward with a twist of his head.

"Special for the lovebirds. Two for the price of one."

The attention was flattering, of course, but Dorothy just couldn't let this go any further. Before she could explain that they weren't a couple, weren't lovebirds, she felt the pressure of Duane's hand on her elbow.

"Let's go," he whispered.

She tried to read the expression on his face while he paid the admission, but found there was nothing to see. He didn't look purposeful or wary, or guilty, or anything relating to the moment. He was just a man buying a ticket to the Hall of Mirrors. A man, a friend . . . no, the fiancé of a friend. A friend who had told her to be aggressive, to reach out for what she really wanted.

Was this what she really wanted? *Was it?*

The short hallway inside the entrance was lined with dark gray drapes. Billows of the same material, which swooped down to the uppermost rim of the smaller entryway that lay ahead, formed a soft roof over their heads. The floor, a linoleum material scraped and scuffed by years of shuffling feet, was printed with black lines that converged beyond the interior doorway in forced perspective. Even in the dim light, Dorothy could see that the floor was dirty as well as worn, littered with discarded cigarette butts. It was depressing and she felt grateful for Duane's heavy arm over her shoulder as he guided her through the entryway and into the maze.

There was a yellow neon sign just inside, glaring its incomplete message: WE COME TO ILL SI N. Below the sign were two squatty people no more than two feet high—a woman whose breasts, under a pale cotton blouse, jutted to spiky points over squashed and rubbery arms, and a man whose dark-jacketed shoulders swelled up behind the woman like a menacing black mountain. The woman's eyes were bruised grapes squeezed together, and her mouth, puckered to the size of a seed, traveled a crazy path over her chin when she spoke.

"I think I'm happier being tall and skinny than short and fat," Dorothy commented. She moved to stand directly in front of Duane. The head of her reflected image swelled as if the brain case were ready to explode. "If my head gets bigger, will that make me smarter?"

Duane's answering smile, in the mirror distortion, made the tips of his teeth stretch out of his mouth like growing fangs. "This way," he said, guiding her around the mirror to the left.

The pathway branched every few feet. The angles of the many mirrors made a dozen image-clones split and walk away from them at one turn, then come back and merge at the next.

The maze was as much a haunted house as a hall of mirrors. Plastic skeletons, lit with eerie blue light, advanced toward them from every side. One could not detect the real skeleton in the midst of all the crazy reflections that bounced and hovered for a moment as the sound of clacking bones echoed on a hidden tape player, then were whisked away to the sound of moaning wind. The wires, however, could be seen even in the reflections.

They walked into a small open area where the mirrors before them were arranged in a semicircle, or seemed to be. Angled mirrors suspended overhead threw an occasional upside-down image that contributed to the confusion. Another sign, this one of red neon, began to pulse: WAR ING GO BACK NO EX T. A loud siren screeched, augmented by haunted groans and wails.

The noise and the blinking light that left the room in deep shadow between its surges, gave Dorothy a real fright and she took an involuntary step backward. Duane pulled his arm from her shoulder, then softly placed his hand on the back of her neck. Even when the red neon flashed, she could barely make him out in the mirrors. He seemed no more than a blur, a dark shape rising tall, very tall, behind her.

"This is scary," she breathed. "We should really get this over with."

"Yes." His answer was deep and breathy, slightly muffled, but his hand began to caress the back of her neck.

She shuddered under the press of his fingers but could not keep from closing her eyes and luxuriating in the touch of his warm flesh. Just to feel another body close to her, to know that someone cared, even . . . *wanted* her?

It was a moment before she realized that the fingers had left her neck and were trailing down her back, pulling open the zipper of her blouse. She wanted to stiffen and pull away, but she couldn't . . . she couldn't.

Am I afraid? Fear, or guilt? Fear, or . . .

She let her head nod forward. The moans on the taped soundtrack reflected the moans of ecstasy that seeped from between her lips in warm rivulets of sound. The moans seemed to flow away, receding—no, not receding, *enveloped* by new sounds, different sounds. Sounds of churning and bubbling, of bodily protest.

Oh God, she told herself, placing a hand on her midriff, my stomach's rumbling.

Dorothy opened her eyes. Her sweater lay on the floor next to her feet. There was something wrong with it. She blinked the drowsiness from her vision, and when the light blinked on once again she saw that her sweater was stained. It was smeared with dark patches, and the floor was covered with droplets that looked like blood.

Shifting her gaze slightly, she could see Duane's left hand dangling limp out of his jacket sleeve. Blood dripped from his fingers, and as she watched, the hand shuddered and—and melted!

A vein along the back of his hand rose through the skin and split apart, the blood flow increasing for a moment until the fingers began to curl up. But, they couldn't curl up like that. *Backward*.

The blood pooled in a cup formed by the twisted fingers. Then the flesh folded over itself, absorbing the blood, its surface texture crinkling, changing into a shiny, scaly thing that writhed like a tentacle before it snaked back into Duane's coat sleeve.

I've fallen asleep, she thought wildly. This is a dream, a nightmare. But the light continued to flash before her eyes, and the primal warning signals from her body at last broke through the haze that clouded her mind.

She could see it in the mirrors as she lifted her head, feeling the horrible pressure of the wet and slimy appendage that slid quickly over her face and neck. She could taste its dampness in her open mouth as it released acid that ate into the sensitive tissues of her face and throat.

Above her head she saw the gleam of silver blades that parted, opening like the jaws of hell. Behind them a black pit of ravenous appetite, closing down over her at last.

She thought of the Devil, who had come to claim his own. In her last instant flashed a picture she had seen years ago, a crude woodcut in which humans lay prone before Satan, who gored them with his spiny tail.

Shock had already erased her senses by the time spikes probed into her soft belly, catching on the surrounding bones and snapping them like brittle twigs. And a moment later the silver teeth had sheared off her head, searching for the meat of knowledge.

fifteen

BETTY FIDDLED WITH the dimmer until she had reduced the kitchen light to a softness that was restful yet not too dim. She returned to the table, where Mrs. Gordon's bowl of bread dough had been left to rise, settling herself in one of the shiny chrome chairs.

Across the table Happy had his hands wrapped around a nearly empty glass. He stared into its bottom as if waiting for the last ounce of milk to evaporate in the warmth of his hands or the heat of his gaze. He didn't even glance up when she sat down.

It wasn't his preoccupation so much as his intensity that worried Betty. She had never been able to get close to him, for he was a man of distance, without much humor. He reminded her of her grandfather, who used to sit on the porch of her parents' home and bask silently in the sun, saying little and seeing all. Like her gramps, Happy was brusque but not unkind, with a mute admiration for young people and their independent spirit.

She reached forward and tapped his glass with her finger. "Some more milk?"

He shook his head, but at least she had broken his spell of contemplation. He straightened, withdrawing his hands from his glass and placing them in his lap.

When he'd come into the kitchen from the patio half an hour earlier, he had looked tired. His teeth were now clamped tightly on his pipe. The smoke, smelling of cherry, wreathed his face but didn't disguise the dark circles under his eyes. He'd asked for the milk, then sat at the table and brooded while Betty tried to look occupied with makeshift duties.

There was no reason for Betty to be here so late, but her boyfriend was gone on a trip and she had nothing to do but go home for another weary evening with her parents, or see a movie. So she had stayed, helping Mrs. Gordon prepare the bread dough for the next day, enjoying the woman's simple chatter and ever-present radio music.

Mrs. Salina was working on the company books in the study, so Betty kept her supplied with tea during the evening. Betty had prepared a pot of coffee and a plate of petite sandwiches for Maria and her friends, but they hadn't returned yet from the carnival. She had been ready to give up and go home when Happy arrived.

Eventually she tired of refolding dish towels, checking the well-stocked cupboards, and shifting Mrs. Gordon's recipe box from one side of the sink to the other. Happy stared at his glass again in private desolation.

"Did you go see the carnival?" Betty asked. She wouldn't have been caught dead at that annual campus display of rubbish, having some odd pretensions about differentiating "good" and "bad" entertainment. Late movies on television, especially the ones starring Errol Flynn or Doris Day, were art; carnivals were cheap and tacky, entertainment for the lower classes.

Happy nodded absently.

"Duane didn't like it much, either, I guess." She had a slight cold and sniffed loudly, then snatched a handkerchief from her pocket and dabbed at her nose in a delayed gesture. The gardener glared at her so fiercely that she thought she had offended him. She stuffed the hanky promptly back into her pocket.

"Duane is here?" he growled, leaning closer, as if he would pull the words right out of her mouth.

"Yeah, sure. He came in just before you did." Betty hopped out of her chair and moved around the table, shifting dishes aimlessly. "Didn't even stop to see the Missus. Went right upstairs, said he was sick or something."

"How did he look?"

"Look?" Betty wasn't sure she understood the question. "He looked okay to me. He went up the stairs three at a time, which is more than I can do when I'm feeling my best."

She thought a moment, then added: "But his clothes were a mess, all rumpled and dirty. Like he fell down on the ground in them and rolled around."

Happy got out of his chair, walked to the hallway door and peered out. He might have been snooping to see if anyone was listening, Betty thought, like somebody in one of those confusing spy movies. He was really acting peculiar.

"You don't like him, do you, Betty?"

"Who?" She knew precisely who he meant.

Happy turned, but stayed by the door. "*Why* don't you like him? Did he do anything, say anything?"

She tapped her finger on the bread dough, testing it, while she gauged just how far she should go, what she should say. It made her even more jumpy with Happy hovering in the doorway like a vulture. At last she pulled the handkerchief from her pocket again and began to wring it.

"He's never said anything to me. In fact, I feel like I don't exist when he's around, that's all. For all he cares I could be a ghost. The first day I thought he was just quiet, a shy man—I actually thought he was kind of sweet.

"But he acts so strange, never telling anyone where he's going, worrying everybody to death. And now he's—well, he's so . . . he's so . . . oh, dammit, I don't know what he is! But I get this creepy feeling whenever he's close."

"And Maria?"

"She knows. *Everybody* knows. That Miss McGregor watches him all the time, too."

Betty was almost in tears, beyond caring what Happy thought of her now. "You can see it, or you wouldn't ask about him. Can't you feel it when he stands next to you? Something . . . *wrong*."

"Why does he want to marry Maria?" Happy's voice held no inflection, probing steadily but without manifest insistence. "Do you think he wants the family money?"

"Mrs. Gordon says he's very rich, but the marriage won't last more than a year, is what she thinks. I wish someone would talk Maria out of it. If I had to spend a year with that man, I think I'd—"

She broke off at the sound of the opening front door. Drying her eyes, she hurried across the room and paused to place her hand on Happy's chest and whisper. "I didn't mean to get so upset. Please don't say anything about this, will you?"

Happy patted her hand and held it gently. He remained expressionless but there was compassion in his eyes. "Nothing, Betty. Don't worry."

Inside the front door Boris Page had his arm around Maria's shoulders. Carolyn, Jenny, and Brad surrounded them, the entire group looking like nothing so much as a cluster of worried refugees. Betty hastened down the hallway to meet them.

Mrs. Salina stepped out of the den, gave them a greeting wave of the hand. She would have returned to the books, but something about the group's forlorn expressions held her. "Well, what's the matter with all of you? Such long faces. You look—"

"Oh, Mama. Mama!" Maria's voice was husky with worry. "Have you heard from Duane? He just disappeared. He's gone, and I, I . . ."

"No, no, don't worry, honey," her mother said hurriedly as she placed a hand on Maria's cheek. "He's upstairs. Betty told me he got in quite a while ago."

There was a collective sigh from the group that immediately broke down into nervous coughs and laughs. Duane moseyed down the stairs to hear it. He was dressed in fresh clothes and looked clean and well-scrubbed. He might have just stepped out of the shower.

"I guess you wonder what happened to *me*," he said as he opened his arms to Maria, who had pulled out of Boris's grasp and hurried to Duane.

"We looked everywhere and nobody had seen you and you weren't in the car and are you all right and what happened to you? . . ." Maria ran out of breath.

"Hold on, hold on. Give me a chance," Duane answered. "It was that carnival food. I told you I shouldn't have eaten so much. I had my head in a trash bin, throwing my guts up. Some lady saw me by the auditorium and gave me a lift home." He hesitated for a second. "I forgot to even ask her name."

With the crisis over, the group talked idly for a few minutes, until Betty and the professors took their leave and vanished into the night. Maxine retired back into the study, while Brad yawned and excused himself, saying he was heading for bed. Maria and Duane said goodnight and followed Brad up the stairs to their rooms.

Jenny stood by herself in the hall, her sight on Duane's back until it disappeared on the landing above, then she headed for the kitchen where Betty had said she had left sandwiches and milk for anyone who wanted them.

The faint light in the kitchen was soothing. Someone had turned off most of the lights and the room was just this side of dark. She found a pitcher of milk and a plate of sandwiches covered with a damp towel in the refrigerator. A large bowl held a blob of something pale and heavy. Bread dough, she thought absently, as she poured half a glass of milk and took a sip.

There was a nearly empty glass of milk on the table, which she took to the sink and rinsed out under the faucet. An impulse made her part the curtain over the window and look out.

A figure was walking across the back lawn. A man. He paused at the shrubs and turned, looking back at the house.

Pale squares of light appeared, falling across the edge of the patio and out over the lawn. Those would be the lights from Duane's room, Jenny calculated. The man looked up—watching?

Jenny leaned closer and squinted, trying to make out who it was. The sky had become cloudy and it was difficult to see. The flare of a lighter illuminated his face for a moment. Ah, the gardener. A breath of relief fled her nostrils.

Yet there was still a hard knot in the pit of her stomach that even the milk could not melt away. It seemed to pulse against the muscles of her diaphragm, looking for an exit.

But there was no way out. No way out.

sixteen

MRS. GORDON RELUCTANTLY reached out and twisted the radio's volume knob. Heirloom china plates, balanced precariously on a shelf above the refrigerator, could be heard to give a final rattle as Bill Haley's "Rock Around the Clock" subsided from a crashing roar to muffled bedlam. The powerful station, her favorite, specialized in musical oldies that pleased her insatiable nostalgia.

There it was again, the doorbell. Where was Betty?

Drying her hands on a terry apron printed with "Love My Food, Love Me," she clutched the edge of the sink and lifted her ample bosom over it to peer through the window. The guests had left earlier in the morning to visit the university museum, well known for its collection of prehistoric artifacts. Maria had elected to stay behind; she wandered beside the hedge at the far end of the lawn, deep in thought.

The missing Betty sat at the long table with Maxine

Salina, writing quickly on a pad of paper as the older woman talked.

The doorbell rang once more. Mrs. Gordon hurried through the narrow hallway, twisting sideways a couple of times to squeeze her substantial hips past an ornate half-table and a wall sculpture that she thought looked like an undernourished Creature from the Black Lagoon. The bell sounded insistently, and she yanked the front door open as if she were snatching a timed egg out of boiling water.

"All right, all right! We ain't lackin' ears, you know—" Her gruffness faded when she saw the woman standing on the porch. "Sorry, hon, but I had to run all the way from the kitchen."

"I've come to see Maria."

"Sure thing." She opened the door and motioned the woman inside. "She's moping around the yard. Why don't you just go on out? Maybe you can cheer her up some."

"Is she alone?"

"Well, there's just the missus and Betty. I guess that's about as alone as you can get around here these days."

Mrs. Gordon put her hand on Dorothy Roosevelt's shoulder and gave her a friendly shake. "My, but you're looking pretty today, all dressed up like that."

Dorothy straightened the lapels of her attractive but not very well-pressed pink afternoon suit. Mrs. Gordon noticed that she didn't look comfortable.

The young woman walked briskly across the hall, pausing at the entrance to the living room. "I'd appreciate it if you'd ask her to join me here. I haven't much time and I need to speak with her privately."

"Whatever you say, sugar. I'll scoot her right in, then bring you girls some coffee."

"No coffee. Just leave us alone," Dorothy responded sharply as she turned her back and walked away.

The tortoise-shell cat woke up as Dorothy entered the living room. Rebecca's ears perked up then went back against her head as she jumped off the cushion on the window ledge and quickly left the room.

Making her way back down the hall, Mrs. Gordon

muttered and snapped her fingers contemptuously when she passed the Creature again. "I'll be double-damned. We try to plan a classy wedding and what do we get—" With growing anger, she counted off on her fingers: "—a peculiar bridegroom, a bride-to-be who sighs more than she smiles, a mother who keeps tellin' me 'Keep 'em happy,' a housegirl whose nerves are shot . . . and now, sweet little Dorothy don't want to be friendly with no one but Maria."

She barged her way into the kitchen just as Betty hurried in through the back door.

"They can all go crazy as hell, but I ain't gonna let it bother me none." Mrs. Gordon grabbed the radio knob and practically twisted it off. The music rose to a screech. "It ain't gonna bother me!" The poor cat quickly abandoned yet another room in search of a quiet place to sleep.

Betty jumped across the room and lowered the volume. She had never seen Mrs. Gordon so upset.

"I *want* it loud!" Mrs. Gordon barked, but the power in her voice seemed to flee even as she spoke. She let her great bulk sag onto a chair.

"Mrs. Gordon—?"

"Sorry, hon," the woman sighed. "I guess all this excitement has got me plumb tired out."

"Are you sure you're all right? Maybe you should see a doctor." Betty knelt on the floor and looked into the older woman's eyes. The wrinkles in Mrs. Gordon's face were deepened by her distress. For the first time Betty noticed that she was really *old*, at least a decade older than she had ever supposed.

"No, no. He'd just tell me I'm gettin' old and crabby. And he'd be right." She straightened in her chair and patted her apron, but she didn't rise. "Would you run out and tell Maria that Dorothy's waiting for her in the living room?"

Betty hesitated, and Mrs. Gordon, with a tone of huffiness, added: "She says she's in a hurry."

"You just sit right there. When I get back, I'll fix you a hot toddy, okay?"

Mrs. Gordon smiled tiredly. "One for you and one for me. And fix an extra one, would you?"

Betty knew Mrs. Gordon was already feeling better. "Who's the third one for?"

"We'll fight over it. Now git."

Because the angle of the house screened the strongest light of the day, the living room was cool and shadowy when Maria entered. Dorothy sat in the wingback chair, her pink suit almost glowing with its contrasting brightness.

Maria fell onto the sofa, letting her breath whoosh out quietly as she kicked off her shoes and placed her feet on the coffee table. "Hi, kid. What's the dope?"

Dorothy's face was passive and serene, her gaze steady. "I have something to tell you."

"I hope it's better than what you told Mrs. Gordon." She stuffed one of the throw pillows behind her back. "Really, Dorothy, she's very upset. Thinks you're mad at her or something."

Dorothy looked flustered and didn't respond for a moment.

"Well, nevermind," Maria continued. "She'll get over it."

Dorothy pressed the lapels of her suit with the flat of her hand. She seemed to be searching for just the right words. Maria lifted her feet off the table and tucked them under her, waiting. The silence lingered.

"Oh, for—c'mon, Dorothy, out with—"

"Why did you tell Duane that I was a doctor?" Dorothy interrupted.

Steeled for an important announcement, Maria found herself stumbling over a question that made no sense. "Huh?"

"You told Duane I was a doctor. Why did you do that?"

"I didn't tell him any such thing! Why would I have? . . . No . . . wait a minute. . . ." She paused, searching her memory, more puzzled now than outraged. "The other night . . . remember when you were leaving? I was joking. I said something about coming to your office if I needed medical care. Nobody in their right mind would think *you* were a . . ." Maria felt the color rising to her face. Open mouth, insert foot, she thought. She was grateful that Dorothy seemed too preoccupied with her own thoughts to have noticed what she had said. Now that that mystery was cleared up, Maria realized there was yet the mystery of why Dorothy had asked the question in the first place. "What happened, Dorothy? Did Duane take my remark seriously?"

"He took you seriously. And so did I."

Maria didn't like the way this was going at all. "What are you trying to say, Dorothy?"

"I talked to Duane—"

"When did you see Duane?"

"At the carnival." Dorothy forced a tight smile. "He looked a little green around the gills, you know. I thought he was going to fall on his face while we were walking."

Maria couldn't help but ask, "Did you bring him home last night, Dorothy?"

"No, he— I thought he was waiting for you."

Was that a harried expression settling over Dorothy's features? It might be guilt, Maria thought, but it might just as easily be bewilderment.

"It doesn't matter. Go on, Dorothy, please."

"We walked along the midway and talked for a long time. I told him quite a bit about myself, about the things we used to do as kids. He didn't speak very much, but he listened. And last night I needed someone, anyone, to listen. It was time for me to make a decision."

"A decision?"

"An important decision. Remember what you told me? Your 'go for it' advice?"

Maria could feel her own frost melt as Dorothy's plain face began to relax and find the facial expressions that were so familiar. "You mean about being assertive and selfish?"

Dorothy leaned forward in her chair. The slightly rumpled suit appeared to catch the room's dim light and reflect it to her face. The illumination could very well have been a gloss of confidence.

Maria couldn't control the delighted interest in her voice. "What did you do?"

"I quit. Just like that. This morning."

"You *what*?"

"I told him what he could do with his dopey patients and his plastic chairs, with his long billings and his short lunch hours and his bad manners. And finally I told him what he could do with his stethoscope—and it wasn't to try and find Irene's flinty heart beneath all that blubber she carries under her chin."

Maria clapped her hands delightedly, then stopped when she realized that she was in a way responsible for Dorothy's drastic actions. It was drastic, but was it realistic?

"Oh, God, Dorothy. That's a decision, all right. I hope I haven't steered you too far over the edge." She didn't want to offend her friend, but she had to ask: "Are you okay, I mean, financially? We could lend you some cash if you need it."

"I'm fine Maria. But I'm not finished yet."

"There's more?"

"Yes, more." Dorothy leaned forward a bit farther and whispered, "I'm leaving. The car's outside, packed and ready to go."

"You mean you're leaving Point Locke? *Before* the wedding?"

Dorothy nodded, sharp and quick.

Maria tried to hide her disappointment. "Couldn't you wait until after the wedding? Surely you . . ."

"No, Maria. I can't wait. If I did, I'd get cold feet and spend the rest of my life under Weitzman's thumb. I know you don't want that. I've got to leave now."

Marie tried to be happy for her friend. "Are you going to Los Angeles? Oh, Dorothy, you'll love it," Maria gushed, regaining her enthusiasm at the thought of having Dorothy nearby once more. "The beaches and the palm trees—it's so different. I could get you *tons* of job interviews.

Dorothy's expression sobered. "No, not Los Angeles. North, I'm going north. San Francisco."

"Oh . . . oh, well, if you can't come to L.A., go to San Francisco, that's what I always say. Really."

"Duane said you would approve. He told me just what you did, that I needed to think of myself for a change. And that's what I'm going to do. A big city. So many opportunities for new experiences, new people, new *knowledge*."

A shiver inched its way up Maria's spine, and the room's daytime shadows deepened as if outside a cloud had just covered the sun. It occurred to her that Dorothy's actions had been more premeditated than she had let on. Not only that, but she had discussed her plans with Duane first. It didn't mean anything, only that she had happened to speak with Duane first, that's all. It was silly to let it bother her. Still, Dorothy had always been so woefully shy, and now she had confided in a *man*, and one she had known only a couple of days.

Somewhere in Maria's mind minuscule neurons snapped crazily, trying to pick up that last fraction of logic that would fold everything neatly into place. Somewhere, something was missing—or was it possible there was one piece too many? Things didn't quite fit, not with ease, anyway.

It all was happening on a subconscious level, but her body made her aware of it. A sense of unease, that shiver up her back.

"I must go." Dorothy stood, reaching into her purse and withdrawing a green envelope printed with tiny white daisies. She handed it to Maria. "Would you mail this for me, or give it to Carolyn if you see her?"

"But . . . aren't you even going to say good-bye to her?"

"No," Dorothy said, "if I see her I'll start thinking about how much she needs me. And that will be the end of it right there."

"Of course, I understand." Maria dropped the sealed envelope onto the coffee table. For some reason, she didn't even want to hold it in her hand. "I feel . . . guilty, somehow."

"Guilty?" Dorothy looked at her quizzically, but her mind already seemed hours away, on the way north.

"As if I'd just thrown a little bird out the window without first checking to see if it was old enough to fly alone."

"This is no little bird, my friend." The pleasure in Dorothy's voice was not pleasurable to hear. "I'm grown up now, and it's time I started managing my life like an adult, don't you think?"

Maria walked her friend to the car, a battered gray Toyota with its back seat piled with suitcases, some of them not even properly closed. Maria brought this to Dorothy's attention, but she only shrugged as she slipped the key into the ignition and started the engine. She had apparently discarded her penchant for neatness along with her inhibitions.

"If anyone wants to steal from the bargain basement, then I say they get what they deserve." There were several layers of irony in her words, and if Maria didn't catch them all, she felt them.

Dorothy leaned out the window and gave Maria a quick peck on the cheek. "I'm sorry about the wedding, but you don't need me."

"You'll write, won't you?"

"As soon as I'm settled, I'll drop you a line. Or maybe I'll call. Would that be better?"

"Yes, please. As soon as you can."

"Adios, *ameega*." Her voice was jaunty but her attention was on the wheel and the driveway. In a moment she was gone.

The car paused at the end of the driveway, but instead of turning left, as Maria anticipated, it turned right, toward the campus. Probably going to pick up some traveling gear at the discount, she thought absently as the sound of the car's engine was lost in the distance.

Maria turned and walked slowly back to the house,

clutching her arms in her icy fingers. The sun was out, but the chill she had felt in the house still clung to her flesh.

The rest of the afternoon Maria spent sequestered in the sewing room with her mother, doing the final hemming on yards and yards of fragile, antique Spanish lace of her wedding veil.

As they worked, Maxine had a chance to study her daughter closely for the first time since the night she arrived. Then she was a glowing, radiant bride-to-be as she should have been. But now? What had happened? The mood of the whole house had changed. Maria's mood had certainly changed. Her face was lined, troubled. The dark circles under her eyes indicated she had not been sleeping well.

And Duane? At that first meeting, Maxine could well understand why her daughter had fallen in love with Duane. His tenderness, gentleness and thoughtfulness had brought back memories of Juan. . . .

But, then things had changed . . . or had they? Had Duane only been putting on an act that first day? No. No one was that good an actor. His friends saw something different, too, especially Jenny. She certainly seemed to be aware of something amiss. She had been very friendly to him before, but now she avoided him like the plague. What was it that she saw?

Maxine would have given a great deal to have known Duane personally before he came to Point Locke—not filtered through Maria's letters and phone calls. If she had known him then, she would be in a position to judge the present situation more accurately.

Of course, no one would know better than Maria, but Maria had thrown an invisible shield around herself and around her relationship with Duane. Maxine knew her daughter well enough to know when she wanted advice. And at present, she was unapproachable behind the barricade she had thrown up.

Maxine was left in a state of mental anguish, wanting to help, but afraid to interfere, and at a loss to know what to do.

Was something really wrong? Or was it all in her mind, Maxine wondered. Maybe it was just all this wedding activity that had changed the mood of the house.

Maria and Duane had been spending too much time alone, but not alone *together*. And yet, Maxine thought, they couldn't get away by themselves when the house had been as active as an airport terminal the last several days. They're nervous about the wedding, a little afraid to get wrapped up in one another when they have visitors to entertain, yet needing to bridge the distance between a man and a woman that demands true and complete privacy to be adquately reduced.

Her own marriage to Juan had been a week-long celebra-tion: an endless parade of relatives who had sprung from the vineyards by the hundreds, their arms joyfully around equally toothless babies and grandparents, parties that soared through the night until the sun soared high. But it was a long time ago, when Maxine Hammond was impulsive and in love with a dark, suavely handsome man who looked a little like one of her favorite movie stars; when the world had survived a major war and predicted, in Pollyanna eagerness, the end of human suffering; when alienation had a simple explanation.

No, the kids saw things differently than she, handled their lives in a fashion that didn't, couldn't reflect her memories of romance. It was middle-age, she reasoned, squeezing out old memories of happy days. Different days . . .

Perhaps it hadn't been such a good idea for Maria to return to Point Locke for her wedding. . . . No matter where she went, people knew her and would stop to talk, asking questions, forcing her to be friendly and alert. Even today, having abstained from the museum trip, she had had numerous phone calls, visits from Mrs. Stimson, her old piano teacher, as well as from Dorothy who had upset her by announcing she was leaving. Carolyn Page had also called to say she'd be stopping by briefly. Too much was going on. No time to stop and think, no time to adjust. No time.

Shapes

Maxine was startled out of her reminiscences by Maria's hand on her arm. "Thinking of Daddy?"

"Old women like to indulge in memories." She put her arm around her daughter's shoulder and hugged. The fresh clean scent of Maria's dark hair enveloped her senses as she pressed her face into it, murmuring, "You'll do it yourself one day, when your children get married. Just wait and see."

"I don't think I want any children . . . right away, anyway." Maria's voice was sad, confused. She turned and looked at her mother, searching for understanding. "—I guess I just want some time. We need time to adjust to one another, you know? Isn't that normal?"

"Of course it's normal. No one should rush into life" (the way *I* did, joyously, with never a regret) "and I think you're being very wise, sensible" (but there's something wrong already, isn't there, my baby, what is it? *What?*) "and adult about it."

Maria sensed Maxine's conflict, but it embarrassed her to be suspicious, to suspect that her mother was hiding emotions. She tried to let her mother know that she needed her confidence, but she was afraid to speak out. Touches of love, hugs of affection, didn't reach the abstractions that haunted her thoughts. They were necessary and they were wonderful, but they were not enough, not now. Words were what she needed now. Words to light the dark shadows, to clarify the ugly things that crawled obscenely from the imagination, to externalize the fears so that their corporeality could be shattered with the sound of reason.

Oh, Mama, what's happening to me? It *isn't* normal and I can't explain. Tell me you know, that you see it, that you understand. Maria's thoughts screamed in private silence.

seventeen

"WHEN I SEE her, I'll speak to her."

Carolyn Page shifted the telephone to her left shoulder, tilting her head so she could hold the receiver in place as she arduously withdrew a butt from her cigarette holder. Her arthritis was acting up again. "But you must realize, Doctor, that I'm not her mother, I'm only a friend."

She lit a new cigarette as she listened to Doctor Weitzman's voice gibber frantically over the line. She couldn't help but feel a rush of satisfaction, hearing the old fool carry on when he found his mousy receptionist had reached her limit and left him hoist by his own petard in a spectacular showdown of expletives. It wasn't an action she would have expected of Dorothy, who often mentioned how she barely managed to hang on from check to meager check. The doctor seemed to be talking about another woman, not the Dorothy who was a model of polite efficiency.

Carolyn heard the front door open. Her lap was soon full of a brown bundle of mongrel energy who slobbered happily all over her tattered sweater, reaching for her chin with his wet tongue. She grabbed Raspy's ear and pulled him down to her lap, patting his head to let him know she was glad to see him. She heard Boris close the door and open the window to let out the smoke she had allowed to accumulate in the room.

"Excuse me, Doctor," she said into the phone, "but I must go. Some guests have arrived." She paused, listening. "Yes, I'll tell her that. I'm sure she'll appreciate it. Good-bye, Dr. Weitzman."

The moment the phone was back in the cradle, Raspy was back in her face, snuffling and whoofing and eager to prove he deserved any affection he received.

"Hear that, Raspy?" Boris called across the room. "Guests, that's all we are. Guests in our own home."

"I had to tell him something, otherwise he'd keep me on the phone until my ears bled. Then he'd charge me for treatment!"

Raspy leaped to the floor as Carolyn lifted herself slowly and somewhat painfully from the chair.

"Bad today?" Boris asked as he watched his wife rub her swollen joints.

"It's the moisture in the air." She crossed the room to help him out of his jacket. "I think it's going to rain this afternoon."

Boris draped his jacket over the doorknob. "Hmmm-mm, not bad for an old battle-axe," he responded when his wife circled her arms about his waist and hugged him tightly.

She pulled her head back slightly and smiled into her husband's parchment face. "What's with you?" she crooned. "You want to fight or make love?"

"What's the difference?"

"Not much, these days." She pulled his face down and kissed him on the nose. "They both tire the hell out of me."

He chuckled as Carolyn turned, removed his jacket from the door and hung it on the rack by the window. Raspy's nose nudged Boris's ankles, reminding him that the animal was ready for a meal.

"Porch." He snapped his fingers and pointed. Raspy bounded across the house, racing for the back porch and his yellow plastic dish. "What did Weitzman want?" Boris asked as he followed his pet at a much slower pace.

"He wants to give Dorothy some Valium. No charge."

"No charge? Weitzman?" Boris was astounded. "What brought on this sudden change in personality?"

Carolyn followed behind her husband, fishing in her sweater pocket for another cigarette. "She quit her job this morning. Told the doctor what she really thought of him, and used a few well-chosen epithets, too, if I must say. The doctor repeated every one of them, verbatim. I think he was shocked, but quite impressed."

Raspy bounced up and down, salivating madly, his nails clattering like castanets on the floor tiles. Boris picked up an open package of dog food shaped into patties that looked like hamburger.

"Dorothy who?" he asked as he opened the back door and followed Raspy onto the enclosed porch. "Doesn't sound like any Dorothy I know."

"No one sounds like anyone we know this morning. It's apparently one of those days."

Peeling a magnetized potholder from the side of the refrigerator, Carolyn carefully removed a pot of boiling water from the stove and switched off the electric burner. She dumped a spoonful of instant coffee into Boris's sculpted cup—made for him by one of his students, a clever design featuring the coil of Ouroboros—and her own kitsch Thrifty special featuring a photo of Gary Cooper.

One at a time she held the cups over the sink as she poured the hot water, working slowly and cautiously, for her fingers twinged in protest when she tightened them in a grip. But it was the twinge in her mind that bothered her more. Today it was Dorothy and Dr. Weitzman. Last night, Duane and Maria.

People were acting peculiar these days. Excessive melancholia and sudden hysteria—was something going on, some sort of psychic breakdown? She thought of June Framington, the town's resident psychic, and wondered if June had responded with any of her unscientific but often uncannily accurate vibrations.

Boris returned from the porch, tossing the empty cardboard and cellophane package onto the breakfast table. He had his metal miner's hat on his head, reaching up to click its light on and off several times. "Time to go to work," he teased.

Carolyn sipped at her coffee but didn't offer her typical rejoinder. She leaned against the refrigerator door. The twinge in her head had become a serious annoyance.

Assuming that his wife was only troubled by her inflammation, he made a big show to distract her, smacking his lips over the coffee with exaggerated television-commercial delight. She eventually cracked a smile when he offered a taste to Raspy, who had raced in from the porch and stood whining on the floor, looking from the cup to Boris and back again, at a complete loss as to what he was supposed to do with it. Prancing in place, he sniffed at the cup and fiercely barked twice, then reared up on his hind feet in a canine *pas seul*, waiting for his kudos.

Boris lifted the delighted dog into his arms as Carolyn retrieved the cup from the floor. They made their way outside, where Raspy wriggled free and raced in circles around a patch of untrimmed shrubs that stood between the house and the garage. The house was loaded with modern conveniences and pleasingly old-fashioned furniture just a hair this side of antique; but the building's exterior siding, worn and weather-beaten, had somewhere over the years deteriorated from rustic to ramshackle. The garage, unpainted and stained with the rust that crept off the tin roof, was even worse.

The plot was comparatively isolated from the edge of town by the woods that advanced from the hills and stopped a few feet from their back door. A quarter-mile of forest burgeoned between the house and the campus, growing wild over property they had owned for many years and were determined to leave in its natural state. The dirt road leading from the town to their home meandered around the edge of the forest, but the Pages seldom used it, preferring a brisk walk through the trees to reach the school and town.

"You want to come sit on an old paint can and talk to me while I work on the Ford?" asked Boris.

She handed him his coffee. "You run and play with your toys, little boy. Mama's got to tramp through the woods on some errands."

"Don't go too far. If those old bones start to act up, you might spend the night out there with the bears and wolves." Boris kept his tone light, but he was truly concerned about her aches and pains, which seemed well on the way to serious infirmity.

"I'm well past worrying about a wolf, but I think I could handle a bear hug." She winked, accepting the best hug Boris could manage while holding the cup. "I'm just going to pay a little visit to the Salina house."

"Ah, you're just nosy. You want to spy on those young people and make sure everything's according to Hoyle."

"You see right through me." She buttoned her sweater and checked the pocket for cigarettes. "That's exactly what I'm going to do."

Raspy was torn when Boris disappeared into the garage and Carolyn moved off into the trees. He yipped indecisively for a moment, then took out after Carolyn, his hoarse bark calling a request for a stick to chase or a squirrel to hassle.

When she emerged on campus a quarter-hour later, Carolyn had to stop and speak sharply to the dog, driving him back to the woods and ordering him to return to Papa. Raspy hovered and peered through the brush until she had crossed the sward and disappeared around the side of Sherman Auditorium. He sat on the ground and waited patiently, but his attention was caught by the chirping and fluttering of a bird, and he was soon back in the trees, searching for mischief.

The carnival had staged a special show for the younger children early in the afternoon, and now the workmen were breaking down machinery and tents, packing the pieces into great silver trucks.

Carolyn paused behind a still-standing tent, the one that housed the Hall of Mirrors, and lighted a cigarette. She promised herself that she would smoke only half of this one. Peeking nosily into the back of an open truck that stood nearby, she saw dozens of mirrors crowded side by side in standing cases. A broad-shouldered, bearded man grunted as he shifted and stacked heavy crates and boxes in front of the mirror cases.

"Good show this year. I really enjoyed it."

The man hopped down to the ground. "Glad you did, ma'am," he said as he tipped his cap. He had a wisp of Slavic accent that went well with the bass in his voice. "But there won't be many more," he added, moving toward the tent, "unless we can find a way to make people interested in carny again." He disappeared through a ragged tear that slit open the tent wall.

Emerging a few moments later, he dragged a couple of crates bound with rope. His powerful muscles gleamed around the skin-tight tank top as he lifted the cases easily and tossed them into the truck. "The profits get slimmer, and the expenses bite deeper every year. Like that." He jerked his thumb over his shoulder, indicating the tent.

"You mean the rip?" Carolyn asked.

"That's it. Some damn kids decided to make a new exit last night. Broke a couple of expensive mirrors, then took a razor or knife to the tent wall. Kids have no idea how much it costs to repair those things."

Carolyn's cigarette burned down to the filter. She extinguished it and pulled it from the holder, wrapped the butt in a Kleenex and stuffed it into her pocket. The man was impressed, but Carolyn hardly noticed.

"Does that sort of vandalism happen often?"

"Oh, sure, all the time. But I think it's the first time we've had any trouble with the mirror show. Those mirrors lock into heavy metal runners. Unless you have the key, you have to shatter them to get them loose. Which is what those kids did."

"Seems to me that would make a lot of noise." Her curiosity had been nicely stimulated. "Didn't anyone hear it?"

"With all the music, people yelling on the midway, you could lob grenades in here and no one would know."

He disappeared back into the tent. When he reappeared he was dragging a single case. It wasn't big but it must have been heavy, for the muscles in his arms and shoulders tightened and bulged with strain. As he tugged it past her, Carolyn could see stains across the wicker lid and the ropes that bound the box. Rusty, reddish stains.

"Goddam, this is a *heavy* mother." He glanced up and tipped his cap again. "Sorry, ma'am." He grabbed the ropes and began to lift the case into the truck.

"Maybe somebody hid a body in it."

The ropes stretched and looked as if they were going to snap. The man used his massive chest to shove the case over the lip of the truck's opening, then fell back with a great sigh and looked at Carolyn. "A what?"

"Maybe we should call Hercule Poirot."

"Hercu—?" Stains from the rope had come off on his hands and he wiped them on his pants as he smiled nervously. "C'mon, lady, you're making a joke, right?"

"When you've been around a college as long as I have, everything becomes a joke." She looked at the stains on the case again. They almost did look like bloodstains. "I hope it's Horace."

"Who?"

"Horace Silverthorn. Medieval Lit." Carolyn puckered her mouth. "If anyone ever deserved to come face to face with St. George's dragon and get eaten alive, Horace is the man."

"Well, if it's this Horace fellow, he'll have to wait till next season to get discovered. They're folding this show until then."

"Oh. Why?"

"It's too expensive to set up and pulls a lot of juice for all the gadgets inside. The profit it's shown so far this year wouldn't buy you a bag of warm popcorn."

"You give me a call next year. I promise to get Poirot out here to solve the case."

"You do that, lady."

As she waved good-bye, he grinned and stood for a moment, wondering who Por-ro was. Then he whistled to a couple of fellows who had just finished folding up the girlie-show tent and indicated that the Hall of Mirrors was ready to go.

eighteen

CAROLYN PAGE'S WALK took more out of her than she cared to admit. Soon she'd have to stop taking such walks and get herself one of those fancy little golf carts. There'd be no stopping her then!

As it was, she limped up to the stone patio of the Salina house like a marathon runner approaching the finish line. Maxine, Maria, and Happy were on hand to fuss over her and prop up her tired feet.

Her short-windedness was not enough to prevent her from enjoying her one vice: cigarettes. She was on her third when Jenny, Brad, and Duane returned from their all-day excursion to the local museums.

The three walked up to Maria with their hands behind their backs. "I understand you're looking for something. Is it me me *me*?" said a bright pink bunny as it sprang forward, covering Maria's face with fuzziness so that she couldn't breathe.

Maria staggered backward, pushing frightenedly at the creature that suffocated her. It was a moment before she realized that it was a puppet slipped over Duane's hand and wrist. The creature moved according to the finger motions underneath and spoke with Duane's strained falsetto.

"Didn't mean to scare you, lady," the bunny/Duane continued, "but there's a bunch of us here who'd like to join your rabbit family."

Jenny stepped forward hurriedly and handed Maria a tiny picture in a delicate oval frame. It depicted a gray hare, *chiaroscuro*, leaping from foggy underbrush, its face straining out of the gloom under the light of a moon partially hidden behind the wingtip of an owl. Brad held a yellow ceramic rabbit, an expressionless shelf-sitter made with more craft than art, and his other hand opened to reveal a brood of smaller bunnies, clay babies painted and fired to duplicate their mother's blandness.

Maria accepted the gifts, which she would add to the collection that dated back to her childhood.

"We can't take credit," Jenny said. "Brad and I spent most of the day wandering through the museums and talking, but Duane left us and spent his time shopping for rabbits."

"Not many rabbits left anywhere," Duane told them. "Maybe they all headed for the hills when they heard the rabbit collector was back in town. The gift shop had a crystal one, but I think you already have one just like it."

"About this high, sitting on its hind legs?" Maxine asked, holding her hands six inches apart, and Duane nodded. "I gave Maria that one for her birthday last year. Wasn't it last year, Maria?"

"Yes, last year," Maria answered absently.

An uncomfortable silence descended on the group. Carolyn, noting the strain, changed the subject. "Oh, by the way, has anyone heard from Dorothy today?" She asked it casually, as if the matter of Dorothy had not been pressing on her mind ever since the call from Dr. Weitzman.

Maria gave a little start that seemed to shake her out of her odd mood. "Oh! Dorothy came by early this afternoon. She . . ." Maria hesitated, wondering if what she had been told by her friend should be kept in confidence.

"Yes, I know, dear, she left Dr. Weitzman." The professor accepted a clean ashtray from Happy with a nod. In a sudden break from character, the gardener did not return to his plants, but stood behind Carolyn, listening to the conversation.

"The doctor called me earlier," Carolyn continued. "He said she was hysterical, created a scene and used some quite, uh . . . uncharacteristic language."

"I know," Maria said. "She told me about it."

"Dorothy Roosevelt?" Maxine exclaimed with wonderment. "Why, I've never heard Dorothy say so much as—"

"No one has," Carolyn said, keeping her eyes on the faces before her. "Strange, isn't it? Of course working for that old goat would be enough to make Shirley Temple scream like a fishwife. But he really is worried, and I must admit that I am, too. She promised to pick up a cake from June during her lunch break today and bring it out to the house, but she never showed up. And if she's at home, she's not answering the telephone."

"She might have called after you'd left," Maxine said, clinging to her belief that no matter what the circumstances, people would abide by polite rituals.

"That's possible. Maybe I should call Boris and ask . . . ah, no, he's in the garage, working on that damned Ford of his. Wouldn't answer the phone if it walked out and wrapped itself around his ears."

Duane backed away from the group. "All that walking today made my feet sore, so if you'll excuse me, I think I'll soak them in a hot tub."

As the conversation was about a local crisis that was probably of no interest to him, Maxine nodded farewell without much obvious interest. Maria started to speak to Carolyn, but the old woman called out after Duane, "Use Epsom salts and make the water as hot as you can stand it."

Jenny kept her eye on him until he had reached the door and opened it. Turning back, she caught Happy glaring at

Duane, his face white with a fierce tension. She imagined it was an expression he wore when he found an insect gobbling at one of his precious plants, just before he severed it viciously with his hoe.

So you don't like him either, she thought. Welcome to the club, mister, it's growing all the time.

"Dorothy won't be coming to see you," Maria said.

Carolyn stubbed out her partially smoked cigarette and let Happy pluck the ashtray from her hand. She looked concerned, but not surprised. "I was afraid of something like this. She's left town altogether, hasn't she?"

"I'm afraid so," Maria answered. "She's not going to be here for my wedding. She left a letter for you. Come with me . . . it's in the living room."

Carolyn followed her through the door and across the hall.

The room was dim and Maria switched on the ornate chandelier. Its teardrop crystals glittered frostily, and Maria turned on a floor lamp as well when she reached the sofa. "Sit here with me for a minute," she said as she stooped to pick up a green envelope from the coffee table. Carolyn took the letter and sat beside her.

"I want you to read it before I say anything," Maria told her quietly.

The letter was not sealed, but Carolyn's gnarled fingers tore the flap as she pulled the single sheet of paper from its envelope. The message was brief, written in Dorothy's neat, unmistakable hand:

This is not a good way to say good-bye, but I can't look into your wise old face and hold on to my resolve. Maria told me to be assertive and I know she's right. I need to examine my life, find out what went wrong. My private demon tells me I should do that far away from the influence of the familiar. Don't fret over me. We'll be together again soon. D.

P.S.—sorry about the cake.

Carolyn folded the letter and tossed it aside. "You told her to be assertive?"

"No! I told her . . . " Maria was flustered and plucked nervously at the nap of the sofa. ". . . I said she should be impulsive. She seemed depressed with her life, and I thought if she did something silly and indulgent that it would . . . that she'd . . ."

"I think she's indulged herself about as far as she can."

"I didn't mean for her to quit her job and run away!" Maria suddenly stood and began pacing. "She acted strange when she left. Distant—as if she was really laughing at me underneath, wanting me to feel guilty." She clutched her arms and shuddered. "Oh, that's a terrible thing for me to say—"

"Not so terrible," Carolyn told her. "Dorothy hasn't been happy for a long time. She was trapped in a rotten, boring job, insecure about her future, her *emotional* future. She grabbbed your suggestion and ran with it, looking for her own happiness. I'm sure she was laughing at her own boldness, not at you, Maria. When she stops long enough to think about it, she'll know that happiness is not where you go but *how* you go."

"Do you think she will?" A glimmer of hope crept back into Maria's voice.

"That's what I said and that's what I meant. I wouldn't waste my breath trying to cheer you up with tall tales." She rose, tugging her wrinkled sweater into place. "Did she mention where she was going?"

"She said San Francisco."

"Ha!" Carolyn was all bustle and cheeriness. "She went there last summer and hated it, absolutely hated it. She's probably in a motel on the edge of town right now, crying her head off and wondering if Weitzman will ever forgive her for the awful things she said.

"And he will. He may like to drool over Miss Watzhername, but when it comes to business, Dorothy's his ace." She took Maria's hand in her own. "Sometimes it's good for us to revolt, to be bold. It may look foolish and dangerous on the surface, but it indicates that a powerful life-force is compelling us to take new measures. It's a survival mechanism, you understand."

They re-entered the hall and Maria glanced at the stairway, thinking about Duane. Her worry over Dorothy may have abated, but there was still an edginess in her manner. She held her body tensely and her hands continually searched for occupation, fingering her pearl necklace, brushing imaginary lint from her skirt, sometimes touching each other and then fleeing quickly, as if they had been caught *flagrante delicto*.

"Honeymoons may sound old-fashioned to youngsters today, but they do allow a man and a woman some time to adjust." Carolyn spoke gently but firmly. "I'm glad you and Duane will be winging your way to Hawaii after the ceremony tomorrow. The longer the better—a month . . . two months. . . . Doesn't that sound wonderful?"

"Oh, I—we couldn't. I have to report back to my desk in three weeks."

"So soon?"

Maria's voice warmed a bit. A dimple appeared briefly as her face searched for a smile. "Jenny and I had to plan six months ahead to schedule a week off work together. Since we're in the same department, we practically had to sign an indentured service agreement."

"But didn't you tell them you were getting married?"

"You haven't met Mrs. Helpmann! She'd have been happier if we'd run to the hospital chapel during the afternoon coffee break—and then she'd have been counting off the seconds."

"You're in cancer research, aren't you?"

"But I'm only a chemist," Maria explained. "Jenny does the hard work—tissue analysis."

"And the doctor?"

"Brad. Cancer isn't his specialty. He confers with Dr. Eisenbaum on the Big Cs. But he told me once that he's learned twice as much from Jenny as from Eisenbaum."

"Jenny's very dedicated." Carolyn didn't make it a question, but Maria didn't notice.

"She's fanatical. She's written lots of papers for the top medical journals. RECRI is very, very lucky to have her."

"Rec-ri?"

"Regard Cancer Research Institute. Jenny and I work for the Institute rather than the hospital. Of course they're affiliated—in fact, the building RECRI uses used to be the hospital before they built the new Mouse—but they're really separate entities." Maria had been successfully distracted. Her hands were relaxed. "It was Jenny who succeeded in getting the government dispensation for marijuana research."

"RECRI, the Mouse, Big C—you have nicknames for everything. What do you call the pot?"

"Shit." Maria actually laughed and Carolyn joined her. "No, really, even Mrs. Helpmann. Except when she says it, she screws up her lips like this—" Maria made a face. "—as if she'd discovered a little turd in her potato salad."

"Maybe," Carolyn gasped out between chuckles, "maybe she's puffing it on the side and just trying to hold it in."

"Prison Warden Helpmann? Not on your life. She weighs and measures that shit so carefully, and so often, that if a single gram of it turned up missing, she'd have the whole department in irons in three minutes flat. And Jenny'd be the queen, 'cause she's got too much influence and Helpmann hates her for it. She'd have Jenny in an iron maiden, toasting over an open fire in the downstairs lobby."

"Are hospital politics really so intense?"

"Maybe I'm exaggerating just a little," Maria admitted. "But they are very strict about the dope. Everyone is under close scrutiny all the time, even the doctors.

"But the government doesn't control everything. I've got my own little supply at home," Maria added with a hint of mischief. "Sometimes Duane and I hole up for an evening and . . ." She wiggled her eyebrows.

"Kids today are incorrigible," Carolyn snorted. "We used to stick with the sensible things—like bathtub gin."

Carolyn felt lighter for the moment. Maria's jitters were surely no more than the jumpiness of a bride-to-be who'd been in the spotlight too unremittingly. She was sure the honeymoon was the answer to what ailed them. They both needed to relax.

The women's laughter brought the rest of the group

back in from the patio. The relief on Maxine's face when she saw her daughter smiling was unmistakable. Jenny and Brad stood with their arms around one another's waists, the pleasure of the moment drawing them together with its spirit of renewal. Only Happy held himself back, lounging in the doorway with his fingers clinging to the frame overhead. He was no longer wearing a grimace, but the sinewy muscles of his thin neck and arms remained corded and rigid.

"Stay for dinner, will you?" Maria clutched Carolyn's arm. "Oh, please. We can drive around and pick up Boris."

"Thank you, dear, but no. I'll have to pass this one up. My automatic timer is cooking dinner at home." She looked at her watch. "Big Mama's Tomato-Paste Meatloaf should be ready in about twenty minutes. If Boris doesn't get his meatloaf, he'll be out under that Ford until three in the morning. And you know I don't like to sleep alone."

Happy stepped from the doorway and took Carolyn's hand. "Let me drive you home," he said.

"No, no, Happy, I need the exercise." She took his hand and tucked it inside her elbow. "But if you'd walk with me a ways, I surely wouldn't mind the company of a brash young man such as yourself."

They could all see that the afternoon was wearing thin when Happy opened the door and escorted the professor through.

Maria had hurried away up the stairs, intending to spend a few minutes with Duane. Tomorrow they would be exchanging wedding vows. In the past few days they had spent so little time together—it almost seemed as if he had had more important things to do than to spend time with her. . . .

His bedroom was empty, but the bathroom door stood open. "Duane?" she called, tapping on the door frame, then peering inside. He wasn't there.

She looked around, wondering. The faucet in the sink was dripping, and she reached to twist it tight. In the sink were splotches of pale powder. Something had been dumped there and inadequately washed away. Maria reached up and slid aside the mirrored panel of the washroom cabinet. The shelves were lined with the usual assortment of items, most of them new and unopened. Her mother had obviously stocked it in anticipation of their arrival.

Below the sink a metal wastebasket, also new and printed with a handsome couple walking through a field of flowers underneath the inscription "You are a child of the universe," stood half-filled with a few days' worth of discarded paper and wrappings. Without quite realizing what she was doing, Maria knelt and sifted through the contents, at last removing from the bottom a crushed yellow box. Its top had been ripped off, but there were traces of powder inside. It was an Epsom salts box.

She stood and looked back into the cabinet. Everything was neat, orderly, ordinary. She took down the box of aspirin. Lifting the flap, she could see the little printed sheet of medical precautions and promotional advertising folded neatly over the top of the bottle. Untouched.

Maria wasn't sure what she felt. A little anger, certainly. Why was Duane creating all these excuses, senseless lies so that he could get away by himself? He seemed to be regressing to the tragic lonely figure he had been when she first met him. But at that time he had been withdrawn and hurt, bruised by life's hard knocks. Now—now, this was out-and-out deception, trickery. And for what purpose?

She wandered back into the bedroom and sat on the bed. The light from the window warmed the cool colors of the room with its burnished glare. In exasperation Maria threw herself across the soft mattress, feeling something crinkle under her hair when her head hit the pillow. She reached under and pulled out a piece of paper. Across it was written, "We're out of Epsom salts. Back soon. D." As had Dorothy, he signed with an initial.

It was like a flare going off in her face. She crumpled the note and threw it across the room, her thoughts a mindless storm of confusion, anger, and—fear? Yes, fear, but fear of what? Of losing Duane? Of finding herself inadequate? *Fear of what?*

She didn't know. Maria lifted herself off the bed and hurried to the window. She needed air. The room was like a bakery oven. She was roasting in the heat of the lowering sun. She threw up the window with a bang and leaned out.

Duane must have taken the van, for it wasn't in its usual place in the driveway. At the end of the drive, she could see Happy and Carolyn disappearing into the woods, making their way toward campus.

I hope he'll walk her all the way, Maria thought. She shouldn't be alone in the woods at dusk. She could fall, hurt herself, and no one would know.

But I'd know, she told herself silently. I'd feel it somehow. And in the back of her mind, she was sure she could hear a call of distress, a plea for help. But it was so faint, so unclear—no more than the tug of a memory that is blocked from the surface.

Then she knew that she was wrong. Monstrously, deadly wrong. It *wasn't* a distress signal or a plea. Suddenly it was as clear as the red sun burning into her eyes. It was a warning, an omen.

The sun was an eye of Cerberus, and she thought she could hear the beast growl.

nineteen

WHEN CAROLYN HAD left him earlier in the afternoon, Raspy had wriggled his way through the underbrush, poking his busy nose into places where he imagined he saw movement. It was almost always his imagination at work, turning the fluttering leaf into a quivering ground squirrel, or grasses bending in a wisp of breeze into a scurrying rat. But if his brain played him tricks, his nose and ears were true, and he was seldom misled by his flights of fancy. He'd never actually caught anything in any of his three years of life, but he'd given a number of woodland creatures, always smaller than he, the invigorating excitement of the chase.

A black crow had done verbal battle with him for the good part of an hour, but Raspy had been the first to tire, crawling into a shaded spot between two tree roots and enjoying the cool wind that would occasionally sigh under the humped root on his right and slide pleasingly over his nose. He sneezed once, then quickly fell asleep.

He woke a couple of times, stretched and shifted his furry body before drifting back to sleep. The Page garage was just a short distance from where Raspy lay, and he could hear the clank of a wrench as it hit the floor or Boris's curse when two hands refused to do what three could easily accomplish. Those familiar noises, so much a part of his life, gave him comfort and security. If the world was going to the dogs, Raspy was convinced it was headed in the right direction.

The sun was bleeding into the horizon when Raspy opened his eyes. In an instant his senses were at their keenest. He used his front paws to pull himself from his hidey-hole, and his muscles tightened like steel to chuck the sluggishness left from his doze.

The shadows between Raspy and the garage were long and deepening by the minute. But it was not so dark that he missed the movement there. It was no squirrel or rat that moved stealthily through the trees, this beast that stood as tall as a man.

Tall as a man, but not a man. Raspy's nose twitched and burned at the odor. It was like nothing he had ever smelled, but his instinct twitched at the danger signals that pried at his brain.

The dog didn't bark but crept forward carefully, moving closer. His fur rose as if it had been combed with a steel brush. The beast ahead of him reached the edge of the clearing that fronted the garage and house. Boris's faint singsong humming drifted through the garage's open door.

Raspy backed up a trifle, raising his haunches, unable to control the low growl that welled up inside him and rumbled in his throat.

The beast turned and looked at Raspy.

The dog growled again, edging closer. Closer again. The beast remained motionless on the exterior, but inside it a fine tentacle coiled tighter. The dog moved again, and a narrow slit appeared on the front of the beast. The mottled gray flesh parted like sliced gelatin, and the tip of the tentacle moved through the slit, a blind white worm peering at the world.

Raspy's ears raised up slightly. He had caught the sound of rippling flesh, the hushed sucking of liquids as they were siphoned into new membranes, new cells. When the new flesh parted with a gentle whisper, and the new tentacle crept through the slit with a wavering tentative movement, Raspy's ears slapped down against his head as his growls gathered in his lungs to become a bark.

The sound, however, could not get past the crushed larynx. The speed of the tentacle, as it shot through the air with unerring precision, was unmatched by any earthly biological creation. It whipped around the dog's neck and tightened in a fraction of a second.

Raspy's neck was broken even before his body was jerked violently from the ground.

The wheels of the Model T had been taken off long ago, and the machine was perched solidly on concrete blocks which lifted it a good twenty inches off the floor.

Even at that, Boris felt cramped. His limbs were a bundle of dried twigs that caught in every crevice, and the miner's hat kept clanging against the motor case whenever he lifted his head to see more clearly. His hands were stained with grease, and his lightweight, bright orange Windbreaker lay on the floor beside him, cradling a shiny puddle of oil that seeped slowly into the left pocket.

Boris pretended the jacket wasn't there. He'd pretend with equal fervor when Carolyn caught sight of it and would fall into one of her sulky pouts. "This little spot?" he'd tell her. "Ahhh, a bit of detergent will take that right out." And then Carolyn would give him the detergent and send him to the laundry room with the order, "Show me." The next afternoon he'd buy a new jacket and that would be the end of it. They'd already played this scene several times, but the plot machinations never varied.

He looked up at his handiwork. The lamp on his hat appeared to be weakening. He couldn't see very well. He peered out from under the car to the room beyond, which was laced with shadows that were barely discernible in the overall murkiness.

Sunset. He was disappointed. He'd had his fun, but soon he'd have to stop. Carolyn would call him to dinner—and tonight was meatloaf night, he thought suddenly, his mouth giving a little twitch at the idea of all that great tomato sauce—so he'd return to the world of sensibility and adult behavior. A healthy meal, some good old sex and violence on television, them maybe a couple of T. Huxley's lay sermons to remind him of his professional standing. The old boy may be dated, Boris thought happily, but he still gives me more entertainment than any of the so-called comedies or trite melodramas on the TV. Soap opera controversies were teapot tempests next to Darwin's Bulldog.

The garage door, which had been partially open, opened wider. Boris saw the slash of dim light fall across the room to his right. In the middle of it lay Raspy's shadow. The angle of the setting sun made it appear huge, he noticed. It seemed to almost fill the doorway. The shadow grew as the dog stepped into the room.

"C'mon, boy." Boris whistled his familiar call. "Come to Papa."

The dog gave a low rumbling sound, halfway between a growl and a bark. The sound was very deep, much hoarser than usual.

"Hey, Raspy, you sound like you've got a frog in your throat," Boris chuckled. "Or did you finally catch one of those frisky squirrels that tease you every day?" He waved the red cleaning rag over his head, out of his eyesight. "Papa's going to finish polishing this case, then we'll head in for dinner. C'mon, boy. Come to Papa."

Boris snatched his hand back under the car, lifting the cloth to clean off a couple of spots of grease that marred the tidy perfection of his handiwork. He reached up, farther. Farther still. I'll be damned, he thought with astonishment. The stupid car's floating right up in the air.

It was then that the shadow fell over his face. He lay there, his hand gripping its cloth and waving stupidly in useless cleaning motions. Raspy's paws lifted the Model T up and up. Only they weren't paws any longer, but red-brown ropes of naked muscle, streaked with patches of Raspy's fur.

The face between them was Raspy's face, but gigantic, twisted into an image of such ferocity and demonic hatred that Boris was frozen into immobility. His eyes bulged as he watched the monster-dog's face lean closer.

Saliva drooled from the widening mouth. A drop of it hit his cheek and burned like acid.

Boris opened his mouth to scream, but the monster's tongue leaped out of its mouth and lodged itself in Boris's throat. The exploratory living wires grew rapidly out of the tongue, which kept expanding, filling the old man's mouth and throat. The face hovered closer, the eyes burning their way into him. Raspy's face—distorted, slobbering over him, *devouring* him.

The elongated teeth lacerated his flesh, just as the living wires pierced the soft membrances at the back of his throat, speeding for the brain. Just as his jawbone broke in half and his face split apart in a splatter of gore.

They made their way out of the trees as the top of the sun slid soundlessly beneath the horizon.

"Raspy!" Carolyn clapped her hands. "Here, boy."

"Maybe he's out in the woods," Happy offered, after the silence continued.

"More likely he's in that garage, sound asleep under the Ford with you-know-who." She disentangled her arm from Happy's. "Let me tell you, don't ever marry an anthropologist who tinkers with mechanics. You'll go crazy if you do."

"I promise I'll keep my head," Happy answered, but his eyes were on the house. He glanced at the garage. The door to it was closed.

"And don't get a dog. They're worse than babies or anthropologists!" Carolyn noticed that Happy wasn't really responding to her attempt at humor. She touched his sleeve and he looked away from the garage reluctantly. "If you'll go wake the master of this quaint household, I'll have dinner for us by the time you herd them into the kitchen. Deal?"

Happy nodded and Carolyn patted his arm, shooing him toward the garage. She turned and walked across the clearing, taking the three porch steps carefully, resting her hand very lightly on the thin banister.

Happy paused at the garage door, then opened it. The inside was gloomy and he could see nothing. He stepped through the door and called, "Boris?" The silence was overpowering.

His eyes were adjusting slowly and he moved with caution. His foot hit against a metal object. He looked down. It was Boris's miner's hat, the light shining feebly from the dying bulb. When he stooped to reach for it, he looked up and saw a bulky dark shape off to the side, against the far wall.

"Jesus," he breathed. It was the Model T, resting on its side. He could just make out the dark concrete blocks, still resting in position in the middle of the room. He rose to his feet, the hat in his hand, and jumped when something hit the floor at his feet with a soft wet sound.

Happy tilted the hat so that the light hit the floor, shaking it to gain the last bit of energy from the expiring battery. The light was faint, but he knew what he saw. Amid the splatters of blood at his feet were chunks of oozing flesh. And in the center, staring up at him sightlessly, a human eyeball.

Happy began to back away, stumbling, his mouth pouring forth a stream: "Oh Jesus God it's true oh Jesus goddammit to hell it's true oh God oh Jesus. . . ."

It was then that he heard the squeaking of the hinges on the garage door.

He turned, groaning. The hat was still in his hand but its light was fainter than a firefly. The door closed and the room fell into a darkness that was worse than total night. The room became a hell of shadows, of half-seen movement.

In front of the door something moved. Its steps were the sound of slime running down a stone wall, its breathing the whisper of an axe. It advanced.

Happy backed into a shelf that jumped with the impact. The tool shelf. He edged along it, running his fingers over the splintered surface, reaching for a wrench, a hoe, anything that would serve as a weapon. His words continued to tumble out in a sobbing, frightened whimper. "Oh Jesus . . . what is this . . . Oh God Almighty! God . . ."

The shelf ended and Happy fell backward. His back hit the wall and there was a clattering sound. He reached, and a wooden handle dropped into his grasp. He knew what it was—the scythe! The goddamn scythe!

He let go of the hat, kicking it across the floor as he pulled the scythe from the wall with both hands. The dark shape was ten feet away . . . six feet . . . four feet. . . .

"Come on, whatever you are. . . . I'm gonna kill you, you fucker—gonna kill you!"

With a cry of rage, he lashed out with the weapon. It seemed to sink into a mound of rubber. And then the handle broke and fell to the floor with the sound of finality. Of death.

Happy pressed back against the wall as the shape moved closer. Boris's hat scraped against the floor, moving forward inch by inch as the thing propelled it with its motion. In a moment of irony its light brightened for a second, the gleam directed upward, glinting against the blade of the scythe that was now held in sticky, veined extensions that were a travesty of fingers.

The sharp edge of the blade cut deep into Happy's chest.

Carolyn stood at the sink in the kitchen, using the knife she had used to chop lettuce to slice the cherry tomatoes. It was a good all-purpose knife, her favorite, and she kept it sharp.

The meatloaf was in the oven and was due to come out in a couple of minutes. She glanced at the wall clock over the stove once again. Sometimes men were beyond her comprehension. Boris was usually sitting at the table, watching the oven like a little boy waiting for the ice cream to be dished out on his birthday.

She heard the front door open and close. At last, she sighed, hurrying to finish with the tomatoes. She turned when she knew someone was standing in the kitchen door. "Sit right down, I've got the salads ready and the meatloaf will be out in a . . ."

Happy stood in the doorway, holding Boris's stained jacket in front of his chest. He looked odd, Carolyn thought. Maybe he didn't know what to do with the jacket.

"Just drop it on the floor, Happy. It'll go in the trash and Boris will buy a new one tomorrow, like always."

Happy continued to hold the piece of clothing.

"Where's Boris?" Carolyn asked, turning back to the sink. In the light of the room, she could see Happy reflected in the window glass before her.

"Do you want to see Boris?" Happy asked.

"Do I want to see Boris! Of course I want to see him. I want to see him at that table, with his hands washed and his hair combed. And you, too. Go on, sit down."

For a moment she wasn't sure if what she was seeing in the window reflection wasn't just a trick of the light. Happy dropped the jacket. There was a great gaping wound across his chest. His shirt was cut open, revealing it.

Carolyn looked over her shoulder, her body turning slowly, the juice of tomatoes dripping from the hand that gripped the knife in a screaming agony of arthritic pain. She couldn't believe what she was seeing.

Happy glanced down at his chest. "How careless of me. I forgot to close that up." The flesh slid together and melded, and the blood was absorbed by minuscule feelers that rose up from the flesh in obscene clumps.

Then Happy's face shifted. The flesh changed texture and crawled over the bones into new positions. She thought she could hear the skull grinding as its form altered to fit the new face that molded itself before her shocked gaze.

In a moment it was Boris's face, staring at her with an expression that had never once been on that familiar flesh in the fifty years she had known it.

Boris spoke. The voice was his voice, but the tone was cold, icy and bitter with wicked amusement. "And Dorothy? Do you miss sweet Dorothy? Maybe she'll come back someday."

And again the face shifted, and it was Dorothy who emerged from the grinding, shifting mess. Dorothy glared at her with inhuman wickedness and malice. The mirth of evil danced in her eyes.

"My private demon, Carolyn," she said as she took a step. "Remember what I told you? My private demon."

The knife fell from Carolyn's hand to the floor and bounced with a racket against the tiles.

But soon it was silent, awash in a great pool of blood.

twenty

JENNY WAS UP and around early Sunday morning, making her bed and getting dressed. This was the last time she would be in this bed, in this house, in this town. Tonight, she thought, I'll be in my own bed, far away from here.

Her heartfelt glee at the prospect brought on a pang of remorse and guilt. Hadn't Maxine been the most gracious hostess imaginable? Hadn't Betty and Mrs. Gordon knocked themselves out doing everything they could to make her comfortable? Even the townspeople she had met couldn't have been more friendly.

Still, there was no denying the fact that she was anxious to leave. Time seemed to crawl here. It weighed heavily, like a millstone around her neck. She felt she had been here a century instead of less than a week.

Small towns were restful and peaceful? You couldn't prove it by her, she thought. But then, she hadn't seen Point Locke under the best of circumstances. Had these past few days not been so plagued with doubt and unfocused suspicions, she was sure she could have come to like Point Locke. It was a beautiful place.

And this room . . . She looked around as she packed her suitcase. It had a pleasant, rosy look in the morning light. The bedspread and canopy had a picture-book beauty that appealed to a child's aesthetic that would never succumb to any overlay of sophistication. Her own bedroom was stylish and comfortable, but it didn't appeal to her fairy-tale sense of wonder as this room did. She remembered when they had arrived Monday night in the dark and listened to Maria's recital of childhood dreams. Although the house never quite shed the gloominess of her first sight of it, this room, at least, retained the optimism of Maria's fantasy.

Jenny took one last look around. She'd left nothing on the nightstand or the dresser. No clothes in the closet. She ducked into the bathroom—no lipstick or comb on the shelf, no make-up smudges on the sink.

Yes, she was going to miss this room, she reflected. How nice it would be to live only in a rosy world, she thought as she opened the door to the hall. But how circumscribed a world it is, she answered herself, closing the door behind her, locking the child away once more from the world of adult concerns.

As soon as Jenny had stepped out into the hall, she was beset by the hustle and bustle of the house. It was like Grand Central Station, with caterers, florists, and other delivery people going busily about their business.

The expanse of grass was now covered with white lawn tables and chairs. A crew was already setting up the white, lattice-work gazebo from which the catered food would be served.

It helps to have money to hire all this work done, Jenny thought. There was enough to do without having all *this* on one's mind.

Jenny tapped softly on Brad's door but there was no answer, so she left her suitcase beside his door and went downstairs. He would be packing the van early—with all the activity of the day, there would be no other time—for their return to Los Angeles right after the reception.

She was amused to find Brad already downstairs. He was on the kitchen phone making a check-in call to Los Angeles. He couldn't quite believe that he had actually spent all his allotted time away from the hospital without receiving one emergency call. Hanging up the receiver with relief that Eisenbaum had not been pushed from an open window by a patient unhappy with the watery oatmeal, and that he could report on schedule on Monday morning.

"Where is everyone?" Jenny asked, getting her own juice from the refrigerator when it became clear that Betty and Mrs. Gordon were occupied elsewhere with preparations for the reception.

Maxine and Duane, Jenny learned, had just left for the airport to await the arrival of the family contingent from Mexico City, including the family patriarch, Jaime Salina, Maria's great uncle, who would give the bride away. "June Framington is up with Maria. Maria's pretty upset. Something to do with the Pages. Seems they won't be here for the wedding."

"Not here for the wedding?!" Jenny repeated incredulously.

Brad merely shrugged. "That's what I heard." He was off to load the luggage in the van before Jenny could ask him anything else.

Maria *was* upset. Jenny found her sitting at her dressing table brushing out her hair. She had been crying. Her eyes were red and puffy. Jenny's heart went out to her. Today was her wedding day, supposedly the happiest day of her life, the day she had so long looked forward to. The mood in the room was bleak and funereal rather than the euphoria normally associated with these events.

Betty worked silently in one corner of the room, doing some last minute pressing of the wedding gown's undertulle. By the expression on her face, she might just as well have been pressing black crepe instead of bridal white.

June sat near Maria, trying to be of help but not succeeding. She was dressed in pale yellow chiffon, a shade too frivolous for the occasion and for a woman her age.

Maria was grateful for Jenny's presence, and motioned her to a chair beside her. "Oh Jenny. Everything is going wrong. Everything. . . ." she said, dabbing her eyes. "First Dorothy and now the Pages and Happy."

"What! Happy, too? What's happened?"

Maria was too distraught for explanations, so June jumped right in. "It was all very odd, I must say, talking to me around the door like I was an encyclopedia salesman." She stopped, sighed, her hips rolling as she shifted her weight, then gave Jenny a hard glance. "Don't you think?"

Jenny was growing exasperated. "Who? What?"

"Why, Carolyn Page. Isn't it strange?"

"I don't know. What's happened?"

June took a deep breath before beginning her story.

Maria sat dabbing her eyes, and listening with Jenny, as if she had to hear June's story again to really believe it.

"I went over to give Carolyn her cake last night, the one Dorothy forgot to pick up. It was just past sundown, and the house was dark. Not even the porch light was on. Well, I know they never go to bed early, so I stumbled my way up the steps and pounded on the door big as you please. I banged until my knuckles were raw but no one answered.

"Finally I peeked through the window, just as Carolyn came out of the kitchen. I could only see her for a second in the light from the open door, but I was sure she was ill. Her hair was a fright, like she'd just been in a fight, and she was wearing that old blue bathrobe she trots around in at night. She opened the door, just a crack, making it clear that I wasn't invited in. 'Carolyn,' I said, 'are you sick or something?' And she told me she was just resting. Resting! What's she doing, sleeping on the kitchen table? Anyhow, she opened the door and took the cake, didn't even say thank you, then Out. Of. The. Blue. says she and Boris are going to Yucatan for the rest of the summer."

"Yucatan?" Jenny was surprised, but not particularly astounded. "Why Yucatan?"

"That's what I said. *Why Yucatan?* Carolyn said something about Boris getting a letter from a professor. Menzel or Wenzel or—"

"Menzel," Maria said. "He used to teach anthropology here."

"Anyhow, she told me it was something very important—her exact words. Very. Important. —and that Happy was going to drive them to San Francisco this morning to get a plane." June paused dramatically and then continued. "Now. Does that make sense to you?" she asked, her attitude making it clear that it made no sense at all.

Maria fought back tears. "I can't understand it. Why would they leave the day of my wedding. The three of them are my oldest and dearest friends. I've known them my entire life." She stopped, blew her nose and then went on. "And why would they want to drive that far when they could just take a plane from here and make connections?"

"Now, now, my dear. You know how attached they are to Happy. They probably wanted some time alone with him before they left." June's suggestion was rational, but there was a shade of concern in her tone that could not be masked by her level-headed explanation.

Jenny was sure she should say something, but she was at a loss for anything to say that might be of help, except for: "They would surely try to call you this morning before they left, don't you think? Or maybe you could call their house," she added with sudden inspiration.

"Oh, they've gone already," June said with finality. "Carolyn said they had to be in San Francisco by noon. As I've been telling Maria, it was too early for them to call before they left. I'm sure Happy will phone from the airport."

Maria didn't look convinced and Jenny was inclined to agree that the entire incident had an odd sound to it.

Everyone meant well. But rare is the wedding that does not have numerous little crises to be dealt with. The morning was not half over and already Jenny was exhausted.

Calming Maria had left her emotionally drained, and

helping her dress had proven to be a detailed, formidable task.

The early morning had been filled with frenzied, last-minute activity, in which everyone was pressed into service. Jenny had been on hand to greet great-uncle Jaime. She had run errands for Maxine. She had dealt with unexpected gifts and unexpected guests that turned up at the house. She had even arbitrated a rapidly heating territorial dispute between Mrs. Gordon and the catering staff.

But now, finally at the church and with everything presumably ironed out and running smoothly, why was her heart pounding? Why were her hands shaking? Why was she verging on panic? Her stomach was tied in nervous knots and she was afraid she was going to be sick.

And as if her nervousness were not enough, contrasting scents assaulted her nostrils, making her feel lightheaded and queasy. There was the acrid smoke and waxy smell of the votive candles that flanked the altar. There was the over-powering, overly sweet fragrance of roses, carnations, and lilies of the valley. She was not at all sure she would be able to sit through the ceremony. "Pull yourself together," she commanded herself sternly. This was, after all, the last item of business here in Locke Point—this and the reception to follow.

Why couldn't she just relax and enjoy this beautiful, elegant tableau before the altar of St. Mary? The morning sun streaked in through the stained-glass windows of the church, bathing Maria's friends and neighbors in a soft golden glow. Cascading garlands of flowers tied with heavy satin bows decorated each of the oak pews.

It simply could not have been more beautiful, and yet this beauty was eclipsed by Maria as she came up the aisle on the arm of her distinguished-looking uncle. She was breathtaking in the ivory Spanish lace gown that had been passed down through four generations of Salina brides. Maria tried gamely to smile, but she seemed nervous.

Jenny's eyes filled with tears at the sight of her friend. She loved Maria. Maria deserved the greatest measure of happiness. She had to be warned! But warned about what?

Jenny reminded herself that there was no rational basis for this anxiety that was dominating her; unsubstantiated but insistent whisperings inside her head were not sufficient grounds to step away from the pew and dash hysterically up the aisle and tell Maria that she was making a terrible mistake.

She could only watch helplessly. Her eyes followed Maria to the altar where Duane awaited her. Was that a slightly befuddled glaze on his face? Or was it just a look of concentration as he filed away every word, every face, every emotion for future reference?

The journey from the church to Maxine's home did much to dispel the solemnity that had enveloped the church and trailed the newlyweds out through the heavy doors and into the street. Once the guests were lodged inside their cars, decorum and inhibitions were pitched out on the pavement with the leftover rice. There were shouts, the honk of horns, and relieved laughter that grew in volume all the way to the reception.

Within an hour the celebration was in full swing. Bottles of champagne did a disappearing act with canapés, and clear plastic cups transformed into makeshift ashtrays displaying burnt-out butts. The patio, yard, and garden swarmed with well-wishers. A couple of photographers wandered endlessly through it all. One was a balding fat man from the local paper; he knew his job, but not well. The other was a young woman in a frothy purple hat, doing her damnedest to look professional and cheerful. If Jonathan Swift and Lewis Carroll could have collaborated, this couple would have been their version of voracious *paparazzi*.

Maria circulated dutifully through the crowd. Most of the guests had known her since she was a child. They repeated her new name, *Mrs. Eastman*, until it began to sound to Jenny like the name of a merit badge. Jenny observed the reception with a sense of detachment that made her feel superior, as well as frustrated. It wasn't a nice feeling at all, and she oozed buckets of dry sweat trying to maintain her outsider status. She smiled politely at each introduction, said a few words now and again. No one seemed to notice her watching.

Duane was at Maria's side. He spoke easily with these strangers, many of whom he would most likely never see again in his life. Even so, Jenny thought, he should be more excited, more exhilarated . . . more *something*!

Jenny eventually drifted away, but her uneasiness persisted. It wouldn't go away.

"He's a killer." June Framington held a glass of champagne out to her.

Jenny took the glass. "He's what?"

"A killer . . . your boyfriend." June nodded at Brad, who was hemmed into a corner of the patio by four young women who fanned him with their eyelashes. "These small-town girls are impressed by handsome professional men. Especially doctors. Especially single doctors."

"Is that a warning, Mrs. Framington?" Jenny cocked an eyebrow as she wrapped a napkin around the stem of her glass.

"That depends on whether he's open to suggestion."

Jenny had to admit to herself that she was mildly annoyed. She did not want to be rude, but she had no intention of discussing Brad or anything pertaining to their personal lives with June. There was an awkward pause as Jenny scrounged for something to say.

"Maxine mentioned that you had some ability to see into the future. Can you see my future? Do you have to look at my palm or something?"

"I'm not a sideshow charlatan, you know. Sometimes I see things, that's all. People's emotions act on me like some sort of trigger."

Trigger—there was the word again. Jenny had a brief moment of vertigo and reached toward a nearby table, stumbling over a dropped cup and spilling most of her drink on her shoes. Something about that word made the world spin and blur. . . .

"Honey, maybe you've already had enough to drink." June put her hands on Jenny's shoulders and propelled her into a wooden folding chair, moving aside a paper plate someone had left behind. "Why don't you sit down here for a few minutes."

"Thanks." Jenny rubbed her hands over her face and smiled wanly. "I'm not stoned. Really . . . it's just that, sometimes, I have these spells. I get dizzy, and I see things, too. . . ."

"Psychic?" June was suddenly interested.

"Oh, no, I don't think so. Just—just pictures that come and go." She tried to laugh, but it came out choked and bubbling. "Odd fantasies."

"Did you see something just now?"

"No, nothing. It was merely something you said. A word." Jenny tried to remember, but her thinking was fuzzy. She *felt* drunk. "I just had this odd feeling."

Jenny appeared so distressed that June decided it would not be a good moment to question her further, or to mention her own disturbing vision on the day the young people went to the beach.

"What you probably need is something to eat. Too much liquor on an empty stomach is an upset to the body processes."

Jenny just wanted to sit and rest for a moment, but the woman was no doubt right. It had been a hectic morning, she hadn't eaten breakfast, and had put a swift end to several glasses of champagne.

"Yes, maybe some cheese or a canapé. . . ."

"I'll be right back with something." June went clattering across the patio toward the buffet table, where she began to pile enormous quantities of food on a sagging paper plate.

The endless movement of the crowd made Jenny's dizziness return, as she tried to concentrate on something specific. Across the yard Maria disappeared behind a screen of shrubbery with Duane in tow.

Jenny would watch that spot until they reappeared, she told herself. Watch the leaves glisten in the early noonday sun, watch them tremble in the slight breeze. Watch . . .

* * *

"How much longer is this going to go on?" Duane's face was rigid, with a beading of perspiration along his hairline.

Maria slid a stiff handkerchief from his pocket and dabbed at the moisture, giving him tiny, nervous kisses as she did so. "We're only waiting for the cake now."

"The cake?"

"Mrs. Gordon's been on the phone for an hour. They swear the cake is on the way."

The caterer's delivery man had received garbled instructions and had taken the cake to the church, after which he instantly disappeared for an extended lunch break.

"All this fuss just to cut a cake?"

"Well, Mama wants the photos for her scrapbook, and the paper wants them to fill up the spaces between ads." She paused, then whispered, "And I want them, too, so I can look at them when I'm old and ugly and can't remember why you liked me in the first place."

Duane didn't reply. The strain on his face had become a definite frown, and when she took hold of his arm Maria was astounded to find that his muscles were like granite. "It'll be over soon, I promise," she said, and then added pertly, "Just think, this evening we'll be in Honolulu! Then we can really relax. We'll have time for each other for a change. Hey! Wait until you see the sexy sarong I have in my trousseau!" She wiggled her eyebrows and gave him a wicked smile, implying that she had more in mind than just modeling. Her efforts at recapturing some of the lighthearted, lovingly suggestive banter of their past was met with a blank stare. She wished she could get him away from Point Locke and begin helping him.

"Why don't you take a sedative, Duane, just to relax. I have some in my medicine cabinet. While you're up there, maybe you can lie down for a few minutes."

Jenny rose from her chair when she saw June propelling Maria across the lawn. They were headed for the draped table in the latticed gazebo, where an enormous white cake stood citadel before a rose-strewn curtain the photographers had draped behind the area. Duane had emerged from the house and now waited behind the table. A small bank of floods washed him in bright light, and Jenny saw him reach out and straighten the little doll-figures on the cake before the crowd thickened and cut off the view.

Jenny elbowed her way through the crowd, finding a station slightly behind the photographer and his camera as Maria finally arrived at Duane's side. Maria whispered something in his ear and touched his forehead. He responded with a shrug and a strained smile.

Edging a bit closer, until she was standing almost alongside the photographer (who was instructing the Eastmans to pick up the knife and hold it over the cake), Jenny could see that Duane's hair was damp. Peering closely, she could detect a trickle of moisture sliding down from his sideburn and scooting along his chin. He was sweating, heavily.

The photographer shouted, his voice a strangled whine: *Smile, smile. . . . Look at the camera, and SMILE!*

One of the visiting children might have been playing with the electrical cord, or perhaps the power merely shorted momentarily, but the following seconds were so fast and confused that absolutely nothing made sense, then or later.

The floodlights flickered and grew dim, flashing on and off several times before going out altogether. Jenny's eyes were fixed on Duane's face. For a split second it looked as if a great vein bulged down the side of his face. She saw his head snap up in the fluttering bright light that seemed to disorient and panic him.

Somehow, Jenny blinked and dropped her gaze in time to see a spurt of Duane's blood surge across the white wedding cake.

In the confusion Duane rushed into the house, alone, and by the time Brad got to him he'd locked himself in the bathroom. When he emerged a few minutes later, his wound was already bandaged. Brad made him show the wound, and he reported to the others that it *was* merely a small nick along the juncture of finger and palm. Duane later said he'd lost his grip and cut his finger on the knife, and promised to keep it bandaged for a couple of days.

Jenny knew better.

Her angle of vision was exactly right and she saw the "accident" clearly. The blood certainly hadn't come from a nick on the hand. It had shot out from under the sleeve with a great deal of pressure behind it, as if an artery had been punctured. One small spurt of blood, then Duane had grabbed his wrist and palm with his other hand and rushed away to the house.

She was sure the blade had been nowhere near his arm—or had it? There was the quick motion of the couple's hands, the falling blade, the red blood spilling over the white icing. Had the strobe effect of the flashing lights fabricated a fantasy to her? After all, her previous fantasies had centered on visions of blood and death.

But this wasn't like her other fantasies. This had been sharp and clear and real, fully in focus with the world around it.

All she knew was that the chill she felt in her flesh whenever she looked into Duane's eyes was growing deeper. She no longer trusted her reactions, and she no longer trusted Duane.

And somewhere deep inside her, a parasite of fear continued to grow.

Part

III

*Los Angeles
Three Months Later*

twenty-one

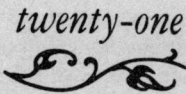

JENNY PUT THE last slide under the microscope and brought it into focus. The phone on her desk rang and she reached for it automatically. "Jenny McGregor. Can I help you?"

"This is Joan Kranz," replied an artificially nasal voice. "The lab reports you requested just came in. Would you like me to bring them up?"

Jenny played along, pinching her own nose before she answered. "Yeah, if you think you can make it here before you asphyxiate yourself."

Joan began giggling. "Good. I wanted to talk to you anyway. See you in about half an hour. Maybe we can go to the cafeteria for lunch?"

"Sounds good to me."

"See you then. Bye."

Jenny felt a certain amount of triumph as she replaced the receiver. For the first time in months she had answered the phone without worrying about who might be on the other end. It was a simple thing, but it meant that she could once more function normally. Maybe she had finally gotten herself together.

She had been feeling paranoid. It had just been her dreams and imagination imposing themselves on reality. *Of course* it hadn't been Duane calling her, watching her apartment at night, she told herself soothingly. She hadn't even *seen* Duane since Point Locke. Although the incidents—the imagined incidents—had stopped over a month ago, it had taken weeks to convince herself that nothing had ever happened, that her problems were her own, and that no one, least of all *Duane*, could possibly be responsible. It was hard for her to believe that she was capable of such intricate, terrifyingly realistic self-delusion, but it was so much easier to accept her own fallibility than to even consider the alternative: that Duane was indeed stalking her.

She went back to the microscope, finished her analysis, and was jotting down some notes when her phone rang again. Exulting in her new-found freedom, she leaned back in her chair and picked it up. "Jenny McGregor."

"Hello, Jenny. This is Duane."

Jenny slammed the receiver down and quickly jerked her hand away. The thought of being connected to him even by telephone upset her far beyond any rational justification. Trembling, she reached over and took the phone off the hook. She had not consciously intended to hang up; it had been a purely instinctive, panic reaction.

Hello, Jenny. This is Duane. The words reverberated in her head. Why was she so disturbed? They were such mundane words, their banality disproportionate to the terror and trauma they sparked in her. It wasn't what he said or how he said it; it wasn't even the timbre of his voice. It went beyond mere auditory perception and made her jump like a frightened animal.

Her old fears instantly returned. *Why wouldn't he leave her alone?* His voice and eyes haunted her day and night. It didn't matter if Brad was lying snug against her, she was alone with her nightmares. She would wake up terrified, but too insecure to wake him and try to explain. Daytime episodes she had written off to her imagination. She all too vividly remembered the state she had been in before going to Point Locke, when she had been unable to distinguish dreams and hallucinations from reality. Even now, she couldn't tell.

Had he really just called, or had the entire scene crawled out of her subconscious? Had he *ever* called her? *What did he want from her?*

Jenny refused to think about what had just happened. If she did, she knew she'd never make it through the rest of the day. The sensible thing to do would be replace the phone in its cradle and get back to work. She settled for the latter.

Automatically, she took the slide out from under the microscope and put it back in its box. The slides rattled as she closed the box's lid and thrummed on it a moment with her nails. Barring the incident from her conscious mind, she forced herself to concentrate on her work.

On her right was the patient's chart: *Jones, Mavelyn K.; Rm. 776; Eisenbaum*. She flipped back the metal cover and glanced through the case history once again. Mrs. Jones had first seen Dr. Eisenbaum last month. Early chem tests had been inconclusive, but the scintiscan indicated the site for biopsy. The liver masses had been multiple, confusing immediate identification, but the elevated LD levels had been specific. And now the biopsy was confirming: carcinoma.

She had met Mrs. Jones only once. She was a graying, middle-aged woman who had sat quietly in her bed, answering Jenny's questions with careful consideration and a rather strained good cheer. The lines in her face were deeper than they should have been, and large, stylishly shaded eyeglasses did not mask the weariness that had settled behind them.

Jenny wrote her conclusions quickly and professionally, but if her hand was steady, her mind still recoiled from the evidence.

Signing her name quickly, Jenny clipped her handwritten notes together. They would be typed, photocopied, distributed to the doctor and to the lab files, becoming simply another entry in a black-and-white written history.

There would be a record of Mrs. Jones's pain, drugs, meals consumed and expelled, nurses' notations of her rallyings, setbacks, and irritabilities. But there would be no record of the look Jenny had seen in the woman's eyes when her son and his wife arrived to visit and she removed her glasses, as if she wanted to see them very clearly, without the impediment of colored plastic lenses. The medical record could never reflect the enormity of her suffering. Jenny's fingers trembled as she slipped the cover over her microscope. She could put aside her problems, but doing so caused her to project her pent up emotions onto whatever she happened to be doing.

She wondered again if she was really in the right profession. Lately, each time she signed a report which indicated a terminal condition she felt as if she were consigning someone to death. Where each new case had been a challenge to her, they now only reminded her of human mortality. Someday, she feared, she would become as hardened as Mrs. Helpmann, who supervised the activities of RECRI with prison warden watchfulness. To her, each case was a name, a hospital number, a statistic—so many pounds of meat to be as carefully controlled and measured as was the variety of dispensed drugs, until at last the container was empty and the history neatly filed.

Jenny glanced at the wall clock in her office before stepping out. No wonder she was hungry; it was nearly one o'clock. Gathering up the chart and slide box in the crook of her elbow, Jenny left her office and headed down the hall toward Mrs. Helpmann's office.

She stuck her head into the laboratory even though she knew Maria wouldn't be there. She usually left for lunch at twelve o'clock. Jenny was quietly, though guiltily relieved that Maria wasn't there. She had purposely pushed herself, and could very easily have started on the slides *after* lunch. That way she'd have been free at twelve.

Things had certainly changed between them, Jenny reflected. Before her marriage, Maria and she had been as thick as thieves. But these days, they seldom talked.

On her first day back at work after her honeymoon, they had had lunch together. Maria had brought her a brightly colored mumu and a ginger blossom lei, and had gabbed nonstop about the sights she had seen. Listening to the breathless, forced Hawaiian travelog, it had seemed to Jenny that Maria was almost afraid to stop talking—afraid perhaps that if she did so, she might have to talk about things that *really* mattered. She had not once mentioned Duane. It had sounded as though she'd gone on her honeymoon alone. Jenny had taken note of this, but had remained silent.

For a while their friendship retained some aspects of its former nature, but Maria was withdrawing. A deepening self-absorption was separating her from Jenny. Jenny accepted the situation and even made excuses for her friend's behavior. Maria was now a married woman. Her interests, her point of view were different now.

Jenny suspected that things were not going well with their marriage, but she was not about to interfere in matters that did not concern her. She fervently hoped for the best and tried to close her mind to Maria's strange depression that had started in Point Locke.

Shortly after Maria's return from her honeymoon, her work schedule had been altered. She now started later in the morning and got off later than Jenny did.

Even their lunch hours were hard to coordinate. When they did see each other around the lab, it was only to exchange hurried greetings and to renew promises to get together very soon.

But that time never seemed to come. Before the wedding, they had seen each other every single day. Now, it had been a full week since Jenny had last seen Maria. That had been a wave across the lab just before Jenny had been assigned to analyze a dull government medical study just completed in San Diego.

Although Jenny missed the close friendship she and Maria had shared, she had gone so far as to formulate—

and rehearse—a string of excuses to have ready in case Maria should happen to ask when she and Brad were free.

But Maria had not asked . . . and Jenny was glad. It wasn't Maria she wanted to avoid. It was just that seeing her would almost inevitably mean seeing Duane. A shudder went through her body at the thought of him.

Jenny entered the small foyer off the main hall that led to Mrs. Helpmann's office. The office was empty. Jenny didn't even try the glass door. It would be locked, as always. She left Mrs. Jones's chart and slides in the wire bin on top of the supply cabinet in the foyer, then turned when she heard her name.

"Hey, Jenny." Joan Kranz came up behind her and tossed a stack of papers into the bin, then peered quickly through Helpmann's door before continuing. "Hope the Bride of Frankenstein chokes on them." The bustling woman brushed her hands together with satisfaction at a job completed.

"Stat work?" Jenny asked as they moved through the doorway and down the hall toward the elevator.

"Routine electrolytes from the Mouse, that's all. But the Bride wanted to check them before they went back to the floors." Joan halted suddenly. "Oh, darn it. I got so mad at Helpmann I forgot *your* papers. Do you need them right away?"

"Not till this afternoon."

"They'll be waiting for you when you get back. I have to run upstairs as soon as I get lunch or else the Bride will throw a fit. She wants me to be 'available' if she finds anything wrong with the electrolytes. Honestly, Jenny, all those results are printed out automatically by computer and *still* she has to check every one."

Jenny laughed. "If it keeps her in her office and out of our hair for a while, then maybe there is a God in Heaven looking out for the welfare of RECRI slaves."

"Bull. She just likes to pretend she's a doctor. She wouldn't know a potassium from a colloidal gold if she didn't have her little black book of normal values."

Jenny knew that wasn't true, and she knew that Joan

was only letting off steam, just as all the technicians did when Helpmann went on a rampage. Helpmann was a registered technologist—Jenny had seen the certificate framed and spotlighted behind the woman's desk—but had given it up years before for her cushy job as Simon Legree in RECRI's main lab.

"Wait a minute." Joan stopped and tugged at Jenny's jacket sleeve, nodding toward the elevator panel that indicated the car was on its way up. "The Bride may be on it. Let's take the stairs. I don't even want to catch sight of the old bitch."

They slipped through a swinging door and clattered down the steps for two floors to the main level, Jenny hurrying to keep up with the little woman who bounced her way along with the nonchalance of a rubber ball. Outside, at the building's entrance, Joan paused and leaned against the bronze plaque bearing the Institute's name and an extensive dedication that few but extremely bored visitors ever bothered to read.

Across the greensward were numerous sidewalks leading to various hospital entrances, most of them marked with signs: *Employees Only, Visitors Use Main Entrance*. The hospital itself was formidable—a great gray structure, seven stories, with extensions on either side that made it look very much like the rodent that had given the building its nickname. Scattered between the sparse trees were small stone benches, at which were seated nurses and various hospital personnel who extracted lunches from brown paper bags and enjoyed the sunny day. Jenny's spirit was lifted by the beauty of the day and the gardenlike scene before her. It made her feel better just to look at it.

"What's happened with Maria?"

"Maria?" Jenny asked, suddenly having to shift mental gears.

"Yeah. Maria!" Joan frowned. "You remember her, don't you? The pretty lady who went away three months ago and came back lobotomized."

"Lob—? What are you talking about, Joan?" The apprehension, the presentiment that Jenny had been so carefully suppressing came surging to the surface as she studied Joan closely. Had the horrible thing she had been dreading finally happened? With great trepidation, she asked, "What's the matter?"

"I asked you first! Anyway . . . Maria looks like she just crawled out of a casket, that's what's the matter! But she keeps insisting she's fine. The circles under her eyes are so dark you need a flashlight to see past them."

"She's probably just tired. She's redecorating her house and she has a new husband to look after . . . not to mention Helpmann's vulture gaze." They both knew, however, that Helpmann admired Maria's work accuracy and seldom bothered her.

Joan was quiet for a moment, as if uncertain she should continue. But her questions eventually tumbled out, inspired equally by concern and curiosity. "What's her husband like? She's never once brought him around to the lab to introduce him. He's very good-looking, judging from the picture of him she keeps on her desk. I think you and Dr. Knowlton are the only ones who have met him. Is he mean to her or something?"

"Don't be silly, Joan. He's a . . . a quiet, ordinary young man. . . ."

"Ordinary, my ass. Patricia said he's richer than shit and they have a cozy little mansion up by Griffith Park."

Jenny simply couldn't let Joan's curiosity run on this way. Her own feelings about Duane were still too close to the surface and liable to slough off if she didn't watch herself.

"Doesn't Maria ever talk about him?" Jenny asked, wondering how much Joan knew. Even though Joan had never met Duane, she suspected there was something odd about him.

"Why do you think I'm asking *you*? Maria's been like clam city ever since she came back. She used to be so outgoing. . . . What the hell happened up north?"

Jenny shrugged uneasily. "A nice wedding, a few days away from this place. Nothing extraordinary."

Jenny searched her pocket for lunch money as she headed

for the Mouse's sixth rib, which led to the hospital cafeteria. Joan stayed with Jenny as they took their place in the rapidly moving line. They both mechanically took one of the orange trays from the stack and began sliding them along the self-serve gauntlet, pausing to gather up silverware and napkins before they had to select from the wide variety of salads.

Joan was persistent, not about to give up now that she had Jenny where she could not escape. "Patricia works in the office next to hers. She says that Maria never talks about her husband. She says Maria's depressed all the time. Doesn't talk to anyone anymore."

"What does Pat think she is, a spy?" Jenny replied sharply, resentful about having her friend speculated about.

"We're asking each other a lot of questions, but I'm not hearing any answers," Joan said as she considered the entrées listed on the felt board. "I know I'm nosy, too damn nosy. But I'm serious, Jenny. Maria really doesn't look well or act well. Can't you talk to her, find out what's the matter?"

Jenny wanted to slap herself for her idiocy. Joan was genuinely concerned—these endless questions and idle gossip weren't characteristic of her, any more than Maria's continuing despondency was typical. It seemed to Jenny as if the whole world were putting on masks, hiding, changing, slipping in and out of personas.

If anything, Jenny should have been surprised that no one had mentioned Maria's withdrawn behavior to her since their return from Point Locke.

"I'll talk to her today, Joan, if I can catch her before she leaves, okay?"

"Why wait? Why don't you see her right now?"

Jenny gave her a quick look. Joan winked and directed Jenny's gaze the length of the cafeteria. Through the large expanse of glass that made up the entire west wall of the cafeteria, Jenny could see into a sun-drenched patio. Maria was seated there, talking to a slim man in a white coat.

"Ah ha!" Joan said triumphantly. "Maybe I've just

answered all of my own questions, Jenny. Do you know who that is she's talking to?" Leaving her rhetorical question hanging in the air, Joan headed back to RECRI for a working lunch.

twenty-two

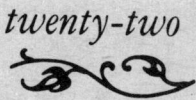

JENNY HELD HER tray securely as she threaded through the noisy cafeteria. It was crowded, as usual, with many white-clad hospital personnel who were making the most of the brief respite from their hectic duties. There was a noticeable haste about the way everyone ate. The tables were rarely occupied for long.

In more relaxed cafeterias, trays were generally unloaded before eating. That was seldom done here. Most people ate directly from their trays. It made things easier if one had to leave in a hurry. Hospital staff members always ate with the expectation that their names might be called over the loudspeaker that paged doctor after doctor in a never-ending litany.

Somehow it seemed a little more peaceful on the patio where Maria was sitting with Justin Harriman. At least it had more pleasant surroundings. Raised flower beds and potted trees and shrubs transformed what otherwise would have been simply a concrete quadrangle into an inviting, restful oasis. Interspersed among the potted greenery were small metal tables, each with its own colorful umbrella rising from its center.

Sparrows and blackbirds hopped around between the tables awaiting the tidbits they had come to expect. The choice morsels that came their way were avidly fought over with noisy chirping and aggressive pecking.

As Jenny approached, the tall, young doctor appeared to be getting ready to depart. Jenny did not know Dr. Justin Harriman all that well, but she liked him. He was well thought of by others in the medical community. She had first met him at a party she had attended with Brad, and she had since run into him at other medical-social affairs. They were a close-knit bunch, these doctors.

It was Jenny who had introduced him to Maria here at the hospital last year sometime. Since that time, he and Maria had become good friends.

Jenny put on her brightest smile as she got to the table. "Hi. Mind if I join you?"

Both turned at the sound of her voice. Greetings were exchanged, and Jenny placed her tray on the table and sat down. She was shocked by Maria's appearance. She *did* have dark circles under her eyes. Her face was haggard and thin.

Still trying to affect a cheerful demeanor, Jenny looked from one to the other. "Say, if I were a suspicious sort and I saw my newly married friend having a serious talk with a doctor whose stock in trade is babies, well, I just *might* put two and two together." Maria gave Jenny a despairing look. "Maria!" Jenny said excitedly. "Is it true?"

Maria's eyes avoided hers as she nodded slowly.

Jenny was dumbfounded. She could not understand Maria's attitude. She had often talked about having a baby. *Babies*. Lots of them. And now this? Her momentary confusion was overruled by the pleasure she felt for her friend. She grabbed Maria and hugged her. Instead of responding to Jenny's enthusiasm, Maria stiffened.

Shapes

Jenny drew back slightly and stared into Maria's face in alarm. Those brown eyes, usually so bright and sparkling, now had a dull, fearful look like those of a trapped animal.

Justin Harriman shifted uneasily in his chair and thoughtfully studied the burning end of his cigarette. He suddenly leaned forward and crushed it out. Jenny's eyes followed the action. There were a number of butts in the ashtray. It must have been some heavy discussion they were having.

It was Dr. Harriman who finally broke the silence when it was clear that Maria was not going to. "Maybe you can talk some sense into Maria, Jenny. She's pregnant, all right, but she won't let me or any other doctor examine her."

Jenny looked at Dr. Harriman incredulously, then at her friend. "Why not, Maria? You should be under a doctor's care. You look terrible! You . . ." Jenny stopped, ashamed of her tactlessness.

The public address system finally caught up with Dr. Harriman. He was needed on the third floor. Before leaving, he covered Maria's hand with his and squeezed lightly.

His concern for her was unmistakable. "Maria," he said gently, "It's this simple. You need help—the sooner the better. Here's my card. I'll write my home phone number on the back." He took a pen from his pocket, scribbled a number on the card and handed it to Maria. "Call me day or night, okay? I want to help you."

As Dr. Harriman left, Jenny turned back to Maria. She regretted having been remiss about looking after her friend because of her own intangible fears. Now she intended to make up for that neglect.

"Maria, what's the matter? I know something's terribly wrong. Can't you tell me about it?"

Maria leaned forward eagerly. "I—" She then stopped and looked anxiously around. "No, I can't, Jenny." She shut her eyes tightly and shook her head, holding back tears.

Jenny could see that Maria was getting more and more upset. She was obviously afraid of something. An inner voice insidiously whispered, "Duane," but Jenny tried to banish that from her mind.

They sat in silence for a long while until Maria began to speak haltingly, confirming Jenny's suspicions. Her marriage was a failure. "I don't know what's made him change so much, Jenny. He used to be so sweet . . . so kind. But now . . . It's as if he's someone I don't know. He resents my presence, afraid I'll get too close to him. Before we decided to get married, we did everything we could to get to know all about each other. Now he keeps trying to push me away." Her voice dropped lower, smothered in misery. "Every day with Duane is worse than the one before. He gets angry over trivial things and then he gets moody and withdrawn. He goes away day after day. . . . I hardly see him, much less get a chance to talk to him.

"I know he's not working at Eastman Hardware. I've called there. Apparently he's ignored the business completely since we got back. It runs itself anyway. . . .

"If I ask him what he's been doing all day he'll say he's been at the library or something equally strange."

"But Maria, surely he's pleased about the baby. I remember him saying he wanted a houseful of children."

The tears began to flow faster than Maria could wipe them away. "Oh Jenny, when I told Duane I was pregnant, he went crazy. He said I couldn't have his child. Then he told me I'd have to abort the pregnancy. When I refused, he wouldn't have anything more to do with me." Maria reached for Jenny's hand and held it so tightly it hurt. "It's not normal, Jenny," she said.

The look of fright on Maria's face almost matched her own. She wanted to say something helpful, comforting, but she was at a loss for words. "No . . . of course not," she blurted out. "A husband should—"

"No, no, You don't understand! The baby. The baby isn't normal. Something's wrong. I can feel it. I'm scared!"

"That's all the more reason to see a doctor right away!"

"No. Duane won't permit it. And he'll be furious that I talked to you like this. He told me I wasn't to tell *anyone* I was pregnant."

"But you need a doctor—" Jenny protested.

"When I refused to have an abortion, he told me that under no circumstances was I to go to a doctor or even tell anyone I was pregnant. He said he would cable the Eastman family doctor to take care of me. There's been a delay because he's in Europe, and since he has a fear of flying, he's on his way home by ship."

As Justin Harriman left the busy cafeteria and headed toward the elevators, he mulled over the conversation he'd just had. *Maria wasn't even his patient!* He had scores of others who were. He really should be expending his energy on *their* behalf instead of getting involved in this case. He should limit his bursts of caring to his *real* patients. *That* certainly drained enough out of him without adding additional emotional involvement. His compassion did get him involved too much perhaps, not only with his patients' medical problems, but with their burdens, their hopes, their sufferings. . . .

He shrugged his shoulders and smiled ruefully. Maria might not be his patient, but she was his friend. He prided himself on being a good doctor, but he was equally proud of being a good friend. Not that it was hard to be a friend of Maria's. She was the best: bright, witty, sensitive, beautiful. . . . He deeply regretted that he had met her *after* she had fallen in love with Duane Eastman. His temper rose in righteous indignation. How could that bastard treat Maria like this?

He was still fuming inwardly when he reached the elevators. He jabbed his finger repeatedly at the "UP" button, and his eyes followed the numbers above the door as they lighted up and then went out. The elevator was currently on the eighth floor and descending slowly—too slowly for Justin's frame of mind. He turned away impatiently and headed toward the stairway.

"Well I'll be damned! Speak of the devil!" he muttered under his breath. He had spotted Duane coming in the opposite direction. Probably meeting Maria for lunch, he guessed.

Feeling as he did about Maria, he could not help but regard Duane as his personal, sworn enemy, even though he had only met him two or three times—all before their marriage. Justin remembered seething in silence as love-sick Maria had gushed on and on telling him much more than he wanted to know about her then fiancé.

It had been well-nigh impossible to harbor any ill will against a man who was so endlessly decent, so unfailingly polite—but he had managed it. And now at last he had something concrete on which to vent his spleen. If it weren't such a serious matter, he would have enjoyed his vindication more. Right now, however, he was a doctor, first and foremost—Maria's health was what mattered most.

He stepped out in front of Duane, introduced himself—in case Duane didn't remember him—and quickly apprised him of the facts: Maria's condition was perilous. She needed immediate medical care. She could not wait for some doctor to sail leisurely across the ocean. And what's more, Maria needed emotional support and understanding from her husband.

He spoke in that exaggeratedly calm, quiet voice that he used with patients he expected would be difficult.

Duane listened to Harriman's deadly earnest speech impassively and noncommittally. He had detected the antagonism underlying the doctor's words.

"What is the name of this doctor Maria told me you had sent for?" Harriman was asking, and when Duane did not answer immediately, Harriman asked again, obviously determined to get the information he wanted.

"Dr. James Robertson," Duane answered, not at all pleased at being pressured, but at the same time not wanting to appear obstinate. "Now, if you'll excuse me," he said and pushed past Harriman.

Duane walked toward the cafeteria. It was no longer crowded, and there were many free tables now. The patio was also clearing out, and he had no trouble spotting Maria and Jenny. They were still deep in serious conversation.

Maria had been explaining her symptoms to Jenny when

she stopped in midsentence. Her eyes, wide and frightened, were fixed over Jenny's left shoulder. When she spoke, her voice was coarse sand tumbling down a tin gutter. "Oh, Jenny! He's . . . he's . . ."

With trepidation, Jenny turned and saw Duane making his way toward them. Her eyes darted immediately around the patio, seeking the quickest way out.

"Don't leave me—*please!*" Maria whispered frantically, clutching Jenny's arm.

The panic in her friend's face held her in place. Jenny tried to hide her own tension, hoping to direct into her face a look of steely confidence. It must have worked, for Maria suddenly seemed to resign herself to the situation.

Duane greeted the two women warmly, bending over to kiss Maria briefly before sitting down. Jenny allowed herself a quick glance and caught him smiling at her. She averted her eyes at once, but could feel his gaze still upon her. There was a pulsing, pounding sensation in her temples, a sense of unbalance.

What was real? What was imagined? She no longer knew. Whatever it was, sitting here near Duane, there was the familiarity of pattern, the same feeling of terror as when she awoke from her nightmares in the middle of the night.

"Well, Maria, what stories have you been telling our friend here?" His smooth tone could not mask the underlying accusatory, even threatening, nature of his remark. Certainly it was not lost on Maria. Jenny listened in horror as Maria stutteringly lied through her teeth, telling him that she and Jenny had been discussing their lab work. She was not very good at deception, Jenny could see, and her face flushed with guilt. Even to save her skin, Maria could not lie well.

"I see," he said, and both Jenny and Maria knew he saw. As they exchanged fearful glances, he picked up the remains of Maria's sandwich and began eating. "I'm glad I caught you, Maria." He spoke between bites. "When I called, the lab people said you'd already left."

He turned to Jenny, his gaze open and level. "I tried to

get in touch with Jenny, to invite her to have lunch with us. But we were somehow . . . disconnected."

Jenny could not look at him. She concentrated her attention on a tea leaf making lazy circles in her Styrofoam cup. Reality . . . nightmare . . . they seemed to be one and the same now. She had to get away from here, had to get Maria away from him so that they could both think clearly once again.

Jenny looked at her watch, gasping exaggeratedly. "Maria! Do you know what time it is? We're late—Helpmann will have our hides!"

Maria bolted from her chair and grabbed Jenny's hand. They fled as quickly as the sparrows had departed when Duane had sat down.

Duane took another bite of the half-finished sandwich. He grinned and licked his lips lightly. For a conversation that had gone essentially nowhere, it left him looking curiously gratified.

twenty-three

JENNY WAS STILL jittery when she finally left the Institute. Being caught in the midevening Los Angeles traffic didn't help her disposition. It seemed that the particularly vicious drivers were out in force, and she clutched the wheel of her 300ZX until her shoulders and back throbbed with tension. Her gaze flicked around each intersection as if trying to keep track of a handful of marbles dropped randomly before her startled face. Each car was a potential assassin, every truck a deadly behemoth. Miles that receded behind her were remarkable triumphs of survival.

Nearly an hour later, after a quick stop at the market, Jenny was in the apartment garage. She slung the strap of her purse over her left shoulder, had to remove it again to get out her apartment key before she slipped the purse back into place. She dropped the keys between the front seat and the door frame while holding the groceries, and broke a fingernail trying to recover them from their impossible entanglement with the seat belt hooks. In the process, she managed to knock over one of the grocery sacks and lose a couple of oranges that had just enough momentum to roll to the exact center underneath the car.

When she stood again, her arms full of groceries, she caught her hair between the purse strap and her shoulder, and was only able to get free by jerking her head and nearly pulling out her hair.

All this left Jenny ready to kill. Luckily, she met no one.

Brad was going to work out at his karate *dojo* tonight, which meant she would be spending the evening by herself. Knowing this, she had put off coming home as long as possible. At the Institute she had even taken refuge in the extra work Mrs. Helpmann had assigned her, using it as an excuse not to come home. Even the odious task of marketing had seemed preferable to facing the evening alone.

Jenny occupied herself by unpacking the groceries, switching on lamps, and straightening the living room, dropping yesterday's newspapers into a wicker basket hidden behind the sofa. Comfortable routine was soothing.

She had just turned on the news when the phone rang. She froze, bent over in front of the television, shaken out of her self-imposed complacency. Maybe it's just Brad, she told herself, not believing it for an instant. Maybe he's decided to come over anyway. The phone rang again. Not to answer would be to accept defeat, to admit that she couldn't cope. That she would not do. Steeling herself, she straightened up and moved toward the phone.

"Hello?" she said, poised to hang up instantly.

Heavy breathing answered her. It did not, however, sound like the stuff of her nightmares. The hoarse breathing gave way to an unknown, relatively normal-sounding voice which solicited her involvement in a variety of sexual acts.

Jenny began laughing hysterically. She laughed until her stomach hurt, until all the pent-up tension drained out of her. In between gasps for breath she hung up the phone but continued to laugh until tears ran down her face. Things were looking up. It was a sad commentary on her life when an obscene phone call could make her day.

After that marvelous phone call, even watching the news failed to depress her. She was still chuckling to herself while she took a bath and prepared for bed. A door slammed in the apartment next to hers, followed by the sound of muffled laughter from the hallway. Must be Vic, she thought, as she pulled on her nightgown. Probably on his way down the hill to a West Hollywood bar.

Maybe she should go out dancing, too. Maybe see if she could still have some fun on her own.

Before she'd become involved with Brad, Vic used to take her out for evenings on the singles circuit, even introducing her to the gay bar orbit that was his special province. She had watched his one-night stands and lovers come and go in a neverending succession.

He was always willing to tell her why he enjoyed the freedom of his lifestyle, and she was more than willing to listen. She'd never been convinced that his life was any worse than other people's, but she didn't believe it was any better, either. She accepted Vic on his own terms, he accepted Jenny on hers, and they had a good friendship.

She hadn't talked to Vic much recently. If she hurried, she could call to him from the window, ask him if he wanted to escort a hopeless traditionalist out for a night on the town.

But the laughter indicated he already had company, and besides, the thought of getting dressed and ready to go out brought yawns rather than excitement. Ah, the hell with it, she decided.

She heard Vic and his friends get into a car and drive off as she padded barefoot around her apartment, making sure the door and windows were locked, pulling curtains closed, turning the lights out. It lulled her into a false sense of security.

Burglars could be stymied by bolted doors; nightmares and visions could not. She knew that even having Brad sleeping beside her was not proof against them. It was a terrible invasion of private moments.

But today had been different. Today, she had met Duane face to face, and had come off only slightly the worse for wear—she was sure that having dealt with him in the flesh, she could even confront her dream images. Tomorrow, she resolved, she would have another long talk with Maria and the two of them would decide what to do. She wasn't going to let Duane ruin her life *or* Maria's. Not if she could help it.

She felt confident, ready to take on whatever might appear. Besides, she hadn't had a nightmare in weeks—three, to be exact.

Jenny tumbled into bed, relaxed, assured, and positive she had a peaceful night ahead of her.

Even though she was exhausted from her full day at the lab, Maria had come home and prepared a fancy meal for Duane. No frozen dinners tonight. The rich aromas of the roast cooking in the oven and the peach pie cooling on the counter had made her nauseous, but she had been determined to fix his favorite dishes, hoping to put him in an agreeable frame of mind. She was certain he would be furious. She knew full well he hadn't believed her at lunch. Besides, she had a lot to tell him, and a good meal under his belt might make him more receptive.

After all her work, he had not come home for dinner. He had not even called. Finally she sat down despondently in the dining room. She pushed her food around her plate, eating little. It didn't matter. She had kept the roast warm so long waiting for Duane that it was dry, and the vegetables were overcooked.

She was trying very hard to keep from giving way to tears. She had done everything she could think of to make her marriage work. She had loved him so much. Since her noontime conversation with Justin Harriman, and especially since her talk with Jenny, she had begun to see the whole situation from a new perspective.

Living with Duane over the past few months, her self-esteem had plummeted. She had almost forgotten that she was an intelligent, attractive young woman. Duane, with his explosive temper and unpredictable rages, had effectively transformed her into a cowering, whimpering, vacillating person who no longer thought for herself.

It had taken Jenny to point out the obvious to her. It was not even what she had said so much as her unquestioning faith in Maria's judgment and sanity. That reinforcement had caused her to begin a quiet, realistic evaluation of her situation.

Maria heard Duane's car come up the driveway and looked up at the bronze Cartel clock on the wall. Ten o'clock. He slammed the car door and entered the house. At once she felt the adrenaline pumping into her system. I shouldn't be so afraid, she told herself. But she was. Nonetheless, she was determined to have things out with him.

She had been living with her self-denigration because of an unreasoning hope that conditions would change. Duane had a strong hold over her. How could she help recalling those good times, not so long ago, when the world had revolved around the two of them; the times of closeness before the Duane she loved had changed?

Memories could not sustain her forever, and the present situation could not continue indefinitely, especially now that she was pregnant and having such a rough time of it. She had every right to expect some consideration from her husband, even though he was less than thrilled about her impending motherhood.

Why had he lost interest in her so completely? She was positive he had been in love with her. What had happened? The thought that he might have a mistress tucked away somewhere crossed her mind again. That would account for his long absences, but she dismissed that thought as she had the other times it had occurred to her. Somehow, she didn't think that was the answer, but still she checked herself out in the mirror over the sideboard.

She was taken aback by the image looking back at her. It wasn't fair. Mothers-to-be were supposed to look radiant. It said so in all the literature. She, on the other hand, looked the way she felt: weak and unwell. Her appearance only served to convince her that she was doing the right thing by bringing the situation to a head.

The door to the study was open, and she could see Duane sitting at his desk, preoccupied with some paperwork. She felt a tightness in her throat as she watched him. He was as handsome as on the day she had first met him.

She was already inside the room before she spoke his name. Duane leaped to his feet, upsetting his chair, and glared at her. She drew back in fear. He had responded like a wild animal cornered in its den. On his face was a look of savage ferocity.

The violence in him subsided quickly, but the anger remained. "Why did you sneak up on me?" he demanded. "What do you want?"

Maria was so shaken by his behavior that she could barely speak. Old habits die hard, she thought, gathering the shards of her resolve. "I just wanted to talk to you, Duane."

"I'm busy! Can't you see that?" he said curtly, dismissing her abruptly. He walked back to the desk and picked up the chair he had overturned.

Maria swallowed hard but held her ground. "Duane, you've got to listen. I'm going to see Dr. Harriman in the morning. I . . ."

"You've *already* seen Dr. Harriman, haven't you?" he broke in.

"I don't feel well." Maria continued in a more determined voice. "In fact, I feel damned sick. And if you were ever around, you'd know it. I can't wait another week for some doctor I've never met! I'm going to call Justin—maybe he'll even see me tonight," she finished defiantly.

Duane looked up from his desk. "'No!" he said with a ring of cold finality in his voice.

"Why not?"

"You'll just have to wait for Dr. Robertson. Women always feel sick when they're pregnant. That's just the way it is. . . . Don't you know anything? Harriman is a meddling fool. Can't you see that he's just trying to come between us?"

"Come between us?" Maria echoed in outrage. "COME BETWEEN US? How *dare* you say such a thing. If anything is wrecking our marriage, it's you!" Her voice was steady. This had been too long on her mind for her to stop now. "Duane, you listen to me and you listen good! You need a doctor as much as I do. Something is seriously wrong with you. It's destroying you . . . and I'm not going to let it destroy *me!*"

"Harriman's turned you against me. You've been telling him everything about me, haven't you?"

"Yes." Maria was so angry that she lied. "'He knows everything!"

Duane suddenly grew still. Maria had expected him to continue ranting and raving—his unpredictability was the most terrifying thing she had to contend with. She would have preferred a blaze of temper from him. At least that was some form of communication. Silence was harder for her to deal with.

Only his eyes moved as he studied her, as if she were a specimen he was about to stick a pin into. It was an ugly thought and she tried to erase it from her mind. Where did he go when he lapsed into one of these—what were they? Spells? Trances? What dark thoughts seized his mind when he entered this private world of his?

There was nothing left for her to relate to. She no longer had any idea what he was going to do, what he was capable of doing. She just didn't know.

The one thing she was sure of was that she was afraid.

Finally, she left him in his strange frame of mind and went into the living room to call Justin Harriman's home phone number. She was relieved to hear his voice, and they arranged to meet at the hospital as soon as they could get there. She hung up and was halfway up the stairs when she cried out and doubled over, clutching her abdomen. Gasping for breath against the severity of the spasm, she had to grab for the banister to keep from falling back. The wave of pain gradually subsided, leaving her weak and soaked with perspiration.

From the landing below, she heard Duane's voice. "Maria, go up and lie down. I'll call Dr. Harriman back and ask him to come here."

His concern surprised her, although she would have appreciated a comforting arm even more. Still, it was better than nothing. Perhaps her hopes were not unfounded. She nodded gratefully and slowly picked herself up while Duane went to call.

twenty-four

IF IT HADN'T been for the fact that Maria was ill and waiting for his arrival, Justin Harriman would have enjoyed the drive. The night was warm and still, the scenery illuminated by a bright moon.

This hilly residential area near Griffith Park was nice. Great place to live, if you could afford it. Duane apparently could, he thought with no small amount of envy.

Harriman could only speculate on what elegant homes lay at the end of the long, winding driveways bordered by manicured trees and carefully tended hedges. Occasionally a whole wing of a massive house could be seen, set back from the road, but usually it was only the roof line over trees that gave a tantalizing hint.

He turned his Porsche onto Evergreen Drive, following the directions Duane had given him. Here the terrain was more rugged and steep. Sidewalks had disappeared and narrow roads led, presumably, up to the houses hidden away behind the protective groves. This stretch of road, an upgrade, had a country feel to it. It seemed incongruous to find such a remote-looking area in the heart of a megalopolis like L.A.

Without warning, bright headlights flashed in his rearview mirror. He was blinded momentarily and clutched the steering wheel tightly as he slowed the car down. "Damn fool!" he cursed, shading his eyes.

There was no need for anyone to follow that closely, especially with their lights on bright. The pursuing vehicle continued riding his bumper for a few moments, as if verifying Harriman's identity, then the headlights dimmed and the car dropped back slightly.

Harriman speeded up again, hoping to put a little distance between them, and the other car accelerated steadily, creeping up on him. Harriman decreased his speed slightly, in case the car wanted to pass. Instead it pulled alongside him. Perhaps, he thought suddenly, the other driver was trying to tell him something. Maybe one of his rear lights was out.

He rolled the window down but there was no answering response. Harriman looked across into the other car and tried to make out the features of the driver, but all he could see was a vague silhouette. He struggled to discern detail in the darkness, but his night vision hadn't recovered from the initial blinding flash. The car was a Lincoln, but the moonlight silvered it with paleness, disguising its true color. The driver was merely a blurred shape, something almost nonexistent.

Before it happened, Harriman had already felt the cold finger of fear caress him intimately. He was about to step on the gas pedal when the Lincoln suddenly swerved into the side of his Porsche with a loud scraping sound. The impact wrenched the steering wheel out of his hands, sending the car veering into the side of the roadcut. Being a doctor and no stranger to the unexpected, he quickly regained control of his vehicle.

The heat of anger burned away the cold fear. The guy's *crazy*, Harriman fumed, slamming his right foot to the floor. The scream of his tires matched the heat of blood rushing to his neck and face.

The Lincoln matched his speed, then rammed him again, edging him so far off the road that his right fender struck sparks off the side of the hill. Harriman risked a quick look backward, hoping to spot another car, but it was as if the mountains of the moon had grown around him, hiding the world in icy shadows and deserts of blackness. He would have no witness to the assault.

The Lincoln's size and weight gave it solid traction. The Porsche was outmatched, the road too narrow and winding for it to have any speed advantage.

Harriman gave up trying to see who his attacker was. He no longer cared. His face was ashen and his hands trembled. All he wanted to do was escape with his life. Up ahead, he perceived a sharp turn. If he was going to try anything, he knew he'd better do it now. Gritting his teeth, he slammed on the brakes.

With a piercing screech the Porsche skidded, and the smell of burned rubber filled the night air. In the seconds it took the Lincoln's driver to react, Harriman was turning his car around. His car had a smaller turning radius and could accelerate faster. The other car had overshot.

The Porsche took off downhill, veering toward every hole of shadow like a jackrabbit hearing the claws of an owl cutting the night just behind him.

He looked for a driveway. Swerve left—no, just a pocket of dark. Back right, now straight ahead. No driveways. *No driveways!* A shard of light stabbed into his eyes and he glanced at the mirror. The headlights were upon him once again.

The big car pulled alongside and started edging him over to the side of the road. This time, there was no wall to scrape against, only the steep drop-off. Banging into the smaller car again and again, each time the Lincoln shoved it farther over, forcing it onto the bumpy shoulder. Harriman clung to the wheel, his slick hands working desperately to keep his car from plunging over the edge.

Ahead, the road curved left. Harriman's eyes grew large

with terror and he hit his brakes, hard, but the car's momentum, combined with the downgrade, was too great. The Porsche skidded off the road.

As it careened down the uneven slope, it gathered speed, plowing through dry, tangled brush. Miraculously, it remained upright throughout its wild plunge. Trying to protect himself, Harriman threw his arms in front of his face, just before the car slammed headlong into a tree.

The bone-jarring halt left Justin Harriman slumped over the wheel in the smoking wreckage. His face was bloody and bruised, but the seatbelt had held him securely in its grip.

His eyes opened a slit, closed, then opened again, wider this time. At first he could see nothing and he almost panicked, afraid he had been blinded. Sight returned slowly as his eyes adjusted to the gloom. A low moan escaped his lips as he focused on the shattered windshield and memory achingly slithered into his numbed mind. His muscles seemed to be trying to crawl right off his battered but unbroken bones.

Acrid smoke assaulted his nostrils, prompting him to force his muscles into activity. He felt his body to assure himself that he had survived intact, taking quick inventory of his injuries. The left elbow was dislocated, but it didn't hurt. It was so numb that it felt like he was examining someone else's arm. His right hand went up to assess the throbbing pain in his head and came back sticky with blood. He was sure he'd have a textbook case of whiplash in the morning. He tried to chuckle at his absurdly professional analysis, but a bubble of red-tinged saliva splattered his lips.

Harriman used his right hand to release the clip on the seatbelt, then pulled on the door handle and shoved outward. Nothing. Whether from the Lincoln's battering or from the impact, the door was jammed shut. The other door was a hopeless mess of twisted, crumpled metal.

Once again he smelled smoke. He knew he had to get out—fast. It would have to be through the window.

Earlier on the road, he had opened the window almost

all the way. He tried to crank it the rest of the way down but now it wouldn't budge. Fighting his growing panic, Harriman shoved his medical bag out, then gritted his teeth against the pain and began the agonizing process of working his tall frame through the small opening. At last he fell through, catching his ankle briefly and sprawling on the ground, almost blacking out from the pain. A glimmer of light and heat as the spilled gas under the car ignited forced him to fight up through the agony and find his feet.

Clutching his bag, he stumbled away from the car. He tried to move faster, but his feet would not respond. He staggered like a drunkard toward the nearest tree, dropped the bag, and leaned heavily against the trunk. His head reeled and he had to fight an overwhelming desire to slide down to the ground, to sink into the bliss of unconsciousness.

There was a sharp report, and his good arm moved up instinctively to shield his eyes from the heat and glare. Someone would surely see the flames and come to his aid.

Which way now? There was no trace of a house or a path. His best bet was the road, he reasoned. The way things looked, he was going to have to climb all the way back up to the road, unless he wanted to spend the night in this gully.

He wasn't at all sure he could make it, but he had to try. His eyes followed the steep slope up to the level of the road. He *was* lucky to be alive—damned lucky.

He pulled out a pocket handkerchief and dabbed at his bloody head. He was still losing some blood, and a kaleidoscope of lights flashed inside his head, just behind his eyes. He had probably cracked his skull against the door. Most likely, he had a concussion. And it was beginning to hurt like hell.

Harriman left his medical bag at the base of the tree and began plodding up the slope, step by staggering step. After only a few meters, he was dizzy and gulping for air. He stopped to catch his breath, and his gaze drifted upward to see how much farther he had to go. There was a car up there—someone had seen the flames after all! He gasped for extra air and was about to call out when some sixth sense made the shout die in his throat. The bloodied handkerchief dropped out of his feeble grasp, but the grip of memory was growing firm.

A wave of terror seized him. It was the Lincoln! That nut in the Lincoln! He wasn't content to force him off the road. He was up there waiting for him in case he happened to survive!

Confusion left him irresolute and helpless. Who could possibly want to kill him? No one, as far as he knew, had anything against him. He hated no one, and no one hated him. Then, why . . . ?

Harriman was stringing these thoughts out in a web of reason when he heard scrambling sounds in the bushes above, near the car. His web disintegrated. Madness was coming down the slope.

He took one step backward, then another, turned, and found himself running toward the dark refuge of the trees before he even knew he was moving. His body had stopped hurting—either that or his brain had stopped acknowledging the pain.

He did not stop until he had gained the protection of the trees, where he slammed into a large tree trunk, throwing his arms around it to keep himself erect. His throat was a dry chute feeding oxygen to the fire in his lungs, but there was already coolness flooding the blaze with each successive breath.

The panic in his mind subsided as well. Perhaps the blow to his head was causing him to hallucinate. He almost had himself convinced that he was behaving foolishly when he heard a rustling in the bushes. He strained his eyes and ears in the direction of the noise, but saw nothing.

The sound grew louder, coming closer. It sounded like an animal, not like the footfalls of a man. A dog? He supposed that was possible, maybe even probable in this area.

He waited a moment, listening, his pulse racing. Perhaps the man in the car was tracking him with a dog! Panic spurred him on. However paranoid the idea was, he was not going to wait around.

He ran awkwardly, his injured knee stiffening with each move. Bushes cut and scratched at his face and body, slowing him down as he made his way through the undergrowth. Once the ground gave way under him when he stepped into a gopher hole. He staggered but he did not fall. He could not allow himself to fall. If he faltered, he knew he would be lost. Behind him he could hear a rapid scuttling, a scampering, as if the animal had picked up his scent and was coming after him.

There was no doubt in his mind that something—*something* was chasing him. Equally apparent was the fact that it was gaining on him. He risked a quick look back over his shoulder. Bounding toward him in the darkness was a flowing shape with two wide-set glowing eyes.

Harriman stifled a cry of terror with his hand but struggled onward. His hand came away wet—sweat? blood?

Terror drove him on, but panic made him look back once again. He tripped and went crashing to the ground. His legs jerked spasmodically, but his feet only slid against wet weeds. The scuttling sound behind him told him that the creature was close. Frantically, he clawed at the ground, dragging himself behind a clump of bushes.

Trying to control his ragged breathing, Harriman contracted himself into a knot as his eyes searched the small clearing he had just crossed. The bushes were black patches in the moonlight. One of the black patches swayed and sidled out into the open. The bright eyes lowered to the ground, as behind it a dark rope of a tail lashed into the air like a whip of doom.

Harriman's eyes bulged. At last he saw what had been tracking him. It was an enormous rat!

He stared unblinkingly as the rat advanced. He recognized the signs of his own delirium. This was a delusion. He was suffering from mental confusion, disorientation, and hallucinations. There was absolutely no way this was actually happening. *Rats did not get as big as panthers*.

Soon it will evaporate into the nothingness it is, Harriman thought calmly, his body still frozen in its knotted position. It's only a phantom of the mind . . . of *my* mind. . . .

The apparition approached, its nails snapping small branches underfoot. It seemed to be grinning hideously, and a stench of foul rot escaped with its hot evil breath. The expression it wore was unbelievable—a look of absolutely bottomless hunger.

It seems so real, Harriman thought, noting how the moonlight made faint highlights on the filthy hair matted along its back. He watched it place each foot with an odd delicacy as it twitched the long whiskers sprouting from its wet nose. Pointed teeth gleamed in the light, and the odor of corruption made his stomach lurch.

How very real. . . .

The sudden weight bore Harriman flat to the ground, and he could actually feel its heavy furry body. His arms went up to fend off the nightmare creature, as if of their own accord. He watched the teeth slashing at his arms, the claws tearing at his body. He felt nothing. He knew it was only a dream.

The last thing Justin Harriman saw was the rat's demonic eyes. And then the dream's razor teeth tore into his throat and ripped one long gash all the way to the pubic bone.

As carefully as a good doctor.

twenty-five

MARIA LAY IN bed, her eyes closed, her dark brown hair disarrayed by perspiration and neglect. She had intended to stay awake so that she would be sure to hear Dr. Harriman's arrival, but she was too ill, too exhausted. Already she had drifted off to sleep several times, each time awakening with a desperate, clutching motion to keep herself from an imaginary fall.

Even through her groggy, fitful sleep, she heard the front door open and close, and was fully awake by the time the footsteps reached her bedroom. She breathed a sigh of relief at the reassuring sight of the lanky young doctor striding across the room. It made her feel much better just to see his familiar face, and now she did not feel so isolated, so hopeless.

Normally solicitous and accommodating, Justin now seemed reserved and very professional, wasting no time on preliminaries.

It was late, Maria reasoned, and this was a doctor-patient matter, not a social visit. Poor fellow, she thought guiltily. He probably gets little enough sleep as it is without having to make house calls in the middle of the night.

He sat on the edge of the bed, his tall frame hunched awkwardly toward her as he took her pulse, temperature, and blood pressure. He extricated a stethoscope from his jacket pocket, plugged it into his ears and moved it from place to place on her abdomen, listening intently. All the while, Maria did not take her eyes off his face. She was watching for any change of expression, any outward sign that would give her some clue to what he might be thinking.

It was impossible to interpret the maddening, noncommittal look in his eyes as he pressed, probed and listened. Since his face betrayed nothing, a glimmer of hope began to replace the fears and dread that had consumed her lately. Maybe things were going to be all right after all.

Dr. Harriman finally sat up straight and removed the instrument from his ears. "You're lucky I came over," he said evenly. "An abortion at this stage is a simple procedure. I can induce it with medication."

Maria was jolted upright. "No!" she cried out, staring with horror into his face. She was going to lose her baby! Stricken, she wrapped her arms around her abdomen protectively.

"Maria," he chided, touching her arm. His hand felt icy cold. "You've got to trust me. There's no choice. I'm sorry. It's best to get it over with right now."

Maria's eyes widened in alarm and she could not stifle a gasp. All this was happening too fast. It was too much to comprehend, coming too swiftly for her to absorb. "How can you possibly tell without tests? Shouldn't I at least go in for some tests?"

It distressed her to have to question his judgment. After all, this was her friend—an excellent doctor—one who had gone out of his way in order to help her. If she could trust anyone, she could trust Justin . . . but somehow, this didn't seem right. Why was he in such a hurry to begin treatment? She couldn't think of a reason, unless . . .

unless it wasn't only her baby that was in danger! A chain reaction was set in motion, as she recalled the most recent symptoms—the constant nausea, the bleeding, the dizziness, the surges of pain.

She had minimized the seriousness of her condition because she wanted this baby so badly. Having a child might have brought Duane back to his senses and saved their faltering marriage. It had been a last, desperate gamble, one she had felt compelled to take for the sake of what they had once meant to each other. Now, everything had gone wrong.

Her brain reeled at the new fears, but despite the emotional confusion, a sensible inner voice quickly surfaced. If matters were so perilous as to put her health in jeopardy, it seemed even more imperative not to rush things.

"There is no need for lab tests. We have to go ahead *now*," he said with grim finality.

"Shouldn't this be done in a hospital?" Maria's voice quavered.

"There's no need for that. This is best . . . in private." There was something cold, even sinister, that she picked up in his voice. That and an absolute determination that his course of action must be carried out. Real or imagined, it turned her unfocused fear to panic.

She was not ordinarily subject to bouts of paranoia, but tonight was not ordinary. She needed time to think, time to calm down so she could make a rational decision. "An abortion is against my religious belief," she blurted out.

"This is strictly for medical reasons. Lie down and relax," he commanded. His annoyance at the delay, at her uncooperativeness, was becoming more and more apparent.

Maria remained sitting up. "I don't know. . . . ." She knew she wasn't thinking clearly, and she tried to explain. "I'm very upset, Justin, and I can't make such an important decision feeling like this. Besides, whatever I do, I'll have to discuss it with Duane. I'm sorry to have dragged you out here like this in the middle of the night, but I need time to think."

"Duane will agree with everything I recommend," Harriman said. His impatience seemed to be mounting rapidly. "I need some things from my car. I'll talk to Duane downstairs."

As soon as he left the room, Maria was moving. She threw back the covers and dressed hurriedly, throwing on the first thing she encountered in her closet. She wiggled into a pair of slacks and pulled on a sweater, her thoughts still churning. She was still trying to make sense of Justin's strange behavior. It was unlike him to browbeat *anyone*. He had always been so informative, so generous with reassurances. He was careful, meticulous, and conservative in his medical judgments, taking no unnecessary risks where his patients were concerned.

She found it impossible to understand the way he was acting, so totally out of character. Whatever the reason, he would have to accept that tonight was not the time for her to make a decision. Not wanting to confront him in her bedroom, Maria went downstairs. She descended quietly, hoping to overhear anything Justin and Duane were discussing, but all was silent. She paused on the bottom landing and looked around. Duane was nowhere in sight, and she surmised that he was outside with Justin.

She headed for the windows in the living room, morbidly curious to see how the conversation between the two men was going. Parting the sheer curtains exposed the entire driveway to her scrutiny. There was only one car outside, and it was Duane's blue Lincoln. How did Justin get here?

As she peered out she saw a figure beside the car. It was Justin, not Duane. Justin slammed the car door closed and strolled toward the house with his black bag in hand. He had said he was going to get something from *his* car, not Duane's.

Maria let the curtain fall and slowly turned away. Her mind was making mountains out of molehills. She was perplexed, but steeled herself to face Justin.

The front door swung open and Dr. Harriman entered. He stopped short when he caught sight of her, fully dressed, standing in the archway of the living room.

Maria saw his brief look of surprise turn into an angry scowl. Refusing to be intimidated any further by anyone, she stood her ground and stated flatly, "I'm going to get a second opinion."

"You need an abortion, and you need one now. There's no time."

She realized that he really meant what he said, but it was too late. She had made up her mind. Besides, any doctor worth his medical diploma would not be opposed to a second opinion. In fact, knowing their own fallibility, they encouraged patients to seek out other opinions. Even Brad did that. There was something inherently suspect about a medical judgment that could not withstand the scrutiny of another physician.

Harriman launched into a tirade, pacing back and forth, insisting that she do as he instructed. Maria stopped listening and waited for him to finish. What had gotten into him? This was a man she would have trusted with her life. Now he seemed to have undergone some strange metamorphosis.

It was the same kind of personality change that had come over Duane.

A terrifying thought crossed her mind. Somehow, Duane had turned Justin Harriman around to his point of view. The idea alarmed her, but the more she thought about it, the more she realized it was true. His words, his coldness, his reactions—they all echoed Duane!

It was almost as if Justin had *become* Duane . . . or vice versa.

Maria shuddered. Bizarre as the thought was, she could not shake it. Her mind rejected such an outrageous conclusion, but in her overwrought state, she trusted her intuition more than logic. And her intuition told her it was Duane in Harriman's body. *He looked like Justin but it wasn't him.* It was Duane, and there was no mistaking the aura of malevolence. He wanted to destroy the child in her womb.

She was going to get away from here, but first, she wanted to try something . . . to be sure.

He had stopped ranting, and stood motionless, facing

the window. Once again, she thought of Duane. Harriman's posture reminded her of Duane in one of his odd fits of silence. Maria took advantage of the opportunity to open the curio cabinet that held her rabbit figurine collection. Dust catchers, Duane called them. She was looking for one rabbit in particular—the fat, wooden one with a sweet, angelic look on its carved face, belying the fact that it was a humidor.

Maria screwed off the top portion of its body and drew out a marijuana cigarette. With a trembling hand, she lifted it to her lips and picked up a cigarette lighter.

Harriman whirled around when he heard the lighter click. His eyes narrowed, clouded with rage when he saw the quivering flame lick around the tip of the joint. "Put that out! Put it out this instant! I hate smoke!"

If she needed proof, she had it now. Justin Harriman smoked as much as she did. The words might have been spoken by Duane . . . it was Duane's tone, Duane's fury.

Before their trip to Point Locke, she and Duane had shared a joint now and then, but since their marriage Duane reacted strongly even to ordinary cigarette smoke, and she had stopped smoking when he was around, which wasn't often. His rejection of pot—the first and only time she had offered him a joint since their return—was best described as violent. And now Harriman was reacting exactly the same way.

When she made no move to comply with his order, he charged across the room like an angry bull. Maria didn't flinch, although her knees quivered beneath her. The smoke curled lazily from the glowing end, and the distinctive smell of marijuana permeated the air. Maria inhaled as deeply as she could and blew the smoke in his face.

He stopped dead in his tracks, then staggered backward, swaying unsteadily. His face contorted frightfully. "No . . . No . . . distorts . . ." It was unmistakably Duane's voice. "No more . . ."

Maria drew back in horror, afraid of what she had done. Guttural sounds, racked with agony, escaped his throat, filling the room with horrible, inhuman noises. Her shock and fear were nearly eclipsed by her desire to help him. She hadn't known the smoke would affect him so radically. She quickly put out the joint and started to move toward him.

The muscles in his face had begun to strain, writhe, stretch. The bones beneath his skin looked like they were moving, rearranging themselves.

Maria stopped. She was paralyzed, as if some iron grip held her in place, forcing her to watch the spectacle unfolding in front of her eyes. It was no longer Dr. Harriman's face. Now it was Duane's, grown twisted and demonic. The veins in his temples and cheeks were pulsing visibly, swelling to grotesque proportions before they burst with flashes of red. His hands jerked up to his face in a vain attempt to hide it from view, but Maria had already seen more than she could believe.

She saw the blood oozing between his fingers, which were clamped tightly against his face in a vain attempt to mold it back into form. Moaning, he weaved across the room, knocking over a chair, sending a lamp crashing to the floor. He fumbled with the doorknob and rushed out of the house.

Maria heard the engine of his car start up, followed by the screeching of tires as he raced down the driveway. She was left alone, pale as death, incapacitated by fear. Other sounds reached her—low, pathetic sounds of wailing—and she realized it was herself.

Had it been a marijuana-induced hallucination?

No. It had been all too real. The drops of blood, starburst splashes on the hardwood floor attested to that.

God, what was it that had taken over Justin and Duane's bodies. A demon? No, she couldn't accept that. But something just as impossible, just as evil.

What should she do? Was there anyone she could turn to? Her first impulse was to call Jenny, but how could she explain what had happened? She would sound as if she had gone insane.

But it wasn't madness that hardened her resolve. Maria knew she had to choose her course of action alone.

* * *

The transition between dream and reality was so smooth that Jenny was never exactly sure at what point she actually woke up.

She was hardly aware that she was moving slowly out of her bedroom, and she had no memory of getting out of bed. Her body might as well be fastened to a taut guy wire for all the control she had over it. She was being reeled in like a marionette by someone, some Svengali lurking in the night.

The louvered windows were closed, the curtains were still. Her living room looked completely normal, reinforcing her growing conviction that what she was experiencing now was reality rather than one of her gothic-influenced dreams. Jenny was surprisingly calm. It was as though her subconscious was trying to show her something—something important.

She reached the window and parted the curtain.

She was not surprised to see the figure standing on the lawn. She had seen him before, in her nightmares if not in reality. He was always in the same place—the place where she had first seen the dead lizard.

The night shadows were much too deep for Jenny to be able to make out his features, but it didn't matter. She *knew* who it was, with a certainty beyond her capacity to understand. It was Duane.

And she knew that this was no dream. She couldn't tell whether he was being drawn to her or she to him, and she realized it didn't matter.

Jenny let the curtain slip back into place. She searched for a handle, a fresh way to grasp the recent flow of her life. But the only connection she could find was the lizard. There were no easy psychological terms to explain it away, to pull the creature from its lair and examine it as a psychiatrist might pluck out an adolescent fear. Her subconscious mind had latched on to it instantly, using it to try and communicate through some sort of twisted Freudian symbology.

She peered out through a crack in the curtains, then

more boldly pushed them all the way open when she saw that the figure was gone. She stood for a long time, staring out into the darkness.

The steady blaze of nighttime L.A. seemed absorbed rather than reflected by an ominous, low bank of clouds. Here in Laurel Canyon, with the bulk of the Hollywood Hills rising behind her apartment, Jenny seldom saw much of the background glow from either the Basin or the San Fernando Valley, and the street lamps seemed mere flecks of soft light, weak as dying fireflies in the darkness.

Jenny shivered. Realizing the futility of trying to go back to bed immediately, she tried to slip into her morning routine, even though it was still the middle of the night. She went to the bathroom and swallowed a glass of lukewarm water, then brushed her hair and inspected herself in the mirror.

The apartment looked perfectly secure in every way as she shuffled to the kitchen, opening the refrigerator and drinking some orange juice right out of the pitcher. But when she put the pitcher back and closed the door, she could no longer fool herself into believing that it was nearly morning.

She wondered if Vic was home yet. Perhaps if she got dressed and talked to someone . . .

Wandering back into the bedroom, Jenny glanced at the glowing dial on the clock radio. Too early for Vic. He never came back before three, if at all. She went back to bed, but didn't get back to sleep for a long time.

twenty-six

MARIA CHECKED HER watch. It was one-thirty.

Mrs. Helpmann would be out to lunch. Maria knew her schedule well. She always went to lunch late, partly because she wanted to be in her office when everyone else was off-duty, and partly because the hospital cafeteria was less crowded after the noon rush.

Maria felt guilty as she walked down the hall toward Mrs. Helpmann's office. The woman trusted her, and now she was breaking that trust. Maria was in a dismal mood. She felt she was betraying everyone—her co-workers, her friends, the Institute.

Last night she had realized that her present situation demanded drastic action. It transcended normal ethical considerations, Maria told herself, still trying to justify what she was about to do.

There was no one in the area at all. The keys she carried slipped out of her trembling fingers and clattered onto the hard tile floor. Maria gasped and turned pale as she looked around, fully expecting a regiment of security guards to descend on her and lead her away in chains.

When they did not appear, Maria quickly scooped up the keys—the keys that Mrs. Helpmann had so trustingly given her to keep in case of emergency—and stepped into the small foyer off the main corridor.

On the right was a row of supply cabinets, and to the left was Mrs. Helpmann's office. The office door, unlike most of the heavy steel, small-windowed doors throughout the old building, was a shiny piece of glass in a metal frame. "Easier for me to keep an eye on the supply cabinets," she had once told Maria, "because you know how the bleeders are." Mrs. Helpmann was referring to the assistants who collected blood samples, but her expression had clearly indicated that no one in the lab was above suspicion.

Maria remembered a day when Jenny had accidentally headed for the elevator with a rubber tourniquet in her white lab jacket. Mrs. Helpmann had snatched it from her pocket without a word, but it might have been a cachet of emeralds for all the ferocity of her action and the look of triumph on her face. Maria knew that RECRI had to be carefully monitored because of its supply of experimental drugs but she had to admit that Helpmann was a bit overzealous.

She stood in front of the door, trying not to look at the intimidating signs that spelled out—in no uncertain terms— the consequences and penalties of unauthorized entry. It was too late to turn back now, Maria thought resolutely.

Even before opening the door, Maria could see into the entire room through the metal framed glass pane.

A heavy steel cabinet, containing RECRI's controlled substances, replete with additional warning signs in case those blatant ones outside the room had been inadvertently overlooked, was to the right of Mrs. Helpmann's desk.

The cabinet would be locked, of course, but Maria was privy to the hiding place of the duplicate key. She was just about to open the cabinet when one of the janitors walked past the door. Seeing her inside, he gave her a big smile and a wave as he went by. Maria swallowed the lump in her throat and managed a brittle smile in return.

Maria found the bottle labeled CONCENTRATED TETRAHYDROCANNABINOL. With it was the log book in which were recorded all withdrawals.

One of the Institute's projects was a controlled study of the effectiveness of THC, the active ingredient of marijuana, in reducing the side effects of protracted chemotherapy.

Maria carefully recorded the subtraction of 40cc's of the powerful, hallucinogenic concentrate, forging the names of Mrs. Helpmann and one of the doctors on the project. Her unauthorized withdrawal would be discovered eventually, Maria knew, but that really didn't seem to matter now.

With shaking hands, she measured the 40cc's into the graduated flask she had brought with her and replaced the rubber stopper. There. It was done. She checked to make sure that everything was as it had been when she opened the cabinet.

She left Mrs. Helpmann's office, carefully relocking the door behind her.

She stuck the flask into the pocket of her lab coat, and walked quickly back to her own office. There she locked the door behind her, and leaned back against it, relieved that the ordeal was over. Several minutes later, after her heart rate had returned to normal, Maria transferred the drug into two 20cc disposable syringes she had picked up earlier.

Hell, she thought, 20cc is enough to knock out a rhinoceros. If just a lungful of smoke disturbed him so much, this ought to *really* wipe him out . . . whatever he is.

Her eyes wandered to a picture of Duane and herself that Jenny had taken last year soon after they had first met. The thought of Duane the way he used to be, and what she had to do now shattered her veneer of control and filled her with sorrow.

She sat at her desk looking at the picture, until she had

the strength to take paper and pen and write Jenny a note telling her what she intended to do.

Jenny was in a rush. Hastily she pushed her chair back from the microscope where she had been working and flicked off the polarized platform light. She made one final notation in her lab report, closed it, then grabbed the sample she had been working with and put it away. She returned to her office to file the report. Jenny took off her lab coat, draped it over her chair, and kicked off the low-heeled shoes she wore while working, replacing them with a pair of stylish high heels she kept in the bottom drawer of her desk.

"Hello, Jenny," Maria said. "Looks like you're on your way out."

"Oh! Hi, Maria. Brad's got to finish some paperwork tonight, so we're having an early dinner." Jenny paused and looked carefully at Maria, who still seemed as overwrought as she had been that morning when they had talked on the phone. It had been a strange conversation—a rehash of the previous day's talk, but there had been a fearful, nervous undercurrent throughout. "After lunch I stopped by to see you but you were out."

"I was . . . busy," Maria said, and then added, "Jenny, I know this sounds strange, but will you do me a favor without asking any questions?"

"I'd do anything for you—you know that, silly!" Jenny gave her a quick hug.

"I knew you would." Maria reached into the pocket of her smock and pulled out a sealed envelope. "This is for you, but you mustn't open it until tomorrow morning."

Jenny gave Maria a quizzical look as she took the letter. She opened her mouth to ask what was going on, but Maria said, "With no questions asked, remember?"

Jenny pocketed the envelope without comment. They stepped out into the deserted hallway, and Jenny locked her office door. "We really need to talk. Would you like to come to dinner with us?"

"No, I really can't. I'm not hungry anyway."

"You should eat better," Jenny said. There was an awkward silence. "You're sure you don't want to talk now? I don't *have* to go to dinner."

"You two go ahead. I'd like to go—I haven't seen Brad in ages—but I can't. Say hello to him for me."

"I will. You try and eat something, all right?" Jenny looked at her watch. "I should be home by nine at the latest. Promise you'll call if you want to talk?"

Maria nodded.

Jenny gave her another hug. "I've got to run. See you tomorrow."

Maria returned to her office and checked the two syringes in their plastic cases, then carefully placed them in her purse. She absently tidied her office and watered her plants. She had started out with only one plant, but she had now accumulated eight. Most of them, sick or dying, had been orphaned at her office doorstep by their "parents" who knew she had a green thumb. She had patiently nursed them all back to health, but no one had ever reclaimed custody, so they remained with her.

Her office was not very large. She would either have to stop taking in plants or get a bigger office.

As she watered the pepperomia on the window ledge, she looked out the window in time to see Jenny and Brad heading for the doctor's parking lot. They were holding hands as they walked and Maria was happy for her friend. She and Brad were obviously working out their problems at last. When they got to Brad's green Jaguar, he gave Jenny an enthusiastic kiss.

Maria smiled. For a long time after Brad and Jenny drove away, Maria stood gazing out the window.

twenty-seven

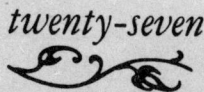

"YOU'LL LIKE THIS restaurant, Jenny," Brad assured her as he steered her toward the heavy oak door. "American Colonial decor—you know, 1776 and all that. The specialty is prime rib."

They had driven to Marina del Rey, an ocean suburb of Los Angeles, for dinner. Every time she and Brad came to this part of town and saw all the assorted types of boats and yachts bobbing at their berths in the marina's sparkling blue water, Brad swore he was going to buy a sailboat. Together they would sail off into the sunset to some tiny, uncharted island where they'd subsist on coconuts and flying fish.

It sounded ideal, Jenny thought. She would like nothing better than to escape reality for a while, and a remote island sounded just fine to her.

"Hello, I'm Daphne. I'll be your serving wench tonight," said the pretty but overly made-up waitress who gave them their menus, concentrating her attention on Brad. She informed him that tonight's pottage was potato and leek. Her low, seductive voice made even that sound like she was proposing a romp in the sheets.

Brad gave her their order, with his eyes firmly fixed on the young woman's half-exposed breasts, which were immodestly pushed up by a tightly corseted bodice.

Jenny knew all too well how easily Brad was distracted by pretty women—she was sure that would never change. At least he had cut out the sexist crap that had irritated her so much.

She was gratified when he turned to devote his undivided attention to her. She drew in a deep breath and began, "I saw Maria today. . . ."

"Oh? How's she doing? We should have invited her and Duane to dinner."

Now that she had decided to tell him what was going on, she was impatient to get to the heart of the matter. "Maria is in trouble. She's pregnant and having complications, and she hasn't seen a doctor yet!"

Brad was looking incredulous. "With all the doctors she knows?"

"Duane won't *let* her see a doctor. He's making her wait for his family doctor to arrive from Europe.

"First he wanted her to get an abortion and she refused. Apparently he got so upset that now she's afraid to try and see a doctor."

"Afraid?" Brad was flabbergasted. His voice had taken on a slight edge that did not bode well for Duane; Jenny knew from personal experience that Brad had a tendency to be a bit overprotective of his female friends. "What exactly has he been doing to her?"

"I don't know *what* he's doing. That's part of the problem. Maria won't talk about it, she talks around it. All I know is that she's scared. I can't blame her. . . . Duane frightens me, too."

"He frightens *you*?" He looked at her reproachfully. "Why didn't you tell me?"

Jenny found it difficult to verbalize her fears—fears that

didn't seem to make sense when considered logically. "It's all so subjective. . . . Every time he looks at me, I get the impression that he . . . wants me."

"You're imagining things!" Brad laughed, but the laugh faded quickly when he saw the look on Jenny's face.

"That's what I thought at first. I thought I was going nuts." She paused a moment, then hurried on. "He watches my apartment at night. I've *seen* him. It's like he's stalking me."

She wasn't even sure what she was trying to say. Only the fact that she had come to terms with the situation the night before gave her the confidence to try. All she really had to go on were vague impressions.

Brad could see that she was deeply troubled. He knew something had been bothering her the last few months, and now he finally knew what it was. He put his napkin down and took her hand. "If he disturbs you so much, we don't have to see them at all."

"Brad, it's not just me. Maria is more afraid of him than I am. I think he might be crazy!"

"Maybe I can talk him into seeing a psychiatrist."

"He wouldn't go." Jenny unconsciously rapped the table with her knuckles. "Besides, it's Maria I'm worried about right now. She doesn't eat, and she looks like hell. We had lunch with Justin yesterday, but Maria wouldn't agree to let him examine her. Then Duane showed up. Maria begged me not to leave her alone with him, so we left right away. He makes my skin crawl."

Brad remained quiet, digesting what she had said, so Jenny plunged ahead. "I have these terrible nightmares . . . visions, I don't know what to call them. They all concern Duane."

"Like that old lady in Point Locke?" Brad asked. "Remember what Maxine told us about her?"

"Mrs. Framington knew when her husband was going to die," Jenny recalled thoughtfully. "Mine aren't that clear, and they're only on one subject."

Brad tried to gloss over it. "Well, lots of people have those . . ."

"Premonitions?" Jenny finished for him, and they looked at each other. Their soup and salad arrived, and by mutual consent they concentrated on their food for a while.

Brad finally asked, "Didn't you tell me a few weeks ago that Maxine was coming down to visit? How did *she* react to Duane?"

"Yes, she came. Maria says that Duane was so rude to her that she only stayed two days."

Shaking his head in disbelief, Brad said, "He always used to be so thoughtful."

"While she was here, Maxine brought Maria up to date on Point Locke. The old couple—the Pages—remember how they left so suddenly? The police are looking into it because they found blood stains all over their house and garage. No one's heard from Happy, either. Same with Dorothy. They all just vanished. It was June Framington who hounded the police until they decided to check it out. They're all still listed as missing. Pretty strange, eh? Things like that don't happen very often in small towns." Jenny said.

"Yeah, that's strange . . . especially since they all disappeared just before Maria's wedding. I'm surprised they haven't called to question us."

"That's what I thought. It's as if the four of us are somehow—" Her voice caught in her throat and she stared down at her plate.

Both Jenny and Brad suspected Duane, but neither wanted to actually verbalize their suspicions. Doing so would endow them with too much reality.

Later, having dropped Brad off at his apartment with an agreement to pick him up early in the morning, Jenny saw that the gas gauge was registering empty. With a muttered curse, she pulled into the first service station she saw and waited patiently while three young attendants fussed around the car. Whenever she had Brad's Jaguar, it always drew admiring attention.

When she reached into her purse for her credit card, she saw Maria's letter. Puzzled, she studied the plain, white envelope, turning it over in her hands. She had to fight with herself to keep from tearing it open on the spot. No. She had promised Maria. She wouldn't open it until tomorrow.

Yet what difference would it make if she opened it now or in the morning? It was such an unusual condition to impose on a friend anyway . . . unless Maria planned to do something foolish. Jenny's hand began to tremble. The feeling of dread which had been hanging over her head for months descended full force, worse than ever before. Maria was so despondent these days. There was no telling what she might do in her present frame of mind. . . .

Concern for her friend won out over honor, and Jenny quickly ripped the letter open. As she read, her expression changed from one of worry to one of sheer panic.

"Oh God, no! Oh no!" she murmured as she tore out of the service station, heading in the direction of Maria's house.

Her face was ashen, her mouth felt dry. The first line of the letter was as pointed as a knife: "By the time you read this, I will have killed Duane. . . ."

twenty-eight

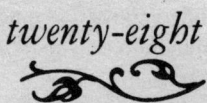

THE BATTERED BLUE Lincoln turned into the Eastman driveway with its lights out. Some distance from the house, it pulled off the driveway and stopped among the trees.

A figure got out, closed the door almost soundlessly, and began the long walk up to the house.

The sun had completely set and the moon was nearly full. Its silvery light enabled him to see quite well, though he chose to travel in the shadows. All his senses were alert. As he walked, the crickets that had been tuning up for the evening stopped, and the night became deadly quiet.

The heavy scent of night-blooming jasmine Maria had transplanted from Point Locke annoyed him. It saturated his olfactory senses, temporarily blunting their usefulness.

The house itself looked totally dark, but the garage light was on. As usual, Maria's car was parked next to the orange van. She had neglected to trip the switch that closed the garage door.

He walked quietly around the house, pausing to peer into each window. He had checked the last downstairs window from the rear patio garden when his attention was attracted by the flutter of soft wings. A large moth had made a fatal blunder and had flown into the web of a spider. Duane had noticed the web in the ferns before, but he had never seen the spider.

The moth's frantic efforts to escape the web brought the monster out of hiding. The spider approached the moth as stealthily as Duane had approached the house. It clambered over its struggling captive and quickly injected venom through its fangs. The fluttering of wings slowly died as the poison took effect.

Fascinated, Duane watched the highly specialized predator exercise her instinctive skills—skills little changed over more than a hundred million years.

He knew predatory skill when he saw it. He reached down slowly, first to touch the web . . .

Maria lay on her bed in the darkness, fully clothed, fully awake. She had been waiting for what seemed like an eternity, listening so hard that she thought she could even hear the blood coursing through her veins.

She had never known a night to be so totally silent.

She was waiting for the thing—whatever it was—that had taken Duane's place. Duane was dead, she knew that now. She had thought through the whole sequence of events: Point Locke, the beach, the raft, the waves catching the sunlight. And then the fin cutting through the water. The Duane she loved had died that day—and something horrible, something evil had come to take his place. However bizarre the idea was, she knew that it was true.

She was under great strain, both physically and emotionally, but she was not hallucinating. And she knew what she had to do.

The room was dark, but fingers of moonlight crept in through her open window, casting an eerie pattern across the bed. The light illuminated her hands tightly clutching her purse. As she looked at it, and thought about the syringes it contained, a shadow moved across the window, blocking the moonlight for an instant.

Maria sat bolt upright, her eyes wide and frightened, but now the light was streaming in again, unbroken as before. It was her imagination, most likely . . or perhaps an owl.

She listened intently, her gaze focused on the window, its white curtains billowing with the gentle breeze.

Imagination or not, she would feel a whole lot better with that window securely closed and latched. She got off the bed and moved slowly, cautiously, toward the window, then froze in her tracks. Something was moving outside near the window. But that was impossible! It was a second-story window, and there was nothing out there but the sheer side of the house.

Still, there was the sound again—a scratching, scrabbling sound against the side of the house.

Maria scarcely breathed. She could hear only the pulse of her blood as it pounded, louder and louder, faster and faster. The pains in her abdomen were beginning again. Incredibly, the sounds continued, but they were no longer near the window. Now they were proceeding upward to the roof of the house. She stared in dread at the ceiling of her room, following the sounds she was hearing. She had once heard pigeons walking on the roof and mistaken their footsteps for rain. But this was something large; an animal, perhaps.

There *were* wild animals in these hills . . . but none that climbed walls.

The noises stopped abruptly, but instead of feeling less anxious, she grew more alarmed. She could see nothing at the window, and with a burst of energy, she ran to it, slammed it down, locked it and backed away as if it had singed her hands.

Looking up, she listened again. There was nothing else, no further sound. After a few anxious minutes of silence, she tiptoed to her locked door. After putting her ear to it like an eavesdropper and hearing nothing, she opened it slowly.

Nothing seemed to be amiss. She leaned out of the room

and looked up and down the hallway. Nothing there. Cautiously she stepped out of the room onto the cool, hardwood floor of the hall and looked over the stairway landing. Nothing there either. There was no movement anywhere except the fluttering window curtain at the far end of the hall. She always kept that window open for the cross ventilation it provided.

She listened again, and heard nothing in the darkness. Maria walked down the hall, her eyes probing the shadows as she approached the window. She shut it quickly, latched it, and listened again.

At first she heard only the grandfather clock in the downstairs hall ticking away the night, but then she heard the sounds again. They were nearer now, and not coming from the roof. They were coming from inside the house . . . from the room next to hers. The room she was fixing up as a nursery.

Maria sank into the shadows, her back pressed against the wall. The door to the room was open. She could feel the presence, could hear a dry, rustling sound she could not identify. A burglar? She would almost have been grateful for that. She had a sinking feeling that it was much worse.

With a shudder, she realized she was trapped. The nursery door stood between her and the stairs. Somehow she would have to get past that door if she was to escape. There was no other way.

She began moving down the dark hall, leaning against the wooden railing of the landing as she went. Her eyes, grown enormous, were focused on the door. With her heart pounding, she edged nearer the room, one hand clutching the purse with the syringes. In the dim light, she tried to make out the furnishings she knew were there. The crib, the dresser, the hobbyhorse—all from her own childhood—were barely discernible, strangely outlined by the moon's pale light.

She'd just finished making curtains for the windows a few days ago, but hadn't put them up yet. They lay draped over the sewing machine by the window.

She stifled a scream as a large, vague form inside the room disappeared into the deep shadow in the corner. She blinked her eyes. Maria knew she'd seen *something*. She took a cautious step forward . . . and heard the rustling noise again. She stopped, and the rustling stopped, too, as if waiting for the sound of her movements to mask those of its own.

Maria mentally calculated how fast she could get past the door and down the stairs. She slipped her purse over her shoulder and was ready to make a run for it when a voice emanated from the dark depths of the nursery.

It was low at first, indistinct and yet strangely familiar. As she strained to hear, the sounds became words, an anguished plea. It was Duane's voice . . . the Duane of old. "Maria . . . Maria . . . I need your help."

It was an appeal that went straight to her heart, an appeal she could not resist. The tormented voice shot her mind back to the day they had met, the day Duane had been in such desperate need of comfort and reassurance. Without thinking, she moved slowly through the open door.

"Duane? Where are you?" She could barely see into the room. "What's the matter?"

She groped for the light switch. No light came on in response. She flicked the switch several times in frustration. "Duane, are you all right?" Cautiously, she moved forward into the room. Her foot hit something and quickly became entangled in what seemed to be thick, sticky yarn. It clung tenaciously to her ankle. She almost fell.

Flailing awkwardly for balance, her arms encountered more of the sticky strands. The gauzy filaments seemed to be everywhere, hanging from the ceiling and walls, and the more she struggled, the more entangled she got. The strands were silky, but covered with a viscid, clinging material. It was like being caught in a huge cobweb. The incredible truth dawned on her at the same time she saw movement in the shadows.

A shrill scream burst from her throat as a giant spider scurried toward her. Unadulterated panic took over and she never thought to question what she saw. Her hands clawed frantically at the strands of web, ripping them away from her face, hair, clothes. Maria pulled free just as one of the hairy, jointed legs touched her. She screamed and tore free.

Her legs felt as though they were weighted down with lead, but she was hurtling down the stairs, counting on her feet to find their own way. One backward look was sufficient to convince her she was not dreaming. The huge spider was crawling down the stairs in pursuit, its eight legs a frenzy of activity.

Maria missed her footing and tumbled down the last three steps, dropping her purse and landing hard on her knees. She scarcely felt the pain as she scrambled to her feet and across the room, heading for the front door. Her tortured gasps erupted into a scream when the spider leapt in front of her, cutting off her escape. She skidded to a halt, but was unable to keep from brushing against one of its legs. It felt like an old, dry branch.

Maria recoiled and fled again, this time to the living room. Once more, the spider got there ahead of her, outlined in all its hideousness against the French doors. It came toward her, the small paired feelers near its mouth working in anticipation. The spider's black, expressionless eyes gleamed in the darkness. It lifted its forelegs, reaching out to gather her into its deadly embrace.

Terrified, Maria backed away, and nearly fell over an end table. Grabbing the first thing that came into her hand—a large ashtray—Maria flung it at the spider with all the strength she could muster. It darted nimbly to the side and the ashtray crashed into the French doors, sending glass flying.

Maria had not waited to see if her aim had been accurate; she had turned and was making a dash for the front door. This time she made it to the hallway. The spider was right behind her, its legs scrabbling for purchase on the smooth, hardwood floor.

She dodged into the first room she came to, the bathroom, and locked the door behind her. Turning on the light, she leaned heavily against the door. The fear, shock, and exertion had gravely exacerbated her condition; the pains in her abdomen were intense, debilitating, far worse than she had ever experienced before. Her breathing was labored and her heart was pounding wildly, but at least she was safe from that thing out there.

Then she felt a tremor run through the thin door. Maria jerked away from it and stood paralyzed, listening. All was quiet, the only thing she could hear was her own panting breath. Perhaps it had gone away. Maria caught a glimpse of herself in the bathroom mirror. She didn't even recognize the wild-eyed, half-crazed woman who stared back at her.

Then out of the silence came a scratching, grating noise. Softly at first, the volume increased as it chewed at the wooden door.

Maria drew a long, sobbing breath and began looking for a way out of the tiny room. There was a small, high window, and she stepped up onto the toilet seat to reach it. Behind her the sounds intensified. She tugged at the window desperately, but it refused to budge.

The door splintered and groaned. Now the spider's mouthparts were visible, tearing at the hole it had created.

Finally the window flew open, only to reveal burglar-proof bars. Maria cried out in despair. She had dropped the purse with the syringes on the stairs, and she had nothing with which to defend herself. Flinging open the medicine cabinet, she searched for something, anything she might be able to use as a weapon. Nothing looked promising.

Maria scrabbled frantically among the cosmetic bottles on the counter as the spider forced one of its hairy, jointed forelegs into the room. She spotted a book of matches in an ashtray. That might be the answer . . . if she could find something to use as a torch. Unable to reach her, the spider pulled its leg back and resumed chewing at the door. Maria jerked open the drawers under the counter, but before she could examine their contents the spider stuck two legs into the room through the enlarged hole. They wavered jerkily in the air, groping blindly.

Pulling the nearest drawer all the way out, Maria used it to fend off the spider's attack until her eyes locked on an aerosol can of hairspray. She threw the drawer at the spider, grabbed the matchbook, and lit as many matches as she could. Then she scooped up the hairspray. Holding the can at arm's length, she pointed it at the door just as the last shards of the wood gave way and the spider began squeezing itself through. She pushed down on the button, raised the matches, and ignited the aerosol, creating a brief miniature flamethrower. The spider screamed hideously.

Jenny pulled up to the Eastman house, flung herself out of the car, and rushed to the front door just as an eerie scream, a shriek like none other heard on Earth before, came from somewhere inside. Jenny pounded on the door, yelling Maria's name. She got no response.

Afraid to wait any longer, she ran around to the back and saw the shattered glass from the French doors. Fearing the worst, Jenny reached in, unlocked the doors and entered, stepping cautiously over the broken glass. Inside, a foul odor, like that of burning hair, filled the air. It was dark, and Jenny picked her way carefully through the house, trying to remember where the light switches were. She saw a dim glow of light from the front hall and headed for it, calling Maria's name.

Jenny had the feeling that someone was watching her. She stopped and whirled around. Something large moved in the shadows. It was only when she heard Maria moaning that she had the nerve to turn and hurry ahead.

Praying that Maria was all right, Jenny entered the hall, looking behind her nervously. She gasped when she saw the broken, blackened door. The light shone through the still smoldering hole, and she could see Maria kneeling on the floor, holding on to a can of hairspray. When she saw Jenny, Maria began sobbing. "No, no, not Jenny, not Jenny . . ." she wailed, trying to struggle to her feet.

"It's me, Maria. I read your letter. I'm here to help you!"

Realizing at last that it wasn't Duane in another guise, Maria slumped back down to the floor clutching her stomach. Instead of crawling through what remained of the door, Jenny stuck her hand in and turned the knob.

Maria was gibbering frantically, and Jenny was barely able to make sense of what she was saying. "It was a spider, a giant spider . . . he talked to me . . . a web . . . in the nursery. He can change into *anything*." Maria closed her eyes as a spasm of pain rippled through her body.

Afraid that her friend was miscarrying, Jenny grabbed some towels and made her as comfortable as possible. "I'm going to call an ambulance, Maria. Don't try to get up, I'll be right back."

To Jenny's relief, she recognized the voice of the person manning the emergency desk at Regard Memorial. "Stan, this is Jenny McGregor. I need an ambulance, fast. I'm with Maria Eastman, and I think she's aborting."

In a precise but leaden voice, Jenny gave the dispatcher careful directions. He repeated them back to her, then said, "We'll have an ambulance there stat."

"Thanks, Stan." Jenny hung up, then picked up the phone again and called Brad. He answered after two rings.

"Brad, I'm with Maria. I'm afraid she's going to abort. I just called an ambulance."

"Are you all right? What can I do?"

"I'm fine. I've got to get back to Maria, so could you call Justin Harriman and tell him that Maria's coming in?"

"I'll try till I get him. He might already be at Regard."

"Can you meet me at the hospital? I need to talk to you."

"I'll call a cab, and be there as soon as I can. I love you."

"I love you, too, Brad. See you at Regard."

Jenny hung up and hurried back to Maria. She seemed more coherent now.

"Jenny, listen. There's something you've got to do for me." Maria looked pale and weak, but she spoke with great intensity.

Jenny took her hand, "I'll do anything I can to help you, you know that, Maria."

"It's Duane. He's got to be stopped. I . . . I can't explain everything that's happened, everything I've seen. . . ." Maria stopped to catch her breath; she was obviously in considerable pain. "Duane has changed, he's some kind of monster now. I don't think anyone would believe me except you. He can make himself look like other people, other things." Maria's eyes pleaded with Jenny to believe her story. "Did you see what attacked me?"

"I saw something when I came in. . . . I'm not sure what, but something sure wrecked that door!"

"I was going to try and kill him, but I can't now. You've got to do it, Jenny."

"How?"

Summoning all her remaining strength, Maria raised herself up, gripping Jenny's arm tightly. "He can't stand anything that hurts his concentration. He won't drink alcohol, he won't even take sleeping pills or anything like that. Pot smoke is the worst. It really wiped him out when I blew some in his face. That's how I first found out he was a . . . a monster. I stole two syringes full of THC from Helpmann's cabinet today. They're in my purse, and I dropped it on the stairs. I've got to get it. I'm sure they'll destroy him."

Maria started to get up, but Jenny restrained her. "I'll get it, Maria. You stay right here."

"Get the syringes! If you don't believe me, look in the nursery. He . . . *it* tried to catch me in a web."

Before Jenny could make a move, Maria shuddered violently. Her eyeballs rolled so far back that her pupils vanished from sight. Her arms and legs stiffened, then thrashed. She was having some sort of a seizure.

Intellectually, Jenny knew that such an attack was not unusual in such a situation and was not intrinsically life-threatening. Emotionally, however, it was very difficult for her to handle.

As quickly as it had occurred, the seizure was over. Maria was simply unconscious, a more peaceful look on her face than Jenny had seen for many weeks.

twenty-nine

Brad gripped the receiver tightly as he waited to be connected with Dr. Harriman's office at Regard Memorial. "Come on, Justin! Come on!" he urged through clenched teeth. His fingers drummed an impatient tattoo on the table top; he observed them clinically. They seemed to have a life of their own. He sometimes felt that way when he was in surgery, as if his hands were operating by themselves without his conscious volition. As if they had no need of *him*.

His impatience turned to concern, as he feared that Harriman might not be in. Despite his grip, he almost dropped the phone when a female voice answered, "Dr. Harriman's office."

"Hello, I've got to talk to Dr. Harriman. Tell him it's Brad Knowlton."

"I haven't seen Dr. Harriman this evening, Dr. Knowlton," she said, recognizing his name, "but I just came on shift. I—"

"Look, this is an emergency. I've got to get in touch with him immediately!"

The nurse reacted to the urgency in his voice. "If you'll hold on, I'll try to locate him for you."

Brad heard the phone being put down on a counter. In the background, he could hear muffled hospital sounds and he wished he were there. He ran his fingers nervously through his hair, fidgeting as he waited for what seemed like an eternity.

The nurse came back on the line. "Dr. Knowlton? Nobody seems to know where Dr. Harriman is. He's supposed to be on duty this evening, but he's not answering his beeper. Dr. Stuart is taking all of his cases."

"Okay," Brad said, fighting to remain calm. "Maybe you can help me. One of Dr. Harriman's patients, Maria Eastman, is being brought in to emergency. Will you keep trying to reach him and give him that message?"

She assured him that she would try, and Brad hung up the phone. He began rummaging furiously through an assortment of medical journals, magazines, and newspapers on the coffee table. Halfway through the first stack, he found what he was looking for—a copy of the hospital directory. Brad flipped through the personnel section, got to the *H*s, and ran his finger down the names as he dashed back to the phone. He punched in Harriman's home phone number, looked at his watch, and waited for an answer.

He and Justin were acquaintances rather than friends. They regarded one another with mutual respect and attended some of the same social events, but they didn't really move in the same circles. Justin was serious, self-effacing, and conservative, all things that Brad was not.

After the third ring, there was a click. Brad cursed as Harriman's recorded voice came on the line to say he wasn't home, but would return the call as soon as he could. Harriman's voice went on to give his office number at Regard Memorial. After the beeping sound, Brad left a brief message giving Maria's status and asking Harriman to get in touch with him at the hospital.

He checked his watch again, then plunged back into the

paper compost pile on the coffee table. This time, he came up with the Los Angeles area phone book and looked up taxicabs in the yellow pages.

The dispatcher promised to have a car at his apartment within fifteen minutes. That was the best she said she could do. Brad hung up and began to pace. The long purposeless strides did nothing to relieve his tension. Waiting was not something he did well. Waiting was for patients, not doctors. His modern apartment seemed cramped and confining, holding him in a frustrating, subjective kind of suspended animation.

The brass clock on the shelf ticked off the passing seconds. Was it his imagination or was the sound louder than usual? The steady *tick tick tick* seemed to reverberate throughout the room.

The most useful thing he could do was to stay calm so that he could help Jenny, give her the support that she needed. She had sounded so frantic. She needed him, and he would not fail her. He just wished the cab would come.

The words of his karate sensei leaped into his mind. Stay calm. Breath control. In and out, slowly. *Feel* the breath, feel the relaxation spreading through your body.

It was no use. He didn't feel the least bit relaxed.

All he could think of was how helpless he was and how badly he wanted to be with Jenny. He began straightening the mess on the coffee table. Stacking magazines and papers was just the type of mindless activity he needed. *That* he could handle. Medical journals in one stack, *Omni*s in another. Toss out the old newspapers and miscellaneous fliers and advertisements that had accumulated. Pile up the *Playboy*s.

As he cleared the table, exposing its walnut burl top, he remembered the day he and Margie had shopped for it. It had replaced the orange crate that had served as their coffee table through their years in med school. It was the first piece of decent furniture they'd bought, and it was the only one he had kept after Margie divorced him. Why he kept it at all was for a psychiatrist to fathom. Maybe it was some perverse form of masochism. Did he keep it to remind himself of his past failures?

It was only in the last few months—after some long, serious talks with Jenny—that he had finally begun to see things in perspective. He was finally taking a good hard look at the quagmire he'd been wallowing in since his divorce.

He had blamed Margie for everything—their break-up, his resultant depression, the lingering bitterness. Blaming her had allowed him to avoid acknowledging his own problems. But it hadn't been Margie's fault. It had been his . . . all his. Deep inside, he had known that all along. It was no longer bitterness he felt, it was deep regret.

Margie was decent, loving, honest. Instead of being proud of her intelligence and her dedication to medicine, he had felt threatened by her competence. Now, he was beginning to understand that she had put up with him longer than she should have. He had failed her, but he would not fail Jenny. At long last, he had his life on the right track. He was finally coming to terms with himself, and everything was going to work out all right.

He had wandered so far into the quiet depths of memory that he jumped at the harsh, jarring buzz of the doorbell.

His eyes flew to the clock. It couldn't have been more than five minutes since he'd called the cab company. Miracles *did* happen in this day and age!

Brad grabbed his jacket and black bag and sprinted toward the door. He jerked it open, ready to blurt out a grateful thank-you to the cabby for his promptness. He stopped short, his mouth hanging open.

It was Duane. He stood on the doorstep, smiling.

Duane walked past him into the apartment. Brad was stunned by Duane's nonchalance, then the answer dawned on him. Obviously Duane didn't know that Maria was in critical condition. It was the only thing that could account for his composure, and it meant that Brad was stuck with breaking the bad news.

Brad shut the door and set down his bag. Duane appeared not to have a care in the world. He was sitting on the couch, his legs crossed and his arms draped casually over the back. An amused smile crossed his lips as he studied the room, as if he'd never been here before.

Something about Duane's smile disturbed Brad. Jenny was right. There was definitely something strange about him, but he couldn't put his finger on it. But now was not the time to worry about it. The important thing was to get to the hospital. "Duane . . ." he began, his bedside manner faltering badly.

"'Yes?" The calm reply. Too calm.

Why did he get the feeling that Duane was toying with him, as though he were playing some strange game with rules of his own making? Brad swallowed hard and tried again. "Jenny just called. Maria is in pretty bad shape . . . she may even be aborting. Jenny's called an ambulance and they're on their way to Regard right now."

"What else did Jenny say?" Duane inquired, ignoring most of what Brad had said.

"Isn't it enough to know that—what's the matter with you?" Brad almost shouted, getting to his feet. "Jenny's got my car, so I called a cab. I don't know when it'll get here, so let's go in your car. Come on!"

Duane made no move to follow him to the door.

What the hell was going on? "Did you hear me? Don't you understand?" Duane's bizarre behavior was unnerving him. Maybe he's in shock, Brad thought.

"Duane, why don't you give me your keys and *I'll* drive. I know this is quite a shock, but we've got to hurry!" Duane got up, his movements slow and deliberate. He led Brad to the door, then turned and leaned against it. The relief Brad had felt when Duane began moving vanished instantly. "Damn it, Duane, this is no time to play games. Let's get going!"

In a cool, untroubled voice, Duane stated, "There's no need for us to go, Brad. Maria is no longer important. I'm much more interested in Jenny."

Brad's mouth dropped open as he stared incredulously at Duane.

Jenny had been right! Brad had made excuses for Duane,

convinced that there wasn't anything serious wrong with him. Now a veritable flood of incidents and fleeting impressions buried in his subconscious came rushing into his mind. Duane after the shark incident, that strange dinner conversation with Professor Page, Duane at the reception, Jenny's reactions to him. How stupid he had been not to see it from the beginning. "Duane, I don't know what's wrong with you, but you better get out of my way."

There was no doubt whatsoever in Brad's mind that he would emerge victorious from a fight with Duane.

He was a karate expert, and though he used it primarily to keep in shape and get out his aggressions, Brad knew how much damage he could inflict. He did not want to hurt Duane—he was reasonably certain the man was mentally ill—but he felt he had no choice. Jenny was counting on him, and so was Maria, and they were much more important to him than Duane.

He gave him one more chance. "I'm going to the hospital, Duane. Now."

Duane smiled, silently sizing him up.

Still, Brad was reluctant to act. He threw an indecisive and rather conventional right cross at Duane.

Even if it had been more than the half-hearted effort that it was, it probably would not have been any more effective. Duane was poised to react, and he evaded Brad's punch easily.

Duane shoved him away. "Surely you can do better than that, Brad," he said mockingly. He spoke too soon.

Brad did a backward roll, came smoothly to his feet and immediately launched another punch at Duane. Still smiling, Duane blocked it with his forearm.

Brad's punch had never been intended to connect; it was merely a decoy. He spun around, pivoting on his right foot, his head and torso low. His left foot caught Duane in the rib cage, knocking the wind out of him and slamming him up against the door. Brad followed up the roundhouse kick with a right hook, which landed solidly on Duane's jaw. The blow hurt his hand, but it wiped the smile off Duane's face and improved Brad's mood considerably.

Duane gasped for air for a moment, then charged at Brad as if to tackle him. Brad stepped aside like a bullfighter, pushing him to the side and tripping him for good measure.

Duane crashed into the end of the couch headfirst, his outflung arm sending a lamp crashing to the floor. He picked himself up slowly, shaking his head as if stunned.

Sarcastically Brad said, "Surely you can do better than *that*, Duane." He could hear the cab driver honking outside. His way no longer barred, Brad gathered up his jacket and bag and turned to leave.

Brad was reaching for the doorknob when he heard Duane's voice. "Just a minute, Brad. . . ." He sounded strange, his voice changing even as the words were being uttered. The words became deep and slurred, only half-articulated, as if a phonograph record had been playing and the power suddenly shut off. The creature was tired of fighting in human form.

Brad turned to see what was the matter, and the shock of what he saw made his body grow weak. Duane was staring at him with demonic intensity, and his face was no longer human. His features were rearranging themselves— elongating, pulsating, rippling grotesquely.

Small vessels split apart, sending blood dripping down the thing's face. The lower jaw spread out and forward, with the blood trickling into an open mouth sprouting countless sharp teeth. Something, perhaps a tongue, rolled around the dark interior of the mouth, as if it were waiting to leap out and attack.

The monster advanced.

Brad felt behind him for the doorknob as he saw the creature's body coalesce into a silver-gray mass of perfectly controlled flesh, growing new tentacles that writhed and snapped with feverish action.

Brad's dumbfoundedness gave way to terror. With time, his courage would have displaced the fear. But Brad had no time for courage. He had time only for the most excruciating of agonies.

The slimy appendages wrapped around him, holding

him securely, drawing him into the deadly mouth. Brad struggled but the teeth split into thousands of writhing cilia that pierced his head from every direction, wriggling into the ears like ravenous worms, shooting through the eyeballs like microfine spikes, filling the mouth with exploding torments as membranes were shredded off a fraction of an inch at a time by an inhuman torturer.

But the creature did not indiscriminately crush its victim, taking special care to keep Brad's heart and lungs functioning. It wanted Brad's memory intact, didn't want the brain cells to die before it was through with them.

Brad's medical knowledge was only of secondary interest. What the creature wanted most was information about Jenny.

The monster's careful precautions kept Brad conscious while his body was destroyed, his memories and personality systematically devoured. Brad's last independent thought was not of the unbelievable pain that was beyond comprehension, but was instead a more horrible pain in his soul— the despairing realization that he had ultimately failed Jenny.

The disgruntled cab driver gave up honking. He parked in the apartment driveway and checked the address he had been given by the dispatcher. He got out of the cab and walked up to Brad's apartment.

He tried the doorbell first. Getting no results, he pounded loudly on the door.

Fortunately for him, it never opened.

With a curse, he stormed angrily back to his cab and drove away.

thirty

JENNY SAT ON the floor near Maria, listening for the ambulance siren. She knew full well that it would take some time for it to arrive from the hospital. And then there was the turnoff that even she, who was familiar with the road, still sometimes missed. Jenny tried not to think about what might go wrong. The reality of the situation was bad enough without conjuring up additional problems.

Stan Bennett was an old friend, and he'd get an ambulance to her as fast as was humanly possible. All she could do now was wait.

Jenny turned her attention back to Maria's unconscious form. She was determined to give Maria the best possible chance of survival. But for all her medical knowledge, Jenny was dismayed by how little she could do. Her experience had been confined almost entirely to the laboratory; she seldom dealt with patients directly.

Maria was her best friend, and she was reduced to

making her comfortable, holding her hand, and waiting for help. She smoothed Maria's dark hair and dabbed her face with a soft wash cloth.

The wait seemed interminable. Off in the distance, she could hear the faint din of traffic on Franklin Avenue, far below. She finally heard the shrill, piercing sound of an ambulance siren rising above the background noise.

Now the ambulance was on Franklin, but it sounded as if it had gone past the Evergreen Canyon turnoff. As she listened, the ambulance got farther away. The driver must have corrected his mistake in a hurry, because the siren soon grew louder as the vehicle snaked its way up the canyon road.

Jenny carefully checked Maria again. She had just decided there was no perceptible change in her condition when she noticed a small trickle of blood on the bathroom throw rug. At the same time, she heard the ambulance turn onto the long driveway that led up to the house. She was torn between wanting to stay with her friend and running to meet the ambulance attendants, who could help Maria more than she could.

Reluctantly, Jenny left Maria and hurried to the front door. Earlier she had turned on all the outside lights she could find. The ambulance came to an abrupt stop, then backed up to the house. The siren and flashing light cut off sharply, leaving the night strangely silent.

Two men emerged from the back, carrying large equipment cases, and Jenny led them into the house. "She's unconscious now, and she just started to hemorrhage."

After a quick calculation, she added, "She's about three months along." Jenny led them to the bathroom where Maria lay.

They noticed the ravaged, scorched door, but said nothing, brushing past Jenny to kneel beside the patient. One of the attendants wrapped a strip around her arm and manipulated a squeeze bulb. "How long has she been unconscious?" he asked as he checked her pulse and respiration.

"About fifteen minutes. She had a brief seizure when she tried to get up . . . hypertensive reaction, I think."

They gave her a brief look, recognizing her, she hoped, as a medical professional.

While one felt Maria's abdomen, the other withdrew a portable radio from one of the cases and contacted the hospital's emergency center.

"Regard Memorial, this is Regard Mobile Two."

"We read you, Mobile Two, go ahead," came the immediate reply.

"Regard Memorial, we have a female Caucasian, about twenty-five, approximately three months pregnant, unconscious, hemorrhaging, apparently aborting. Telemetry strip attached, transmitting now." The other medic flicked a switch, activating the tie-in that allowed the doctors at Regard Memorial to evaluate Maria's heartbeat and other vital signs directly. "Pulse 120 and thready, respiration shallow, around 30. Over."

"Mobile Two, administer an I.V. of five percent glucose and Valium. Transport as soon as possible!" There was no mistaking the urgency of the last instruction. While one of them started the intravenous feed, the other left, returning almost at once with a stretcher.

The ambulance was soon screaming back down the winding canyon with Jenny and Maria inside. Jenny sat beside Maria, holding her hand. It felt cold and damp. She was afraid that she was losing Maria, and she was powerless to do anything.

One of the attendants rode in back with Jenny, checking Maria every few minutes. His face seemed emotionless.

Her friend was dying and the ambulance attendant seemed cold and indifferent. Jenny wanted to scream at him, to *make* him care. She calmed down, knowing that to do the job they did, day after day, they had to keep themselves detached. It was simply not possible to show all the compassion each case merited and still be able to respond efficiently when called upon. She had learned that the hard way.

The trip seemed to take forever. When the ambulance

arrived at Regard Memorial Hospital's brightly lit emergency entrance, the vehicle's doors were flung open and Maria was handed down to the emergency staff who began ministering to her even as they wheeled her into the hospital.

Jenny, along with the ambulance driver, trotted after them. "You can fill out the paper work over there," he said to Jenny, indicating the main desk. "I'm sure they'll be moving her up to Obstetrics. Don't go away—you're the only one who can give us information about the patient." Jenny nodded her head feebly as she caught one final glimpse of Maria's face before the double, swinging doors closed behind the narrow wheeled cart.

After filling out countless forms, she slumped into one of the orange vinyl chairs in the emergency waiting room. She watched as the scene repeated itself, with minor variations. The same swinging double doors continued to swallow people into the mysterious, antiseptic realm beyond, leaving anxious, frightened friends and relatives behind.

Like Jenny, they were helpless in their vigil. Some of them paced around like animals in a zoo, but most sat, staring straight ahead.

In one of the curtained examination rooms, Dr. Campbell, a tired-looking, red-haired young man, was examining Maria. As he applied his stethoscope to her abdominal area, a perplexed look came over his face. There was no longer anything tired about Campbell's expression. Raising his voice, he said, "Call Obstetrics and have a team standing by in an operating room. Get her up there *fast!*" The two orderlies seemed rooted to the spot, momentarily startled. "Stat!" Campbell shouted, and they finally responded. He barked out other orders, and Maria, her face now covered with an oxygen mask, was wheeled to the elevator. The young doctor made the trip, too, keeping a tight check on Maria's vital signs and muttering to no one in particular. "God, that's the weirdest thing . . ."

When they reached the obstetrics wing on the third floor, Dr. Campbell was met by Dr. Stuart. "Is that Maria Eastman?"

"Yes. Her pregnancy seems to be very abnormal. Here, you better check her right away."

Wondering why the doctor from Emergency was so worked up, Dr. Stuart put on his stethoscope as Campbell lifted the sheet to expose Maria's body. After listening for a few seconds, Dr. Stuart frowned and moved the stethoscope, then repeated the procedure. He replaced the instrument around his neck and palpated her swollen abdomen. Stuart straightened slowly.

"I see what you mean," he said.

Every eye in the waiting room, including Jenny's, focused on the doctor who strode down the hall to the reception desk. He leaned over the high counter to talk with one of the night nurses. Jenny's heart leapt when the nurse pointed him in her direction.

We were too late, Jenny thought. That must be what he's going to tell me. She felt faint, staring at him wide-eyed as he approached.

"Jenny McGregor? I'm Dr. Campbell. We've moved your friend, Mrs. Eastman, up to Obstetrics. Dr. Stuart is with her now. He'd like to talk to you."

Upstairs, Jenny paced back and forth in the corridor. Every time a door opened, she hoped to see Justin or Brad. They should be here by now! What could have happened to them? It wasn't like Brad to disappear like this, especially when she needed him. In the back of her mind was the thought that he had had an accident. She continually had to wrench her mind away from thoughts like that.

She went to the phone and tried calling Brad's apartment. There was no answer. She hung up, turned, and found herself face to face with a white-jacketed doctor.

"Ms. McGregor, I'm Dr. Stuart," he said, extending his hand. "I work with Dr. Harriman."

"I've heard your name," Jenny said, trying to gauge how much she could tell him. He had a square, friendly face, complemented by gold-rimmed glasses. "Both Maria and I work over in RECRI. How is she?" Jenny asked with considerable trepidation.

"She's in very serious condition, as I'm sure you know," he said. "Does her husband know she's been brought in?"

"I don't think so. I don't know where he is. . . ." Her voice trailed off nervously.

"Is there anything else you can tell us about her medical history or her condition?"

Jenny shook her head in answer. She knew she should talk to him, but what could she say? That Maria's husband was some sort of monster? That she was afraid Maria's child might also be monstrous? Should she warn him to be careful, or tell him to be prepared for anything? "I know she talked to Justin a couple of days ago, but I don't know what she told him. Do you know where he is?"

Dr. Stuart frowned. "'No, he hasn't come in today." Scrutinizing her face closely, he asked, "Are you related to her?"

"No, I'm just a close friend." The instant the words were out of her mouth, Jenny regretted them. She should have lied. Now he wouldn't tell her anything. Trying to rectify her mistake, she volunteered, "She doesn't have any relatives down here; they live up north."

"We're prepping her for surgery right now. It looks like we'll have to do a cesarean section as soon as we get her stabilized."

thirty-one

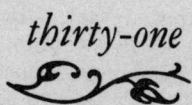

Dr. Stuart couldn't help feeling reluctant to prepare for surgery in such an unusual situation. From what he'd gathered from his initial examination, there were several abnormal fetuses. He felt sure that Jenny wasn't telling him all she knew, and he couldn't figure out why.

He changed methodically into the green, V-neck, short-sleeved top and matching pajama-type pants, then began scrubbing down.

Many times in the past, Dr. Stuart had saved patients he thought were beyond hope, but he had no illusions about the extent of his knowledge. Obstetrics was an unpredictable field, and cases like this certainly kept him from becoming overconfident.

A nurse came in to help him get all his hair underneath a surgical cap and reported, "They still haven't been able to reach Dr. Harriman."

Dr. Stuart swore under his breath. He hated going into

an operation in an even greater state of ignorance than usual, but he had very little choice in the matter.

He bowed his head so the scrub nurse could tie on his face mask, then entered the operating room.

Maria's draped figure looked small, surrounded by monitors and stainless steel instrument carts loaded with clamps, scalpels, aspirators, forceps, needles, sutures, specimen jars, and sponges. The whole scene was lit by the cluster of surgical lamps above her. A cart bearing fetal monitoring equipment was being wheeled away as Dr. Stuart came in. The intern pushing it said, "Her cervix is hardly dilated; there's no fetus in the birth canal to attach the electrode to. She's having contractions about once every five minutes, but they don't seem to be normal."

Dr. Stuart consulted briefly with the others in the room. Their reports were not encouraging. Maria's heart beat was weak, and her blood pressure was low. The team of interns, nurses, and anesthesiologist had hooked up the various monitors, and all told the same story—the patient's condition was deteriorating rapidly. The doctor had few alternatives open to him.

Ordinarily, he would have let nature take its course. She was miscarrying, and from what he had heard and felt, the fetuses were too abnormal to survive even if carried to term. The problem was that the patient was weak and getting weaker. The contractions were sapping her strength but had not yet begun to expel the fetuses. If he did a cesarean, got in and out quickly, he had a good chance of saving the mother. He had decided to operate at once.

Before anyone could make ready, the nurse assisting the anesthesiologist blurted out, "She's stopped breathing!"

As the nurse and doctor began working to get Maria's lungs going, the rest of the team stared down, transfixed, as flecks of blood became visible on the drape covering Maria's abdomen. A quivering, palpitating motion began in the center of the drape, which was rapidly growing dark with blood. The movement slid to the side of the cloth and a small, bloody tentacle crept into view, undulating like a grotesque snake.

Everyone in the room watched in stunned disbelief. They were all seasoned operating room veterans. They had seen enough blood, abnormality, and suffering to desensitize anyone, but what they saw completely unnerved them. The anesthesiologist was able to resume his attempt to save Maria's life only by refusing to believe what he saw.

Dr. Stuart was the next to recover. Regaining a measure of self-control, he grabbed a pair of forceps from a nearby cart and shouted "Get me a bottle of formaldehyde!"

His sharp words broke the spell holding the others motionless, and one of the nurses ran out of the room. Stuart leaned forward, grasped the questing tentacle, and pulled the larva out of Maria's abdominal cavity.

He held fast to the loathsome creature, revulsion only partially held in check by medical interest. It was about the same size as his hand, and had three tentacles, all writhing madly, spattering blood in all directions. Suddenly, it sprouted needlelike teeth and slashed out viciously at the forceps.

The nurse came running through the double doors, carrying a large bottle of formaldehyde. "Put it on the cart," Dr. Stuart advised. After she had done so, he tried to pry the creature off the forceps and into the bottle. It held on tenaciously, but he finally managed to force it in. The creature shriveled up immediately and sank to the bottom of the jar. An audible sigh of relief was heard as the lid was screwed on tightly.

Their relief was short-lived. Dr. Stuart put the bottle on one of the carts and turned his attention to the anesthesiologist, who was still laboring over Maria.

"There's another one," yelled one of the interns. The frantic cry drew all eyes back to the hole from which the first larva had emerged. The sheet was quivering again.

"Get me a vat of the acid they use to destroy C-waste," Stuart ordered. Two of the technicians glanced at each other and took off at a dead run.

Dr. Stuart tried to grab the second tentacled creature but it eluded him. Hissing and spitting, it batted at the forceps.

One of the interns finally caught it from behind, and carefully dropped it into a large, steel pan.

No sooner had the second larva been removed than a third popped up. Dr. Stuart deftly seized it as it pulled itself onto the sheet, then dumped it in the container with the other one. The two larvae began fighting, eating each other and simultaneously regenerating themselves. Stuart turned away in disgust—and saw that yet another tentacle was rising from Maria's body. "Dump the instruments and bring me another container!"

His directive proved unnecessary, as the two technicians wheeled in a large, covered crock of concentrated sulfuric acid. They removed the heavy cover as he caught the fourth creature up with his forceps and dropped it into the acid. An intern followed suit with the two in the metal pan.

A high-pitched, unearthly scream came from the larvae as they hit the corrosive liquid. There was a violent hissing and bubbling as they slowly dissolved, and an acrid, stomach-turning stench emerged from the crock.

Mopping his brow, Dr. Stuart turned his attention once more to the operating table. The anesthesiologist shook his head sadly and pulled the sheet over Maria's face.

Everyone in the room stood silently, wondering if the preceding events had really taken place or if it might all have been some horrid shared nightmare. But one look at the blood-spattered body of the young woman on the table gruesomely reminded them it was no dream.

Dr. Stuart gradually regained his composure and asked one of the nurses to bring him the specimen. The spell was broken, and the operating team resumed their duties.

The nurse who had picked up the specimen bottle glanced at it out of morbid curiosity, and was shocked to see that the creature seemed to have revived. "I think it might still be alive," she said. Everyone stared. The larva was indeed squirming around in the formaldehyde.

She lifted it up to eye level, and a single, horrible eye opened and stared directly at her.

She screamed and dropped the jar. It shattered on the

floor, and the creature was free. Though small, it slithered rapidly across the floor, propelled by its tentacles.

An intern scrambled to get out of its way and slipped on the wet floor. His foot lay in the larva's path, and it moved to attack. Its sharp teeth slashed his shoe open and took off two of his toes.

The man screamed in pain, and kicked madly, dislodging the creature.

The room was once more thrown into noisy confusion. Reacting quickly, one of the technicians seized a large pair of forceps and managed to grab the larva, which thrashed violently.

The vat was opened once again, but the creature had twined itself around the forceps and refused to let go. It reached a tentacle up toward his hand, and he dropped both the larva and the forceps into the acid.

The limping, bloodied intern was bandaged and helped out of the room, and for the second time, the devastated team stared in stunned silence at one another.

With shaking hands, a nurse put a clean sheet over Maria's body.

Jenny was frightened by the expression on Dr. Stuart's face. He was exhausted, and he seemed to have aged considerably since she had seen him less than an hour before. Although he wore a fresh white jacket, there were flecks of blood on his glasses. Even before he spoke, she knew what he had come out to tell her.

"She's dead, isn't she?" Jenny said, her voice low and shaky.

He nodded his head.

The two stood in uncomfortable silence, each unsure of how much to tell the other. Jenny didn't know what had happened in the operating room, but she had been aware of an ominous undercurrent on the floor as clusters of doctors and nurses spoke in hushed tones.

"It . . . it wasn't a normal pregnancy, was it?" stammered Jenny. She had to know.

Dr. Stuart looked at her, long and hard. "No, it wasn't," he said softly. "There were four . . . abnormal fetuses."

Jenny felt faint and closed her eyes. Dr. Stuart's arm steadied her. "Are you sure there's nothing else you can tell me? The circumstances were so unusual that there's bound to be an investigation."

Jenny wanted to confide in him and relate the whole story, suspicions and all. She could certainly use any help she could get, but there was nothing more she could say. "No, I'm sorry. There's no more information I can give you."

"For now, then," Dr. Stuart said, "the cause of death is 'complications due to abnormal pregnancy.'" He paused, then asked, "Uh . . . do you know the father?"

Jenny could tell from the way his eyes searched hers that he was after more than a simple yes or no. Before she decided how to respond, he continued. "Have you been able to reach him?"

"No, but I'm going to," she said, grimly.

"Thank you for your cooperation—I'm very sorry about your friend." His eyes were sad, but not as sad as Jenny's.

She left Dr. Stuart and walked back to the public phone near the nurses' station. Jenny knew she should call Maxine, but she couldn't think how to tell her what had happened. She would do it in the morning . . . after someone from the hospital had already broken the news to her.

She punched in Brad's number automatically—so automatically that she could not remember having done it, but it was ringing nonetheless. He didn't answer. She tried again, and let it ring, over and over. Jenny stared dully at the wall of the phone booth. Finally, she hung up.

She took the dimes out of the phone and stuck them back in her purse. Her hand touched the two syringes that Maria had forced her to take, and a cold shiver went through her. She withdrew her hand quickly.

thirty-two

GRIEF-STRICKEN, JENNY walked slowly out of the hospital. She had never been this close to death before, had never faced it head on like this. Until tonight, death seemed vague and distant, something that happened to strangers, something that her lab tests predicted and confirmed.

Now her dearest friend was dead, and Jenny still did not really believe it. It seemed impossible.

She was standing in front of the hospital, shivering in the cool night air. What should she do next? She was about to go back inside and call a cab when she remembered that her own car was still in the RECRI parking lot where she had left it that morning. It seemed like ages ago.

Jenny slid behind the wheel of her sports car and sat staring straight ahead for a few minutes, her hands clamped tightly on the steering wheel. Finally, she turned the key in the ignition.

She drove aimlessly, no destination in mind. Jenny thought about going to the police, but what could she tell them? That she knew a man who could turn into other people—into a monster who had just killed her best friend? It wouldn't take them long to lock *her* up as a looney if she went in with that story.

She couldn't even count on Brad. Something must have happened, otherwise he would have met her at the hospital. A feeling of intense, chilling cold gripped her, and she fought back new tears. She could not stop to wonder about Brad. Everything was on her shoulders now. Duane was *her* responsibility.

How could such a horrible thing have happened to Maria? She drove carelessly, lurching ahead at each green light, then screeching to bone-jarring halts amid honks and shouts. *She was so young. It wasn't fair. It just wasn't fair!*

It was stupid to expect life to be fair. All of us play the game, she thought, but Death holds the wild cards, plays the unexpected hand. Everything depends upon our courage . . . and our guilt.

Self-reproach pushed away Jenny's numbness. She blamed herself for not having paid sufficient attention. She should have done more—if only she'd kept in touch with Maria, despite Duane. . . .

And it was *Duane* who was responsible for what had happened. He was the wild card—Death's winning hand.

Jenny drove on. With considerable surprise, she realized she was on Hollywood Boulevard. It was almost as strange as being on another planet.

Most of the businesses were closed now. The heavy iron security gates across the entrances made parts of the street look like prison cellblocks. A car pulled away from the curb in front of her. She decided to park and consider what to do. Driving around aimlessly was not getting her anywhere.

Jenny sat in her car, her face illuminated from time to time by the harsh lights of passing cars and flashing neon signs overhead. Overcome by feelings of desolation and remorse, she finally broke down and wept.

Back at her apartment, Jenny realized that there was, truly, only one solution. She would have to confront Duane. She picked up the phone and dialed the Eastman number. She didn't really expect an answer, and was not altogether sure what she would say if there were one.

She had to determine for herself what was real and what was not. Maria had given her the means to destroy whatever it was that was now inhabiting Duane's body, but before she tried to kill him she needed something substantial to justify it. What did she know about Duane from firsthand experience? It amounted to very little. He had changed drastically in Point Locke . . . after the shark incident. A shiver made its way down her backbone whenever she recalled how he had touched her when he came out of the water. More concretely, four people had disappeared at Point Locke; she didn't believe it was only coincidence.

It was nevertheless pretty flimsy evidence. Maria had lived with him, and there was no doubt in Jenny's mind that Maria had believed Duane was a monster; but then, she had been in critical condition and might have been delirious. Jenny wished Dr. Stuart had told her what had happened in the operating room.

She almost dropped the phone when the receiver was picked up at the other end and she heard Duane's all too familiar voice. Self-control, she told herself furiously. Self-dammit-control.

"This is Jenny. I was at your house earlier. Maria was very ill and I had her taken to the hospital."

"Yes, I know. You went with her."

"Do you know that Maria . . . died?"

"No, but I'm not surprised."

Her mind instantly seized upon his statements. *Brad* was the only person who knew that she had gone to the hospital, and Duane would have known about Maria's death if he had called Regard. That left only two possibilities. Duane had learned about it from Brad, or Duane had been at the house while she was there.

"Your wife is dead, and it doesn't seem to upset you!" Jenny's voice was shrill.

"Jenny. Jenny, I want to explain everything to you. I want to answer your questions. I've wanted to talk to you for a long time, but you've been avoiding me. We need to talk, but not over the phone. I'll come by and pick you up."

"No . . . I'll come to your house. I think you're right. We do need to talk. . . ." After a long pause she added, "I'll be there in an hour."

"Good. I'll be waiting for you, Jenny." The line went dead.

Jenny tried to pull herself together by taking a big swig of Scotch straight from the bottle Brad kept in her pantry. She grimaced, her eyes tearing as the liquid burned into her throat and stomach.

Her hands were shaking as she applied her makeup and dressed with minute attention to detail. There were few enough weapons at her disposal, she thought, and she'd better make the best use of what she had. Everything she selected was black: bikini panties, a skimpy lace bra, and sheer stockings. From her closet, she chose a seductive black cocktail dress, low-cut and slit to midthigh. Brad always liked her in black—he liked the contrast with her blond hair and fair complexion.

She slipped on a pair of high heels and stepped to the mirror to assess the full effect. It this didn't do the trick, nothing would, she decided after giving herself a hard, scrutinizing look.

It was clear to her that he wanted her in some extraordinary way—she had known it from the beginning, but had not been able to admit it even to herself. His looks and actions had repeatedly confirmed her earliest instincts. Now that she had accepted the reality of the situation, the pieces were starting to fall into place.

Her brave resolve evaporated when she transferred the two syringes to a small black purse. She hoped the outfit would throw him off his guard . . . at least long enough to use the THC. In order to buy even that much time, she would have to go along with whatever he had in mind.

thirty-three

FOR THE SECOND time this evening, Jenny was headed for the Eastman house. The first time had been a frantic, desperate rush to get to Maria. Now, only the dread, nauseous feeling in the pit of her stomach was the same. She was both anxious and fearful of reaching her destination. But she drove cautiously. It wouldn't do to have a policeman stop her . . . not with what she carried in her purse.

Jenny felt a strong impulse to ditch the syringes, go back to her apartment, pack her belongings, and leave Los Angeles. If she did that, she might be able to block out the last few months and return to some normal kind of existence. She concentrated on her driving, resisting the temptation, and was again trapped by memory. Images sprang vividly into her mind's eye. It was a Saturday, shortly after Maria's engagement. Maria had driven her up this same road to give her a comprehensive tour of the house.

Maria had been so cheerful that day, bubbling over with enthusiasm and love of life. Jenny's eyes stung, and she knew she couldn't run away without at least trying to keep her promise to Maria.

As she rounded a curve in the winding, climbing road, Jenny saw road flares ahead. Accident, she thought, as her foot depressed the brake. Three police cars and a tow truck had reduced the already narrow road to a single lane. Officers stood at the edge of the road, their floodlights aimed down the steep embankment. A battered sports car, blackened by fire, was being eased up with a winch.

She drove past, taking her eyes off the road only long enough to search for the landmark that would let her know she was near the Eastman turnoff. It was Maria who had pointed it out. On a hillside, sticking up above the high trees, was what appeared to be the ancient stone turrets and battlements of an English castle. It had been built by a film director in the twenties, and it wasn't hard to spot, even at night.

Jenny had to be alert now. The Eastman driveway was not much farther. She slowed to a crawl even before she got to the turnoff, greatly agitating the lone motorist behind her.

The headlights illuminated the rural-type mailbox with the Eastman name on it, and she brought the car to a stop. Her eyes followed the driveway. Beyond the beams of the headlights, there was only darkness . . . a darkness that filled her with terror.

The house was not visible yet. It was situated a few hundred meters up the paved driveway, past a veritable forest of trees.

Jenny put the car in motion once again and headed up the dark driveway, moving at a snail's pace. Up ahead the trees finally parted, and the outline of the house loomed into view. She had been nervous before, but now her hands were icy as they held tightly to the wheel in an effort to keep her body from trembling.

Jenny parked the car and turned off her lights. A feeble porch light offered scant illumination.

It was a large, wood-frame house in what was generally known—for want of a better designation—as Victorian, but actually combined the classical elements of Gothic, Georgian, and Italianate in the ornamentation of its exterior. Jenny tried to remember how the large covered porch gave it such an inviting look in the daytime. The house looked anything *but* inviting now. It seemed to be breathing, listening . . . waiting.

Jenny took a deep breath, picked up her purse, and stepped out of the car. The night was cool. It was like being out in the country. Crickets chirped, and up here, above the smog, stars twinkled brightly. She winced at the sound of the gravel crunching beneath her feet. She smelled the jasmine, strong and sickly sweet.

Her eyes focused on the large, beautifully carved front door as if it were a guillotine waiting for her at the top of the wooden steps. Jenny pulled on the macramé bell rope that Maria had so carefully handcrafted, and inside the house, tiny brass bells responded.

She stiffened and stood rooted, hearing her respiration coming faster and faster as footfalls inside approached the door. Duane pulled the door open, looking relaxed and friendly. This was the old Duane, her friend.

Only it wasn't. The eyes . . . she seemed to be falling into them, drowning. It was like a whirlpool, and she was powerless. "Come in." His voice startled her out of the strange cataleptic state. Awareness flooded back into her mind. Bewildered, she blinked a few times and pushed her hair back from her face. Only tension, she thought, Nothing more than that. But the smile on Duane's face changed her mind. He had deliberately instigated the brief capture of her mind, and he had terminated it just as deliberately. She felt violated and afraid, but was also, strangely, intrigued.

"Come in," he repeated. "I've been waiting for you." He stepped aside to let her pass. "Let's talk in the study—I have a nice fire going."

She led the way, pointedly keeping her gaze from the

bathroom door which was a silent testimonial to the earlier violence.

Jenny's eyes scanned the study quickly. The crackling fire cast a warm orange glow over the room as a flickering pattern danced on the walls and ceiling. The velvet couch picked up the deep blue of the Persian carpet that was a gift from Maxine Salina to the newlyweds, and the ornate oak desk standing against the book-lined wall had been shipped from Maria's bedroom in Point Locke.

The lights were low, and classical music was playing softly in the background. On an antique table near the couch was a bottle of wine and two glasses, framed by a pair of silver candle holders supporting two thick, unlit yellow candles.

Something troubled her about the room, but she couldn't put a name to it.

"You're looking exceptionally lovely tonight, Jenny," he said. His eyes moved appreciatively down her body. Without taking his eyes off her, he lit the candles, then uncorked the wine and poured them each a glass. The deep red wine caught the firelight and sparkled in the crystal glasses.

As they lifted the glasses to their lips, they sized each other up. Jenny allowed no movement to go unnoticed. Every syllable he uttered, every intonation was dissected and analyzed in her mind for possible hidden meanings.

He seemed amused at her vigilance. When he motioned toward the couch, she complied. He sat down also, but at a reasonable distance, for which she was grateful.

The wine tasted good. She felt its warmth spreading through her and tried to relax. "I see you've been studying," she said, pretending an interest in the books stacked underneath the coffee table.

"Yes, I've been reading a lot about instinctive behavior lately. Insects fascinate me. . . . They are controlled almost entirely by their instincts. Unlike humans, the differences between individuals are of practically no consequence. They are little more than biological robots."

Jenny stared at him. "What's your point?"

Duane smiled. "I'm talking about instincts, a very relevant subject."

Relevant to whom? Jenny wondered if he was trying to throw her off guard.

"A cat, for example," he said, "is not really intelligent. Its learning ability is practically nil. But a cat *seems* intelligent because it relies on highly developed instincts. It is very good at being a cat. That's the way I have always functioned."

"You certainly don't sound like the Duane I used to know." she said. It was a calculated statement, and she was afraid she knew how he would respond.

"I'm not really Duane . . . but you already knew that, didn't you?"

His admission and the enormity of its implications was overwhelming. "Oh God," she moaned, covering her face with her hands. "Maria was right!"

"Calm down, Jenny, and listen to me," he said quietly. "You came to hear my side of the story and have your questions answered, didn't you?"

Jenny was inwardly terrified by his statement, but she had to hear him out. Whatever it was she was talking to obviously had a definite reason for talking so candidly to her—he had a plan, and she had to keep a tight grip on her emotions if she hoped to defeat him. She nodded her head in agreement.

"What *are* you? Where did you come from?"

"Think back," he said. "You actually saw the spacecraft that brought me to Earth. It was reported as a meteor shower over Point Locke, but it was actually the wreckage of a spaceship."

Jenny remembered the meteors and she remembered the feeling of great sadness that had swept over her at the time. "Are you saying that . . ." She stopped herself. Best to let *him* tell the story.

"I was abducted from my native planet by advanced alien beings. They wanted to experiment with me, to change me into something they could use, but it worked out much better for me than it did for them."

Jenny wondered what he meant. Had any of the other aliens survived? Even while she considered the possibilities, a part of her refused to believe what he was saying. It was too incredible. Things like this just didn't happen! Yet she felt that he was telling the truth—as he perceived it.

"Go on," she insisted, motioning him to continue.

He smiled at her encouragement. "The reason I'm so fascinated by instincts is that for most of my existence they were all I had. They enabled me to survive in an extremely competitive environment. In my original form, I had nothing like the upper brain you humans pride yourselves on—I was a totally instinctive being. What you would call a monster. Then I . . . absorbed one of my kidnappers." He paused, seemingly caught up in his reminiscence.

Absorbed? It sounded like a euphemism for "killed" to Jenny. Before she could bring herself to ask, he continued.

"Even though the particular being I merged with was retarded by their standards, he would have been the greatest intellect you humans had ever known. He was as far beyond your species as you are beyond the apes."

Jenny weighed his statements carefully. The concepts he presented were not new—she had long been convinced that there was intelligent life on other planets. Still, it was difficult to really accept that the creature sitting next to her was an alien when he looked so human.

"Can you imagine what that was like, trying to integrate a powerful intellect with my purely instinctive capabilities?"

No, I can't, Jenny thought. Information was coming too fast for her to make any reasoned response. She tried to project some degree of sympathy.

"Besides the problem of their intelligence was the *way* they had developed culturally. They had chosen to reject their instincts and repress their emotions—to glorify only the intellect. I couldn't begin to assimilate their knowledge at first. I had to reject most of their capabilities just as they had rejected their primitive instincts and emotions." His hands clenched in a very human gesture. "I hated them for what they tried to do to me."

Jenny could feel how much he wanted her to understand

his ordeal. Then it occurred to her she might be misreading his gestures, mistaking them for genuine emotion. She realized how alien he was to everything she was familiar with. It would be foolhardy to project her own emotions onto a being who was so totally unlike anything she'd ever known. Jenny didn't know enough to question him about his planet, so she tried another tack.

"And what happened when you 'absorbed' your first human being? It was Duane, wasn't it? At the beach."

"Yes." He answered without regret, without remorse. "The ship disintegrated in the earth's atmosphere, and I landed in the ocean."

"But it was a shark that attacked Duane!" she interrupted.

"The first thing I encountered and absorbed was a shark. It was a stupid animal, but it helped me find something better."

"Something human . . ." she whispered. The real Duane had died that day and no one had known. No one had mourned.

"At first, all my faculties were concentrated on making the deception work. I knew immediately that humans were a far more difficult audience than I had ever had to fool before. Even with Duane's memory, it was hard to imitate him well enough to maintain reasonable credibility."

"Yes . . . Duane seemed odd after that," she agreed sadly.

"It was quite some time before I learned to use any of the human abilities I had acquired for anything but mimicry. When I realized that human intelligence could be used effectively for my own benefit, it was like waking up after being in a coma. I soon needed more knowledge and experience than Duane possessed."

"Those people—the ones who disappeared in Point Locke—it *was* you, then? You killed them for the *knowledge* they could provide you?"

"Jenny, you don't understand. They're not dead. They're a part of me now. They will live as long as I do."

That was the verification she had needed, and it had come from his own lips. He had killed them, *absorbed* them—it *was* the same thing. He was a cold-blooded, murdering beast with no sense of right and wrong.

Jenny's gaze shifted from his face to his hands as he leaned forward to refill her glass of wine. She noticed that his glass was still full. He was just pretending to drink. What was it that Maria had said about disrupting his concentration? She mustered her courage and decided to try a small offensive. "You haven't been drinking your wine at all," she accused. "That isn't fair. Finish your glass and we'll both have another."

Duane looked at her intently, as though trying to ascertain her motives. Repressing a shudder, she blinked innocently and smiled as calmly as she could. He appeared to relax, then lifted his glass and drained the contents.

Jenny watched, cheering inwardly. Chalk up one small victory for her. If Maria had been right, it might make her job easier.

Duane set his glass on the table and filled both glasses to precisely equal levels. "To us," he said pleasantly, holding up his glass.

She decided her best strategy was to keep him talking. "Go on, Duane. You were saying?"

"I've been spending most of my time in libraries. Reading is certainly a less strenuous way of obtaining knowledge than I had been using before." He smiled.

It looked almost like Brad's smile. The thought behind that observation was hideous, and she tried not to think about it. She had to remain cool and collected.

"My abductors were far superior to humans, but I don't think they took the best path." He paused, remembering the outlandish philosophy of his former captors. "Can you believe they wouldn't even eat *plants*? Their diet was entirely synthetic!" His tone of genuine wonder made it clear that their behavior was very nearly incomprehensible.

"I think you humans can surpass them with my help." He stared into the fire pensively for a long while before he continued. "You are taking a more dangerous approach. You're much more primitive, of course, but you don't reject your emotional instincts. That's good—there is much of value there."

Jenny realized he was trying to present himself as a possible savior of humanity—and she didn't believe it for a minute. She didn't like being patronized, but she smiled at him attentively. Convinced that she was hanging on his every word, he went on.

"Your species prides itself on its superiority to animals, and yet your so-called rationality was superimposed on a primitive, bestial brain only a few million years ago."

She was sure that he had attained some of this knowlege from the professors. She remembered how they had fascinated him.

"Your species is still grappling with the same problem I had—how to reconcile primitive instincts and emotions with the relatively new ability to reason." His eyes were still on the fire. "The mistake my kidnappers made was in relying too heavily on their higher brain functions. Logic by itself is quite limited, you know. It cannot set values or tell you anything really new. It is, however, excellent for analyzing what you already know and deciding what to do about a given situation.

"Humans often make the opposite mistake—using emotions when you *should* use logic. To make the best use of your abilities, it seems clear to me that instincts and emotions must be the primary source of values and goals. Logic and reason are useful in determining the possible consequences of actions. The trick is getting the proper balance between thoughts and feelings."

Jenny nodded automatically. She understood what he was saying, but wasn't sure what he was leading up to. He seemed to have been so caught up by what he was saying that he had lost sight of the point he was trying to get across.

"What I'm trying to do is use my acquired ability to reason as a check on my natural instinctive reactions."

"In other words," Jenny said, "you admit to being a predatory beast, but you're trying to change. Is that it?"

"I cannot help what I am. Any living creature is exactly what it is."

He took a drink, keeping his eyes on her face all the while, trying to gauge her reaction. It seemed important to him that she understand. "Jenny, my ancestors evolved on a world you would consider hideous. Yet they managed to survive. I was born an instinctive predator, but now I have new capabilities and I'm trying to become something different. Maybe I'm not very accomplished at it, and maybe I will fail, but I have no choice on this planet but to try. Can you understand that?"

Of more concern to her was the fact that the wine seemed to be mellowing him.

"I am learning much from humans. Just looking at you tonight with my human faculties is giving me tremendous pleasure," he said with an all too human smile.

With a supreme effort of will, Jenny took her eyes off Duane for a moment and took a deep breath, inhaling the subtle lemon scent given off by the candles. Suddenly she understood what had troubled her when she had first walked in. Everything seemed so preternaturally familiar—the fire, the soft lights, the wine—even the Brahms symphony playing softly in the background. It was an exact duplicate of her first night with Brad, right down to the lemon candles!

There was no way Duane could have known all this without Brad's cooperation . . . or Brad's memory. Tears rushed to her eyes and her voice was barely audible. "What have you done to Brad?"

Duane's gaze was sad, almost contrite. "I'm sorry if I've frightened you. Brad is here."

Jenny was stunned. Before she could say anything, Duane had turned and left the room, closing the door behind him.

thirty-four

JENNY STOOD SHAKILY and paced in front of the fireplace, never once taking her eyes off the door through which Duane had just left.

Could she have been mistaken about Brad's fate? She didn't think so, but she dared to hope.

She saw the doorknob turn, heard a muffled click, and watched the door as it opened. The breath caught in her throat.

Brad closed the door behind him and leaned against it, grinning. "Hi, cutie. I guess we're in this together, huh?"

Jenny stared. She'd been wrong—so wrong. Brad was here, really *here*. She ran into his outstretched arms. "Oh Brad! I can't believe it. When you didn't come, I was afraid that . . . I thought . . ."

She could not get the words out. It didn't matter now that she could see his face and feel his body pressing against hers, now she had help, now that she would not be facing the nightmare alone. He held her in a deep embrace and his mouth moved on hers, warmly seductive and familiar.

But as his mouth opened on hers, she was seized by a feeling of indescribable wrongness. Her body stiffened and her eyes snapped open. It . . . wasn't . . . Brad.

"What's wrong?"

She pulled herself from his embrace and backed away warily. "You've killed him, haven't you?"

He calmly scrutinized her with—Brad's eyes? They *looked* like Brad's eyes. Why then was she remembering her lizard dreams? There had been a man inside the lizard— but now, who was real? Her eyes revealed the flesh, but his eyes revealed the truth.

Brad, the *real* Brad was dead.

He seemed almost to read her mind. "I *am* Brad, but much more than that. Brad is not dead, he is a part of me now.

"Poor Jenny," he continued, sounding touchingly sympathetic. "You still don't understand yet, do you? I am Brad. I have his body, his mind, his skills, his desires . . . everything." He paused and his eyes traveled the length of her body. "I'm as much Brad as he ever was."

"You're not—you're not!" Jenny could no longer contain her anger. "You may look like him, but you're not Brad. Maria was right—you're a monster!"

He moved toward her and Jenny stepped back fearfully. He shrugged and sat down on the couch. "I've been reading your newspapers," he said. "Today's, for example."

He reached into a magazine rack and pulled out a *Times*, shaking it open and glancing at the headlines. "Terrorist bombings, sectarian violence, guerrilla warfare, sexual abuse of children, ethnic hatred, mass murder . . ." He paused and looked up at her. "And you call *me* a monster?" His voice had grown cold. "Why shouldn't I feel right at home with the human race?

"You think your lofty values are so important. You're as hypocritical as the beings that brought me here. Who are you to judge me? You don't have the slightest conception of what alternatives I had."

Jenny didn't intend to judge him. Given the chance, she was just going to kill him.

Until this moment, everything had been relatively low key, but now the creature was upset. It frightened her, knowing how many people he had killed without a hint of remorse.

He paused and Jenny could see he was struggling to control himself. He took a deep breath, held it for a moment, and sighed. "I know you can't help being influenced to some extent by your feelings," he said. "I won't deny that from your point of view I am a monster. I must use the bodies of those I've absorbed because my own form would be . . . frightening. But I don't have to kill anyone again—even if I want to take their shape. Theoretically, I just need a few skin cells. I'm adapting rapidly, becoming progressively more human. I need your help, your advice. Come sit down and we'll have some more wine."

Jenny breathed a sigh of relief. He was calm again, and she was still in his good graces. She smoothed her hair and sat back against the softness of the velvet couch, her confidence increasing even more when she noticed that he was drinking again. She decided to put her plan into action.

"Do you mean it when you say you're becoming more human?"

He smiled. "I never had any concern for the feelings of others before I encountered humans. It would have slowed my inherent survival mechanism. But that's changed now."

As she sipped her wine, her fingers began moving rhythmically up and down the stem of her wine glass, sensually fondling its smooth roundness.

He watched her movements, mesmerized, then cleared his throat and tore his eyes away before speaking. "I've learned more from humans than from the aliens that kidnapped me—their attitudes were incomprehensible . . . so incredibly different from mine that I . . . could not understand them at all."

He could not keep his eyes off her, and each time he looked at her he seemed to lose his train of thought.

Jenny was sure that her femininity was working its magic on him . . . or maybe it was just the wine. Perspiration beaded on his forehead as he watched Jenny dip a finger into her wine and then seductively place it to her lips.

When he stopped talking, she brought her eyes up, gave him a questioning smile, and whispered, "Go on, I'm listening. . . ."

He cleared his throat again. "Your species is so far from using even what capabilities you do have that—" He stopped again when she crossed her legs—the slit in her dress parted to reveal her shapely legs. He was breathing harder now, and moving closer to her on the couch. It definitely wasn't the wine.

Jenny tensed, and in the dim light, her hand felt for the purse at her side. "But I still don't know what you want from me," she asked. *Like hell I don't,* she thought.

He moved still closer. "Like all successful living things, I have a strong desire to survive. But here on Earth the threats are not so immediate. Other, long-term possibilities are open to me."

"You mean you've discovered sex?" she said, giving him what she hoped would pass for a teasing smile.

"*That* I've known about," he whispered huskily. He lowered his head to touch his lips to hers—gently, tentatively, as if expecting resistance, then with a hungry possession when he encountered none. She had willed herself not to be repulsed by his touch, but it had been exciting and arousing. Now Jenny was the one fighting for control. She willingly submitted to the smooth caress of his hand as it slid along her shoulders and explored the warm curve of her throat before slipping inside her dress to cup the soft warmth of her breast. Jenny closed her eyes, caught up in the fervor of his desire, forgetting that it wasn't really Brad. The anguish she had felt at learning of Brad's death faded, replaced by the reality of the moment. Her body denied his death—how could he be dead when he was here, now, making love to her?

She reminded herself that the creature had killed Brad and Maria, and the illusion was shattered. She gathered up his roving hand and held it securely, still shaken by the storm he had aroused in her. Jenny pulled away slightly and flicked her eyes over him appraisingly. "Certainly you can't mean love?"

He carried her fingers to his lips and smiled. "I won't claim that yet, but perhaps in time. What I have in mind is a mutually beneficial alliance."

"What do you mean?" Jenny's smile was wary. Being a child of her time, she certainly knew what *that* meant—he wanted to shack up with her—but she wanted to know more. "How will it benefit me?"

"You will be able to do anything you want . . . have anything you want . . ."

"In exchange for . . . ?" she prompted, trying to keep the skepticism out of her voice.

His face took on a sincere, almost inspired look, his thoughts on some distant philosophical plane that Jenny could not fathom. "In exchange for being responsible for a whole new species of superior beings . . . beings with tremendous physical and creative capabilities. Jenny, you and I can create a whole new species—a species that is more than human, a species that is powerful, flexible, with the highest probability for long-term survival of any in the galaxy."

His eyes searched hers for a reaction, but she simply stared, stunned and shocked. He was deadly serious, and she cursed herself for her stupidity. She had never considered the possibility that he could reproduce, that he could unleash more of his kind on an unsuspecting world, even while she was waiting for Maria in the Obstetrics wing. She felt dizzy. She'd had too much to drink and she had to clear her head.

Jenny stood unsteadily and walked to the fireplace. More was at stake than she had realized, and no one else knew what was going on. No one even knew where she was. Idly, she began poking at the coals, just to have something to do. The fire was soon crackling and burning brightly, but her hands still felt icy cold.

"Why do you want *me*?" On one level it seemed a question that hardly needed to be asked, but she was after another answer. He rose and came to her.

"Don't you know? I wanted you from the moment I came out of the water and saw you for the first time. We have an affinity in certain areas—no, don't bother trying to deny it. You knew Duane had changed right from the beginning. It was just that nothing in your human experience prepared you to deal with the situation. You weren't going crazy, Jenny—you have latent telepathic abilities. They only work with me, though, don't they?"

Jenny nodded mutely, her eyes wide.

He reached out for her and drew her against him, his hands roaming over her soft skin, his lips seeking hers greedily. He murmured against her mouth. "You're beautiful, adaptable, and extremely intelligent for your species."

"Maria was all those things, too!"

"Maria was flawed. She couldn't have even carried a human child."

His callous dismissal of Maria angered Jenny, but she kept her face blank.

He continued with hardly a pause. "My species is extremely flexible in reproduction. My genetic material can combine with that of almost any species—not unlike your concept of recombinant DNA. Our offspring, Jenny, will look exactly like humans at birth, but they will also be able to change shape.

"My abductors modified my reproductive material, but I didn't realize that until too late. Since my genes couldn't combine successfully with Maria's, they switched to an asexual mode of reproduction and developed into my genetic duplicates. When I discovered that something had gone wrong, I tried to talk her into getting an abortion. She refused. Believe me, the last thing I wanted was to let

Maria die. I was afraid that an examination of her condition would give me away."

Jenny could tell that he felt Maria had got what she deserved. She remembered the hushed commotion in the hospital corridor, and Dr. Stuart's face when he told her about the "abnormal" fetuses. They weren't abnormal—they were his genetic duplicates. What did he look like when he wasn't hiding within the bodies of his victims?

"Let's not talk about Maria. Let's talk about us." He put his arms around Jenny and she shivered with revulsion. He grinned, attributing her trembling to passion. He pushed aside her long hair to nuzzle her throat.

"What if I don't agree to all these plans of yours?" Jenny asked, trying to make it sound as if that were furthest from her mind.

He broke off his caress and looked at her through narrowed eyes. "But Jenny, you have no alternative."

She had never thought he would allow any. "Well," she said, putting her arms around him, "you *said* I was adaptable."

His passion was instantly resurrected. "Jenny, Jenny . . . you won't be sorry." He kissed her lingeringly, a kiss to seal the bargain. While his eyes were closed during the kiss, Jenny's were open and alert, trying to locate her purse.

She spotted it on the couch where she had left it. "It's too warm here by the fire," she whispered to him. "Let's sit down. We'll be more comfortable." The smile she gave him hinted broadly of forthcoming delights and he followed eagerly, taking off his shirt before sitting down.

The firelight bronzed his broad shoulders. His body—Brad's body—was beautiful, and she closed her eyes to shut out the sight. After tonight, she would never see it again. She refused to acknowledge the possibility that she might fail.

His lips traced the lines of her eyelids, mouth, and chin. He knew she liked that. He was breathing heavily, insistently. She could feel the tempo of his heartbeat increasing with each kiss. Jenny felt a certain superiority over him in his aroused state. She was gambling. As long as he was intent on sexual gratification, she had the advantage. Desire, combined with the wine, would make him vulnerable—she hoped.

Slowly, so as not to alarm him, Jenny reached toward her purse. She had just managed to turn the clasp when he straightened up. She drew back her hand, afraid of being discovered.

Murmuring her name over and over in a passionate incantation, he trailed kisses down her neck and eased the strap of her dress off her shoulder.

"Let's take this off," he said thickly, as he began groping at her back for the zipper.

Jenny shivered, her skin puckering into tiny goose bumps all over her body. She was breathing as hard as he was, but it was fear and dread that *she* was feeling. The time was right. While he was preoccupied, she felt blindly for her purse. It wasn't where she had left it!

A little involuntary cry of panic escaped her lips, but he mistook it as evidence of the heightened excitement she was experiencing.

Cautiously, Jenny felt for the purse again and found it had fallen between the cushions. He was still fumbling with the tiny hook fastener—perhaps the liquor had slowed him down, made him groggy. She almost ceased breathing as her hand closed around one of the syringes.

Her hand trembling, she withdrew it and prepared to plunge it into his muscled back.

He had finally unhooked the clasp, and she could feel her dress parting as the zipper eased downward. With her thumb, Jenny flicked off the protective cover, exposing the needle.

He looked up just at that moment, and with a dexterity and swiftness—predator reflexes—that she did not expect, he slapped her wrist sharply. The plastic syringe flew across the room, hit the oak desk, and rebounded to land on the brick hearth.

Terrified, Jenny sprang to her feet, clutching her dress to her. Her one chance to take him by surprise was gone.

thirty-five

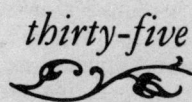

JENNY STUMBLED BACKWARD, clutching at her clothes. His eyes glared at her as he turned and moved quickly to the only door in the room.

With a flick of his wrist, he twisted the old-fashioned skeleton key that protruded from the lock and pocketed it. He turned to confront her again. Jenny could see that he was fighting to control himself, fighting his anger.

Shaking his head, he calmed himself. "Poor Jenny . . . you still don't understand, do you? Things would have been so much easier if you'd accepted my offer."

His eyes were compelling and hypnotic, like those of a reptile intent upon its prey. Her attention was riveted, and she felt as though she were being sucked into the vortex of his irises, into his very being—into infinite blackness. She wanted to tear her eyes away, to run, to do anything, but her muscles refused to obey her frantic commands. Only her eyes and her mind were functioning, and they told her she was helpless against him.

He approached her slowly. The trapped look in her eyes seemed to delight him as much as her previous willingness. He took her face in his hands. "I really don't need your cooperation . . ." Leaning forward, he brushed her unmoving lips with his own. ". . . but I do need *you*."

His lips moved on hers, lightly at first, and then again with deepening intimacy. As if she were a department store mannequin, he began undressing her. Jenny felt him drawing the zipper down—all the way down this time. He peeled her dress over her hips and it slid to the floor. She was left standing in the scantiest of undergarments. He walked around her slowly, looking her up and down with satisfaction.

"You see, Jenny, the aliens who kidnapped me were very powerful telepaths, and even the one I absorbed had some little ability of his own. Unfortunately, it's hard to use his telepathic powers while in human form—so I need your genes to help fix the trait in my . . . excuse me, *our* children. I'd take care of the problem myself, but my abductors severely disrupted my ability to manipulate my own reproductive material—they were afraid I'd escape." He chuckled. "Telepathy is a very valuable survival trait, even though it didn't help *them*."

He undid her tiny black lace bra and slipped his hands around the warm softness it had concealed. He fondled and teased the rosy nipples of her breasts with languourous sensuality, first with palm and thumb, then with his eager lips.

She could feel his urgent hunger, his growing need for her. His hands moved downward, over the rounded swell of her hips and the smoothness of her thighs as he guided her pantyhose down.

Jenny closed her eyes, waiting for the inevitable. Would he take her then and there on the carpet in front of the fireplace? Would he carry her to one of the bedrooms?

He was in no hurry. His lips moved in an intimate trail of kisses along her belly, moving slowly, sensuously downward. Her thighs were spread apart, and his relentless tongue probed the most sensitive of places. She tried to ignore what he was doing, told herself she was feeling none of the arousal he was experiencing.

An image—from a dream?—of a long tongue darting from a lizard's mouth flashed through her mind. He was right. Telepathy *was* a powerful trait. She knew that this was what her dreams had been warning her about, but ultimately what good had they done her? What options did she have left?

The fire was still burning. She could feel its warmth on her bare legs. She looked down at it, trying to think of something, anything but what he was doing to her, and saw the syringe lying on the hearth. If only she could move! Her only hope for salvation lay right at her feet, yet she was powerless to avail herself of it.

He guided her to the couch, then sat down to remove his shoes and socks, releasing his grip on her momentarily to unbuckle his belt. Jenny looked away. An inner voice told her that if she were to break the creature's hypnotic hold, she had to concentrate on something completely different, fix her consciousness on something he couldn't reach.

She remembered her grandfather. She imagined herself back on his farm, feeding the ducks by the pond, petting the rabbits, playing in his huge hay barn. Only a memory could offer her an escape.

If you can't keep your finger off the trigger, you shouldn't play with the gun.

She fantasized squeezing the forbidden trigger. Again, and again, and again.

She wanted more than anything else to destroy the creature who had killed her friends, who was holding her paralyzed. Recalling the lizard dream, she let the hatred she had felt then possess her, channeling it into a will to move. Suddenly, she was free.

Jenny kicked the syringe into the orange, glowing coals. It lay atop the hot coals for a moment, seemingly impervious to the tiny flames that licked around it.

"Brad" was taken completely by surprise. He had been sure she was totally under his control, yet she had broken free. He lunged at her, just as the syringe burned and released a churning, blue-gray cloud of smoke.

The creature imitating Brad growled and drew back as the potent smoke reached him, his tight repression of bestial impulses failing rapidly. Jenny could see that it was only with great difficulty that he maintained Brad's shape long enough to speak. "I don't need you. I can have anyone . . ." His voice degenerated, so low-pitched and slurred that it was barely intelligible.

What had been Brad's handsome features were distorting grotesquely, so much so that she could scarcely believe it had ever looked like Brad. But she was unable to take her eyes off the hideous change taking place before her.

The texture of his face was changing, becoming squamous. His blood vessels had begun to pulsate and distend. As they burst, the blood flowed in rivulets from his ears, nose, and eyes. His mouth was stretching, erupting rows and rows of shiny objects that looked like giant daggers to Jenny. The eyes bulged, lizardlike, and the pupils were now elliptical.

Jenny gasped in horror. It was uncanny how much he looked like a medieval painting of a demon she had seen in a museum.

The creature expanded up and out, as if some tremendous inner force had been locked inside his body for too long and was forcing its way out.

With a hideous rending of flesh and muscle, Brad's body split open and seemed to turn itself inside out. The seething mass of glistening, pustulant viscera became tentacles that stretched and writhed. On what had been Brad's arms, flesh folded over flesh, rippling, as the bones that supported them dissolved, leaving ropes of undulating flesh. Deadly sectioned tentacles reached out, grasping for Jenny's body.

The grisly transformation was complete, and now the creature moved toward her.

She tore her eyes away from the repulsive monster and looked for a way out. The door was locked. That left the windows. She ran toward the nearest one, but the thing was faster. The arms that had held her so tenderly just moments before were now long, slimy tentacles that blocked her escape. She threw herself to the floor and scrambled behind the couch.

The creature could have killed her in an instant, but it was enjoying her terror. Frightened though she was, she knew it was toying with her, obtaining a perverse pleasure from her torment. How long did she have before it became bored with the game?

Maria had been wrong, Jenny thought. The THC made it revert to what must be its original shape, but it hadn't stopped him. Then she realized that the fireplace flue was drawing most of the smoke up the chimney.

Jenny crawled backward, the creature advancing as she retreated. She waited until she felt the warmth of the fire on her bare skin, then whirled around and looked frantically for the handle that pulled the damper closed. She found it and yanked down hard, and the smoke began gushing back into the room. The creature flinched backward, its tentacles waving wildly.

One of them must have swung over the table, because Jenny heard the wine glasses shatter. Through the smoke, she could see that the candles had also fallen over. One of them rolled under the drapes near the door, and she could see a tiny ribbon of flame climbing delicately up the fabric.

She had to get out of here! She grabbed her dress and edged toward the windows again. That was her only hope. Her eyes were beginning to sting from the smoke.

The drug-laden smoke was getting to the creature. It was having trouble holding any well-defined shape at all. It thrashed wildly in the smoke-filled room. A blood vessel of some kind, near the surface where Brad's chest had been, bulged to enormous proportions as Jenny watched. It pulsated hideously a few times, then burst with such force that the stream of reddish fluid sprayed out across the room. The next spurt caught Jenny on the chest, covering her breast with a reddish ooze that looked like blood. It was considerably stickier than human blood, slimy and thick.

The drapes were now engulfed by flame, adding to the smoke in the room. She dodged a swinging tentacle and lunged for the window. Numerous coats of paint over the years had formed a seal, but desperation lent her strength and the wooden frame squealed as it shot up.

Jenny felt the slimy touch of alien flesh on her bare shoulder. She recoiled, dropping the dress, but the tentacle passed her by and reached for the window ledge.

It's trying to get out!

She couldn't allow it to escape and regain control of itself. She slammed the window down with all her might, severing the tip of the tentacle. The creature drew away as if it had been stung.

It was weakening now, Jenny thought. This was her chance for the *coup de grace*.

Coughing as she groped around the sofa, getting high on the pot smoke, Jenny found her purse, which held the second syringe.

She approached the flailing, maddened creature, unsure where to make the injection. Holding her body as far away as possible, she stabbed the needle in low, under a bulb of flesh that suddenly split open and oozed more "blood" onto her hand. Jenny jammed on the plunger, pumping the full 20cc's of THC into the monster's already malfunctioning system.

The creature wailed in agony, and Jenny leaped away, leaving the syringe dangling from its pulsating body. Its moaning ululations continued as she felt her way back to the window, climbed out quickly and closed it behind her. The air was chill, but she gasped it desperately into her smoke-filled lungs. Her head began to clear.

At last she was free, but now she was compelled to look back, to make sure it didn't escape. Through the blue-gray smoke, she could see only part of what was happening in the burning room. The blood-curdling howls continued, and what she could see through the haze sickened her.

The concentrated drug was having a devastating effect. Lesions were opening up all over the creature's body. Between the ulcerations, oddly shaped, tumescent cysts formed, then ruptured to expose bits and pieces of previous victims, based on random bursts from the monster's disintegrating mind. It had withdrawn its tentacles into its body, and all of its absorbed patterns were tangled together in one self-destructing mass.

Jenny stood transfixed, unable to look away from the window. She could see parts of assorted people and animals all mangled together in a writhing fury.

Within moments, moments that seemed an eternity, the creature lost cohesiveness and began to come apart. Pieces fell off—a large spider leg, a dog's head, a human arm, a rat's paw, and more she didn't recognize—all distorted, all covered with ichor. The fire from the drapes had spread to the wood-paneled walls and was burning fiercely.

The creature was melting into a ghastly porridge made from the body parts of its terrestrial and alien victims which poured out on the floor as from a monstrous caldron. The fire raged over everything now. She watched the room become a crematorium. It looked like a window into hell.

For one instant she saw Brad's face peering through the slime. His lips formed her name, making one last plea, then the vile ooze on the floor caught fire and his features were consumed by flames.

The nightmare was finally over.

epilogue

JENNY AWOKE, CHILLED to the bone. The living nightmare that had died in the flames refused to leave her mind. In the loneliness of the night, every night of these past weeks, memories of horror haunted her.

It was agony enough to experience the creature's disintegration night after night, to see Brad's disembodied head calling her name. Yet what tormented her the most was that she could not be sure what was real, and what was not.

Had she *really* seen a rat crawl out of the bushes that night, by the window where the piece of tentacle had fallen, or was that only a drug-induced hallucination?

Had it stopped and boldly stared at her with those terrible intense eyes, or was it just a fever dream of delusion, a trick of memory?

Jenny stared at the dark corner of the ceiling above her

bed. She lay quietly, listening for the sound of the dream beast scuttling along the floor.

Listening.

Forever listening.

And all she could hear was her own scream.

DEAN R. KOONTZ
A master of spine-chilling terror!

With more than 3 million copies of his books in Berkley print, Dean R. Koontz is one of today's most popular horror writers. His chilling tales catch you by the throat, grip the pit of your stomach, and dare you to turn the page. The terror is just beginning...

__	09217-8 Strangers	$4.50
__	09760-9 Whispers	$4.50
__	09864-8 Night Chills	$3.95
__	09501-0 Phantoms	$3.95
__	09502-9 Shattered	$3.50
__	09278-X Darkfall	$3.95
__	09931-8 The Face of Fear	$3.50
__	09860-5 The Vision	$3.95

Prices may be slightly higher in Canada.

Available at your local bookstore or return this form to:

THE BERKLEY PUBLISHING GROUP
Berkley • Jove • Charter • Ace
THE BERKLEY PUBLISHING GROUP, Dept. B
390 Murray Hill Parkway, East Rutherford, NJ 07073

Please send me the titles checked above. I enclose _____. Include $1.00 for postage and handling if one book is ordered; add 25¢ per book for two or more not to exceed $1.75. CA, IL, NJ, NY, PA, and TN residents please add sales tax. Prices subject to change without notice and may be higher in Canada. Do not send cash.

NAME_____
ADDRESS_____
CITY_____ STATE/ZIP_____
(Allow six weeks for delivery.)

ENTER A WORLD YOU MAY NEVER ESCAPE

Mesmerizing tales of horror from The Berkley Publishing Group

__ **Buried Blossoms** by Stephen Lewis	0-515-05153-5/$2.95
__ **Halloween III: Season of the Witch** by Jack Martin	0-515-08594-4/$3.50
__ **Blood Sisters** by Mark Manley	0-441-06799-9/$3.50
__ **The Playhouse** by Richard Levinson and William Link	0-441-67071-7/$3.50
__ **Tomb Seven** by Gene Snyder	0-441-81643-6/$3.50
__ **Last Rites** by Jorge Saralegui	0-441-47185-4/$3.95
__ **Nightwing** by Martin Cruz Smith	0-515-08502-2/$3.95
__ **The Piercing** by John Coyne	0-441-66310-9/$3.50
__ **The Touch** by F. Paul Wilson	0-515-08733-5/$3.95

Available at your local bookstore or return this form to:

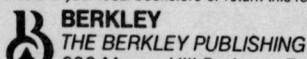

BERKLEY
THE BERKLEY PUBLISHING GROUP, Dept. B
390 Murray Hill Parkway, East Rutherford, NJ 07073

Please send me the titles checked above. I enclose _____. Include $1.00 for postage and handling if one book is ordered; add 25¢ per book for two or more not to exceed $1.75. CA, IL, NJ, NY, PA, and TN residents please add sales tax. Prices subject to change without notice and may be higher in Canada. Do not send cash.

NAME_____
ADDRESS_____
CITY_____ STATE/ZIP_____
(Allow six weeks for delivery.)

423/B